The
Broken
Yarns of the Knitting Witches
Circle

ALSO BY CHERYL POTTER

Handpaint Country : A Knitter's Journey

Lavish Lace: Knitting With Hand-Painted Yarns
with Carol Noble

Rainbow Knits For Kids

Ribbon Style: Knitted Fashions And Accessories

Skein For Skein: 16 Knitted Projects

Special Little Knits from Just One Skein

The Broken
Yarns of the Knitting Witches
Circle

CHERYL POTTER

POTTER PRESS
Vermont

Novel ISBN: 978-0-9856350-0-8   Book Set ISBN: 978-0-9856350-2-2

Novel eBook edition ISBN: 978-0-9856350-3-9   Pattern Booklet ISBN: 978-0-9856350-1-5

Novel ePub edition ISBN: 978-0-9856350-7-7   Pattern Booklet PDF edition ISBN: 978-0-9856350-4-6

Novel Kindle edition ISBN: 978-0-9856350-6-0   Pattern Booklet eBook edition ISBN: 978-0-9856350-5-3

First edition

Printed in the United States of America by Versa Press

All illustrations except where noted by Frank Riccio
Map by Joe Wilkins
Icons and graphic design by Mary Joy Gumayagay

www.potluckyarn.com

To my husband Tim, who puts up
with knitting witches everyday

and for knitting witches everywhere

CONTENTS

ACKNOWLEDGMENTS

Welcome to *The Broken Circle*, a fiber fantasy filled with Yarns of the Knitting Witches. I began writing this first book of the *Potluck Yarn Trilogy* five years ago and abandoned it in discouragement a few years later, convinced that my desire to combine a fantasy novel about knitting witches with a pattern book that featured magical garments was foolish. Combination books like this one are called "cross genre," which is jargon for "not desirable" by commercial publishers.

I was undaunted at first. I hand-dyed my witches' colorways and put together their patterns. I wrote most of the novel. I referenced patterns in each chapter, and then took them back out when everyone I consulted told me my idea would not work. Then I gave up on the book completely and resolved to return to the familiar terrain of writing pattern books for hand-dyed yarns. Then I met the Visionaries.

Without Cat Bordhi and the Visionary Authors Group, this book would never have been published. I am grateful beyond words to the Visionaries, whom I think of as my personal group of knitting witches. Thank you for your unending support, carefully chosen comments and sound advice. I owe a special thanks to Deb Robson who edited the book not once but twice, and provided me with sound counsel long after her work with me was finished. Many of the words and phrases used in the book do not appear in Webster's and I have Deb to thank for the Potluck style guide.

Special appreciation goes to Donna Druchunas, who managed the production of the novel and edited the companion pattern book simultaneously, giving me the advice and support that only a true friend can offer. Kudos to Mary Joy Gumayagay for the beautiful book design, and thanks to Reed Glenn for her careful, efficient copy editing.

I am especially excited by the visuals in the book. Thanks to artist Frank Riccio for the beautiful cover and interior line drawings and our resident cartographer Joe Wilkins, who designed the map of the Middlelands.

Finally, thanks to everyone at Cherry Tree Hill Yarn and Plymouth Yarn Company. I was so pleased to have the opportunity to work with all of you.

CAST OF CHARACTERS

THE ORIGINAL POTLUCK TWELVE
Aubergine: The Potluck Queen
Smokey Joe
Esmeralde
Indigo Rose
Lavender Mae
Lilac Lily
Sierra Blue
Tracery Teal
Mamie Verde
Ratta
Winter Wheat
Tasman: The Dark Queen

THE BLUE FAMILY OF TOP NOTCH
Kendrick: Sierra's husband
Warren: Sierra and Kendrick's oldest son
Skye: Sierra and Kendrick's daughter
Garth: Sierra and Kendrick's youngest son

THE FOSSICKERS
Trader: The Fossicker leader
Clayton
Ross
Micah

OTHER CHARACTERS
Miles from Nowhere: A traveling bard
Ozzie: The Banebridge Trading Post proprietor

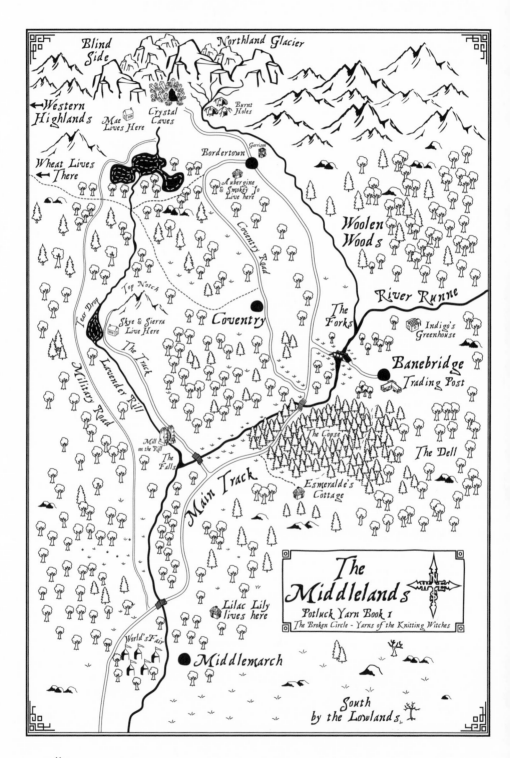

Blind Side

Northland Glacier

Western Highlands →

Crystal Caves

Mae Lives Here

Burnt Holes

← Wheat Lives There

Bordertown

Garrison

Aubergine & Smokey Jo Live here

Woolen Woods

Coventry Road

River Runne

Top Notch

Tear Drop

Skye & Sierra Live Here

Coventry

The Forks

Indigo's Greenhouse

The Track

Banebridge
Trading Post

Military Road

Lavender Rill

Mill on the Rill

The Copse

The Dell

The Falls

Main Track

Esmeralde's Cottage

The Middlelands

Potluck Yarn Book I

The Broken Circle – Yarns of the Knitting Witches

Lilac Lily lives here

World's Fair

● Middlemarch

South by the Lowlands

INTRODUCTION

When the creation of this *Potluck Yarn Trilogy* began, and Book One, *The Broken Circle: Yarns of the Knitting Witches*, came into being, two parallel creations were conjured together: the novel you hold, as well as a sequence of magical handspun and knitted items—shawls, bags, mitts and gloves, a cloak, and more. The handcrafted textiles came to figure prominently in the story of a world where the powers they represent are no longer welcome but are desperately needed. Knitter or not, our goal is to add a healthy mix of fiber to your fantasy. One project per chapter, these talismans and useful garments play significant roles in the narrative. The yarns of the story and the yarns in the fiber creations grew to the point where they could stand alone, although each enhances the other.

The book you hold is the novel: formatted in standard trade-paperback size, it encompasses a map of the fantasy world, a broad cast of characters, and a prologue that precedes the twenty chapters of the trilogy's first volume. Whether you are a knitter or not, we trust that this first book will pique your imagination and stir your creative impulses, allowing you to read for entertainment without being distracted by knitterly details.

If you are a knitter, we have an extra dose of good news for you. The patterns have blossomed into a separate book of instructions, prepared in a larger format and in full color, with beautiful photos and easy-to-read charts. The Companion Pattern Book to *The Broken Circle* will give you, if you are so inclined, the opportunity to make enchanting projects like those created by Sierra, Lavender Mae, Ratta, and the other knitting witches whose lives, challenges, journeys, conflicts, and alliances you are about to encounter. For those who would like the enhancement, the companion book also includes a color version of the map of The Middlelands, where the novel's action takes place.

I am not the first author to believe that magic and knitting share certain mystical qualities for those who choose to look for them. Examples of those who have noted this connection before include Anna Zilboorg (read her *Knitting for Anarchists*) and Cat Bordhi (whose *A Treasury of Magical Knitting* brings out her perception right in its title). Debbie Macomber's best-selling novels about the fictional shop on Blossom Street in Seattle called A Good Yarn have given rise to coordinating pattern books. Throughout the *Harry Potter* series, many of J. K. Rowling's characters wield knitting needles as well as wands.

In *The Broken Circle*, you will meet the knitting witches, who have been called to circle the dye pot once more and rekindle their magic, scattered for more than two decades and faded in a society where its colors and powers have become unwelcome, in an effort to save their world from destruction. In the intervening years, each witch has, however, practiced her singular talent and kept its flame flickering, even if in a diminished form: spinning and dyeing yarns for specific purposes, or coloring these efforts with crystals and plants that have magical qualities. In addition to maintaining the skills and knowledge that they cultivated together in the Potluck workshop, they have also been tellers of tales, serving as the carriers of stories that have been handed down through the years. In both these ways, they are guardians of the last vestiges of magic in their threatened homeland.

We hope that the spirit of the knitting witches inspires you to follow them on their colorful quest through the entire trilogy, and that your hands find delight in the working of the designs in the Companion Pattern Book. (Some of the patterns are well suited to aid the nonknitter in becoming an apprentice to the craft, while others are more appropriate for the adept practitioner.)

It's clear to me that each of us has the potential to experience some of the magic of the knitting witches in our own creative power. And now it's time to pack up some yarn, real or imaginary, and begin the adventure. . . .

Some say the world will end in fire,
Some say in ice.

ROBERT FROST

Red sky at night, sailors' delight.
Red sky in morning, sailors take warning.

FISHWIVES' TALE

A yarn is naught but a tall tale,
a continuous string wound around itself into a ball,
sometimes knotted, sometimes tangled,
or so the story goes.

SIERRA BLUE, KEEPER OF THE TALES

A dim form stole from the back of the dye shed.

The Gathering has begun.... Who will come?

BARELY VISIBLE IN THE PREDAWN LIGHT, a dim form stole from the back of the dye shed. Wrapping a shawl tight against the wind, the figure shuffled along the snow-packed path through the frozen herb garden and opened the gate to climb the knoll behind Merchants' Row.

At the top of the hill, the slowly blooming light revealed a woman, gray-haired and hunched—perhaps by age, but certainly against the wind. She scanned the snow-crusted rooftops that spiraled from the center of the city like wagon-wheel spokes. Then she directed her gaze toward watch fires that shone from the garrison bordering the Northlands and beyond. In the far distance, a plume of dirty smoke rose from the Northland Glacier. She felt certain a new band of Lowland raiders had passed unseen through the Blind Side of the glacier during the night. The air smelled faintly of fish oil, the odor cast by the smudge torches borne by the Southern invaders. She wondered if they had yet breached the Crystal Caves, as they burned out the belly of the ancient glacier in their quest for water.

An acrid wind caught a corner of her handspun shawl, threatening to snatch it from her grasp. From the straggly line of buildings that wound along the base of the foothills beneath her, a wooden sign groaned on its hinges. She knew without looking that it was the sign above her own shop. The screech of iron on iron sounded ominous.

The old woman searched the gray horizon for answers and found none. She fingered the shawl that she called her magic wrap. Old and worn, even though made from sturdy mohair, it was lavender and plum tinged with black, hand-dyed in a colorway called "Aubergine," a combination to which she had given her own name. This familiar shawl provided warmth and comfort, as well as courage sometimes.

This blustery morning she felt nothing but sorrow. If she had just searched her heart twenty years ago, she could have prevented the Lowlanders' desecration of the Middlelands. Before the water in the great pot in the dye shed had grown cold and the Middlefolk ceased to believe in her yarns, she could have prevented the damage. Yet she had been younger then, both strong and foolish.

She felt like a marionette whose strings had been cut. Smokey Jo was right: It was time to call the Twelve. It was past time. She knew not all of them would recognize the summoning fire in the sky. Of those who took notice, not all would heed its command. The circle of Twelve would remain broken, as it was before. Even broken, though, the circle might contain enough power to prevent the destruction of the world as they knew it.

She reached a veined hand to the skin of her neck and she felt the pain afresh, as if the betrayal had happened last night. How could she have chosen to trust that young woman, the one who on that last night of the Twelve ripped the amethyst circlet from her throat, then spurned the power of the group and fled south to the Lowlands, knowing none of them would follow her there? Then, coaxing some magic from the crystals she had stolen, she had learned to bend the Lowlanders' greed to her will. As the years passed, rivers raged and whirlwinds struck and forests burned. Now a grown woman, and no longer merely a novice, this former apprentice had become Aubergine's enemy. Known as the Dark Queen of the South, she had stripped the fields and forests, siphoned the rivers and lakes, and polluted the seas with the foul sludge that remained. Then the Lowlanders had been forced to invade the Northland for food and water. The old woman shook her head, unwilling to even think the name of her adversary.

A tiny, round gnome toiled up toward Aubergine from the path below, holding a tinderbox in hands warmed by felt mittens. Just last week she had rediscovered the silver container, shelved among dyestuffs in the back room, and glowing as it had not for decades.

Wheezing, the gnome gently lifted the delicate chest toward Aubergine. Dawn was beginning to send a hint of brightness above the horizon, but the old woman found she had no strength to open the box she now held. Made of seamless hammered metal, it had no lid.

The gnome clapped her hands together to warm them further against the morning chill. She coughed. "It's time," she said. "Quickly, before the dawn obscures the stars."

The old witch shook her head. "Poor little one, we are only two tired crones whose time has gone." The glowing chest remained closed between them, like an unanswered question. A loud crack startled them, just as the ground trembled under their feet, followed by an after jolt that jerked the tinderbox from Aubergine's hands and cast it into the snow. Clutching each other for balance, the women looked north, unable to see the distant avalanche but not surprised. Lowlanders had been mining the Northland Glacier for years, chipping away at ancient ice with sledgehammers, dumping frozen chunks into washes where they melted and flowed south. Now the entire border was unsafe. The Glacier Guard was useless, their ranks having dwindled to a few feeble oldsters playing dice outside the Burnt Holes. Even with fresh conscripts to swell their ranks, they were no match for the raiders.

The wind stung tears into the corners of Aubergine's eyes. She watched as Smokey Jo dug the glowing box out of the snow. Drops of water beaded across its top and ran down its sides, melted by the cold fire within.

The witch grasped her shawl tight against the buffeting wind, trying to muster enough strength to open the box. "Fire and Ice," she murmured, tasting the words that had the metallic flavor of war. Some would live, and some would die. But the Middlelands, caught between the Northland Guard and Lowland invaders, were about to change forever.

The gnome raised her dark eyes hopefully as her mistress scanned the horizon, searching for signs of sun.

"Everyone knows," Aubergine said. "Everyone knows to leave the glacier alone. Let it dwindle to the south as new snow packs it from the north, as nature intended." Her eyes sought out the gnome's. "When I was young, each year the glacier would disappear a little further down the rock-strewn valley and fossickers would collect the slow trail of treasure it released. And that was true and good."

"Fossickers would pan the rivers," Smokey Jo added, remembering. "Some would follow the trails of mineral-colored freshets that spilled each spring from the Crystal Lakes to pool behind the Teardrop Dam at the Top of the Notch. And that was true and good."

A gust ripped the magic wrap from Aubergine's grasp, leaving it held only by the amber stickpin at her throat. The shawl fluttered behind her like a cape. "The Lowlanders don't care what they unleash from the frozen past."

"That is why it is time," the gnome repeated, gently.

Aubergine nodded. Summoning what power she could muster, nothing like what she had known when all this began, she ran her fingers over the box until they remembered how to release its top. An inner spring clicked, allowing her to pry the cover.

The gnome leaned over to look closely at the fiery crystals inside. "I wish I could do that," she whispered.

"You have other talents," Aubergine said softly, her face rosy in the light. Was this enough? She asked herself. Could a broken-down band of aging women silence an army led by a traitor, formerly one of their own, who thought she could conquer all? "The day will dawn red as it has not for twenty years," she said. "And then we must wait to see who will answer its call."

Aubergine gathered the small handful of crystals in her bare hands. They glowed through the cracks formed between her fingers by her swollen knuckles. The colored shards felt strangely light and alive with cold fire. With a deep breath, she threw the jagged bits into the air. For a moment, nothing happened. Smokey Jo gazed skyward helplessly, and then looked up at Aubergine in confusion.

"The spark's gone out!" Smokey Jo cried. "The crystals have gone old and useless, like us!"

Aubergine's breath caught in her throat. "No, little one," she said. "No, they haven't." Both felt the warm rush of fire before they saw it. One by one, each blood-colored crystal burst over the horizon, wresting dawn from the day.

"Red sky comes morning. All take warning," the gnome whispered, her face shining pink with each flash of light as she bent to lift the empty tinderbox from the snow.

"I doubt there are more than nine of us left," Aubergine said, as they picked their way carefully down the icy hill to the yarn shop.

"Nine or all Twelve, we have to make ready." Smokey Jo cheerily blew a frozen cloud into her mittens. "Maybe enough of us will come that we may yet circle the great pot and meld crystal to fiber as we once did."

"It is time for a simmer," Aubergine nodded.

"Luck of the dye pot," the gnome said. "May we have the luck of the dye pot."

 *Aubergine's Magic Wrap*

A WRAP PATTERN

*This reversible wrap requires a beginner skill level,
and size after blocking measures 30" by 55".*

Get the pattern from PotluckYarn.com/epatterns

"Keep this mohair covered."

CHAPTER 1

Trouble at the World's Fair

SKYE THRUST THE LAST BURLAP SACK of colored fleece through the doorway of her mother's dye shed, and waited for her father to pull up with the wagon. It was early and chilly even though spring had recently touched the mountains of the Middlelands.

As her father approached, the only sound Skye heard was the soft *chuff chuff* of the two mountain ponies hitched to the wagon. The pair wore no silver bells this year, for they did not want to call attention to their journey.

"Whoa," Kendrick called, halting the dun geldings, Chuffer and Shep. Steam rose from their broad backs and their breath looked like the ragged smoke that rose from the unseen chimneys of the lower valley.

As Kendrick jumped down from the bench seat to help Skye load the wagon, the sun crested the eastern slope of Top Notch. It bathed their narrow pass in white light that glinted from the icy outcroppings at the base of the Teardrop Dam, sparkled across the Lavender Rill and struck the drifts of rotted snow that dotted the pastures like sheep. Skye blinked in the glare, her eyes beginning to water. She looked at her father, who had pulled out his handkerchief to wipe the tears that streamed down his face.

Before them, the freshly washed fleeces shone brightly, for the mohair locks were tipped mauve and baby blue from the crystal-swirled waters of Lavender Rill, which flowed past their farm. Swollen with the spring run-off from the colored freshets of the Northland Glacier, the rill had grown from a stream to a river. It thundered through their valley from the Teardrop Dam above. Their mountain goats favored the icy glacier water and the colors of the river clung to their fleeces. While the crystal shadings might fade with age, they never washed out completely. These whimsical stains had never been a problem before.

"Keep this mohair covered," Kendrick warned. "You don't want it confiscated before you get to the fair."

"These fleeces harbor no magic," Skye grumbled, securing the tops of the burlap bags and pulling the flaps tight. "It's not like they can spin and knit themselves."

The whole family was trying to pretend that this year was the same as the last. In truth, it could hardly have been more different. Over the winter Skye's older brother, Warren, not two years her senior, had been conscripted by the Northland Guard to help defend the glacier. The Lowland raiders ventured north to burn out glacial ice for its crystalline mineral water, at the same time that they searched for plunder and ancient secrets. Warren had been gone now from Top Notch for two passes of the moon. No word of him had traveled up the river valley to relieve their anxiety. Skye's younger brother, Garth, slight for his fifteen years, proved no substitute for his brother. And Skye could see that he would never be, at least in Kendrick's eyes.

Absentmindedly, she twisted her corn-silk hair into a loose bun and turned in the doorway, adjusting her eyes to the dim light of the shed, where she and her mother had toiled through the long winter. Sierra's dye pot was dormant for once, and the air now held little of the heavy lanolin odor of sheep and mohair. The spinning wheel stood silent, and warped wooden drying racks stretched bare before the cold hearth. Skye had piled the hanks of homespun yarn into split-twig baskets that now leaned against the porch rail outside.

Even the ripple-stitched afghan that usually lay rumpled on the window bench sat neatly folded on the rush stool. Skye had spent much of the previous winter on the window bench, tucked into the afghan, preparing for the Middlemarch World's Fair. In the disarray of her cozy nest, Skye passed the evening hours with a mug of honeyed cinnamon tea, spinning crystal-dyed roving into yarn before the fire. Nearby, her mother felted garments by boiling them in a pot brimming with the colored waters of the high glacier ponds. As they worked, Sierra told fanciful tales of the legendary Potluck Twelve, stories Skye and Garth loved to hear. Sierra called them her yarns. Each day as she listened, Skye knit row upon row of headscarves, vests, hats, and mittens, as well as clogs, slippers, shawls, mufflers, and the odd cardigan or pullover. The stories seemed to become part of the knitted fabric she made.

Now they were ready for the fair, which should have been simply a joyous prospect, yet this year was not like any other.

Working side by side, father and daughter loaded bags of raw fiber shorn from their alpine goats into the wagon bed. Each snowy fleece was skirted and tagged, the long silky staples tinged with color, the exact shade depending upon which glacier-fed freshet each mountain goat had drunk from. They made space behind the bench seat for the prepared fibers, the batts, and the rovings, all ready to be spun into yarn. These were shaded aqua, teal green, lavender, and light blue. The natural hues were random, products of the rock flour that tumbled ceaselessly through the ponds and streams each spring. As the tinted run-off melted from the Northland Glacier, it flowed through a succession of Crystal Lakes, deepening in color as it went, until finally it ran down the Lavender Rill.

These days, dyeing anything with glacier crystal was forbidden, Skye knew. She wondered if the judges at the Middlemarch fair would be learned enough to distinguish between Sierra's fleeces, tinted through the natural effects of the animals' grazing, and other fiber, illegally dyed with ground-up stone. During the war, all forms of crystal use had been outlawed by the Northland Guard, lest someone mistakenly unleash bad magic that the invading Lowlanders could harness. Because of this risk, the Northlanders had decided to stop the Southern raiders with armies of men unaided by witchery, especially in the form of crystal magic. The regulations had much support in the Northlands, but were considered foolish here in the Middlelands, where using the odd crystal to hex or heal had been a way of life for generations.

The Northlanders' approach was not working. With almost nothing to hinder them, bands of Lowlanders boldly raided north. As they burned out the frozen underbelly of the glacier, it was said that they left behind pestilence and disease and worse.

As if real magic even existed any more, Skye thought. The ponies snorted. If there was magic in the air or water, or in the rose quartz crystals she kept on her bedside table, she would certainly like to see it. No amount of pink crystals under her pillow or blue crystals in her bath had been able to rescue her from the constrained life of Top Notch this past fall and winter. Even though she enjoyed the fibers, the yarns, and the stitching, she was so starved for conversation after Warren left that she felt like screaming.

Skye glanced at her father, afraid to voice her fears, lest he confine her to the farm. At daybreak, as they breakfasted quickly on goat's milk and porridge laced with dried berries, Kendrick had made a sudden announcement. Neither he nor Garth would accompany them to the fair, a family outing that Skye had not missed in her seventeen years, nor Garth in his fifteen.

Although he seemed surprised, Garth had not raised his voice to complain; he never did. Garth was slight and wiry compared to Warren, who had been as tall as Kendrick when he left for the Northland Guard, and was an avid outdoorsman. Last year, Kendrick had allowed Warren to compete in the Winter Games in the Northlands, where he had placed first in the bobsled division, outrunning grown men. As soon as that happened, Warren Blue became known far and wide as the best sledder in all of the Middlelands. Youths from all over had asked to train with him.

But that had been before the war began again. Not even this fame had kept Warren from being one among the many boys taken from their homes against their wills to defend the northern border.

Only Sierra had questioned her husband's decision. "Kendrick," she protested, smoothing Garth's sandy hair away from his face, as was her habit. "The boy has not set foot off this farm since last fall. Surely he can spend a day or two days at the fair?"

As Sierra raised her face to look at Kendrick, Skye noted the flecks of gold that stood out in her mother's irises. They reminded Skye of a mountain cat's eyes. Sierra's children had always called the knowing look she gave them her lion eyes, for little escaped her notice.

Kendrick shook his head. "How can we all go?" he asked, begging Sierra to understand, or so it seemed. "The goats are not down from the highlands, and the Teardrop Dam threatens to flood the Rill at any moment." He lowered his voice—not angry, Skye could tell—just afraid. "What will become of the farm if the Rill floods the valley and we are all a day's ride away?"

While what he said was true, what remained unsaid was their shared uneasiness now that Warren had been taken from them like a convict. The Guard had put him, along with other boys they had rounded up, into a rolling cage that waited on the Military Road. Later a rumor had reached them, even as high as this small valley at the top of the Notch, that one male from each family to serve the Glacier Guard would not be enough. The Northland Border Patrol threatened to pick up any man or boy who dared to show his face along the main track into Middlemarch. Skye thought of Katarina, her friend, whose family owned the Mill on the Rill in the village at the bottom of the Notch. Katarina's brother, Averill, was no older than Skye herself. She wondered if he was still safe. She wondered if she would see him this day.

Skye handed the final bag, stuffed with pale lavender fleece, up to her father and waited until her mother went inside to gather their traveling cloaks, out of earshot. Then she asked the question that had been burning in mind her all morning. "Do you think the Lowlanders really mean to harm us with bad magic, father? Or do they merely come to burn out the glacier for water, as the Northlanders say?"

"I do not doubt the folk of the Lowlands are already here among us," he replied. Grunting, Kendrick loaded into the back of the cart three forkfuls of hay and a bucket of sweet feed for the ponies. He brushed off his sheepskin coat before he continued. "Southerners want the water—they need it badly. They will do whatever it takes to free the ice and funnel fresh water down to their parched lands."

"But it is said that melting the glacier will unlock old secrets," Skye replied, giving her father a troubled look. "According to mother's yarns, it could unleash dark things, too, things that have lain buried since the last age of ice." Skye lowered her voice. "Such ancient magic could destroy us all, mother says. Is that why magic is forbidden in all the lands?"

Kendrick shrugged uneasily, sweating so that he had to push up the brim of his Potluck hat and give his forehead some air. "Some say the world will end in fire," he admitted. "Others say yet again in ice." He sucked in a deep breath. "Mean times, you do what you feel you must."

Her father's Potluck hat was one of the originals, Skye realized. Only recently had she been blessed with the discernment to tell the difference between the old and the new. The rare, hand-painted, crystal-dyed fiber in her father's hat came from a shop called Potluck Yarn, located in Bordertown, a city on the northern border. There, it was rumored, a much younger Sierra had apprenticed at a dye house, intending to forsake farm and family to master the magical dye crystals.

Skye had never been able to prize from Sierra what had prevented her from following that path farther. The deep, multicolored blues and greens of Kendrick's hand-knit hat melded together in a swirl of jades and teals that made Skye think of the calming strength of deep, still waters. Her father, who otherwise often had an air of worry and of not trusting his own instincts, always seemed strong and sure of himself when he wore the hat, which had lately become all the time.

"Have you ever seen the Lowlands, father?" Skye asked.

Kendrick looked away from her, as if looking at something she could not see. Finally, he said, "It is a wasted place." He sighed. "A burning dustbowl with all the goodness of the land used up. It is no longer a place to grow crops or to hunt or fish for food."

"You have been there," Skye said. This time it was not a question.

Kendrick took off his hat, turning it around and around in his hands before giving a slow nod. "Don't tell your mother."

Then the rumors might be true, Skye thought, biting her lip. But it all could make sense, couldn't it? Someone had been leading bands of Lowlanders past Top Notch, up the far shores of Teardrop Lake, and then to the base of the Northland Glacier. And back. Once last fall and then again this winter before the Glacier Guard had come for Warren, Kendrick had set out fully provisioned to hunt elk and had come back over a week later from their hunting lodge, known as the Sleep Out, with nothing to show but grimy clothes and an empty pantry sack. *I wonder if Warren knew*, Skye thought. *I wonder if that is why the soldiers came for him so suddenly.*

The door of the farmhouse creaked, and her mother came out carrying their alpaca traveling cloaks piled atop more bags and bundles. *All I want is a little fun, even if only for a day at the fair*, Skye thought, dismissing her dark conjectures as she hurried to help Sierra. Carefully, she had packed the sky-blue ribbons she planned to wear to the Spring Carnival dance, hoping she would meet up with Katarina and entice her bashful brother Averill to join them for the Sugar on Snow. But maybe he was gone, too, Skye worried, as her mother handed her the basket of potato bread and goat cheese with dried apples, and then the flask of mulled cider. Skye stored their food beneath the plank seat of the pony cart. Or maybe Averill was hiding at his family's mill-side farm at the bottom of the lower valley, just as afraid to drive the family's wagon into Middlemarch as her father seemed to be.

Skye had not been away from the Notch since the road filled with snow the fall before. Since then, the only other folk she had seen were sledders, rangy youths from the Northlands who climbed the Notch trail with Warren, a master at guiding the quick runner sleds through the narrow mountain passes. The hunters came up, too, to drink hard cider in the Sleep Out and track the elusive alpine moose with her father. But they came less often, and now not at all since the Glacier Wars started. Sometimes Garth would trail along to help clean and quarter the moose, and to skin the precious gray-white hide that could later be sewn into windproof garments that made their wearers nearly invisible.

The mountain ponies stamped impatiently in their black leather harnesses that gleamed with dull silver. Sierra slipped back into the house and returned with her rucksack, which contained a precious bundle wrapped in waterproof cloth.

None of the family needed to ask what was rolled in the cloth. For their quality of workmanship, the garments inside were prized more that any other handcraft in all the Middlelands. The traveling cloak and cinch bags and knapsacks were virtually seamless; the caps and mittens fit any wearer. Sierra's hand-knits lasted forever. There were those, too, who said that her glacier dyes gave the garments certain qualities. Surely not magical qualities, for no one that Skye knew took magic seriously any more, but unusual qualities nonetheless.

It was true that Sierra's garments were warmer than most and windproof, but Skye attributed this to the way her mother boiled and finished the pieces in the clean mineral waters that trickled south from the glacier. Water and snow failed to penetrate Sierra's felt, but then their alpine goats yielded finer fibers than most, and the mohair yarns they made had a higher twist than other homespuns. The natural blues, lavenders, and grays that colored the yarn made the wearer almost invisible against icy outcrops and snow. Perhaps this was because the snow itself looked blue in shadows, and the appearance of invisibility was nothing more than an optical illusion, but perhaps it was not. Some said that when Sierra was accepted to study at the famed Potluck Yarn Fiber Cooperative as a child, she apprenticed to the legendary dye mistress, Aubergine. In those times magic had flourished, and Aubergine was the undisputed queen of the magical crystals she had gleaned from the underground rivers that flowed south from the Northland Glacier.

Aubergine's Potluck Yarn, a fiber arts trade school for girls, provided craft education for all, but hardly any were chosen to learn how to meld crystalline dye to fiber and how to harness the resulting magic. These handpicked few were allowed to circle the great pot that simmered in the back room of the dye shed and to witness the swirl of colors called luck of the dye pot. Such apprentices were commonly known as knitting witches, but in more knowledgeable circles they were referred to as the Twelve.

Skye did not know now if Aubergine ever existed. Sierra always claimed that the Potluck Yarn where she was working when she chanced to meet Kendrick was just a simple fiber cooperative. There was no witchery, and there was no Twelve. There were merely classes where students spun yarns and knit garments to sell in a studio not bigger than a glorified yarn shop. Although Sierra was free with fanciful "yarns" she told as bedtime stories before the fire at night, Skye learned not to ask her mother more about her past. When she did so unbidden, she received a warning glance from her father.

What unlikely forces had brought her parents together when they were young? Kendrick had no family or friends in the Middlelands, the Western Highlands, the fisheries of the Far East, or even the Northlands. He seemed to have appeared out of nowhere during Sierra's apprenticeship at the Potluck. Soon after, she had forsaken the life of a magical witch for the bucolic existence of a fiber-farm wife.

"This is the last of it." Sierra loaded her bundle into a secure space in the wagon. Skye slipped into the knitted cloak that matched her mother's, both garments spun from a combination of alpaca and llama down dyed in the opaque shades of sun-touched frost flowers, a colorway they called Glacier Ice that blended with the snow on this spring morning. Skye pulled on her moose mittens and climbed up to join her mother in the wagon. Sierra's hair was tied back in a practical ponytail with a multicolored strand of yarn. The only sign of age around her unlined face was a touch of gray hair at her temples, a few lighter strands mixed in with honey blond.

"Better get a move on," Kendrick said, with an eye toward the fields. From the hillside a patch of red approached; even in the glare, Skye knew it was Garth, in his old red barn sweater, on his way back from feeding the goats.

"We'll at least say goodbye." Sierra accepted the reins from her husband as Garth slammed the gate and rushed over, his cheeks flushed from running and the empty grain bucket banging against his legs.

"Can't I go?" he begged his father.

"Maybe next year," Kendrick said gently. "By the look of the rill, I think we will have to move the goats to higher ground before dark. Did you see the rim of the Teardrop from the slope?"

"Higher yet," Garth admitted, with a quick nod, dragging his eyes from the wagon. "And the water's darker, almost purple. It's flush with the top of the sluice board." Chuffer nuzzled at the grain bucket and Garth stroked the pony's head, letting the small, soft muzzle sniff his felt mittens.

"Then there is your answer," Kendrick said. "Dark water means that the caves deep in the glacier have flooded and even the Crystal Lakes are not able to hold back the water."

"It happens every spring," Garth muttered.

"Not like this." Over the top of Garth's head, Kendrick gave his wife a worried glance. "I smelled smoke last night."

"And I as well," Sierra said. "It had the fishy odor of something rotten burning."

"The rank smolder comes from the smudge fires the Lowlanders light to burn out the glacier," Kendrick said. "I've seen them time and again." He gave Garth's shoulder a rough squeeze. "We've already lost one son to this war. We'll not lose another."

Garth said nothing, just looked down and stroked the pony's neck. Skye could see that although his eyes were rimmed with tears, he would not let them spill over in front of his father. It had been months since Garth had left the pass, too, Skye reminded herself, and he sorely missed his older brother—to say nothing of the added chores that he'd had to shoulder.

"See you in three days?" Sierra asked it like a question.

Kendrick seemed not to notice. "Be careful," he reminded her.

"And you," Sierra replied, then, more gently, to Garth, as she paused to lay a hand on his arm. "And you."

She slapped the reins and the ponies stepped out surefootedly. The wagon wheels creaked in the snowy ruts.

An unsettling fear gripped Skye as they left the yard and she looked back at the little farmhouse with its sturdy stone foundation beneath its timbered walls and cedar-shingled roof. Lavender Rill Farm, her parents had named it, after the river that ran the length of the pass. After building the main house the summer he and Sierra had first moved to the Notch, Kendrick had added a chicken coop and a live-stock shed. A few years later, after the children were born, he had built a little ell onto the kitchen. Skye had never lived anywhere else.

Skye put her hands to her cheeks, for her face felt flushed. Warm feelings were always coming over her whenever she wore her travel-ing cloak. This one panicked her, for she felt as if she would never return to her family life at the Notch, and would never see their farm-house again. But the feverish thoughts were gone as quickly as they had come. She shook off their aftereffects with a shiver, and pulled her cloak tighter.

The sun rose in the sky and burned through the morning mist that hung over the valley. As they made their way toward the Lower Notch, the road widened into a muddy track and the snow disappeared. The Lavender Rill rumbled off to their right as it spilled grape-colored water down the mountain. A cluster of stone buildings hugged the narrow defile of the lower pass, dwarfed by the great grain mill that straddled the river. Mill on the Rill it was called, and almost everyone in the lower valley had something to do with it. Skye flung back her hood, breathing deeply of the aromas of winter wheat and cherry that scented the air from the bread ovens. The delivery wagon was missing from the mill yard, and there was no sign of Katarina or Averill. Their grandfather, the Gaffer, was at the wellspring near the hitching post. Sierra turned the ponies into the low enclosure and halted at the watering trough.

"How goes it, Gaffer? What news?" She called, as the ponies drank deeply.

"If it isn't Sierra Blue," the old man smiled, bringing them a pitcher of water. "And young Skye Blue, the perfect image of her mother."

"Where is everyone?" Skye's smile faded to a frown, as she looked around at the deserted mill yard.

"Gone," Gaffer's blue eyes flashed under snowy brows as he retrieved the pitcher from Sierra and handed it to Skye. "Katarina and her mother left before daybreak, to set up their stall at the fair while the loaves of bread were still warm."

"And Averill?" Skye asked anxiously.

"Gone, too," Gaffer said, and this time there was no light in his eyes. "The Northlanders took him away this past fortnight. With barely sixteen winters behind him."

"Younger than our Warren," Sierra nodded sadly. "Warren's two months' gone and we've had no word."

"Nor us. They say the Northland border is where they take conscript recruits." Gaffer gave a bitter laugh. "I guess they figure it's too far to run home. I've never been to Bordertown, but 'tis a rough place, from what I hear. Full of water fouled by the glacier burn." He gave them an unblinking stare. "How can you live in a place where you can't drink the water? I don't care what they say about magic being forbidden. That whole city's full of it. And it's bad."

As Gaffer ranted on, Skye saw something flicker in her mother's golden brown eyes. A knowing look? A glimmer of fear? It couldn't be fear.

"Well, it's old magic, anyway." Gaffer said. "The rest of your men? Safe, are they?"

"Hiding," Sierra said brightly. "Tending the goats."

"You'll have that." Gaffer nodded, looking toward the swollen river and the mountains beyond. He took off his hat and swabbed at his forehead. "The air is warm, too warm this time of year. There's smoke in the valley, which bears no good tidings. Take care on the road."

"And you," Sierra replied, picking up the reins, and backing the ponies away. "It would not surprise me if the Teardrop Lake spills over the dam this day."

They made good time through the lower valley and before long they were able to turn onto the main road, where their mountain ponies fell in behind heavier wagons pulled by mules or teams of oxen, headed south from the mills of Woolen Woods and the trading-post town of Banebridge. The junction was known as the Falls, for here their fierce Lavender Rill emptied from the hillside into the River Runne below. The waterfall was a favorite fishing spot, and the ledges were nice for picnics, for you could watch the pretty purple water dilute instantly to a near-colorless hue as the rill splashed into the wide, flat Runne. Skye scanned the makeshift food stalls and tents set up along the river's edge, and caught a whiff of fried eggs and bacon that made her realize just how long ago they had eaten breakfast. She glanced at her mother, but she knew Sierra would not want to lose their place in the line along the crowded track. She dug a handful of dried apples out of their lunch basket.

The going was slow along the main road. Everywhere Middleland-ers like themselves rode horseback or trudged on foot, driving sheep or leading a prize bull or calf. Ahead of them and behind, as far as Skye could see, carts and wagons were piled high with handmade quilts and jars of mountain berry jams and jellies, as well as crates of protesting goats and lambs, yipping shepherd puppies, and piglets. There were spinning wheels and looms, iron pots and hearth brooms, and even a wagon bearing a portable forge and blacksmith's bellows. But some-thing was amiss; and whatever it was involved more than the stench that grew stronger as they headed into the valley—a fetid scent of rot and disease.

"Mother, there are no men," Skye realized all at once. "No men at all, and hardly any boys."

"As I feared." Sierra nodded grimly. "The world is about to change again. Do you smell that smoke?"

Skye wrinkled her nose and nodded.

Sierra turned to scan the sky behind them from beneath the brim of her hat. "It looks to be coming from the northwest. A glacier fire, I believe, though many would deny that to keep the peace." She shook her head in frustration. "No matter that we hide in the mountains of the Notch, change still reaches us. We are sadly unprepared."

"What are we to do?" Skye asked. "Conscriptors march down from the Northlands and arrest our men. Raiders sneak from the south to steal our water and foul our air."

"It is the sad plight of the Middlefolk," Sierra said, attempting to soothe her daughter without dismissing her concerns. "We are forever caught between the north and the south, through no fault of our own."

"Then why do we hide?" Skye asked. "Are we more leery of the north or the south? I've yet to set eyes on a Lowlander. Are they really terrifying?"

"No, no, not as a race," Sierra said, her lion eyes scanning the distance as the ponies slowed to a stop behind the train of wagons that snaked toward the Middlemarch bridge. "But there is one person who rules the South, one who would drive the Lowlanders to mine the glacier in the hope of stealing the secrets of the ancients at any cost."

"Who is he?"

"Not he, but she." Sierra's gaze assessed the hold-up at the bridge. "They are inspecting wagon loads ahead. Ready yourself."

"She?" Skye searched her mother's face. "Do you mean the raven-haired girl you mention in your yarns? The one who stole the necklace and left in the night? She is real?"

Sierra nodded. "She is a grown woman now. And she controls the South."

"I thought those were just old stories," Skye said, recalling nights by the fire, the enchanting tales of the Potluck Twelve. "The Guard controls the north. The Lowlanders control the south."

Sierra shook her head.

"So you spin your yarns from the truth?" Skye asked in disbelief. "Your Tasman is real, as is Aubergine? All the rest of them, too?"

"Shhh," Sierra hushed her as their wagon approached the entrance to the bridge. "Do not name them aloud." She watched as a young soldier wearing a gray uniform beckoned them toward the checkpoint. She lightly slapped the ponies' reins and the wagon pulled forward. "This is neither the time nor the place."

Skye stiffened as two men of the Glacier Guard approached, one on either side of the wagon. Chuffer snorted and backed away, almost pushing the back of the wagon into the mule cart behind them, until Sierra calmed him. The men wore short tunics embroidered with the white crest of the Northland Glacier, and stiff leggings tucked into nailed glacier boots. Skye had seen such garb just once before. Men like these had taken her brother.

"Good morning," Sierra said, coolly.

"And you." The taller soldier's distinctly Northland accent reminded Skye of her mother's way of speaking. Climbing gear hung from his leather belt: an ice pick and a length of thin braided rope. He must have been a scout in the Northlands, or maybe a sledder like her brother.

"Where do you drive from this day?" he asked.

Sierra appraised him. "The top of the Notch."

The tall guard cast a questioning look at the other soldier.

The shorter man explained. "It is a small mountain pass here in the Middlelands, which begins at that grain mill and goes up to the Teardrop Dam. A handful of families raise mountain goats and hunt moose along the lake. There are a few farms and a sleep-out lodge at the top of the Notch, and not much else. A forsaken place."

"Teardrop Lake," the tall soldier repeated. He gave Skye a curious look. "There is good sledding up there, I have heard."

The short soldier held only a long pike, although he had a wicked-looking knife strapped to his waist, and a shield and a broadsword were propped against the bridge abutment. This one had the look of a bully, Skye thought.

"What is your purpose here?" The short soldier began to swat his pole at their bags and bundles.

"We've come to sell our garments and yarns." Sierra turned in alarm as the short bully stuck his pike into a bag of fleece. "Take care," she warned. "You'll spoil the roving."

"We have a stall in the main tent every year," Skye said, feeling her anger begin to rise. She watched as the taller guard unlatched the top of one of the twig baskets, spilling hanks of lavender and blue yarn into the wagon bed. He jumped back as if stung.

"Shards!" he swore.

"Why do you spit oaths and spill yarns?" Sierra asked, ever calm.

Skye reached out quickly to save the skeins.

The short guard flicked a hank away from her with the tip of his pike. "Are these not dyed with magic crystals?" he asked slyly. "I hear you folk up in the Notch do things your own way. You guide Lowland parties disguised as moose hunters to hidden sleep-outs. You sled on the Military Road without a pass."

Sierra gave him a sharp glance but said nothing.

Skye took the bait. "Do you know of my brother Warren? Warren Blue of Top Notch?" She asked. "You must have heard of him. He won the Winter Games last year. He is the best sledder in all of the Middlelands." Her eyes turned from the short soldier to search the face of the taller guard. She sensed that the tall foreigner from the Northlands was not mean-spirited like his companion. He looked out of place here. "Do you have any news?" she decided to ask. "Any word at all?"

"We know of your brother," the tall guard confirmed before the short one cut him off.

"Warren Blue the great sledder, is a now a deserter." The short soldier's curled lip exposed a row of crooked teeth as he laughed. "He is wanted, perhaps by both sides."

"Warren would do no such thing," Skye shot back.

"It must be that you get no word at all up at your Notch," the short soldier mocked. "Magic has been outlawed in all the lands. Traveling the Military Road without a Northland Pass is a punishable offense. Lowland guides and defectors alike are considered traitors with prices on their heads."

"Enough, Maynard," the tall soldier warned.

The short soldier snapped the tip of his pike again, and the hank of yarn impaled there seemed in danger of being tossed into the river. His eyes narrowed as he glared at Sierra. "Using magic crystals for any purpose is forbidden. You could go to the darkest chamber of the Burnt Holes for this."

The tall soldier reached out a sturdy hand to stay the short one's pike. "Enough, I said."

"These are not crystal-dyed," Skye said hotly. "And they have no magic." She picked up a skein of yarn and shook it at the guards. "Watch closely. Nothing happens."

"Our goats drink from the freshets spilling from the Teardrop," Sierra explained, stilling her daughter's arm. As her lion eyes gazed at the short guard, she spoke slowly and carefully. "These glacier waters are most pure. Some ponds are blue and purple, even pink from the rock flour that swirls through the water. This powder tinges the locks of hair on the mountain goats. That is all." She pulled her traveling cloak tighter, her eyes on the taller guard. "It is just natural dye, not magic."

"Natural dye, not magic," Maynard repeated, looking a bit dazed.

Skye was growing warm in her traveling cloak, whether from her anger or just sitting here in the balmy air before the bridge she did not know. She began to unfasten her wrap, but her mother's hand reached out again to stop her.

"I don't like it," the short guard murmured to the tall one. "What with new fires from the glacier and the sledder gone missing." He motioned to a pair of foot soldiers loitering at the checkpoint. "These are two of the ones we seek. Detain them."

Skye began to sweat but could not shrug out of her cloak. Her mother's hand gripped her arm hard. When she opened her mouth to speak nothing came out.

Sierra's lion eyes focused on the short guard. "You do not seek us," she told him calmly.

He gave her a quizzical look, and held his hand up to slow the approaching soldiers. "No?"

"No," she answered. "We are mere goat farmers. Hand spinners and knitters who know nothing of magical dyes."

"Nothing?" The guard motioned the foot soldiers away. "Nothing at all?"

"Nothing," Sierra confirmed. "There is nothing to fear."

Skye felt a surge of warmth flowing from her mother's fingers.

"Our yarns are entered in the Goat to Garment contest," she heard herself telling the guards. "If they harbor magic, we will be disqualified and detained."

"Let the judges decide," Sierra suggested. It was not a question.

"Let the judges decide," the tall soldier echoed as the other guard gave a slow nod.

Sierra pointed down to the colorless water that thundered beneath the bridge, waiting until both guards glanced down at the swollen river. "Up at the top of the Lavender Rill, the water really is purple."

The tall soldier nodded to his companion. "The judges decide, then?"

"They don't know anything." The short soldier sneered. He lifted his pike to let them pass. "Women."

Skye stayed silent until their wagon clattered across the bridge and passed under the arch of the fairgrounds. Above them flapped the blue and pink banner of the Middlemarch World's Fair, held each year as a celebration of spring.

"Mother, I've seen you do that before," Skye said softly, looking straight ahead. Soldiers were everywhere, dotting the sodden grounds with short tunics of gray. These were simple foot soldiers, she could see, with short swords or knives strapped to their belts, or pikes in hand. She saw no others dressed for climbing or sledding, like the tall guard who had detained them at the bridge.

"Do what?" Sierra brought the wagon to a halt before the grand hall, a great tent adorned with pennants snapping in the breeze.

She smiled, knowing their empty stall stood within, waiting to be stocked with their garments and yarns as it had been for twenty years without fail.

"Get people to do what you want," Skye said. "Is that part of the magic that ugly soldier was yelping about? Did you see his twisted teeth? I know when Father wears his Potluck hat—" She broke off, not wanting to reveal the conversation of this morning. "Well, things just seem a bit different."

Sierra shrugged. "I just used a little power of persuasion." She paused. "It is a womanly ploy."

"But I grew so warm," Skye complained, shedding her outer garments at last. "And you wouldn't let me take off my cloak. I could not speak."

"Well," Sierra laughed, also laying her cloak aside. "Mayhap there is a little magic simmering in the dye crystals yet?"

"You've known all along," Skye accused, as they got down from the wagon and began unloading their bundles. "There was more to that Potluck than yarns!"

Sierra sought out her precious bundle of garments, while Skye strapped on the first of the twig baskets. "Yes, there was," she said at last.

"You've known forever."

"I've known since my days at the Potluck," Sierra admitted. "But that meant nothing until now, and now I fear nothing I do will matter." She turned to face her daughter directly. "Skye, I cannot protect you here. If anything happens to me, you must make your way north to the border. Promise me."

"But what of Father?" Skye asked. "And the farm?"

"There will be nothing he can do," Sierra said, calmly. "It will be too late."

"I thought I saw him shedding tears this morning," Skye murmured.

Sierra nodded without comment. "There is a yarn shop in Bordertown, in the borough of Merchants' Row. You will find it near the end of the main thoroughfare. The sign does say Potluck Yarn. Go to the side gate through the herb garden and bang on the summer-kitchen door until someone lets you in. That someone will be a gnome called Smokey Jo. Have her take you to Aubergine."

"Aubergine," Skye breathed. "You mean she is real as well?" She gave her mother an appraising look. "It must be they all are."

"She will know you on sight," Sierra assured her daughter. "Now let's go see who is about."

Inside the main tent, the air was rich with the smell of lanolin and sheep's wool, of fresh bread and eucalyptus soap. Skye breathed deeply, listening to the festive trill of flutes and pipes from one of the booths.

"Katarina!" She called, spying her friend at the bread stall just inside the east entrance. A familiar small banner strung over the booth announced Mill on the Rill, with its emblem of a stone hut straddling a lavender river.

The dark-haired girl looked up and wiped her floury hands on her gaudy show apron and came around the wooden table to hug Skye. She smelled of rye and honeyed oats.

"Skye," she said, stepping back out of the hug to look at her friend. "How have you fared? I have been so worried since the soldiers. . . ." She trailed off, glancing at the line of buyers surrounding their table. "Oh, let me cut you a slice of bread. It's still warm."

Skye glanced at Sierra, deep in conversation with Katarina's mother, who was weighing sacks of milled grain for a waiting farmer's wife. "But you're so busy!"

"Those soldiers, they are ravenous." Katarina plopped a half dozen tarts onto a scrap of paper and twisted it loosely before handing it across the counter to a guardsman, who began to eat as he walked away. "And they have Northland silver." She showed Skye the newly minted coins stamped with the glacier on one side.

"But aren't you afraid?" Skye asked, accepting a slice of bread spread thick with honey. "They are everywhere."

Katarina shrugged. "They have to eat." She paused. "You heard about Averill? I know you cared for him."

"Your grandfather told us." Skye demolished the bread, realizing that she hadn't eaten since the handful of dried apples, hours ago.

"He wanted to go, that is the truth," Katarina said, slicing more bread. "He couldn't wait to leave, ever since father died."

"I hope he comes back," Skye said. Two years earlier, the miller had died in a terrible accident, when the great grinding stone split and heaved to the ground, crushing him.

"Averill has been gone only a fortnight," Katarina shrugged. "Maybe he's still in training at the great garrison in the Northlands; who knows?"

"We've heard no word from Warren. But did you see that guard at the crossing, dressed as a sledder?"

"Really tall," Katarina nodded, refilling the breadbasket.

Skye took a big bite of bread. "He seemed to know something. And he wasn't from around here."

"Lots of folk aren't from around here, silly." Katarina shook her head, and smiled as she waited on another customer. "We're at the World's Fair. I've seen Northlanders, Middlelanders, folk from the Western Highlands, and even from the fisheries of the Far East."

"He knew more than he was saying. I thought maybe he knew something about Warren."

"Did you get into trouble for your yarns?" Katarina asked, distracted, as she turned to open another jar of honey. "They have been throwing people out of the fair left and right for supposed use of magic."

"That's ridiculous," Skye said, with growing worry.

Sierra appeared to summon Skye back to the tasks at hand. "Come, we must let these ladies do their work and get to ours."

A group of armed soldiers passed them as they reached the center aisle and turned the corner toward their stall. "Trouble is brewing," Sierra murmured to Skye. "Be watchful of the Guard."

As they reached their booth space, they saw that the stand to the right of theirs, which sold buttons and clasps handcrafted of metal and wood, shell, and bone, was already half set up, but the spot on the left that usually sold herbal remedies stood empty.

"Chloe," Sierra greeted the robust lady in the adjoining booth, "All is well with you?"

"Sierra!" Smiling, the woman looked up from arranging cards of matched buttons. She wore a huge black shawl, fastened with a stickpin of hammered copper, over a flowing crimson dress. "Yes, and you?" She forged out into the aisle to give Sierra an ample hug. "I wondered if you would show this day."

"Nothing could keep us away." Sierra glanced toward the empty booth. "But where is Esmeralde?"

"Never showed yet," Chloe replied. "Every year she is here before me, already selling herbs and teas while I set up. Many have been looking for her." She lowered her voice. "Not all of them friendly."

"Oh, Mother, Esmeralde is so old," Skye said. "You don't think she passed on?"

"No." Sierra's eyes flashed. "Did soldiers come looking for her, too?"

The plump woman nodded slowly. "Word is she's afraid of being arrested for misusing magic in her colored syrups. Some say she was one of those Potluck witches way back when."

"So Northland soldiers would arrest an old woman for selling cough medicine," Sierra said in disbelief. With a quiet shake of her head, she covered their table with a cloth and stowed her precious bundle underneath. "These are strange times."

They had almost finished unloading the wagon when trumpets sounded and they heard the announcement for the Always Alpaca judging.

"Should I still enter my shawl?" Skye asked as they hurried back to their stall with the last of the burlap bags of roving. In the main aisle of the tent, a stream of soldiers passed on their right, while others walked behind them, checking vendors for contraband crystals. Inside their booth, Skye's Suri lace shawl laid airing across several baskets of yarn.

"Of course." Her mother lifted the featherweight garment of shaded amethyst. "It is your winter's work. Take it to the judge's stand."

"They will say it is crystal-dyed," Skye whispered.

"You will just explain," Sierra replied, handing her the shawl as a group of soldiers turned down the main aisle and headed for their stall. "Everything will be fine."

Skye looked up in alarm, recognizing the short Guardsman from the bridge who was leading the pack. "Go," Sierra shooed her away with a wave of her hand. "Go!"

Skye hurried from the booth with her shawl and made her way to the judges' pavilion. As she waited in line to enter the contest, Skye saw that in addition to yarns prepared for the Goat to Garment Competition, the craft tables were already loaded with fleeces and furs for the Sheep to Shawl, the Moose to Mittens, and the Bear to Blanket. As she surveyed the array of shawls and scarves at the Always Alpaca table, Skye's breath caught in her throat. None of the projects were naturally shaded like her own. She was about to step out of line when abruptly it was her turn to stand before the judges. Perched behind the table heaped with garments, they gazed at her expectantly. She focused on the one with snowy eyebrows. He reminded her of Katarina's grandfather, the Gaffer.

"I would like to enter the Always Alpaca judging," she faltered, spreading her shawl across the others.

"Nicely knit," the old man admitted, fingering the intricate Fair-Isle pattern. "But crystal dyes are forbidden, under the new guidelines. We cannot qualify you under the World's Fair rules."

"The yarn is not crystal-dyed, it is natural," Skye said. "Our animals drink from the colored freshets below the Teardrop Lake, and their locks keep the color. Have you heard of the Lavender Rill? It flows right by our house and the water really is purple."

"I have never heard of it," the judge replied. He turned to another old man, seated at the next table. "Have you heard of naturally dyed fleeces, pink and blue and purple?"

"I have heard," the other man acknowledged, giving the garment a cautious glance over the top of his ground glass spectacles. "It is nothing but an old woman's tale. Take the shawl and hide it well," he admonished Skye, "before you are thrown out of the fair."

"But last year. . . ." Skye began.

The first judge raised his hand. "There is nothing that likens this year to the last," he insisted, not unkindly. "Do you not see the soldiers and smell the sour smoke in the air? The Middlelands have fallen under the rule of the Northland Guard; we just do not know it yet."

"We will not admit it—is more likely," the other man agreed with a nod. "Times will get worse before they get better. Some say soon you will see signs that say: Do not drink the water, for fear of pestilence and death. Do not drink the water!" He pushed his eyeglasses up the bridge of his nose and shooed Skye away with a wave of his gnarled hand. "Now go."

Skye's eyes stung with tears as she made her way back to the main tent. One glance at the judging table had told her that her patterned shawl was easily the best-executed wrap in the competition, and the most original. Skye had worked out the motif herself, following the web of fine-lined frost flowers that had decorated her windowpane on winter mornings. It was a fanciful design that she called Elfin Lace. Lost in her disappointment, she failed to notice the commotion at the east entrance of the main tent. Katarina was standing watch outside and pulled her into the bread stall as soon as she walked through the door.

"Katarina," she said woodenly, as her friend parted the drape so that they could crawl under the table. "The judges disqualified my shawl. They said it looks like magic."

"Skye," Katarina hissed, as they hunkered under the stand, hidden behind the tablecloth. "The soldiers have arrested your mother. They're looking for you!"

"What?" Skye exclaimed, hitting her head on the underside of the table. "This day can get no stranger."

"Shh," her friend cautioned. "They say Sierra uses magic. They say she was one of the Potluck Twelve, from the old stories."

"Mother worked at a yarn store at the Northland border when she was young. She was an apprentice at a fiber cooperative. That was all," Skye said stubbornly, remembering her mother's earlier admission. "Where are they taking her?"

"To the Northlands, most likely, everyone says," Katarina said. "Even Bordertown maybe. Nobody really knows."

Katarina's mother lifted the cloth. "Shh," she said. "Soldiers."

The girls watched the rough boots approach. They were so close that Skye could touch one. Then the questions began. Who was Sierra Blue? Where was Skye? Where were they from? Katarina's mother offered frightened one-word answers until finally the boots stepped away.

The tablecloth lifted and the girls stumbled out into the dim light. Katarina's mother took Skye's shoulders. "You must go," she insisted, "Quickly, before the soldiers find you."

"But where?" Skye asked with terror. "Where should I go?"

"Home to Top Notch?" The older woman asked. "To your father? Perhaps he will know what to do."

Skye shook her head tearfully. "No," she said quietly, remembering the promise she had made to her mother such a short time ago. "He would not." She untied her show apron and wiped her face with the edge of it. "Mayhap I should follow my mother to the Northlands."

"You cannot walk all that way. And the soldiers will find you with the wagon." Katarina began to cry. "Skye, I fear I will never see you again."

"Nor I you." Skye trembled. She turned to Katarina's mother. "Will you unhitch the ponies? I will ride one and lead the other in hopes of finding my mother."

Moments later, Skye stole to the side entrance of the main tent, the hood of her traveling cloak pulled low over her eyes. Wooden stools held back the great canvas flap; on one of them sat Chloe, the button lady.

"I managed to save these," she said, pulling Sierra's precious rucksack of felted garments from under her crimson skirts with a grunt. "The soldiers took all else."

Skye hugged the knotted bundle to her chest. "Did you overhear anything? What did they say?"

"Sierra is to be detained for misusing magic. They will take her to the glacier and imprison her with the other witches in the burnt part of the Crystal Caverns." Chloe frowned. "I do not know what any of that means, do you?"

"The Burnt Holes," Skye said slowly. "Of course I've heard of them, but I didn't think they were real. I thought they were a make-believe place your parents threatened to send you if you were cross to your brothers."

"Oh yes, to scare you with the spirit voices of the ancients," Chloe nodded. She fixed Skye with an earnest look. "I think these soldiers were speaking of different caves. They sounded like a jail. Now look," Chloe lowered her voice and patted the rucksack. "Your mother said: Let nothing happen to these, no matter what." She studied Skye intently. "They took her cloak away. They said it was magic." She narrowed her eyes. "Sierra was one of those knitting witches, wasn't she? And Esmeralde, too."

Skye shouldered the rucksack, her eyes cloudy with tears, saying nothing.

Muttering, Chloe heaved herself to her feet and turned to lumber back to her stall. "All these years, set up beside two of the Twelve and I never knew it."

A few minutes later, Skye slipped from the tent and crept toward the stables at the edge of the fairgrounds, careful to keep the hood of her cloak up and her eyes on the ground. The ponies had been unhitched from their traces and stood tied to the back of the wagon. Scavenging what little she could carry, Skye fashioned makeshift pack straps from one leather harness and hung both her mother's rucksack and her own split-twig baskets from either side of Shep's withers. She fitted Chuffer's bit into his mouth and climbed onto his broad back, holding his mate's lead rope in one hand. Slowly, she urged the ponies to pick their way through the maze of carts and cook fires in the encampment that had sprung up along the river. She and Katarina usually spent the first night of the fair visiting the campfires where traveling minstrels sang the old tales anew. No one knew yarns like Sierra, and by the end of the evening she would always be sought out to tell the last tale.

There would be no storytelling tonight, Skye thought sorrowfully. She kept her head down, even when a little boy with a squirming puppy peeped at her from a tent flap. "Can I pat your ponies?" he called. "I'll let you hold my new dog."

Behind her, horns heralded the start of the midday fair events. Cheers rose over the bleachers as the sheepdog trials began, while from the mead tent the strains of lute and flute gave way to music promising afternoon revelry. The whole array of noises was nothing but a dull roar to Skye, whose only thought was to escape unnoticed from the fairgrounds, so that she might rescue her mother. She left the shelter of the last tent and rode along the riverbank past the far side of the campground. The rushing torrent was the same River Runne that she and her mother had crossed this morning. The high expansion bridge they had traveled over was guarded on both ends by Northland soldiers, and Skye had little hope of using it without being stopped. She walked the ponies slowly along the river's edge, scanning the water for a place to ford, but it seemed impossible. Spring run-off swelled the river. It looked too fast and deep for small mountain ponies, even ones as sure-footed as Chuffer and Shep. A few rocks poked above the water, but they looked too slick to use for stepping stones. Discouraged, Skye turned away from the raging river to find herself face to face with the tall sledder she had met at the bridge this morning.

"Where are you going?" he asked softly.

Skye looked about wildly but there were no others. "You've been following me!"

"It wasn't difficult, if that's what you're thinking," he said with an easy smile. "That cloak may allow you to pass unseen, but those two fat ponies are less easily hidden."

Skye's face flushed. "What do you want?" She demanded, backing Chuffer away from the soldier. They were still too close to the river's edge, and as Chuffer backed into Shep she saw that the pack pony could easily slip down the embankment through the slick muck along the water. "Leave me be." She tried to urge Chuffer past the tall sledder. "Don't follow me."

"You have the wrong idea," he protested, holding his bare palms out to show he bore no weapons. "I am a friend, an ally."

"Not likely." Skye strained at Shep's tether, but it was too late, the pony was beginning to slide over the edge of the riverbank. If she held on, he would take her and Chuffer with him. She began to sweat inside her cloak. "Get up, Shep," she urged. "Get up!"

The tall soldier lunged for Shep's halter but missed just as the lead left Skye's hand and disappeared down the muddy bank after the pony. For a fleeting instant Skye considered escaping with Chuffer but she could think only of the rucksack strapped to Shep's back, along with Chloe's admonishment, a message from her mother, to let nothing happen to the garments within.

Helpless on her pony, she watched the soldier flail clumsily down the embankment. What did he mean about passing unseen in her traveling cloak, she wondered? Because there was another one in the rucksack; she had seen Sierra pack it. It was probably fortunate that there was another—Sierra would need it now that the soldiers had taken hers.

Slipping and sliding, the sledder led Shep up to the grassy knoll where Skye waited. The soldier was covered in so much mud she wanted to laugh. His words were ridiculous, she decided, for she had never passed unseen in all of her life. She opened her mouth, but the laughter died in her throat as she realized her self-deception. She had passed unseen, more than once; she had simply not realized the act for what it was. How easy it had been to explain the magic away as coincidence or circumstance.

The memories came back to her like fragments of dreams. As a child, she had once taken a loaf of her mother's fresh-baked bread to the hunters at the Sleep Out lodge. It was cold, so her mother had dressed Skye in her traveling cloak, a miniature of the one she wore now. How startled the moose hunters had been when she appeared, once she took off the garment inside the lodge. How uneasily they behaved toward the small girl they believed had purposefully snuck up on grown men who hunted the most elusive moose in the Middlelands. Skye had been confused, because all she had done was take off the cloak inside the lodge when it made her feel unbearably warm.

Another time, she had chanced upon Katarina in the mill house, while Sierra visited with Katarina's mother in the bread kitchen. She remembered standing in the doorway waiting for Katarina to notice her, but the stone wheel ground loudly and Katarina never looked over. The mill house was warm with the yeasty smell of wheat and rye, too hot for her traveling cloak. Averill passed by with a sack of grain and still no one appeared to pay attention to her. She decided to sneak over and tap Katarina on the arm, to surprise her. But instead her cloak slipped off her shoulders and Katarina's eyes lit up as she beckoned her friend to a pile of burlap sacks next to the grain bins. "Skye, come see! Poppy had her kittens!"

The tall soldier reached the grassy knoll, holding Shep's lead rope. "Now tell me what happened," he insisted, dirty and out of breath. "Where are you going and where is you mother?"

"You don't know, soldier boy?" Skye asked, curious now. "Some of your so-called Northland Guard took her away to who knows where because they say she uses magic."

"They are not my Guard." The soldier thrust Shep's tether into her hands. "I am not one of their foot soldiers, in case you haven't noticed."

"Your clothes," Skye reasoned, heat rising in her face. "Your accent. You're not from around here, are you?"

"No."

"You're a sledder from the Far North," Skye guessed.

"My name's Niles," he said. "And if you are Skye Blue, I'm a friend of your brother's."

"I had a feeling," Skye insisted, flush with the familiar heat that only her traveling cloak offered. "I knew it when I saw you."

"And I you. Warren's spoken of you oft enough," Niles smiled. "He never said you were so pretty."

Skye grew redder. "Why did you act that way at the bridge?"

"Maynard, he's trouble," Niles said. "He fears anything to do with magic, crystal or other. And I've been in more than enough trouble already to want to cross him. He is dying to report me and draw a new partner."

"They're a small-minded lot here in the Middlelands," Skye offered. "Sometimes narrow valleys make for narrow vision. Let me tell you something: Where I live at Top Notch, you can see for miles."

"How could Maynard like me?" Niles agreed, with a laugh. "I'm from the north."

Skye threw back the hood of her traveling cloak and loosened the tie. "We got past you on the bridge because of our cloaks, didn't we? But we had no power to pass unseen, just the power of persuasion."

"One and the same if rightly used," Niles replied. "Your mother showed us what she wanted us to see: a mother and daughter with yarn to sell at a fair."

"Maybe crystals do harbor magic."

"More than you would believe, and none of it's been used for much good by either side."

Skye's brow furrowed. "You mean the north and south?'

"According to the ancients, it was men and women," Niles said.

"I know my yarns. And that's nothing but a tale of old." Skye gave Niles a level glance. "I really need to find my mother."

"And I your brother," Niles agreed. "What Maynard said is true. No one has seen him. He is called a deserter."

"Warren, a deserter?" Skye gave him a troubled look. "Never."

"Maybe not," Niles shrugged. "But he's gone. He slipped out of our unit after a battle between the Lowlanders and a Middleland detachment in the foothills beneath the Northland Glacier. We watched from above with our sleds and could do nothing. He left without a word."

"That doesn't sound like him at all. There must have been a reason."

"When I reported back to the garrison at Bordertown, no one had seen him for days,"

Niles said. "Our detail was broken up and we all were reassigned lest there be more traitors and deserters among us. So now I am here." He wiped sweat from his brow. "It's too warm down here."

"We can find him," Skye insisted. "And my mother. Come with me!"

Niles shook his head. "Then I would be called deserter, too. The best way for me to help is to stay with the army. I'll hear more that way. Maybe I'll see something." He scanned the fairgrounds and then the sun, no longer high in the sky. "You need to go. Quickly."

"How am I ever going to ford this river?"

"There is only one way." Niles turned toward the checkpoint. "Come, let's get you across that bridge."

"The soldiers will see me." Skye patted Chuffer's neck. "You said yourself that I can't pass unseen with mountain ponies."

"No worries," Niles grinned. "This soldier will lead you. I may not hail from around here, but I do know how to ride a mountain horse. Does this pack pony have a bridle?"

"In the saddle bag."

Niles fitted Shep's bridle and swung a long leg across the stout pony's back. He looked so comical that Skye laughed.

Ignoring her, Niles flashed a grin and kicked Shep into a mountain pony's lilting trot. "Come on," he urged. "Let's get you out of here."

46

HAT PATTERNS

These magical hats require a beginner skill level and are sized to fit adults, with a circumference of approximately 20" unstretched.

Get the pattern from PotluckYarn.com/epatterns

"How much for the coin?"

CHAPTER 2

The Road to Banebridge

ESMERALDE, DRESSED IN BLACK, limped up the roadside. She seemed oblivious to the stream of fairgoers traveling in the opposite direction. Her heavy medicine satchel, which she called her Possibles Bag, smacked soundly against her side with each step. The others on the road ignored her, just a crone in dark raiment at the side of the road, giving way to swifter foot traffic but still plodding along stolidly. Her old boots, trodden down in the back, gave witness to better days. A finely knit beret perched at a crazy angle on her head, over unbrushed hair, dark but lightly threaded with gray. Only her clear gray eyes betrayed her as something more than she seemed.

After a fitful night, Esmeralde rose to consult the resources in her felted bag. All signs had pointed north toward Bordertown, as

Indigo Rose had foretold. Esmeralde would have preferred that the signs point south to the Middlemarch fair, full of frivolities. She loved the music and dance, arts and crafts, fiber and frolic, and, best of all, visiting with old friends. A few rounds of the fermented wine called Crystal Cordial that she carried in her flask would loosen tongues and lighten hearts. She often came away from the fair days having gained useful information.

Thinking of her stall mates in the great hall, she sighed. She could do without the affectionate prattle of Chloe the button lady, but she yearned for the lore of Sierra Blue and the chance to trade for one of Sierra's whimsical garments. Esmeralde knew that talk of the Twelve was unsafe at a fair filled with folk from all the lands, especially now that magic crystals had been forbidden. But Esmeralde still treasured Sierra's tales of old, retold around the campfire at night. She never grew weary of the legends of the ancients, known in these parts as the First Folk. They had ruled the north, which had been the only land. Eventually, they discovered the magic crystals and stumbled upon ways to harness the stones' power. According to fable, ruling nature was not something the First Folk were meant to do, and it was their ancient folly that sent the world into the first age of ice.

Sierra was a born storyteller. Esmeralde didn't care whether Sierra's well-told tales were true or merely fables. As a child, Esmeralde had watched as Sierra sat close to Mamie Verde, when the old woman could still utter enough words to teach the tales, and learned each story verbatim. Tales of the ancients were just musty yarns no one heeded these days. Esmeralde believed all would do better to notice what she perceived as veiled warnings hidden in the stories. No matter whether the stories were true or not, Sierra was entertaining and knew her yarns well.

This morning, before she set out on the road, Esmeralde had pulled out of her pack the medicinal herbs and salves she would have sold in her stall at the fair. They were simple remedies for childhood ailments and common colds. Then she had rummaged in the back room of her cottage and ransacked her dark pantry—for what? What had Indigo Rose said to bring? She could not remember. There were too many wax-sealed tinctures and corked vials on her dusty shelves to make a wild guess. She brought them all, and thus was now walking heavily on her right leg, balancing the weight of the clanking vessels that rhythmically slapped in the bag she held against her left side.

Esmeralde was not really lame, though she had discovered it helped to look that way. Already this morning, a farm family had made space for her to ride a distance among squirming sheepdog puppies in exchange for a few coppers' worth of soothing mint tea. Numerous others along the muddy track had glanced her way to inquire about stronger remedies, but she had averted her eyes and feigned ignorance. The sun had risen high in the sky, while dark clouds in the west threatened rain. Once she crossed the broad trestle bridge into Banebridge, she would be just a short hike from Indigo Rose's greenhouse garden, which overlooked the river valley. Together, over the bubbling dye pot, both women hoped that all would be made clear—or as clear as things got these days. So far, she and Indigo had seen nothing over the dye pot other than cloudy shapes; and the night sky had yielded only an ordinary display of moon and stars. The vision they had been expecting for almost twenty years had failed to show itself.

Yesterday Esmeralde and Indigo had made a pact. They would search for the Fire in the Sky one last time, and if it did not come they would take matters into their own hands. To play it safe, Esmeralde had journeyed to her cottage below the wooded Copse, where trees tore at travelers who strayed off the track. There she scanned the night sky to the south, while Indigo looked to the north from her greenhouse garden above Banebridge. Esmeralde had watched until the stars began to wink out at dawn, a dawn that yet again lacked the red call. Esmeralde had become increasingly certain that Aubergine would never call them all together, as she had promised. Maybe the frozen crystals had lost their fire. Maybe they were just lost. Perhaps they were tucked on a rafter in the back room of the Potluck, out of Smokey Jo's reach.

Esmeralde was done waiting. She and Indigo would decide this day how best to take matters of the Twelve into their own hands.

Any of the remaining Twelve had most likely gone to the fair.

Esmeralde imagined that Sierra had journeyed down from Top Notch, unless the Teardrop had spilled—and if it had not already, it would this day. No one needed tea leaves or potions to forecast flood. The wet air and the whiff of smoke that burned her throat as she walked the broad track toward Banebridge were signs enough.

If Sierra had trekked to Middlemarch to sell her garments, then Esmeralde believed she had put herself in danger. The clear crystal Esmeralde employed as a compass had definitely pointed north when she pulled it from her Possibles Bag this morning. In fact, when she turned the jagged point of the stone south, it had clouded, which was a sure warning to any who wielded magic shards. Whether soldiers from the Northland Guard had halted Sierra at the Middlemarch bridge and had discovered her crystal shaded garments, or whether they had waited and stolen everything in her stall that was Potluck-dyed, Esmeralde felt sure that the magical knitwear had been seized.

Perhaps Sierra, blithely unaware as she sometimes was, had also been taken captive. As always, Sierra would have been too complacent, too certain of her disguise as a farm wife, and too far removed at Top Notch to sense the unrest brewing and the trouble that would come with it.

Not for the first time, Esmeralde pondered Sierra's husband Kendrick, who had been inexplicably placed in Sierra's path twenty years ago and diverted her from her destiny as Aubergine's successor. Esmeralde had never been able to fully divine where Kendrick's allegiance lay.

That troubled her. Almost immediately after the circle of Twelve broke apart, Kendrick had wooed and wed Sierra, and taken her to a remote area full of secret snowy trails to the north that Esmeralde suspected were now only used by the Lowlanders. In the villages along the main track to Bordertown, rumors of the Twelve had begun to surface recently, and not by accident. Esmeralde had heard that Northlanders intended to hunt down and imprison the legendary knitting witches for supposed misuse of magic. In addition to assembling the remnants of the Twelve, Esmeralde sought to discover who had infiltrated their broken circle and was now informing the Northlanders.

Hearsay along the track had revealed nothing. Yet she and Indigo Rose had witnessed something mysterious in a shared vision a few nights earlier. They thought they had recognized the lost crystal, regal in its broken beauty, found at last in a most unlikely place. Whether what they had seen was wishful thinking—or perhaps too much Crystal Cordial—they believed they had watched the jagged amethyst edges fit back into Aubergine's original necklace, and the hammered silver circlet made whole, uniting all once again with a power great and terrible.

Could it be that the influence of the Twelve was beginning to resurface after so many years? The only one of them able to verify this possibility would be Lavender Mae, except nobody knew where to find her. She was the only one of the Twelve who knew each crystal and its properties. When they had scattered, Mae had become morose, a tiny figure muttering in the back room among the crystals and dyestuffs or smoking in the kitchen garden with Indigo Rose. Unable to shed her deep funk, she finally fled north to the abandoned mining camps of her youth. From time to time she had been spotted foraging among the freshets that pooled and repooled above the Crystal Lakes, searching for a gemstone to replace the lost one. Finally, she had disappeared.

Later people reported sightings of a scavenging river rat with fierce claws and a mane of flying hair that shielded a pouch, said to contain rare crystals, slung around its neck. Stories also surfaced of a genderless old creature, skin burnished brown by the fierce alpine sun, who smoked the crazy weed that grew in the shadows of the Northland Glacier. Esmeralde could not imagine how this could be their beloved Lavender Mae, the sweet being who had ground the crystals into Potluck powder.

Esmeralde's eyes clouded. There might not be an interloper at all. There might still be a traitor among them, one other than the dark one who had fled south to the Lowlands when the circle broke. If Aubergine no longer had the sense to shush Smokey Jo when she spoke out of turn in the yarn shop, or if Lilac Lily was not able to keep quiet about the Potluck secrets, Esmeralde would know soon enough. This very evening, she and Indigo would seek to reveal the infiltrator. This was the reason she carried all the potions and vials in her pouch. Yet Esmeralde was worried. While she was bringing everything, many of the labels had fallen off, many of the blown-glass vessels looked alike, and some appeared empty, their contents dried up from neglect. In the old days, she knew what was in every bottle without a second glance. Now she was not certain.

The wide trestle bridge that crossed the River Runne into Banebridge loomed to her right. Esmeralde broke away from the midday crowd, turning toward the familiar track with relief. Across the river stood the Trading Post and Granary, where flatbed wagons backed up to loading docks. The mules hitched to the wagons were held by boys too young to be swallowed up into the Northland Guard.

Ever hopeful, Esmeralde scanned the opposite bank for her favorite fossickers. Although she saw none, it looked like a small group had made recent camp under the shelter of the bridge. She had formed a grudging truce with the ragtag boys after several had tried to rob her one evening as she traveled alone from Banebridge to her cottage. Though these youths were able to elude the recruiting soldiers, they were no match for the contents of her Possibles Bag. In the end, they had given up far more than they had stolen to be cured of the pox in one of her glass vials.

Among the plunder the boys had fossicked from the riverbeds, mostly small crystals and relics that had melted free of the Northland Glacier, Esmeralde found a few useful bits. She had made the young thieves an offer they could not refuse. Now the band that roamed the river valley sought her out for the newly minted silver she was willing to pay, as well as the remedies she could provide. Often Esmeralde would go out of her way to cross paths with this band of misfits, who were led by a slight but fierce boy called Trader. As always, she looked among their findings for shards of cold-fire crystals or any other sparkly fragments. None of the fossickers had come to her this past fortnight. She feared that they had been caught. Esmeralde went so far as to leave word at the Trading Post. This was risky, for sometimes soldiers lay in wait for fossickers, eager to round them up and transport them by caged wagon to the Bordertown garrison, where they would be trained and fit for Lowland fodder.

By the time she reached Banebridge, Esmeralde decided to stop at the Trading Post for a short rest and to slake her thirst. The first floor of the lodge was cool after the heat of the midday sun. Esmeralde lingered near the cases of crystal jewelry and silver bangles before she began to finger the beaded pouches and bags. Nothing caught her eye. She glanced through the vials of snake oil and other so-called medicinal herbs.

"What's in the satchel?" the storekeeper asked, pointing to her heavy Possibles Bag. Esmeralde knew him well. He had a penchant for hard cider and mind-numbing herbs to counteract the eyestrain he caused himself by going over ledgers in poor light.

"Nothing for sale, Ozzie," she replied, with an eye toward the bar-room and the cold cup of cordial she felt certain awaited her there.

A handful of foreign coins lay on a tray behind the counter. Ozzie slid them toward her without comment. Obligingly, she rummaged through them until her fingers came across the likeness of the Dark Queen, a newly stamped circle of gold.

"Where did this come from?"

"Dead Lowland soldier," Ozzie shrugged. "One of the body-pickers brought it in."

Esmeralde eyed him keenly. "A fossicker?"

"Yes, but not the ones you seek," he replied.

Esmeralde fingered the likeness of Tasman, already seeing the haze of thinly veiled magic. "How much for the coin?"

"What's in the bag?" Ozzie repeated, rubbing his eyes. "Headache powder? A vial of mind-ease, perhaps?"

Grumbling, Esmeralde pulled out a roll of felt and unwrapped a pair of ground-crystal spectacles linked by thin metal. "These will calm your eyes forever."

"Never in my life had I hoped to cast my weary orbs on a set of magnifiers." Ozzie lifted the glasses reverently and snagged the hooks around his ears. He blinked at her through the lenses. "I can see all," he declared.

"I know," Esmeralde said. "I've been saving them for a special trade."

"How much?"

"Not so fast," she said. "Such spectacles are worth more than ten pieces of your Lowland gold." She fingered the coin. "But I'll take it." She turned toward the tavern.

Ozzie ushered her toward the bar with a sweep of his hand. "Drinks are on me."

"As always." Esmeralde flashed him a cunning smile before pushing open the double doors of the mead hall. "I'll let you know what else."

After a brief rest and a few drops of Crystal Cordial at the bar, Esmeralde left the Trading Post. Soon she turned off the track for the steep hike to Indigo Rose's greenhouse and cottage. Nothing had come of her inquiries in the bar. There was no news of the fossicker known as Trader.

Esmeralde's Possibles

A BAG PATTERN

This beginner-skill-level medicine bag comes in one size with finished measurements of about 8" square, after felting.

Get the pattern from PotluckYarn.com/epatterns

"You don't run after ponies!"

CHAPTER 3

The River Runs High

TWO GUARDSMEN WHOM SKYE DID NOT recognize barred entry to the Middlemarch bridge. With Niles as her escort and her traveling cloak wrapped around her, though, she had little difficulty crossing.

"Our wagon has cracked a shaft," she explained in an easy lie to the gray-clad foot soldiers. "I must fetch my father."

The guardsmen looked toward Niles, who waved them off. "It is as she says. Let her pass. She must ride into the mountains past nightfall as it is."

After they reached the checkpoint on the far side of the river, the lanky young man slid from Shep's back and handed Skye the pony's lead rope. He scanned the clouds that were beginning to form and whistled quietly. "It looks like rain. You'll not make it to your Notch before full dark."

Skye eyed him silently, remembering her mother's instructions. Could she pass by The Falls without turning up the familiar road toward their farm? Wouldn't she do better to ignore her mother's wishes and ride home to tell her father what had happened? Surely Kendrick would know how to rescue her mother.

"There is a flour mill in the Lower Notch, just up the turnoff to our track," Skye began, her face growing hot as she again searched for a way to forge a lie from truth. It was more difficult to tell a falsehood to someone she was tempted to trust. "Did you see the Mill on the Rill at the fair? Their stall is in the main tent."

"Under the purple banner," Niles nodded. "I tasted their honeyed scones."

"Nothing compares," Skye said with a wistful smile. "They are friends of my family. The grandfather, Gaffer, stayed home to mind the mill. I may overnight there with the ponies."

"Overnight there with the ponies," Niles echoed, agreeably. His eyes had the same glassy look they had on the Middlemarch bridge this morning, when he had been under Sierra's spell. Skye flushed, pleased. She decided to test the persuasive powers of her traveling cloak even further.

"It's a good idea," she suggested.

"A good idea," Niles confirmed. "Take care of yourself, then. If I find Warren, I will try to get word to you."

"And I you," Skye replied.

"To Top Notch," he conjectured. "Or mayhap your Mill on the Rill."

Skye nodded, thinking that she would be unlikely to see Niles ever again. With a satisfied wave, he loped back toward the bridge.

With every step, Skye fought the traffic that streamed into Middle-march. She and the ponies were forced to a walking pace up the side of the muddy track, as she rode one and led the other. She had a feeling that she would need both ponies if she came upon the soldiers who had arrested her mother, so she plodded on with determination. How far ahead of her were they? Did they have a cart or horses? Had they even taken this crowded track? Skye knew that a private military road wound through the Western Highlands, on the far side of this valley. The steep trail was well maintained and less trafficked than the public thoroughfare, but closed to all who did not wear the Northland Crest on a tunic or jacket or possess a special token that allowed passage. If you knew how to avoid the Northland Guard, you could travel swiftly on the broad, empty military roads. Skye knew that Warren had often used the army's sled trails beyond Top Notch, always returning to the farm winded and elated. Even when the Guard had spotted him, he had eluded capture by guiding his bobsled off the road and onto one of the moose trails that twisted and turned and petered out into drifted snow. He knew the area well and they did not. In the end, Skye realized sadly, the Northlanders had conscripted him to fight their war anyway.

As the day waned, traveling vendors no longer clogged the muddy track, although food traders still lined the road. With afternoon chores done, a few farm families drove buckboard wagons south, while others passed by on foot, hurrying to join the festivities around the May Pole as the fairgoers welcomed spring to the Middlelands. Most of the men looked old or infirm and the boys very young—no older than Garth. Could the Guard really have taken all others, as they had Warren? If so, they must have seized all the able-bodied men while her family was trapped at Top Notch over the winter. Last fall, when she and her father and Garth had traveled to Banebridge for provisions, there had been plenty of men in the Trading Post barroom. Boys her own age had been loading sacks of feed at the Granary. Now they were gone.

As the sun dropped in the sky, the clouds she and Niles saw gathering earlier began to roll in and the wind picked up, prompting some food-vendors along the road to hastily dissemble their stalls, while others merely boarded up for the night and left. Fewer and fewer folk passed her, until finally Skye had the road to herself.

The temperature began to drop quickly. Skye fastened her traveling cloak tightly around her throat, but even that warmth could not quell the fear that gripped her heart. When she reached the foothills in the valley below the Notch, daylight was only a dim halo on the horizon. By the light of the rising moon she searched for the turnoff to her beloved Lavender Rill Farm, but in the half-light nothing looked familiar.

The River Runne thundered by on her right, as turbulent as the silent battle inside her head. Sierra's words urged her to forsake family and farm, and to flee up the long road north to Bordertown. Her own thoughts pulled her toward home and what should be safety. The ponies were tired. They instinctively slowed as they approached the fishing hole below the falls, which marked the track to the Notch. Frosty breath came in ragged mist from their nostrils. Skye hesitated, too. How would she fare on the mired thoroughfare to Bordertown? She carried scarcely a day's worth of food and had no way to defend herself from soldiers or roving bands of fossickers. Her quest seemed careless and foolish. Yet her mother was neither. Skye called into memory Sierra's words, trying to piece them together as exactly as she could: *There is a yarn shop in Bordertown in the borough of Merchants' Row. It is called Potluck Yarn, and you will find it near the end of the main thoroughfare. Go to the side gate through the herb garden and bang on the summer-kitchen door until someone lets you in. There will be a gnome called Smokey Jo. Have her take you to Aubergine.*

Skye wondered if anything in the bundle of knitted garments tied to Shep's back possessed any magic that might help her to journey to the Northlands without being waylaid or robbed. If so, she wished her mother had offered her a clue. She was not sure how far her newfound skills in lying would serve on the journey, and she was unsure of her ability to pass unseen. As she approached the Lower Notch road, she paused the ponies and calculated the short ride to Katarina's family homestead and the grain mill. Gaffer would have a mug of hot tea and buttered bread for her, plus a warm stable for the ponies.

But as she neared the falls, Skye sensed that something was wrong. The Lavender Rill did not arch gracefully from the falls to the river. It thundered, and great chunks of road had washed away. She guessed that her father's prediction had been right: the Teardrop had spilled, inundating the rill. The track to her family farm was submerged under churning water.

The ponies snorted and backed away from the roiling torrent. Even if she wanted to, there was no way to get home. She thought of Garth in his red barn sweater and her father in his Potluck hat, and wondered if they had been able to herd the goats to higher ground or if all had been lost. She hoped that they had all climbed the Notch to the Sleep Out, where the goats and alpaca had higher pasture. Maybe in a week or so the spring runoff would subside and all would be as before. The sharp odor of smoke in the valley quickened her heartbeat, and the rising wall of brown water left her feeling that nothing would ever be the same. The Lavender Rill looked like muddy sea spitting dirty foam. A sickly haze rose over the water, like mist or the halos she sometimes glimpsed around magical things. There's your answer, she told herself, reining Chuffer around and urging him forward, then bidding Shep to follow. Hugging the edge of the track Skye turned toward the border, regaining the main road by the light of the moon.

The next village north was Banebridge. Many times Skye had traveled there in the wagon with her family to buy supplies at the Granary. Next door at the Trading Post, they always heard news of some sort.

Missives and parcels could be posted there for further passage on mail coaches headed north or south.

Lingering before the cases in the Trading Post, Skye and her mother might spend an hour marveling at the wares others had brought for barter. Skye loved to finger the handmade birch knitting needles, the crochet hooks carved from bone or antlers, and the pins and darning needles forged from precious metals. They both admired the bobbins of bright threads and the yarns plant-dyed with logwood or cochineal. After much haggling with the nearsighted storekeeper, Skye and Sierra would trade their own crystal-dyed alpacas and mohairs, tinged lavender and light blue, for the knitting and spinning supplies they would use over the winter.

Skye remembered how Kendrick had waited months for the ponies' hand-hammered silver bells to arrive at the Trading Post from a smithy in Coventry. Often he had shipped a bundle of moose hides north to sell to a tannery in Woolen Woods, where they were fashioned into leather jerkins and breeches, gloves and laces.

As important as it was in their lives, Banebridge was in truth nothing more than a small outpost, its defining feature a large trestle bridge that crossed the River Runne. Attached to the Trading Post was a barroom, frequented by locals and travelers alike. Upstairs there were rustic rooms for hire. Beyond the village, a few scattered farms dotted the lush valley.

All looked bucolic, but hiding out in graveled shallows along the riverbank and in thickets beyond the tangled Copse were fossickers. These teenage boys eluded conscription by the Northland Guard by staying on the move. According to her father, fossick boys supported themselves by stealing and scavenging. They raided fields and orchards at night, and spent their days picking through the riverbeds for bits of crystal and relics washed south from the Northland Glacier.

Whenever she sighted fossickers, even one or two, Skye steered clear of the river.

Even if she could reach the outskirts of Banebridge village by dark, Skye knew that it would be difficult to cross the creaking bridge at night. It was a narrow span, with only low rails between her and deep water, and was best traversed by daylight. She would need to wait until morning, because she needed supplies. Perhaps Ozzie, the storekeeper, would have heard news of her mother. It would be likely that somebody at the Trading Post had.

Riding slowly as the darkness grew ever deeper, she searched for shelter, careful to keep a safe distance from the tumbling water. Here above the Lavender Rill Falls, the river was not as angry, although the water was high along the banks and the current rushed along. Young trees torn from their roots sliced through the water like boats torn from their moorings, and Skye knew that to slip into the icy river would mean almost certain death.

It began to rain. Skye halted Chuffer and Shep under a stand of birches budding with leaves and dismounted wearily. She looked around and decided to stake the ponies next to a vacant food stall, hoping that the owners would not mind her trespass under its overhanging roof. The ponies stripped the greening branches ravenously; prompting her to untie the knotted grain sack she had taken from the wagon and feed each pony a measure of sweet feed from her tin drinking cup. Unfortunately, there had been no way to carry along the hay Kendrick had loaded this morning, and the shaggy ponies were hungry. They lipped and nipped at her fingers, searching for treats. They all would have water in abundance, but the oats laced with molasses would soon be gone. The small pouch of seed money Sierra had brought to the fair, to make change at their stall, was all Skye had to buy grain with. None of it was newly minted Northland silver like the coins Katarina had shown her. Hunched against the rain under the slanted roof of the stall, Skye sorted through her handful of worn coppers sprinkled with thin wafers of silver by the light of the moon. She wondered if these old Middleland coins, depicting bucolic sheep and goats from happier times, would be accepted as legal tender along the northern border. She would find out at the Trading Post in the morning. She would also ask if there had been sightings of Northlander soldiers with prisoners, or anyone in uniform who might have detained her mother. Surely someone would be able to show her which way they had gone. If she learned that her coins would be worth nothing in the Northlands, she would spend them on provisions here. Skye realized that she did not know how long it would take to get to Bordertown. It must be more than one day's ride; she had overheard as much from the sledders who came down from the Northlands to train with Warren.

Skye spread her traveling cloak on the damp floor of the stall and reached for the goat cheese, bread, and dried apples Sierra had packed for their lunch. She was so sick with worry she feared she could not sleep, but the bread and most of the cheese disappeared quickly, and soon she was dozing, surrounded by the distant roar of the river and the close *chuff, chuff* of the sleeping mountain ponies.

As dawn broke, she woke with a start. She had used her mother's bundle of garments as a pillow and something lumpy inside had given her a crick in the neck. She rubbed sleepily at the ache below her jawbone, discovering the pain was not what had awakened her. The ponies were acting fractious, stamping their feet on the sodden ground and pulling at the stake line. Adjusting her eyes to the dimness, Skye crept to the open doorway of the stall, just as Chuffer snorted another warning and Shep's furry ears pricked, his eyes rolling back with fear. Skye froze. Someone or something was near. In the gloom, she could not make out what.

Suddenly they were upon her, five or six of them, dirty boys in muddy cast-off coats, wrestling her packs from Shep's back. She kicked and flailed as one of them lunged into the stall for her mother's garments, aided by the dim glow of a magic crystal another boy held lashed to a stick overhead. Screaming, Skye got in several swift kicks before they seized her wrists and feet. In the fray, Chuffer reared and pulled his stake, whinnying to Shep, who neighed back. Evading grasping hands, Chuffer charged past the boys and flew along the riverbank, followed by Shep, his lead rope trailing.

"Chuffer," Skye called, but to no avail. "Shep!" The ponies galloped toward the river bend. She turned to her captors and spit, "You stupid, stupid fossick boys!"

"Trader!" cried the boy holding her feet, "There goes our ride!"

"Your ride!" Skye yelled, kicking free. "Your ride! Those are my ponies."

"We'll get them," the one called Trader said. Slight and sinewy, Skye could see he was their leader. He looked about her own age.

"You have put them in danger," Skye said angrily. "What if they drown?"

Trader pointed to two of the bigger boys. "Ross, you and Clayton run after them. They're too fat to get far."

"You idiot." Skye pulled first one wrist and then her other arm from the grimy hands of the red-haired boy called Clayton, who had not, after all, gone after the ponies. She rubbed her right hand, which had gone numb in his grip. "You don't run after ponies!"

"No, you don't," a familiar voice agreed. "You let them run after you."

Skye gasped in surprise as a familiar red sweater came into view within the light of the crystal. "Let her up, mates. That's my sister." Although Garth's face was peaked and drawn, he was smiling at her.

"You look like a drowned rat," Skye scolded, hugging him. Tears stung her eyes as she took in his soiled clothing, and the wet hair plastered to his face. "What happened to you?" She demanded. "What are you doing with this stinking lot of juvenile bandits?"

"Stinking lot?" Ross said. "Did you hear that, Trader? She called us a stinking lot." He sniffed at his coat sleeve.

"You do smell," Clayton said.

"Aye, and juvenile bandits," Trader jeered, his dark eyes smoldering. "Just how old are you, little miss?"

"Old enough to know a thieving fossicker when I see one," Skye retorted. She grabbed her mother's bundle from a rail-thin boy who was trying to examine the contents. "Give me back my clothes."

The boy turned to his leader for direction.

"Micah, hand it over for now." Trader gave Skye a veiled look before he nodded toward Garth. "Seeing as she's his sister and all."

"Garth, let's get out of here," Skye said, tying up the rucksack.

"But these fossickers saved my life. Or at least Trader did."

Hugging her bundle, Skye glared at Trader. "I'll bet they did."

"We brought you your brother," Trader said. His eyes shifted toward the rucksack. "Now we are here to collect our profit."

Ignoring him, Skye turned to Garth. "What happened?"

"When the Teardrop spilled," Garth began, "I was down at the farmhouse. Father had taken the goats up to the Sleep Out. He said he was coming back with the dogs to get the alpacas, so I went down to the barn and WHOOSH!" He pantomimed with his arms. "There was no warning at all. The dam didn't spill like it usually does. No, the sluice board broke and the whole thing let go. Water started coming over the fields in waves."

"What about Father?"

Garth avoided her eyes. "I climbed up on the chicken house and searched for Father, but I couldn't see him anywhere. The water swirled around and around, and then it pulled the roof clear off the chicken house and there I was on this raft, but it wasn't a raft, really, just the roof of the chicken house. It was going down this river that used to be our track beside the Lavender Rill, and then turned into a big muddy river, full of branches and fence posts," he lowered his voice, "and boards from our house. . . ."

"Our farm?"

Garth's eyes grew glassy. "Parts of it anyway. The wood parts. They flew by me, and I was holding on, holding on . . ." Struggling to keep from whimpering, trying to be older than he really was, Garth paused to catch his breath. "It was so scary," he said quietly, hugging her hard. When he let go, two huge tears trailed down his face. He wiped them away swiftly with the back of his hand.

"I imagine it was scary," Skye agreed, recalling her own brush with the Northland soldiers at the Middlemarch bridge and how inconsequential it seemed now that her mother was gone and their farm had washed away. She decided not to mention Sierra's capture to Garth until later.

"Oh, it was scary, a little," Garth nodded, his bravado returning as he noticed the other boys had stopped talking among themselves to listen. "But the worst part was next. I came around a turn where the road was all washed out and the water dropped to rocks below and . . ."

"A waterfall?" Skye asked. "Where was this?"

"Just above the Mill on the Rill," Garth said. "I knew I was not going to make it over that thing, not on a chicken-coop roof." He sighed with a shrug and a small smile. "Then I saw the fossickers along the river bank. Trader caught me with a snag, and him and Clayton and Micah pulled me up beside them, and I never want to go down the rill on a raft again." He gave her a solemn look. "They saved me, Skye. I would be drowned dead."

"Dead or not, they still would have dragged you out of the river, looking for loot," Skye said, scanning the circle of ragged boys. They looked tired, she thought, and hungry—certainly not the predators her father had made them out to be. "They're scavengers, Garth. They did not come looking to save you."

"At least we came looking," Micah said.

"We like to look," Ross chimed in. "Got anything to eat in one of them baskets?"

"Carrion birds, the lot of you," Skye muttered, digging out her sack of dried apples and tossing it to the little boy. "Garth, they knew the Teardrop would spill so they came to the rill for spoils." She watched the boys share the apples. "They almost robbed me."

"And may yet," Trader said, scuffing one small, booted foot in the dirt.

"I dare say you've stolen enough for one day," Skye argued, "Especially if you think you've convinced my brother to join your dirty little band."

"Skye, it isn't like that," Garth said. "I want to be a fossicker."

"You'll do no such thing," Skye declared.

"He owes us," Ross said, stubbornly, chewing the last apple. "Don't he, Trader?"

Skye whirled on her brother. "You owe them nothing. Come help me catch the ponies."

Without looking back, she started toward the bend in the river. Grumbling, Garth followed, trotting to catch up. As the other boys fell in line, Trader held up a hand. "They'll not try to leave without their packs," he told them, motioning to Skye's twig baskets and Sierra's bundle.

As soon as she was sure they were out of earshot, Skye grabbed Garth's arm roughly. "What really happened to Father?"

Garth pulled a sodden lump from his pocket. "Trader found this."

Taking the wet wool from Garth's hands, Skye gasped. It was the Potluck hat Sierra had knit for Kendrick. "In the river?"

Garth nodded. "Caught on a branch."

Skye's eyes began to water. "Do you think he drowned?"

Garth shrugged. "I think he's just gone, and not coming back, just like our farm." He shook his head and leveled his eyes at his sister. "I hated that place. The never-ending chores and the loneliness and Father's disappointment that I wasn't who he wanted me to be."

"I know," Skye said, ruffling his hair.

"No, you don't," Garth shot back. "Do you know what he made Warren do? Do you know what I had to do?"

"I can guess. You didn't go moose hunting those last few times, did you?" Skye asked quietly as they approached the ponies, who were cropping green shoots of new grass next to the river.

"No," Garth said. "We broke trail so filthy Lowlanders could pass through the Notch unnoticed. We built a sled track that was a secret route to the Northland Glacier, called the Blind Side Loop. Then the Guard came and took Warren. They knew something, apparently."

"Our brother is missing now. Some say he's a deserter," Skye said. "At least that was the rumor I heard from soldiers at the fair."

"Warren would desert no one, willingly," Garth disagreed. "Whatever happened, I'll bet it had to do with Lowlanders or Father." Garth bowed his head. "I won't go back to the farm," he said. Then he cocked his eyes at Skye. "Don't make me go back."

Skye squeezed his shoulder. "It doesn't sound like there's much to go back to," she said. "Chuffer," she called in a singsong voice. "Shep!" Both ponies raised their sturdy necks and glanced over, chewing idly. Skye looked at Garth. "Are you ready?"

He nodded, and quickly they turned and sprinted away from the ponies, slowing to let the ponies overtake them as they rounded the bend toward the group of boys, who hooted at the edge of the track. Soon they grasped both lead ropes and rejoined the fossickers.

"That was quite a trick," Trader grinned.

"Mountain ponies love to chase," Skye said, letting Ross and Clayton pat Chuffer. "You don't know much about horses, do you?"

"Nope," Trader said. "Do they always come in pairs?"

"No," Skye laughed. "These were hitched to our wagon."

Garth gave her a sick look. "The wagon," he realized. "Skye . . .?"

She turned to her brother. "I guess you're finally wondering what I am doing here alone with the ponies, without Mother or the wagon."

"Now that you mention it," he replied in a small voice. "Aren't you supposed to be in Middlemarch, tending our booth at the fair with Mother?"

"See?" Micah shot Trader a sulky look. "Some folk get to go to the fair."

"Trader wouldn't let us go," Ross complained. "Because we're boys."

"Trader was right," Clayton argued. His eyes flickered over Skye's tall figure. "Look at her, she's nothing but a girl! She'd not have the Northland Guard trying to round her up in a rolling cage."

"Oh, the Guard came after me, all right," she said. "The soldiers captured my mother and took her away. If I hadn't hidden under a table, they'd have found me, too. Here I am, sworn to find her, except I don't know where to go."

"This day can get no stranger." Garth shook his head. "The Northland Guard arrested Mother? What for? Making the wrong change? When were you going to tell me?"

"When you asked," Skye replied. "They tried to detain me, too, but a sledder friend of Warren's helped me escape with the ponies."

"You got away from soldiers?" Clayton asked, with admiration. "Trader, this girl outran the Guard."

"I heard."

"And she has a wagon," small Ross added. He plucked Skye's sleeve. "Where is that wagon?"

"Back at the fairgrounds." Skye watched Trader, who said nothing. "A long ways off."

"Too bad," Ross grumbled. "We all could've ridden in it."

"You'll not get far on this main track with ponies," Trader said, looking from Garth to Skye. "Neither of you. The Northland soldiers patrol it day and night." He lifted his chin toward Skye. "They would throw your brother into a rolling cage and confiscate your ponies to pull it, or another one like it."

"Do you think that is where our mother is, in a prison wagon?" Skye asked.

Trader shook his head. "No, they only use those for rounding up the likes of us."

"Speaking of which," Micah warned, scanning the road both ways. "It's time to scramble."

Clayton nodded. "We need to scatter."

"One moment," Trader raised his hand. His black eyes snapped at Skye. "Do you know why the soldiers took your mother?"

Skye looked at him and felt her face grow hot with a good lie, but instead found herself telling the truth. "They believe she misuses magic. They think she was one of the original Potluck Twelve."

"A knitting witch?" Micah asked.

"Can't be," Ross grumbled. "No such thing."

"Hush," Clayton knocked him on the head.

"Oww," Ross protested.

"The Guard is arresting all of the witches," Clayton told Skye. "That's the rumor up and down this road."

Trader raised his brows. "If the Guard thinks your mother is a Potluck witch, that means they believe that she's committed a crime against the Northland. In that case, they would smuggle her up the military track. It's faster, less traveled, and you can avoid the walls of

Bordertown altogether. They'll probably try to take her to the jails of the Burnt Holes."

"No one ever comes back from the Burnt Holes," Ross whispered. "That's what they say."

Micah gave him a little shove. "No, that's what you say."

Trader held up his hand again, silencing them. "Clayton's right. All of a sudden, there's lots of talk of the Twelve up and down this track. None of it good. If you want to avoid the Guard today, come with us." He motioned Clayton and Micah to help Skye pack her belongings onto Shep's back.

"Why should I trust you?" Skye asked. "We need to find our family."

"We're all of us without family," Trader shot back, not unkindly. "What you need to do now is avoid getting caught. Look about, boys. It's full day now and we're easy pickings for the Guard."

"Time for us to scatter," Clayton said. "Want to meet at the fossick camp under the big rocks upriver?"

"No," Trader shook his head. "Not with a girl and ponies."

"In the dell?" Micah suggested. "There's green grass in the dell."

"I'll take the girl to the dell, and you take the boys to the rocks," Trader decided, waving Clayton away as he took Skye's arm. "Eat up and pack the gear, plus all we can fossick for trade," he said. "We'll meet at dusk under the bridge. Now go."

"Scramble," Clayton said, as he and Micah and Ross melted into the tall grass on the other side of the track.

"Scatter!" Ross turned back to grin at Garth, who stood alone in the road, holding Shep's halter. "That means you. Come on!"

Once within the safety of the tree line, Trader let go of Skye's arm. "Keep close in the Copse," he warned.

"Copse?" Skye snorted, leading both ponies. "It's just woods."

Trader pulled out a walking stick with what looked to Skye like a dull bit of purple glass lashed to its top. He tapped it on the ground and the glass glowed, lighting their path. Their way was lined with overgrown firs whose branches blocked out the daylight.

"Right," he grinned at her surprise. "And that's just a cloak you're wearing."

An evergreen branch reached across the track to snag Trader's leather jerkin. Quick as lightning, he warded it off with the light from his stick.

"Now help me onto one of these mounts," Trader said. "We need to pass quickly, before these trees catch us up in thickets so dense that we lose our way."

Skye's Traveling Cloak

A WRAP PATTERN

This cloak requires an intermediate skill level, and one size fits any traveler. Approximately 50" long (from the neck) by 74" (bottom edge).

Get the pattern from PotluckYarn.com/epatterns

The smell of death hung heavy in the sun-warmed valley.

CHAPTER 4

The Killing Field

SQUINTING IN THE SUN'S GLARE, the sledder standing on the icy outcropping watched a lone figure far below scavenge the newly dead. Trained as a scout, the tall and well-muscled youth had spent most mornings honing his sled craft at the snow bowl practice slope behind the garrison. There wasn't anything else to do. Pulling his fine horn snow goggles from his pack, he adjusted the straps over his army-issue toque. Even so, his curly hair escaped beneath the cap and caught on his goggles. If only he had his Potluck hat. Right now he could use its ability to make him serene or to pass unseen. But the cap had been taken away, along with his other personal possessions.

The thin and ragged form below darted from one to another of the downed soldiers that lay in the bloody snow. It dug through uniforms and packs, most often finding nothing. The sledder had been tracking the forager for two days, since he'd noticed the ransacking of bodies. Caught unaware, soldiers from his unit, mostly farm boys from the Middlelands who knew nothing of war, had been slaughtered by Lowlanders coming through the lower passes hidden by the Blind Side of the glacier.

Horrified, he and the other sledders had watched the carnage from above. His scouting party could do nothing from the heights but sled back to warn the rest of their company, camped to the east. The sledder had stayed behind and looked on as their unit was crushed like ants. Scant hours later, he had seen this person creep out into the rock-strewn valley and begin to pick over the bodies, slowly, methodically. When he returned to his unit that night, the mood around the camp-fire had been sullen and the talk bitter, laced with glacier beer. It grew worse when he told the other scouts about the creature he had seen among the dead. Several in his detail had vowed to sled down through the foothills and kill whoever dared to desecrate their kin.

Although they called the scavenger an old witch, the sledder was certain that no one else in his unit had any idea who it was. He did. These green recruits had not grown up hearing the yarns, told and retold around the fireplace before bed. If he was right, this lone soul could be not only a witch but also one of the Potluck Twelve, as his mother was. When the Northland Guard had come for him last winter, Warren had sworn to his mother to protect her and her brethren at any cost. Sierra had given him a puzzled half-smile, for she had not known why he would pledge such a thing. But his father had. One look at Kendrick's stony face told Warren that he had much to make amends for, despite, or perhaps because of, his father's part in the Glacier Wars.

Before dawn on the morning after the carnage in the valley, Warren pulled his sled out of line from the entrance to his assigned route for that day, which was the main trail that wound through the foothills on the eastern side of the glacier. Flipping the bobsled over his head in a single move, he traversed to another chute that meandered south before cutting west. The path would mask his route through the glacier pass. He knew the risk. Leaving his unit would brand him a deserter and render his comrades suspect. His detail would most likely be questioned and detained, and then broken up and scattered, lest another traitor remained in their midst. He had seen it happen, even though he had been a scout for the Guard for less than two months.

Warren left silently, not daring to tell his friend Niles that he sought to find the old hag and keep her safe. If Sierra's tales rang true, the river rat had been an apprentice at the Potluck, chosen to become one of the Twelve. If he was wrong—well, he was in enough trouble already. His father had seen to that.

Ever since he had been conscripted by the Northland Guard, Warren had been privy to the restless gossip that flew from bunk to bunk inside the training barracks when all should have been sleeping. New recruits were locked inside their dormitories like prisoners at night, although it seemed he was the only one suspected of a crime. Everyone knew that he hailed from Top Notch, rumored to be a wild place where mercenaries sledded the military road without passes, and sledders for hire broke track for Lowland raiders. Whispered words like turncoat and traitor had floated boldly around Warren's head in the dark—names no one had dared to call him by day.

Even here along the northern border, everyone knew Warren was the best sledder in all the lands. As a boy, he had won tournament after tournament in the Middleland Games held in the Runne River Valley, and last year he had won the adult division of the larger Winter Games. Now all competitions were canceled due to the war, and ironically here he was riding lead sled in the Northlands against his will. He had been handpicked by the garrison commander to break trail for the army. There was no sport in that.

The other recruits in Warren's barracks had no doubt that he would rise quickly through their ranks and soon be regarded as too valuable to send on scouting missions. Although sledders rarely saw combat, the garrison leaders would not want their most skillful guide hurt or missing. Conscripts with much less talent than Warren had escaped into the snowy foothills, where they were waiting out the war. Many had joined the roving bands of fossickers. Warren had been warned that as soon as a fresh group of recruits arrived in Bordertown, he would be assigned to train novice sledders at the snow bowl inside the safety and confinement of the garrison walls.

Not all the murmured accusations directed toward Warren had been true, but enough were. However crude, there was secret track called the Blind Side Loop hidden below the slope of the backside of Top Notch that was used by the Lowland army. Warren's father had forced him to help build the section of it that passed through their land. What gain Kendrick had expected or received from the South, Warren had never discovered. Not once or twice, but three times his father had faked moose hunts at the Sleep Out, where his so-called hunting parties consisted of mercenary road crews who risked their lives for newly minted Lowland coin.

Although Sierra said nothing, Warren was not sure his mother had been fooled. As the secret sled trail grew from a riverbed connector to a track heading north, Warren became afraid for Kendrick, who at times seemed like a complete stranger, not kin, much less father. Warren knew now that Kendrick had used his own sons as Lowland decoys, and he thanked the luck of the dye pot that he had been the one spotted by soldiers, not Garth. The Northland Guard had come for him a week later. Now he was a deserter from an army he had never joined and involved in a war he did not believe in.

Warren watched intently as the figure made its way around the killing field. Once in a while the creature secreted her finds into a pouch slung round her neck. Most often, her plunder went into a pantry sack she at times dragged behind her and other times hefted across her back. He feared that the dead soldiers she robbed this day had been another detachment from the Middlelands. Their torn banner bore the emblem of a World's Fair tent, its pennants flapping against a bright sky above a blue swath of river. He knew he had to investigate, if only to satisfy himself and the families of those who might otherwise never know what happened to their husbands and sons. His biggest fear, one he could not voice even to himself, was that he would come across the bodies of his father or his younger brother in the snow.

He positioned his bobsled at the top of the pass and began slow easy slaloms across the slope, using the switchbacks to control his speed and direction down the steep mountainside. Last night's snow, just a light dusting, sprayed fresh powder around him. It glittered and hissed across his horn goggles. Hunkering down inside the sled's cavity, he picked up speed as the wind resistance lessened. He felt confident that the hide of the Alpine Moose that formed the bob of the sled would allow him to pass relatively unseen among the snowy outcrops. He came to a halt and left the sled high enough on the mountainside that when he returned to it the downward slice would allow him the momentum to mount the next pass without a carry—or so he hoped. Tightening his nailed glacier boots, he began the task of sidestepping carefully down the slope.

The smell of death hung heavy in the sun-warmed valley. Working as a scout, he had never been directly involved in a skirmish. The reddened snow and thawing bodies made his stomach churn.

Taking slow, deep breaths to still his innards, he focused on the torn banner flapping in the breeze partway down the slope. He made his way across to it, through the deep drifts. Pulling the stiff canvas

from the snow, he ran his moose-hide mittens over the familiar emblem and feared he would recognize youths he knew among the slain.
With growing dread, he trudged from body to body, forcing himself
to look for the jackets of Northland blue and gray, to turn over those
forms lying face down in the powder.

The bruised purple and burnt gold uniforms of the Lowland dead
were easy to spot and avoid. He'd seen few Lowlanders at close range,
and most of those had been dead. Even without the sunset-hued uniforms they would be easy to identify. The Lowlanders were short and
muscular, with red skin burnished copper from the desert sun and dark
eyes under hair streaked russet and gold. Their words were few to
none. It was rumored that they had mastered the ancient language
of Mind Speak years ago, during the conflagration that resulted in
the Burnt Holes. Some said they talked more with their eyes; others
said they communicated with secret hand gestures. Warren hoped he
would never get close enough to a band of them to find out. Among
the Middleland dead he recognized a few ruffians from the mead halls
in Middlemarch, as well as a boy from the Granary in Banebridge,
who used to hold the ponies when Warren backed the wagon to the
loading dock for feed. Warren forced himself to look at the young
face frozen in a wide-eyed grimace, thinking to honor the boy's life by
paying attention to his death. Warren trudged down the icy incline,
seeing no sign of his father or brother. He recognized no one else until
he rounded the last drift on the slope. Across the field the scavenger
rummaged on, seemingly in a world of her own. At his feet was another
infantryman, facedown.

When he turned the body over, as he had been doing with many
others, his heart clenched. Dark cropped hair lay unruly across the
peaked brow of his childhood friend, Averill from the Mill on the Rill.
For the pan of a breath Warren fooled himself into thinking Averill lay
asleep. Then his gaze dropped. A series of gashes made by a Lowland

short sword severed the uniform, now blotched with rusty red. The surrounding fabric was as blue as Averill's lifeless lips and eyes, and almost as blue as the hair ribbon clutched in the boy's bloody hand, a torn length of silk that could only belong to his sister, Skye. Warren tugged the ribbon free from Averill's grip and tucked it inside the lining of his mitten. How would he tell his sister that her childhood sweetheart was never coming back?

He straightened Averill's jacket for no reason he could think of, and turned away, blinking back tears. Would Averill's sister Katarina learn of his fate? They had already suffered the loss of their father. How would their mother and grandfather take the news? Shaking his head and fingering the piece of sky-blue ribbon inside his mitt, Warren realized there was nothing left for him to do but walk away.

It took him less than a quarter of an hour to scout his quarry. Soon there were only a few stunted trees and snowdrifts between him and the searcher. He could see clearly now that she was, indeed, a woman. A bone-thin hag, she had a mane of ragged white hair and skin browned and wrinkled by the high alpine sun.

He stole closer and hunkered down behind a juniper bush. She had her back to him and was singing a tuneless ditty that sounded like a nursery rhyme with the words "Mae, Mae, Mae," where the verses might go. Oblivious to the carnage, she picked through the bodies with the glee of a child sorting pebbles on a beach. She had donned several army jackets, layering them like quilts. Warren spotted the light blue-gray of a Northland Guard tunic hanging below a vest of maroon and burnt gold of the Lowland Infantry, covered in turn by a mercenary coat of arms he had never seen.

Pins and medals the old woman had foraged were arrayed down one sleeve of the coat, where they winked garishly in the sun. As she swung toward the next body, Warren glimpsed a small but heavy drawstring pouch slung around her scrawny neck on a fine, braided cord.

Warren knew then who she was, for he remembered the tale of the pouch and the story of the lost crystal supposedly hidden inside.

With a hasty look around, the crone tucked the swinging sack back inside her shift, the yellowed nails of her clawed hands scrabbling at her throat. Although he was sure she could not see him, Warren froze when she abandoned the body she was kneeling over and let her tune dissipate into silence.

Rocking back on her haunches, she sniffed the air like a wild dog, and Warren's breath caught in his throat. Warily, she rose to a half crouch, like a wolf sensing prey. Warren squeezed himself lower behind the juniper bush, so that he could barely glimpse her between the dense branches. Slowly she turned, sniffing, coiled like a spring. As she stretched her arms to the skies, the pantry sack slung across her back slid to the snow unheeded.

In one fluid motion she sprang and Warren gasped. Suddenly they were face to face, with just the juniper branch between them.

"Mae," she screamed, smiling in the sun. "Mae, Mae, Mae."

"Ma-Mae?" he stuttered. For now he thought he understood. "Lavender Mae? You are Lavender!"

"Ha!" she screamed, her smoky breath blasting his face. He quickly opened his eyes again, but she was gone.

Lavender Mae's Precious Pouch

A BAG PATTERN

This intermediate-skill-level pouch is available in two sizes,
depending upon how many crystals you wish to secret inside.
Size small is 4" long by 3 ¼" wide and size large is 5 ¾" long by 3 ¼" wide.

Get the pattern from PotluckYarn.com/epatterns

The crystals began to pulse with the footfalls of many booted feet.

CHAPTER 5

Thieves of the Frozen Tombs

WHEAT HAD NOT WINTERED WELL. Last fall, the Lowland invasion had forced her to stray far to the Western Highlands with her flock, and now she was having a tough time shepherding her Jacob sheep back to the Middlelands. The little black-and-white spotted ewes were heavy with lambs, and the paths were uncommonly steep. Sudden spring rains had swollen the rills and streams to block her usual route, further delaying her return. To add to her uneasiness, a rank scent of smoke increased as she trekked closer to the Northland Glacier.

She knew the stench was burn-out from the ice caves, yet she could not hazard a guess as to what the Lowlanders had set on fire, or why. Finally she hiked near enough to glimpse the layer of sooty fog that settled into the valleys under the shadow of the ice. She feared that the secrets the Potluck Twelve had sworn to protect might have been unearthed, although there had been no summons from Aubergine. It wasn't as if she could have plainly seen any sign in the sky anyway, she reflected, because she was so far from her usual route.

Wheat's tardiness meant that she would miss the World's Fair for the first time in two decades. It was a crying shame, since the fair committee depended on her to judge the skirted fleeces and the finer handspun yarns. Known throughout the lands as a fiber savant, Winter Wheat had only to touch animal fiber to identify its origin, staple length, subsequent loft, and best future twisting structures. She could even envision possible finished garments and the properties they might have, although she almost always reserved this knowledge to herself.

To stay safe, Wheat kept her true identity a secret. Always large, she had grown in girth through the years and doubted anyone from her past would recall her as one of the Twelve. Only the contents of the felted backpack under her oilskin cloak or the two crystals knotted around the curl of her shepherd's crook could give her away, if anyone were near enough or old enough to recognize these things. After a close encounter with the band of Lowlanders last fall had sent her scurrying to the western prairies, Wheat had not seen a Middlelander or Northlander. Winter snowstorms soon blocked the migratory footpaths through the prairie. The shepherds in the Western Highlands seemed to have no knowledge of the Twelve or the fabled yarns. Even so, Wheat had dared to reveal nothing about herself to them. Magic was forbidden everywhere, even in the untamed west.

The amber crystals hanging from her staff clacked together in the breeze, chattering to each other in a way she had not heard in decades. In fact, the last time Wheat had witnessed the slightest glow from either of them was years ago, when she caught Smokey Jo playing with them in the alley behind the Potluck dye house. No bigger than quail eggs, the cabochons were crystallized amber gleaned from glacier tunnels that some said led to the legendary Crystal Caves. Each orb encased a large beetle that had been imprisoned when the crystal had not yet hardened. These two rare jeweled coffins lay dormant now, and weathered by seasons past. Yet Wheat could recall when each golden scarab had cast an opaque fire, and the beetle preserved for eternity had been lit from within. Catching the spheres in her plump hand, Wheat gave them a gentle squeeze and thought she might have felt a replying pulse of warmth. But when she scrutinized the crystals, they remained dull. With a sigh, she let them loose to swirl around her staff. She had more immediate concerns.

As she trekked east, Wheat worried about simple day-to-day quandaries. She needed to cull several rams from her current herd; many of her ewes were due to lamb, and she was sorely short of the shiny new coin of the realm. She hated to even conjecture the handsome price her yearling rams would have brought in the exotic-breed auction at the fair, but she gritted her teeth and calculated the loss in her head, for she had counted on that money. Her Jacobs had distinctive horns and grew glistening patterned fleeces, and her rams were genetically perfect for stud.

Her favorite male was little Tracks. The young ram knew his path from the Middlelands into the highlands instinctively. Such was her fondness for this animal that she treated him like a pet dog, and he was the one sheep she could never part with willingly. His silver bell was the first tinkle she heard at daybreak before the hungry bleating of the ewes began outside her tent, signaling time to move to fresh pasture. The winter grasses had been plentiful in the western prairies, but now the sheep grew hungry as they foraged in the snow. Having missed the auction, Winter Wheat had no choice now but to herd her sheep east through the glacier lands, then south into Bordertown, and finally from there to the stockyards in the borough of Butcher's Block.

Ahead of Wheat loomed the landmark she had been looking for: the signposts of the Crossings, a campsite where she would choose the high glacier route that would take her to Bordertown rather than her usual easier trek into the southern valleys. Often other shepherds were camping at these four corners, and sometimes she found a peddler or two selling wares. But when Wheat finally reached the Crossings not one wisp of smoke curled from the rings of blackened rock that marked the vacant tent sites. New snow dusted the cold ashes of the cook fires. Wheat tried to brush her worries aside. She had hoped to pass through here days ago. Perhaps the campground always emptied out during the fair.

Wheat stuck her shepherd's crook into a snow bank next to a crudely lettered sign offering food and drink at the General Store in Coventry, a community in one of the southern river valleys. Coventry was known for fine ironwork. As she blew into her gloved hands to warm them, the crystals on her staff clinked once more. There was not much daylight left, and even to her practiced eye the high track ahead looked daunting. Climbing the switchbacks to the mountain passes below the Burnt Holes would add two days to her trip, but taking the southern route only to arrive after the fair ended would prove useless. As if reading her thoughts, Tracks trotted up, his black-and-white face nosing at her oilskin coat, his bright eyes seeming to question the difficult path that loomed ahead.

"Two more days, along the ridge track," she said to him, scratching the fur around his three tiny horns as the other sheep milled restlessly around the camping grounds. "It can't be helped, even if the ewes lamb before we reach Bordertown."

Tracks turned and trotted toward the familiar trail to the southern pass.

"Tracksie," she scolded, as the other sheep began to follow him. "Tracks, come back here."

With a turn of his fine head, Tracks offered her a questioning look, his bell tinkling merrily, before he continued down the lower trail. Soon the entire flock was ambling along behind and he had disappeared around a snowdrift at the first bend. Wheat could not understand what Tracks was doing. He never defied her. Shaking her head wearily, she plucked her staff from the snow bank and tapped it on the ground, the crystals clacking.

"Tracksie, now look what you've done," she called after the retreating sheep. Soon she would have to hurry to the front of the flock to ward them off, or she would end up chasing her own sheep down into the flooded valley. She rapped the crooked staff on the ground again, and then pounded it, this time with authority. "We need to take the high road."

The crystals hit and sparked as she spoke. Startled, the sheep moved off more quickly, the downward slope offering them momentum. "There's too much water down that way," she called after her disappearing flock. "I don't want to hike into the valley only to find we have to ford some new river or go round another freshet."

Winter Wheat was alone. "Fire and ice," she swore softly. What she wouldn't do now for a mug of mulled cider around a friendly campfire at the fair.

Though darkness was falling, Wheat felt the weak glow before she saw it. The amber crystals tied to her staff sputtered, like tiny oil lamps whose wet wicks almost refused to catch, and sent a beat of warmth through the wood that reached her curled fingers even through her sheepskin gloves. Wheat watched the golden glow spread through the orbs, outlining the scarab beetles, which shone with jeweled radiance. Tilting the staff experimentally, she focused the light on an icy drift. The circles of amber met with a sizzle, searing through the snow in seconds. Wheat smiled in satisfaction at the hissing sound.

The insects within the crystals looked luminous, as they had when alive.

Over the many years since she had last seen the magic cabochons look like this, Winter Wheat had grown to believe that, like many other forbidden things, the beetles would remain forever dormant. She chuckled at the memory of how so long ago she had punished that red-haired kitchen wench with this same staff, burning holes in the sleeves of the serving-maid's dresses whenever Ratta turned her fiery tongue on Sierra or Aubergine. Mesmerized by her staff's renewed powers, Wheat almost failed to recognize the insistent glow for the signal it was: danger.

But suddenly she became aware of the smell of bitter smoke, and then the crystals began to pulse with the footfalls of many booted feet. Then she glimpsed the dark outlines of soldiers heading toward her in the settling dusk, marching down from the trail above. They looked like Lowlanders, short and muscular. If she had taken the high road, she and her sheep would have met them head-on. Had Tracks known? Had he heard the footfalls, or caught a whiff of the smoke?

She had no time to wonder.

The group above was a large raiding party, fifty or more foot soldiers. Scouts lit the way with smudge torches. Behind them, six squat soldiers with shoulders as broad as draft ponies were harnessed to a sledge. They strained to haul a load that looked like plunder encased in ice.

In one swift move, Wheat pulled off her oilskin cloak, unshouldered her felted backpack, and loosened the drawstring. The Lowlanders would see her as soon as they reached the clearing. She had no place to hide but in plain sight. She dowsed the crystals with the hooded staff cover, made by Sierra many years ago. Thank heavenly hand knits I throw nothing away, Wheat thought, hurriedly pulling the rumpled traveling cloak from her pack and throwing it across her broad back. Both garments had been fashioned for emergencies such as this, although Wheat had not needed to hide the amber crystals from anyone in twenty years. The cape was snug and would barely close in front. Flipping up the hood, Wheat stood stark still, hoping she would be unnoticed and therefore unseen. Two Lowlanders with smoldering torches came to the Crossings and halted not ten yards away.

Too late, Wheat noticed her oilskin cloak, which she had hastily discarded in a dark heap atop a snow bank. She hoped that the torch-light would fail to reveal it, but the scouts picked out the slick garment right away. One of them hooked it on his pike and sniffed it disdain-fully before he swung it around as an offering to the leader of the group that followed. Refusing to touch it, the man gave it only a desul-tory glance. Instead, he scanned the clearing, searching for the wearer. The fish-oil smoke of the torches tickled Wheat's nose. She held her breath, willing herself not to sneeze, her hand gripping the hooded staff, ready if needed. She looked intently at the ground. To seem like part of the landscape, it was best to avoid eye contact. Even knowing this, she could not help but steal glances at the Lowlanders. She could feel their leader's gaze, but he seemed to look right through her. Out of the corners of her eyes, she noticed a few dismissive hand gestures. Then her dark oilskin dropped to the ground. The scouts moved on.

As the six-man team pulling the sledge entered the clearing, Wheat let her breath out slowly. Confident now that they did not see her, she examined the Lowlanders with fascination. Their skin was a burnished red brown, and each had a curly crown of brick-colored locks streaked gold from the sun. All wore boiled-leather helmets and short, belted tunics the color of sunset, with matching leggings of a cloth that looked too thin to withstand winter.

Although she had heard rumors that Lowlanders communicated in the silent language of the ancients, she was close enough to see that the rumors were not true. Dark eyes blinked as the soldiers lifted their chins toward each other, sending messages through eye movements and facial expressions, accompanied by brusque hand gestures.

Further head shaking and hand waving made it obvious, even to Wheat, that these underdressed southerners had seen the sheep's tracks and meant to steal her flock along with whatever else they had plundered. She realized with dread that if her Jacobs were herded to the Lowlands they would not be shorn for fleece, but slaughtered to feed hungry soldiers. It was all she could do not to reveal herself, but she had to remain hidden if she wanted to save herself or rescue her flock.

As the Lowlanders moved down the southern track, Wheat retreated silently to let them pass. It was full dark now. As the sledge slid by, she saw it held a huge chunk of ice, yellowed with age, perhaps chipped from a frozen wall that had taken eons to form. Although the ancient ice was opaque, Wheat thought she could see the outline of a large darkened form inside. She bit her tongue to keep from crying out. This could not be. But somehow she knew it was. The form trapped in ice was an undead creature, straight from the old tales.

Wheat had never believed those ancient legends, even though she had sat at Mamie Verde's knee listening to the stories, just like the other girls. Now fear stabbed her heart.

Wheat did not remember the yarns as Sierra Blue did, yet she mustered a vague recollection of what had happened to the First Folk. According to Mamie, who had been the Keeper of the Tales, the last world had ended in a sudden ice age that froze everything. For eons, the world had stood still while snow fell silently. Ice caves formed and became graveyards lost in time. Finally, for some reason Wheat could not recall, the lands began to thaw. According to lore, the Northland Glacier had been young, and much larger than it was now. The glacier began a slow trek south, sculpting mountains and scraping valleys as it reshaped the lands. All evil lay entombed deep within the huge glacier's belly, along with the civilization of the First Folk, everything frozen solid. All beings encased in ice while they lived were hidden in unnamed, labyrinthine caverns that had formed beyond the Crystal Caves in the thousands of years it took for the world to wake again.

Wheat did not believe in the undead, yet she knew she had just seen one of them. After the Potluck broke up, the Dark Queen's first act was to send Lowland forces north to burn an opening in the south face of the glacier. People said she wanted to find the monsters called Watchers that some claimed were guardians of the Crystal Caves, but the Lowlanders did not discover the caves or the creatures.

Eventually the Northland Guard gathered enough soldiers to turn the Lowlanders away from glacier's south face. The fires burned out and the gap froze over. The yawning caverns left behind became known as the Burnt Holes, and later were used by the Northlanders as a prison of sorts, to isolate those who had committed crimes against the realm.

Wheat feared that the Lowlanders must have infiltrated the Crystal Caves and stolen deep into the glacier. Surely they had thieved this entombed form from beyond the lost caverns.

Wheat recalled that there had been a tale about the frozen grave-yard, a tale that Sierra could not recall but that Ratta, the sharp-tongued kitchen maid seemed to know. That tale told what would happen if the ancients were disturbed.

How had the Lowlanders found a way into the secret places? The ice was reported to be impenetrable. Wheat glanced up the high track that wound down through Glacier Pass to the Crossings. The Low-landers had come from the northwest. They could have trekked around the back of the glacier, known as the Blind Side. Yet, as far as Wheat knew, there was no Blind Side passage through any part of the glacier.

Wheat unhooded her staff and gazed at the glowing beetles. No wonder her crystals had roused themselves. She had to reach the

Potluck—and quickly. There was no time to waste if Lowlanders were robbing ancient graves or planning to harvest magic crystals from the caves. She must convince Aubergine to summon the Twelve soon, or the world might end again as the legends foretold, in fire or ice.

From the smoke in the air, Wheat thought it would not be ice this time. But first she must see to her sheep. Perhaps she also might get a closer look at the frozen form on the sledge. As the last Lowland soldier disappeared, she picked her oilskin from the snow and stuffed it in her sack, and then followed the raiding party—and, in front of them, her wise ram, Tracks—down the well-beaten path to the south.

Winter Wheat's Felted Backpack

A BAG PATTERN

Keep your belongings safe during travel with this intermediate-skill-level project, which is approximately 13" high, 12" wide, and 6" deep.

Get the pattern from PotluckYarn.com/epatterns

Like the fresh flowers Lily favored,
all of the novices had opened up to her in time.

CHAPTER 6

The Road Less Traveled

LILAC LILY FILLED THE STONEWARE PITCHER with fresh-cut daffodils to set on the harvest table. She and her sister Lorna had spent all morning shopping the flower stalls at the World's Fair, and had tucked into their market bags a bevy of spring blooms as well as bulbs and seeds to plant. Tonight their lovely old rooming house, just past the fairgrounds, would be packed with half a dozen out-of-town guests. She had just enough time to set the table before seeing to supper. Lorna had found a basket of early greens in a food stall, and among the outside vendors Lily had discovered a flask of wine vinegar to dress the tender shoots. With a nicely salted ham and sweet potatoes from the root cellar, they would all eat well tonight.

Lily pressed her damp hands to her apron and slipped into the warm kitchen to check the oven. The ham was crisping nicely. She plunged the sweet potatoes into a bucket of cold water and scrubbed the dirt off with a hog-bristle brush before pricking them with a fork and settling them around the ham. Helping her sister run a country inn was a far cry from managing the large and boisterous household of the Potluck Twelve, but it kept her busy. She liked her simple life, and she could no longer imagine any other.

No, that was not quite true. She could imagine her previous life, but dared not dwell on it. Even at each year's fair, she avoided the center aisle of the main tent, where she might run into Sierra Blue and her yarns or Esmeralde and her remedies. She also ignored the exotic-breed tent, because she wanted nothing whatsoever to do with Winter Wheat. And, heavenly hand knits, forbid that she would have the misfortune of running into Indigo Rose or Lavender Mae smoking glacier weed behind the Mead Hall. The thought of red-haired Ratta pushing mute Mamie Verde around in a wheeled chair along the midway, coupled with what Lily knew about their odd relationship, often threatened to send her into a panic attack. For although the circle had broken up, and all who remained at the time had said they forgave her, she could not help what she held: their secrets.

When Lily had become the Potluck housemother all the girls confided in her freely. Aubergine was preoccupied with the crystals, and Mamie Verde with the tales. As the only other adult in the house, it had been Lilac Lily's job to keep the peace or stir the pot among the girls, as she saw fit. Like the fresh flowers Lily favored, all of the novices had opened up to her in time, revealing their hopes and dreams, their plots and schemes. As the warden of the Potluck and its secrets, Lily's own talents seemed like nothing more than well-placed suggestions. Yet she alone held the uncanny ability to guess who to approach for answers or where to find something amiss. And she had never second-guessed herself until the end. Because she had known all alliances and disputes within the house, she had the power to mend or build fences. Nonetheless, confessions she had been under oath not to reveal had at times brought on headaches so extreme that even Esmeralde's strongest tinctures could not soothe them.

Lily's gift had been both blessing and curse. She knew all but was able to reveal nothing unasked, without tempting fate. The one time she broke her oath, the magic of the Potluck had turned on the Twelve. Lily blamed no one but herself for the Potluck's demise. Because of her desperate foolhardiness, life had changed dramatically for everyone involved.

Lily remembered that horrible night like it was yesterday. All that day, Aubergine's amethyst necklace had flashed in her mind's eye. She knew of Tasman's consuming avarice for the power held by the twelve rare jewels. She had known Tasman would attempt that very night to don the circlet of crystals and abandon the Potluck. But instead of warning Aubergine right away, Lily waited and watched. Tasman's scheme to steal the necklace from right under Aubergine's nose was unbelievable, and the veiled threats Tasman shot Lily's way petrified her. Lily let precious minutes pass until it was too late. As Tasman fled with the necklace, Lily made a desperate move to place nearby Tracery Teal in her path, and that decision cost them dearly. No one had since seen traces of Teal, or Tasman, or the crystal necklace. In the fray, the silver clasp had broken open and one of the crystals was wrenched from its setting and lost.

The door creaked as Lorna stepped from the back porch into the kitchen with the greens. "All cleaned," she said, handing Lily the basket and the paring knife. "It smells like the ham is well under way."

"And the sweet potatoes as well."

"Too bad we didn't pick up any sourdough bread, or yeast rolls," Lorna said. "That Mill on the Rill was just inside the main tent. How did we miss it?"

"The line was too long," Lily explained, although it hadn't been.

When she had peeked inside the tent, Sierra Blue and her young daughter had been conversing with the owners. Sierra had sent a meaningful look Lily's way, and her serene face recognizing her yet revealing nothing, made Lily anxious. Turning, she had lost herself quickly in the throng, conscious of the felted market bag she carried, a bottomless pit of a satchel that Sierra had fashioned from potluck wool in shades of rose and lavender, named for Lilac Lily. No matter how much produce or dry goods she stuffed inside, the bag had never become full or any heavier than a normal shopping bag. Sierra had made one for each of them, in their own colorway.

"I can roll out a batch of soda biscuits," Lily said.

"I'll do it," Lorna replied, reaching into the flour bin. "You look a bit peaked."

"A headache," Lily said, feeling the familiar tightening across her forehead. "A small one."

"I did stop by the remedy woman's booth for more of your headache medicine," Lorna said. "The button lady said she did not show this year."

Lily smiled weakly, troubled at the news of Esmeralde. "I'll set the table, and then have a lie-down with a cool cloth."

Her sister nodded absently, busy with the biscuits. "Don't forget the extra china and silver. We've a full house."

In the dining room, Lily opened the cupboard. Out came the cloth napkins and serving pieces, the teacups and tall mead glasses. Pausing, she put her hand to her temple, hoping to still the growing ache. She really should take something, or she would not be able to finish setting the table, let alone serve supper.

Her first few years here at the inn had been fraught with headaches like the one now building. The day-to-day adjustment to hosting on a smaller scale had only been part of the difficulty. She didn't have to freshen as many rooms as there were at the Potluck, which threw her timing off. She set the table for too many guests, somehow expecting there would be twelve, and she prepared far too much food. Yet what had bothered her most had been the secrets that milled around in her head, still looking for a way out to do good or bad. But she could do nothing. Like the wild animals she had seen caged at the fair—striped horses no one could ride, and great arctic birds with wings too small for flight—Lily had lived these past years imprisoned in a foreign landscape, devoid of magic.

"It is the end of the world as we know it," Aubergine had told them all.

That last day at the yarn shop, just ten of them remained around the table. The shop was closed, as it had been since the night when Tracery Teal vanished and Tasman fled south. All eyes were on Aubergine's. No one was knitting.

"It may take years, and it may take longer, for Tasman to strip the South of all that is true and good." Aubergine's eyes simmered from blue to violet with anger. "Magic will be outlawed. Men will once more come to think they rule the world through death and war." She paused. "And we must let them."

"I won't stand for it," Esmeralde said. "Middlefolk will die needlessly without my magic tinctures."

"Without my herbs and teas, they will no longer remember childhood dreams, or even the scent of happiness," Indigo added.

"What of our remaining crystals?" Smokey Jo asked anxiously. "And the shared visions we seek above the great pot? I love the magic of my traveling cloak and my bottomless bags!" She pointed an accusing finger. "Aubergine, even you enjoy passing unseen. It is our way."

"Without belief in magic, how will people heed the yarns?" Sierra asked quietly, before Aubergine could say more. "The legends of the First Folk will be lost. All lore will be lost."

"That is what you think," Ratta glared at them all, her hands gripping the back of Mamie's wheeled chair. Mamie slumped like a sleeping baby, her head resting on the table. "I know tales of old that none of you can tell. Not even you, Sierra, and you think you've heard them all."

"Enough of such talk," Wheat snapped. She pointed her staff at Mamie, who was beginning to snore. "Why don't you hush up and put your mistress to bed?" The amber crystals tied to the crook danced and sparked.

Lily remembered how Ratta had shrunk away from Wheat's cabochons.

Then Lavender Mae let out a howl and clutched the pouch of precious stones that hung around her neck.

"No," she shrieked in Aubergine's direction. "No, no, no!"

Above the din, Aubergine had to shout. "I am not telling you to abandon the magic of the crystals and the dye pot." Standing, she held up a hand for silence. "Magic will be outlawed, and so you must go about your lives in secret. Search for the lost crystal. Practice your lore. When it is time, watch for the sign. There are many things I don't know about the strange events we are about to witness. But one thing I do know is that for this time, only women's magic can stop the world from ending once more in fire or ice."

She turned to Lilac Lily, the only one—other than the dozing Mamie—who had not yet spoken. "Lily, what say you?"

Lily shook her head. "I have said too little at times, and then too much. For that, I beg your forgiveness." She had given Aubergine a pleading look. "I dare not say more."

"Is that all?" Smokey Jo asked impatiently. Even though she perched on stacked cushions, her chin just cleared the table edge. She reached up to smack its wooden surface with the flat of her hand. "You have not even given us a clue. Aubergine, make Lily tell us what we would ken!"

Aubergine gazed at Lily, who looked down at the table. "We need to hear what you would have us know."

"Then you must ask a question," Lily said.

"What else will come to pass?" Aubergine asked gently.

"All that you have predicted and more," Lily answered dully. "Tasman has fled to the South where she will use her powers to bend the Lowlands to her will, along with the laws of nature. She will squander everything. In time, she will be known as the Dark Queen. All will fear her. Conquering the Lowlands will cost her dearly, and will take time. First there will be fire and famine and death. Then a great thirst will come across their lands, for they will have no water that has not been fouled by their own hands or salted by the seas. The folk of the Lowlands will march north. They will seek water, and power, and plunder."

Aubergine nodded, and seemed unsurprised. "They will try to breach the Crystal Caves in search of the secrets of old," she guessed.

"And more," Lily nodded. "The first attempt will be unsuccessful and the caves will ice over, leaving great black holes. I have heard. . . ."

"You are under oath not to say," Ratta spat. "No one has asked such a question."

Lily gazed levelly at Ratta. "It has been asked and I will answer."

"By whom?" Ratta demanded, glancing around the table.

Esmeralde glared at Ratta. "I thought you were told to hush."

Indigo turned to Sierra, ignoring Ratta. "Is there such a tale of these ancient tombs?"

"Yes," Sierra said. "The dead guard the caves with the usual assortment of spells and curses. Additionally, familiars called Watches protect Tombs of the ruling class." She frowned. "But I don't know what will happen when the graves are disturbed." She glanced at Mamie sadly. "She never said."

"She never said to you," Ratta sneered. "I alone know all."

Winter Wheat stood and pointed her staff at Ratta. "You had your chance," she said. The swinging amber crystals came together and Wheat focused a beam of light on the sleeve of Ratta's shift. Fabric sizzled and a black hole formed. The room smelled of burned wool. A few chuckles were heard as Ratta wheeled Mamie's chair from the table and swiftly retreated toward the door.

"What else can you tell us?" Aubergine asked Lily.

Lily glanced at Ratta, who lurked in the doorway. "I dare not say, lest I tempt fate again. But Aubergine, you know the time will come when you alone must choose whether to save the world we are left with or let it end again."

"When last it ended, it ended in ice," Smokey reminded them all. "The ancients wanted it that way."

"The ancients wanted no such thing," Sierra objected. "Men who wielded the power of the crystals fought among themselves as we do now, and the end happened."

Lily nodded. "Remember that." She pointed a finger at Ratta, who lingered just outside the door to hear Lily's final words. "You may think you know all, but sadly you don't. And what you do know unchallenged, you would be wise to share. The ancients fought over twin suns. In the end, both went out and the world was plunged into frozen darkness." She turned to the others. "Watch for fire in the sky at dawn."

"That will be the sign?" Aubergine asked. "Are you certain?"

Lily met Aubergine's violet eyes. "You will call us all with cold-fire crystals. When we see red sky in the morning, all of us will take warning—even the one who will become the Dark Queen. There are only enough stones in the tinderbox for you to summon us once."

"I know where the box is, and the crystals," Smokey interrupted eagerly. "When do we make the call?"

"You will know when the time has come," Lily replied, before turning toward the rest of them. "Sadly, not all of you will be able to answer." She laid a gentle hand on Lavender Mae's arm. "They will need you. Try to come."

"See if I come!" Ratta sneered from the doorway.

"I don't give a smashed shard whether you come or not," Esmeralde said. "We've plenty of magic crystals and tales of old to go around without your two coppers' worth."

"Me, neither," Indigo added. "Take that never-ending shawl you never finish knitting and frog it, for all I care."

"You will come," Lily told Ratta coldly. "And gladly, for otherwise you will have to watch your mistress die with no hope of passing to the land of dreams."

Ratta yanked Mamie's chair away from the doorway and wheeled the slouched form toward the kitchen garden.

"I need a private moment," Sierra whispered to Lily. They rose and went to the back of the yarn shop. Lily listened to the talk of the others as Sierra broke down in silent tears, mouthing fears of what Lily already knew. There was one yarn that Sierra still did not know, which seemed impossible, because she would be named Keeper of the Tales on Mamie's passing.

"Pay the kitchen wench no mind," Lily heard Wheat saying. "Ratta's always having a knit fit."

"You must stop burning holes through her garments," Aubergine said.

"It's just a little sting," Wheat grumbled. "Just enough to keep sheep in line."

"Ratta talks so out of turn," Indigo complained. "She arrived as Mamie's nursemaid, and now she acts like one of us."

"Her and her private language," Esmeralde added, as Sierra and Lily returned to the table. "She cannot read Mamie's mind."

"I fear she can," Sierra murmured. Everyone could see she had been crying. "I can never become Keeper of the Tales if some are known only to Ratta," she explained tearfully. "I should know the yarn of the ancient tombs. I do not."

"Yes, you do. You will remember it in time," Wheat said. Her eyes blazed at Lily and she reached for her staff. "Lily, what did you tell her?" she demanded.

"Only what Sierra asked," Lily said. "And no more. So you can keep your clacking crystals to yourself, unless you want me to tell everyone your unsavory thoughts."

Sierra rose. "I am taking leave of you all, now and forever. Another path has been chosen for me, a simpler, narrower, safer path, and I will take it."

"Sierra, things are not what they seem," Lily said. "Try to come when you are called."

Tears still streaming down her face, Sierra hurried out of the room and up the stairs to the dormitory. Esmeralde and Indigo stood to follow her. Outside, Ratta pulled up to the garden gate driving a pair of mules hitched to Mamie's old covered wagon.

Taking her staff, Wheat moved toward the kitchen garden, while Lavender Mae ran through the shop and down the hall into the dye shed, howling in dismay.

"Everyone's leaving," Smokey said, when only she and Lily and Aubergine remained. "Everyone's mad."

"We'll not leave," Aubergine said. "And they will come back."

It was then that Lily stood to take her leave as well. "No one will come back for a long time," she said. "Maybe never. If Tasman ever comes back here to war with the Northlanders," she hesitated. "If she breaches the Crystal Caves. . . ." She shut her mouth. "I can say no more. But you must call us back to the circle. You must."

"You said that not all will come." Aubergine had a grim look on her face.

"No," Lily replied. "You will be surprised at who does not arrive. And who does. We all will."

And so events had come to pass, Lily mused, somewhat as she had predicted. The Glacier Wars began with the Battle of the Burnt Holes, and the men in charge decided to fight with might rather than magic. Women suspected of using crystals were detained and arrested. During the first years, smoke constantly drifted up from the Lowlands. Then it also blew down from the north.

Even though she knew the world was ending, Lily had not yet seen fire in the sky. Perhaps Aubergine had decided to let the world die down as it had before, without summoning anyone for help.

Lily had practiced her lore in the intervening years, forming unspoken answers to the questions she hoped the others would ask her. She alone knew how to quell the ravaging fires, but with no one to tell, she could only watch helplessly as Middleland soldiers marched north up the track, past her rooming house and toward certain death. If she was right, the crystal was not lost. If she was right, it was merely damaged and hidden in plain sight—in a place no one would think to look. Without Lily's guidance, Lavender Mae's wild foraging among the Crystal Caves to cull amethysts for a replacement necklace would go unrewarded. Without Lily's insights, Esmeralde's and Indigo's shared vision to locate the original would be fruitless.

But if she found the courage to offer the others clues, without actually telling tales or breaking oaths, would any of them heed her warnings? The problem was that they had to ask her and she had avoided them all, because she was afraid they would not like the true answers to their questions.

They would ask if she could loosen Tasman's death grip over the lands.

Although she could not, Lily knew that the Dark Queen's hold could be unraveled like the split seams of an old sweater—if she could find a way to show them how. But the original Twelve would not be there, and that was another problem. There had to be twelve—and there could be—but two of them would arrive unwanted, and perhaps too late. To this day, untold secrets gave Lily such headaches that sometimes she felt as if she had drunk an entire flask of Esmeralde's Crystal Cordial.

Coming back to the present, Lily quickly finished setting the table and returned to the kitchen to fetch a cool cloth for her forehead. Lorna had set the biscuits out on the sideboard, ready for baking, and wiped the counter clean.

As she often had before, Lily questioned her role at the inn. Although she knew that Lorna and her husband, Evan, wanted her here, she was not needed. It had been the same at the Potluck. After the Twelve disbanded, Aubergine and Smokey had invited her to stay, and for a time she had, but finally she could not bear walking into the dusty rooms or seeing Aubergine's neck bare of the amethyst crystals and their power.

Dipping a washcloth in a bucket of cool water, Lily wrung it out and pressed it to her eyes. She could tell the cloth wasn't going to help. Her head was pounding as if it would explode from the inside. Desperate, Lily reached into the back of the spice cabinet for the bottle with the last of Esmeralde's tincture. She drank the bitter syrup straight, without diluting it. The ache abated, but only slightly.

Shaking, she took off her apron and hung it on the pantry door. It was time to do the other thing she had known all along she would do some day, fire in the sky or not. She must head north to the Potluck. The secrets wanted out. They would be told around the big pot once more, and she understood finally that she must let the questions be asked and answered. But why now? Had the catalyst been Sierra's idle glance at the fair? Or the throngs of Northland soldiers roaming the midway? Or perhaps the fact that Esmeralde had failed to show to tend her booth?

Lily slipped up the back staircase to her room in the attic. She opened the lid of her dusty trunk and shook out her traveling cloak. She stuffed everything else she needed into her market bag, and snuck back down the stairs. The kitchen and back porch were empty. She could not explain her departure without telling secrets. Lorna and Evan knew nothing of the Potluck. For all those years, they thought that Lily ran an inn over a yarn store, which explained the myriad garments and yarns she brought home on holidays. Lily quietly made her way up the garden path toward the main road.

Inside, Lorna hurried from the dining room to the front room, where her husband was filling the firebox. "Something's wrong with Lily," she said. "She set the table for twelve. She knows we have six guests."

Evan looked out the side window toward the street. "There she goes. Did you send her to the root cellar?"

"No, we've got the cream and butter for supper," she said, heading toward the kitchen. She returned with Lily's discarded apron. "Did you ask her for an errand?"

"Not I." Evan watched Lily in her traveling cloak swing her market bag into the front of a milk wagon and then climb up herself. "Lorna, love, she's leaving." He turned with a troubled glance. "I don't think she's coming back tonight."

Lilac Lily's Going-to-Market Bag

A BAG PATTERN

This is an intermediate-skill-level bag with wooden handles
and a button, designed to carry your purchases on market days.
It measures about 28" around and 13" high.

Get the pattern from PotluckYarn.com/epatterns

"It might be her time to pass into the land of dreams."

CHAPTER 7

Lost without Mamie

RATTA TUCKED THE SPARKLING SHAWL around Mamie Verde and left the old woman to sleep in the sun at the edge of the garden while she finished her morning chores. She threw bread crusts to the chickens, then swept the coop and refilled the water bowls, all the while with a watchful eye on Mamie. She gathered the eggs. There were more than a dozen.

Folk from the village hooted at the rolling chair Ratta had made for Mamie from a broken rocker and a set of wheels from a child's wagon. Ratta was pleased with her work. It allowed her to wheel Mamie around the village of Coventry when she brought eggs to sell. Mamie slept almost all the time now, and Ratta was afraid to leave her alone. She dreaded the possibility of returning from errands to find Mamie dead in her cot by the wood stove. Ratta knew her fear was selfish. She was afraid of living alone in an unknown world, bereft of magic.

Because of the many wildfires up north, this winter had been so warm that daffodils had already poked their heads through the snow, while green shoots showed at the garden's edge. Soon it would be time to turn the earth and plant seeds. Ratta grabbed a rake and worked savagely on the dead leaves next to her cabin. The signs of spring made her so angry she had to shout, even though she knew Mamie could not hear her.

"The world's waking up, and you're dying," she raged, her red hair flying wild.

Only the shawl sparkled in reply. It was the same never-ending shawl Ratta had started to knit when she thought the magic of the crystal-dyed yarns would keep Mamie alive forever. The shawl held a lot of history. Ratta had made it from a ball of bouncy bouclé yarn that never ran out. Sierra had spun the yarn from Merino roving she had bartered a few felt hats for at a fiber festival, and Indigo Rose had dyed it in the soft crystalline colorway she called Dusty Rose. Cocooned in the shawl, Mamie had only to transform into the butterfly of her next life to offer Ratta peace of mind. That had not happened yet. Ratta was afraid, with her spotty interpretation of the tales of old that it might not happen at all. She knew she was supposed to do something to ease Mamie into the afterlife. She could not figure out what.

Ratta propped the rake against the garden shed and crossed to the bench beside Mamie's chair. A flask sat beside her knitting bag. Ratta sat down, uncorked the top, and sipped the still-warm honeyed tea. She gazed at Mamie and sighed. The old woman hadn't stirred all morning.

Life had not been this dismal when Mamie had first ceased to speak, for that had happened years ago when they all still lived at the Potluck. The big bay windows of Mamie's chamber overlooked the kitchen garden. Ratta's space was a small adjoining anteroom. Day after day, Mamie and Ratta sat in the sun, creating conjoined magic in secret. Their enchantment did not require spoken words. The other Potluckers became envious. Sierra, who had learned Mamie's tales verbatim, was outright rude, for she could not fathom why Ratta no longer listened to her yarns.

Only Lilac Lily had guessed the truth, and she could reveal nothing unless asked. Why should Ratta have to listen to Sierra's rehashed tales when the voice of her mistress, inaudible to the others, echoed in her ears? When Mamie directed her gaze at Ratta, Ratta could hear the old woman's slow, careful words reverberating with the wisdom of the legends. She felt no need to linger at breakfast with the other acolytes, debating the underlying meanings of the old tales or discussing the will of the ancients. With Mind Speak, Mamie's silence told Ratta everything she needed to know.

Although Ratta's attention to Mamie's health never wavered, Mamie's decline quickened when the Potluck broke up. Mamie became convinced that she must return to her abandoned farm outside the ironworks of Coventry. Her attendant had been more than grateful to load the wagon. Ratta understood clearly that Mamie wanted her back at the old cabin in the woods as her successor and the guardian of the tales, not as the lowly farm maid she had been when they arrived at the Potluck. Although she would not be able to recite the stories as well as Sierra Blue, and she did not understand some of them, who else was left? Tasman had broken the amethyst necklace and run off, Teal had disappeared, as had the largest stone, and Sierra had escaped to a dreamy life along the Lavender Rill. Who else would offer the legends a safe haven? Certainly not Lilac Lily, who could hardly keep a secret, or Aubergine, now painfully disillusioned, or everyone's little pet, Smokey Jo. Lavender Mae could not stand to leave the pipe leaf alone, and Indigo had her own set of delusions if she thought she and

Esmeralde could rival Aubergine's authority with visions obtained by sipping Crystal Cordial and smoking Glacier Weed.

The only one of the Twelve that Ratta had ever crossed paths with again was Wheat, whom she liked least. One day last spring, when she was in town alone selling eggs, she had seen Wheat leading a flock of spotted sheep along the migratory foot path that wound down to Coventry from the Western Highlands. Wheat had grown stout and used her staff as a walking stick. The amber crystals tied to the crook looked dull, and Ratta assumed they had gone dead. Still, she steered clear of Wheat, lest she was mistaken and the scarab beetles were only sleeping.

Ratta noted Mamie's sunken cheeks. She would like to believe that the old woman was just sleeping, too. There was one among the Twelve who might be able to help Mamie. Ratta had been mulling that idea all winter. According to rumor, her classmate Esmeralde had grown from selling homemade cough syrup in her dormitory room into the most powerful healer in the Middlelands. Her simpler remedies were sold everywhere, even the Coventry General Store. Yet rumors suggested that Esmeralde practiced more serious lore in the back room of her cottage south of Banebridge. Now that the roads were finally passable again, Ratta considered seeking her out.

Ratta picked up her knitting, and then set it aside. When they had all gone their separate ways, she had been excited about following in Mamie's footsteps. Preserving verbal history, like Sierra wanted, was one thing. Possessing the power to ward the legends against those who would destroy them was quite another. Ratta had hoped that with the entire body of the tales at her disposal, there would be no need for visions over a dye pot or conjectures around a table. Even before she left the Potluck for good, Ratta had been able to recall one tale that Sierra had never heard. She thought Mamie knew even more yarns, darker stories yet untold. She believed that if she returned Mamie to her homestead, they could practice uninterrupted and she could learn those mysterious tales.

But things had not gone as she envisioned. On the journey to Coventry, Mamie suffered a shock of some kind, or maybe a stroke. The old woman's hearing began to wane, and then disappeared.

At the homestead, Ratta closed up the big house and brought Mamie to the small cabin in the woods, where she could watch the old woman constantly. This move caused an uneasy stir back east, among Mamie's nieces and nephews who all wanted to lay claim to the homestead. For a time, the family tried to place Mamie in an old-age home in Bordertown until it became clear that Mamie would rather die. The baleful hate in her watery eyes needed no translation into words.

With each passing year, Mamie had become more unresponsive. Ratta could no longer hear the Mind Speak voice, which had dropped to an unintelligible murmur. With dread, she realized that—short of some kind of miracle—there would be no more secret tales.

A few days earlier, in desperation, Ratta had stopped knitting her never-ending shawl. It was unfinished, of course, but she hoped the wrap's weak power could keep Mamie from getting worse. She knew it could not make her better. She began to bind what would become the last row off the needles.

Horse hooves crunched on gravel and Ratta looked up expectantly. No one ever visited the wooded cabin unbidden, so even before he came around the side of the dwelling she knew the rider would be her childhood friend, Tyler.

He waved. "I thought I'd find you in the garden."

Ratta watched him dismount, balancing on his good leg while he slid his walking cane from its holster under the saddle. "The eggs are gathered," she said. "I can drop them off at General Store on my way through."

"There's no need for that." Tyler said, looping his old mare's reins around a low branch of an apple tree. His twisted leg did not hinder his movement. It had been this way since he was young, and now he was glad of it because it made him unfit for war.

"I thought I told you to leave the chores for me."

"I wanted to do them one last time," she said.

"You have enough to do."

Leaning on his cane, Tyler limped to the chair in which Ratta had nestled Mamie's still form. He put a hesitant hand to the old woman's translucent skin.

"She lives," Ratta said. "But I don't think she knows we're here. For a time now, she hasn't noticed me even when she's wakeful. Her eyes seem to stare at nothing."

Tyler pulled on his short beard. "Will she eat?"

Ratta shook her head. "She refuses all food, even when I touch a spoon of honeyed porridge or warmed milk to her lips."

He watched her carefully. "It might be her time to pass into the land of dreams."

Ratta nodded silently. These past few days had led to loneliness unlike any she had ever known and given her too much time to contemplate how little her life would hold after Mamie died. Would her family return from the fisheries of the east and take over the farm? Would they banish her from the cottage where she had cared for Mamie these twenty years past? Or would they ignore the old woman's passing as they had ignored her life and let the boarded-up buildings rot away, leaving Ratta to practice the remnants of Mamie's lore alone?

"Mamie is unable to pass, for the never-ending shawl I knit is magic," Ratta said. "Wrapped in it, I fear she will remain in limbo until she is either reborn or dried up to a husk."

"What is her will?" Tyler asked.

"I don't know." Tears welled in her eyes and one slid down Ratta's face. "If only she could offer a clue."

"Take her to the remedy woman," Tyler urged. "Surely there is something Esmeralde can do."

As they watched, Mamie's milky eyes opened slowly, and blinked in the sunlight like those of a week-old kitten.

"Ask her," Tyler said.

Ratta knelt before the wheeled chair and stared into the old woman's face. "Mamie," she said silently in Mind Speak. "Mamie Verde, what would you have me do?"

"Use your special language," Tyler interrupted.

Ratta gave him a frustrated look. "I'm trying."

The old woman was unable to focus her gaze. Her unseeing eyes offered them an impression of such complete despair that Ratta immediately regretted not having left for Esmeralde's cottage this morning at first light.

"She wants to pass," Tyler murmured, as Mamie's eyes closed once more.

"But she can't." Ratta looked at him. "Something's undone."

She rose to her feet. Tyler put a comforting hand to her shoulder, as she stared down at Mamie in dismay. Here Mamie was, wrapped in a magic shawl that kept her alive against her will. What Ratta had done to prolong her existence was little better than the old-age home Mamie's relatives had threatened.

"I would do anything for her," Ratta told Tyler fiercely. "Even let her go, if I must."

"Then take her to the remedy witch." Tyler gave Ratta's shoulder a squeeze. "I'll watch things here."

Leaving Tyler with Mamie, Ratta hurried to the barn and hitched up the mules, blinking back tears. Tyler helped her lay Mamie gently among quilts in the back of the wagon, still snugly wrapped in the shawl.

As she slapped the reins and waved, Ratta vowed to find a way to waken Mamie's voice once more—or let her die trying. There were still tales to be told, tales of vast icy graveyards and of frozen dead entombed in palatial caverns. She had seen these things through Mamie's eyes, but she didn't know where.

Ratta's Never-Ending Shawl

A SHAWL PATTERN

This "never-ending," intermediate-skill-level shawl will take you safely to the afterlife. Shoulder line measures 73" with a depth of 52" after blocking.

Get the pattern from PotluckYarn.com/epatterns

"Ever hear of hiding in plain sight?"

CHAPTER 8

The Fossickers Scatter

THE DELL WAS RICH WITH SPRING GRASSES. The ponies hungrily cropped the tender shoots while Skye washed in the nearby streambed. Lifting her face to the midday sun, she became aware of how much she had disliked the Copse, where branches caught at her skirts from the sides of the narrow track, barely kept at bay by the light that shone from the jewel lashed to Trader's walking stick. The ponies had rolled their eyes and whinnied nervously at the dark branches waving at the edge of the trail, and no matter how many times Trader urged her to keep close, Skye lagged further and further behind.

With relief, the two people and two ponies finally broke through the ferns into the warm and sunny river valley that the fossickers fondly called the dell. Shaking the icy water from her hands, Skye rose and trudged back to where Trader had a cook fire crackling in the blackened crescent of rocks before the lean-to. She spread her damp traveling cloak across a bush to dry and pulled her lace shawl close. This was the fine shawl she had meant to dazzle everyone with at the fair. Now the fabric, with its intricate frost-flower design, served only to warm her shoulders around the campfire. The campsite beyond was all but invisible, hidden by tall bushes bright with new leaves.

Various fossickers had camped here over the winter. A footpath to the spring and a privy were evident as were fishing spots along the stream. Trader's lean-to looked sturdy to Skye, though worn. The heavy oiled canvas stretched over the notched wood frame was soiled and threadbare, likely from having been broken down and moved in haste so many times. Tucked beneath the awning, bedrolls lined the sloping wall. Cluttered among them were packsacks and pantry bags, ready to be carried off at a moment's notice. From the amount of truck piled against the canvas, Skye thought the band of fossickers must be larger than she had first imagined.

"It's a nice spot," she said, approaching the fire, near which Trader sat on a bare log. Water boiled in a battered kettle into which he was stirring birch bark and honey for tea.

"It's home," Trader eyed her with a grin. "To us filthy fossickers."

"Come off it," Skye said, sitting beside him. She smoothed her torn skirt around her ankles. "I can't help what I hear."

"Nor I," Trader admitted. He pulled strips of dried jerky and a rind of cheese from an open pantry sack. "You hungry?"

Skye nodded, taking the cheese and knife he offered, plus the bit of planking the boys obviously used for a cutting board. Trader pulled the kettle off the fire and poured the tea into mismatched mead cups.

"How long have you been out here?" Skye asked, as he handed her a cup. He was younger than she had first thought—no older than her brother Garth, or maybe just scrawny for his age. She blew across the rim of the cup to cool the steaming tea. "Living like this."

"Off and on," Trader said. "When need be. It was easier before the Guard started hunting us like wild game."

"Looking for conscripts?" Skye asked, slicing cheese, and he nodded. "They took my brother Warren. He's a winter older than me. Warren was the best sledder in all of the lands. He won the Winter Games last year."

"No doubt." Trader bit off a piece of jerky and offered her the rest. "Soldiers slinking around are always after me and my mates. We have to look sharp." He nodded toward a corner with a pile of surplus bedrolls. "Some of us are not so lucky."

"Were they taken by the Northland Guard?"

"Who knows," Trader sighed. "Boys come and go. Everyone wants to make their fortune as a fossicker until they find they have nothing to trade, and the weather turns cold, and the rivers icy. Then the family farm they ran away from and Mother's stewpot looks good once more."

"What about you?" Skye asked softly.

"I'm always here," Trader shrugged, chewing a rind of cheese. "I got nowhere to go."

"But you get by," Skye conjectured. "With stealing and thievery?"

"Finds," Trader corrected her, waggling a finger. "I know where to find things. And what to look for—that's the difference. There's brisk trade in fossicks the glacier leaves behind, if you know the right folk looking."

"Fossicks like that magic rock atop your walking stick?" Skye asked, sipping tea.

"No." Trader gave her a sharp look. "That's mine unchallenged."

"Unchallenged?" Skye smiled, seeing she had hit a nerve.

"At least for now," he mumbled, looking away.

"Well, have you ever found fossicks? I mean, real ones?"

He smiled slyly. "I do discover the odd crystal now and again. Once I found a jeweled beetle inside a piece of amber. Traded it for leather boots and this new jerkin." He showed her his leather jersey, laced at the top. About to go on, he caught himself. "Lately there's better trade in the truck the soldiers leave behind."

"Weaponry?" Skye asked. "Uniforms?" She looked at him with dawning horror. "Do you scavenge from the dead?"

Trader shook his dark head. "Mostly it's just camp stuff the Guard leaves behind when units move on. Tools and broken bits, dishes and bedding. That's where this kettle came from, and the mead cups." He started laughing. "Once we came across a raiding party of Lowlanders and raided them back while they slept. Oh, the food! We had beans with bacon ends for days, black bread and mustard, gallons and gallons of hard cider." He looked around. "It's all gone now."

"The cheese, too," Skye laid the knife across the barren plank.

Trader sucked on his lip. "There's nothing more. We ate all else."

Skye dumped out one of her twig baskets. "I've no apples left," she said, picking though the empty sacks. "And the ponies ate all the grain." Worriedly, she looked to Trader. "What now? There's a little coin in Mother's change purse, but it's not Northland silver."

"We'll meet up with the others at dusk under the bridge," Trader assured her, "after the soldiers are off the road. Clayton and Micah will bring our barter." His eyes drifted toward Sierra's rucksack beyond the baskets. "We'll need all sorts of truck to trade if we expect to reach the Border Lands."

"We? What is your sudden interest?" Skye asked, emptying her other basket. It held nothing but a clean blouse and pantaloons, her show apron and hair ribbons, a drinking cup and a few odd comforts. There was nothing to sell. Her eyes narrowed as she followed Trader's gaze to her mother's bundle of garments. "Besides, the Trading Post closes at nightfall. Even I know that."

"What I have for barter will not be seen by the likes of them at the Trading Post," Trader boasted. "There's an old witch who owns a greenhouse up in the hills, fond of herbs and twigs, the odd dried thing. She'll give us Northland silver for what I've got."

"What is it?"

Trader shrugged. "Dunno. Clayton's bringing it from our stash in the rocks. It looks like a medicine bag or portent bag. We found it all frozen, lost along the military road."

"I've only ever seen a portent bag once," Skye said, remembering Esmeralde's Possibles Bag. "My mother's friend brought one to the fair last year."

Trader brightened. "So you know what they look like! Well— mayhap we will get a better price." He turned to her. "I'll pool whatever trade I get in order to venture with you and your brother up to the Northlands."

"Why us?" Skye asked. "What about your boys?"

"They'll be fine with Clayton," Trader answered easily. "He'll not let things run amiss."

"Ours is a fool's errand," Skye confessed. "Truthfully. We don't know how to get to the border. We've never been north of the River Runne Valley."

"I know the Border Lands well," Trader said. "I was born in the back streets of Bordertown in the borough of Butcher's Block. From here it would be a long walk, but only two days' ride on your ponies." He lowered his voice. "I would see you to the jails of the Burnt Holes if that's where you would go."

"I thought no one ever came back from there," Skye said, with growing suspicion. "And besides, my mother told me where I should go once I reach Bordertown. I'll not be needing the likes of you."

"You need me," Trader insisted. "You do. There's more to me than meets the eye."

"You tried to steal from me." Skye shook her head. "I won't share the company of anyone I can't trust."

Trader watched her silently. "You're going to have to lose the skirt, first thing," he said, finally. "You can't hike the mountain passes or sled down a slope in a dress."

"Well, I guess I mislaid my mountaineering outfit," Skye shot back angrily, repacking her basket.

"You'll not make it alone," Trader said. He got up as if to go. "Think on it."

"I won't agree until I hear your reason." Skye faltered, afraid of being left alone with the tangled Copse between her and the main track to Bordertown. "What is up there? Some fabled treasure fossick to steal from the Crystal Caves?"

"There's something I need to know." Trader stirred the dying fire with a stick and looked across at her with glittering eyes. "You're not the only one missing a relative or two."

Skye caught her breath. "I am sorry, Trader. I meant no offence."

Trader held up his hand. "None taken."

"You just seem. . . ." she hesitated.

"Shifty?" Trader interrupted. "Crafty? Untrustworthy? I'll tell you what, miss, I have been running my entire life," he said harshly. "And I can tell you this: Nothing is as it seems."

"Big words coming from a boy," Skye retorted.

Trader's voice grew cold and quiet. "Is that all you think I am, a boy?"

Unable to back down, Skye nodded, her eyes widening with fear.

"Because that is what I want you to think, silly girl," he growled, advancing. "I make it look that way."

Skye began to tremble. "Trader, I didn't mean to make you mad."

His black eyes glared at her. "Ever hear of hiding in plain sight?"

Skye nodded, stepping back. "Yes, my mother told tales." Although short and slight, Trader was quicker than she, and would catch her easily if she tried to flee, encumbered by her skirts. Wildly she searched for a stick, something to defend herself with. "There was a group called the Twelve."

"And what could they do?" Trader hissed, baiting her.

"Pass unseen," Skye whispered.

"What else?" He grabbed her arm.

"Hide in plain sight," Skye began to cry. "Trader, what are you doing?"

"Hiding in plain sight." Letting her go, Trader loosened the laces at the top of his jerkin to let her see the small curved breasts flattened by the tight leather.

"You're a girl!" Skye gasped.

"Just a girl," Trader laughed. "And no older than you. So what are you scared for?"

"But you seem so . . ." Wiping her eyes, Skye search for words. "Conniving and mean."

Trader nodded soberly. "That's my disguise. That's how I hide."

"And you boss those great big fossick boys around." Skye gave a weak laugh. "Oh, that is just so precious."

"The world isn't ruled by men," Trader said solemnly.

"It just looks that way," Skye agreed. "How many times has my mother told me that?" She gave Trader an intent look. "Do any of the boys know?"

"No, and they can never know." Trader said frankly. "There, now you know my deepest secret." She let out a dramatic sigh. "Or one of them anyway. If I betray you, you in turn can ruin me."

"So why did you tell me?" Skye wanted to know.

"You said you needed to travel with someone you could trust. I just showed you I trust you," Trader reminded her. "Can you trust me now?"

"All right," Skye agreed. "But I don't understand one thing. Why in all the lands would you want to pass as a boy?"

"It wasn't so bad before the soldiers came," Trader joked. "I always hated skirts and dresses."

"No, really," Skye prodded.

"Hiding as a boy was the only way I escaped imprisonment in the Burnt Holes with the likes of your mother," Trader admitted.

"Who was after you?" Skye said. "Are they still?"

"Oh, yes," Trader said. "But I'm not sure who they are." She paused. "All I know is that they are evil. Pure evil. And they don't look for boys, so I was safe. But then along came the Northland Guard, who do look for boys." Trader rolled her eyes. "Mayhap it is time to become a girl again."

Skye laughed. "A girl in breeches, though."

"There's breeches enough left behind in those bedrolls that neither one of us ever has to wear skirts again." Trader said. "Now your mother. She was one of the Twelve, was she not?"

"I think so," Skye breathed. "I don't really know. Her name was Sierra Blue."

"Sierra Blue." Trader said the name thoughtfully. "What was her talent?"

"When we were young, she told us tales from the days of old," Skye said. "Like fairy tales. She called them her yarns. But her magic lay in crystal-dyed garments." Skye blinked back tears. "Listen to me, I am speaking as if she is dead."

"She is just in trouble," Trader said gently. "Perhaps the magic part of her is dead, and we need to help her get it back. Let's see her sack."

Skye reached for Sierra's bundle. "Do you think there is something in here that can help her?"

"Or us," Trader said nonchalantly. "We all need our magic."

"Your name is not really Trader, is it?" Skye asked, as Trader untied the knot at the top of the bundle and unwrapped it slowly.

"Nope," Trader said. "Some call me Turncoat. Some call me Traitor." She pulled out Sierra's traveling cloak and settled it around her shoulders. "This will do nicely." She flashed Skye a brilliant smile. "Some call me Traces of Teal."

"Teal. . . ." Skye searched her memory. "I know that name. She was one of the Twelve."

"Some say she disappeared as Tasman fled," Trader prompted.

"You do know your yarns!" Skye realized.

"I should," Trader snorted. "Teal was my great aunt. It is traces of her I seek, although some wish me dead. Thus I hide." She pulled several Potluck Hats from the bundle. "Are these real?"

"What do you think?"

"Just checking." Trader gave a low whistle. "The old hags who barter with me for fossicks will know how to dispose of these, I ken," she said. "I've never seen a pink one, only blues and greens."

"Blues and greens are for calm and confidence in the face of danger," Skye said. "My father had one. Pinks and grays allow the wearer to pass unseen." She paused. "Do these witches have Northland silver?"

"Plenty." Trader assured her. "We will see them tonight. What's this?"

At the bottom of the bundle, she pulled out a market bag and a felted knapsack.

"That's one of those bottomless bags, for marketing," Skye explained matter-of-factly, "and the knapsack is one that shepherds use. It never gets heavy or wet, no matter how it rains on the highland trails."

"No, I mean this," Trader said, showing her a dented silver box that looked like it had no lid.

"That is what was hurting my neck!" Skye exclaimed. "I was using the bundle as a pillow last night, and this little thing kept giving me a crick."

"What is it?" Trader asked, turning the box over in her hands, looking for a seam line.

"I don't know," Skye said. "It must have been my mother's."

"But you have never before seen it?"

"No. But look," Skye ran her hand over the smooth surface. "There's no way in. Is it as good as a fossick?"

"It's better than a fossick," Trader grinned. "If it was your mother's, it's yours unchallenged." She shook the box and they both heard the rattle.

"There's something inside," Skye said.

"We should leave it be."

"Will your witches know how to break the seal?"

"Mayhap," Trader set the box down gingerly. "Get your ponies. Let's pack up this truck and go."

Trader trying to ride Shep was a comical sight, but by dark they had made it through the foothills of the small river valley and up to the trestle bridge leading across the Runne to Banebridge. Both girls wore riding breeches underneath their traveling cloaks, and they had a pack bag stuffed with Sierra's remaining garments. Skye carried the silver box inside the pocket of her cloak, while their few pooled coins hung in a change purse around Trader's neck, hidden beneath her jerkin. As darkness fell, they led the ponies down the steep bank to the sandy apron under the bridge and found themselves alone at the river's edge.

"Late as usual," Trader grumbled. "And they have all of our grub and my barter." She squatted on the ground and glanced up at the rising moon. "It should not have taken them this long. The high rocks are not as far as the dell."

"But we rode," Skye pointed out.

"Hadn't thought of that," Trader admitted, shivering. Afraid to light a fire, they put up their hoods and huddled against a piling while the ponies foraged nearby. High overhead, the nailed boots of the odd foot traveler rang out or a cart rumbled across, sending a hail of frozen dirt through the trestles. Otherwise the bridge was silent.

It was not long before they heard the boys arrive, pushing and bumping and shushing each other with loud whispers as they clambered down the bank.

"Clayton," rang the voice of young Ross, "they ain't down here. It's just them strange ponies that like to chase people."

"Shhh!" Micah hissed. "Before you get us caught."

Garth came into the pool of moonlight and caught up the ponies' reins without noticing Trader or Skye. "Something's wrong," he murmured.

Trader looked at Skye, who grinned and pointed at their cloaks, and then put a finger to her lips and motioned Trader to back away. Trader smiled and retreated soundlessly.

Down the bank clambered Clayton and a few other boys Skye did not recognize. Skye guessed they came from the camp in the high rocks. Several carried packsacks.

"What now, Clayton?" Micah asked, as Trader and Skye circled the group.

"We wait," Clayton said, shrugging out of his packsack.

"They've been here," Garth said, tying the packsacks onto the ponies. "They can't be far."

"Maybe the Guard took 'em," Micah said.

"Or them witches." Ross began to whimper.

"Nobody took anybody," Clayton said, helping Garth secure the straps. "Now shush."

"Trader likes swapping truck with them witches," Ross told Garth. "And I'm scared of witches."

Nailed boots rang out on the bridge above and torchlights shone down over the bank.

"Hey!" A man's voice rang out. "Who's down there?"

"Shards," Clayton swore softly. "It's the Guard."

Skye looked at Trader in alarm. Trader put up her hand and then motioned to Skye to open Sierra's bundle of garments.

"Scramble?" Ross asked in a small voice.

"Softly, like eggs scramble," Clayton reminded him, as Skye ferreted through Sierra's garments without a word. Trader pointed out the pink Potluck Hat and Skye understood immediately.

"Scatter?" Micah queried.

"Like we scatter sap buckets in the spring come sugaring season," Clayton confirmed. "Don't worry, boys, we will all meet up again. You know where."

They melted into the grasses along the banks, leaving Garth with the ponies and packsacks. "Oh, wonderful," he said, hearing the call of men's voices over the side of the trestle bridge as the lights got closer.

Suddenly a Potluck hat clamped over Garth's head, and Skye's voice hissed in his ear. "Put on the hat and ride," she said.

Skye's Elfin-Lace Shawl

A SHAWL PATTERN

This intermediate-skill-level lace shawl has stunning details in every stitch. It is a triangular shawl about 72" wide by 28" deep.

Get the pattern from PotluckYarn.com/epatterns

"The brew pot will reveal the traitor only if she is one of us."

CHAPTER 9

IN THE DARKNESS INDIGO ROSE SHUT the greenhouse door quietly and made her way back to her cottage by lamplight. By force of habit, she lifted her eyes to scan the stars for signs, but saw only the glimmer of a clouded moon, promising more rain. Taking a last draw from her handrolled Smokie, she dropped the smoldering butt to the wet ground, where it sizzled out. Esmeralde had asked Indigo not to smoke in the cottage while they were steeping tinctures, arguing that the glacier weed tainted the brew pot and addled Indigo's head.

Indigo felt like she should not have to smoke like a criminal on her own porch, yet during Esmeralde's frequent visits she found herself rolling her bundles of glacier weed in the potting shed and puffing them under the slant of leaded glass in the attached greenhouse, which was at least out of the wind and cold. This past winter, her seedlings had seemed to thrive on the sweet curl of smoke, and so, thought Indigo Rose, had she.

Reaching the cottage door, Indigo paused, momentarily afraid of what she might find on the other side. Wisps of smoke seeped under the threshold, and she heard the dull roar of the brew pot bubbling over, accompanied by Esmeralde's shouted oaths. Indigo knew she should not be surprised. When Esmeralde had shown up yesterday afternoon on the heels of several cups of cordial she had evidently enjoyed at the Trading Post, Indigo had been working in the greenhouse, with a flowered bandana tied over her graying braids.

"You were right." Esmeralde had been red-faced from climbing the steep track. "It is not safe to go to the fair. All signs point north to Bordertown, as you foretold."

"How in cracked crystal can you tell?" Indigo pulled off her fingerless gloves to help Esmeralde with her clanking Possibles Bag. The gloves were of her own design, knit from fine merino spun in the grease. She found them wonderful for pottering among the hanging planters and flats of berries in the garden on cold days.

"I sifted through some Possibles this morning." Esmeralde wrestled the heavy bag from her shoulder to Indigo's workbench. "Everything I tried told me not to go south toward the fair."

The Possibles Bag bulged so full of glass vials that Indigo had been amazed that they had not spilled or broken. Fortunately, Esmeralde had packed them in soft rolls of moss.

"Did you bring what I asked?"

"I heeded your advice," Esmeralde's voice was small, like a child's. "I couldn't remember what you wanted, so I brought it all."

"You've been drinking." Indigo pushed her bandana a little higher on her forehead. "This early in the day?"

"I did stop for a flask at the Trading Post," Esmeralde squinted at the sun. "Ozzie was buying. And it's well past noon."

Indigo had nodded and shut up the greenhouse. For what they were about to undertake, they needed to have no interruption. She had turned her business sign from DOING TRADE to TRADING TOMORROW. "Let's go up," she suggested, her arm around Esmeralde's neck as she led the way to the cottage. "I have a few thoughts about how to catch our traitor."

Once inside, Indigo took off her bandana and gardening coat, and stepped out of her muck boots. With a grunt, she helped Esmeralde shift the Possibles Bag to the kitchen table without spilling any vials or cracking any wax seals. Then she broke out her Smokies and a jug of Crystal Cordial.

The night had passed in a blur, and they were still no closer to discovering the identity of their quarry.

"I've changed my mind about the Potluck," Indigo had said, lighting a Smokie. "I think we should wait for Aubergine to send the signal."

"We'll die of old age first." Esmeralde waved away the thick, sweet wisps of smoke. "Do you have to puff that inside?" Reaching for the jug, she glanced around the cluttered kitchen. Finding no mead cup, she took a swig directly from the earthenware vessel.

"I'll stop smoking when you lay off the jug." Indigo found two used mead cups, which she swiped at with a dishcloth. "Pour me some."

"We need to send our own sign." Esmeralde filled their glasses. "Isn't that clear? There's talk of the Twelve all up and down the track, and you and I are not saying anything." She turned unsteadily. A little cordial slopped onto the floor. "Knots and tangles," she swore.

"Never mind that," Indigo said, with a wave of her hand.

Esmeralde settled onto a kitchen stool. "Unless we discover the interloper, we will be found out and rounded up and banished to the Burnt Holes."

"Or the traitor among us."

"Exactly." Esmeralde reached to clink her mead cup against the one Indigo lifted toward her. "Let us call all to ourselves as Aubergine would have done, and see who comes." Her eyes glistened. "Or doesn't." Merrily she shook the contents of her Possibles Bag onto the table. "Like I said, I brought everything."

"So you did," Indigo's laugh released a trail of smoke as several blown-glass vials rolled to the floor. The stopper fell out of one, which emitted a peculiar odor. "Shards, what was that?"

Esmeralde shrugged and bent down to retrieve it. "Something gone bad."

"I don't think we have the power to call all to ourselves," Indigo cautioned. "But there's another way to find out who among us has loosened her tongue."

"Go root around for your packets of herbs," Esmeralde waved her off. She pulled the stoppers from more glass tubes, sniffing them for rot. "We'll find a way to make our own fire in the sky."

"By the shards and cracked crystals that made them," Indigo swore, searching the cupboards. "How do you propose to do that? None of us is Aubergine."

"Not even Aubergine is Aubergine," Esmeralde argued, grimacing at odor emitted from an open vial before she replaced the cork a bit overcarefully. "Anymore."

"My point exactly. The brew pot will tell us who is not herself, and we will find our traitor." A green cloud rose from the lip of another tube. Indigo eyed it warily from across the room. "We don't need to attempt any fire in the sky."

"The brew pot will reveal the traitor only if she is one of us." Esmeralde said, watching the haze from the vial curl into a lazy S. "I've a feeling she is not. That is why you keep on saying traitor, but I say interloper."

"Semantics." Indigo blew a smoke ring at the green fog and it dissipated.

"Not really." Esmeralde set her empty glass aside. "What if this interloper is a he, not a she?"

Indigo took a long puff. "I hadn't thought of that."

Esmeralde gave her a crafty look. "And that's another reason for us to renew the power of the Twelve. Let us dawn the day with fireworks and see who comes, if any."

"We have no cold-fire crystals. Even if we did, we have not the skill to use them!"

"We have raw amethyst culled from the Crystal Caves." Esmeralde shook a vial of rocks. "And amber." Her voice drifted off. "I used to know what was in this one." She glanced at Indigo, who was now rummaging in a deep chest for her trove of herb packets. "It was something interesting that one of those fossicker boys found in the riverbed of the Trickle."

"Fossickers," Indigo muttered.

"The fossicker boys have not been by, have they?" Esmeralde asked, hopeful. "The one called Trader?"

"Esmeralde, we don't even have half the ingredients we need for a cold-crystal fire, let alone fire in the sky. Did you bring any hematite?"

"No, but I have red ocher."

"It's not the same." Indigo finally found her bundle of herb packets and cleared space on the table. She laid out the folded papers like playing cards in an intricate game of chance.

"It's not as difficult as Smokey Jo and Aubergine try to make out," Esmeralde insisted. "You will see."

But even though they tried all through the night and into the next morning, neither Esmeralde nor Indigo did see. They had searched through Esmeralde's glass tubes and Indigo's dried herbs, but somehow they did not have the right ingredients, or, if they did, they could not find the exact combination.

"I used to know what was in every vial," Esmeralde said blearily after they had emptied the jug of cordial.

"And I, these sorted papers," Indigo added. "I can put pen to paper—why didn't I think to scribe things along the edges? I could at least have given myself a clue." She unfolded a twist of parchment and shook out a few yellowed leaves. "I have no idea," she admitted. "This no longer even has any scent."

Esmeralde continued to unstopper vial after vial, upending each. "I think there is nothing more inside any of them."

As morning dawned, they had stumbled to bed, discouraged, only to repeat the entire process when they had risen from sleep in the afternoon. There had been no fire in the sky, just a fire in the hearth under the iron brew pot, hanging from its hook. From time to time, Indigo swung the bubbling pot away from the blaze to add more water, hoping that finally they would come across the combination of herbs, dyestuffs, and crystal that would promote heavenly fire.

But there was nothing.

Outside the cottage door, after her retreat to the greenhouse for a smoke that took longer than it really needed to, Indigo sighed. It was past midnight again. She took a deep breath of damp air and checked the sky. There was nothing up there but darkness, which meant there was nothing to do but get back to work, despite her misgivings. Summoning what little resolve she had left, Indigo pulled the cottage door open to reveal the chaos within. The brew pot, boiling over onto the hot hearthstones, hissed steam into the fetid air. Smoke rolled into the room, forced downward from the chimney's half-closed damper. Unmindful, Esmeralde sat sweating at the table, sorting sprinkles of crystal, like colored sugar, into piles: powdered green malachite, rare jet ground into silt, milky crushed opal, golden amber.

Coughing loudly, Indigo adjusted the damper so that the smoke rose up the chimney. Even though it had begun to rain, she opened the windows to clear the kitchen and inhaled deeply as a cool rush of night air filled her lungs.

"Aren't you hot?" she asked.

"I am hungry," Esmeralde said. She stuck her finger into a trail of rock flour that had spilled across the table, and brought the granules to her lips. "Do these crystals resemble rock candy to you?"

Indigo suddenly realized that they had not eaten all day. "We have salad greens." She peered into the pantry. "Early tomatoes. I can heat some soup."

"Swing out the brew pot." Esmeralde ignored her, motioning toward the fireplace. "I think I have concocted it right." She swept the crystals into an untidy pile.

"Esmeralde, you will blow up the cottage with that lot." Wild-eyed, Indigo watched the colored grains begin to smolder. "Don't you dare burn a hole through my hardwood table."

"I will not. Just get out of the way!" Esmeralde scooped the whole mess onto a dinner plate, where it snapped and crackled with a sulfurous stench.

Laughing, she tilted the multicolored grains into the brew pot. "It's working!"

They watched the crystals fizzle and then spark out as they submerged. The simmering water turned a cloudy green.

"It is going to work," Esmeralde insisted. "It might take a moment or two." She watched the pot expectantly.

"Right," Indigo said, letting one minute pass, and then another. "Right," she repeated.

"I did everything right," Esmeralde said. "I did!"

"You mucked up the water is what you did." Indigo swung the brew pot out away from the fire. "Do you want to start over? Again?"

"I forgot to add the jet," Esmeralde brushed the black silt into the pot. She grabbed a large wooden spoon from the sideboard and stirred vigorously. "It makes all the difference."

Slowly at first the pot began to simmer again, and then to boil, until it suddenly burst into a roil, spewing green bubbles that burst into sparks.

"Holey socks!" Indigo shouted, quickly swinging the iron pot back into the fireplace, where it clanged against the stonework. "Stand back!"

"It's working," Esmeralde cried with glee, as licks of green leaped from the pot, sending flames up the fieldstone flue. She gave her friend an anxious look. "Isn't it?"

"It is not." Indigo pulled the spoon from the pot. Half of the wood had been eaten away, and the rest was on fire. Hastily she threw the remains into the fireplace as tendrils of the burgeoning emerald flame licked the hearthstones, threatening to scorch the floor. "Can you quell it?" she shouted over the roar of the blaze. The heat became stifling.

"No," Esmeralde cried, sweating profusely. "I thought only to get it started."

"The chimney is burning up," Indigo coughed. "Shards! What if the kitchen is next?"

"We better get outside," Esmeralde scurried to the front door.

They watched in the rain outside the cottage as great green flames leaped from the chimney top like fairy dancers.

"So much for my fire in the sky," Esmeralde muttered, as rain soaked her beret and drenched her dress. She turned her sooty face to Indigo. "It is more like a fire in the chimney."

"A chimney fire," Indigo agreed, gulping breaths of cool air. "And not even red."

"Hopefully the rain will put it out." Emerald sparks spit from the lip of the stonework. "But just in case, you do have baking soda?"

"Some place," Indigo slumped onto the stone bench with her back to the cottage, facing the greenhouse.

"The day will dawn soon." Esmeralde sat down heavily next to her. The rain was abating. "What will we do next?"

"Who knows," Indigo said. "But we are done with this sorcery—promise?"

Esmeralde nodded without complaint. "I used to be pretty good with diseases. I could put a pox on a whole village." She paused. "Cooking with magic crystals just was not my strength."

"Nor mine," Indigo said. "But if you want tea that makes you sleep like the dead, or a flavor you can only dream of, or a smell from your childhood to help you remember. . . ." She yawned. "If you want those things, I am your witch."

The rain tapered to a drizzle. Sobering, Esmeralde turned toward her friend. "Remember that vision we had over the brew pot the other night?"

"Vividly." Water dripped from Indigo's gray braids and soaked her vest.

Esmeralde eyed her closely. "Was that real, or just the cordial talking?"

"I believe it was real. I don't think that crystal is lost. We both saw it, the one from Aubergine's necklace that Teal broke away as Tasman fled. Teal had the amethyst in her hand just before she disappeared."

"When we saw it, the gem was not broken, either." Esmeralde turned to face Indigo. "We both know the amethyst is broken."

"Or was broken," Indigo reminded her. "That was decades ago, and no one has seen it since."

"I wish we could find Lavender Mae. She would know."

Indigo looked toward the chimney top, merely sputtering now, sending an occasional spark of green to drift outward from the roof and then fall toward their booted feet.

"Do you think she would have come if our fire had been red in the sky, instead of green in the chimney?" Indigo asked.

Esmeralde shook her head. "They say she is nothing but a crazy old hermit now. She can answer no one's call. She is too far gone."

"Mayhap we all are." Indigo yawned.

"Crazy?"

"No," Indigo heaved herself to her feet. "Just too far gone. Let's go to bed."

Esmeralde rose and pulled her wet skirts away from her legs. She paused. "Do you hear that?"

Indigo froze. "Sounds like hoof beats."

"Horses," Esmeralde said. "Just before dawn." She raised her eyebrows. "That can't be good."

"Soldiers, or somebody hurt. Did you bring your medicines?"

"Always," Esmeralde peered into the predawn light, looking down the slope past the greenhouse. "But we won't be needing any. I don't see riders."

Indigo walked to the edge of the hill. "Just horses?"

Esmeralde nodded. "Two runaways, all bridled up. Not even horses."

They stood back as two chunky mountain ponies cantered up the steep trail and came to a halt, lathered and spent, in the cottage clearing. The sturdy ponies' sides heaved as they fought to catch their breaths.

"I know these mounts," Esmeralde said. "If I'm not mistaken, they are Sierra Blue's wagon team, from Lavender Rill Farm. Stolen, I'll bet."

As she spoke, the air rippled and a slight figure, swathed in a cape and mounted on one of the ponies, became visible. Throwing back the hood of the traveling cloak, Trader smiled broadly. "Hiya!"

"I should have known," Esmeralde laughed. "The same fossicker I've been seeking, delivered to me in a found traveling cloak with a pair of ponies. Trader, boy, where have you been hiding?"

"Sometimes in the high rocks, other times in the dell," Trader said nonchalantly, dripping water.

"Looks like you've been up to the Teardrop," Esmeralde said, eyeing Shep and Chuffer.

"There, too. Handsome prizes, are they not?"

"That traveling cloak was crafted by Sierra's hand," Indigo murmured quietly to Esmeralde. "She would not offer it willingly to the likes of him."

Esmeralde nodded shrewdly. "What say you, Trader? Are any of these prizes of yours unchallenged?"

"Prizes?" The air stirred again, and a second cloaked figure materialized, perched on the other pony's back. Loosening her hood, Skye gave Trader a scathing look. "I lent him the cloak. And these are my ponies, Chuffer and Shep." She threw back her hood. "Esmeralde, it's me."

Trader's jaw dropped. "You know the witch?"

"Skye!" Esmeralde hurried to the pony's side. "Look, Indy!"

"So it is!" Indigo exclaimed. "Skye, I've not seen you in ages. How are you, child?"

"Cold," Skye admitted. "Wet."

"You know both witches," Trader said, glumly.

"Esmeralde is no witch, just a remedy woman." Skye gave Trader a withering glance. "The one I told you about from the fair. And Indy is a gardener."

"They are witches." Trader insisted.

"They are friends of my family." Turning, Skye tugged hard at something they could not see and the air rippled once more. Her hand came away with a pink Potluck Hat and another figure appeared behind her. "Look who it is!"

"Hey, Esmeralde!" Garth slid off Chuffer's back onto the ground. "Indy." He rubbed his backside. "That was a ride. I'm cold and wet, too."

"Sierra's own," Esmeralde grinned. "What a surprise! But where is your mother?" She eyed Trader fondly. "And how did you come to travel with this ruffian?"

"The soldiers arrested Mother at the fair," Skye said. "They accused her of using magic. I barely got away with the ponies."

"See?" Indigo nudged Esmeralde. "I was right about the fair."

"You're always right," Esmeralde admitted.

Indigo smiled. "Well, I may not always be right, but I am never wrong."

"Trader saved me from the flood," Garth interrupted, and then frowned. "But then he tried to rob my sister." He turned to Skye. "You're not still mad at him, are you?"

Skye shook her head wearily. "I'm way past that."

"Sierra's been taken," Indigo said glumly. "Shards, I knew it."

"So much for calling the Twelve." Esmeralde turned to Indigo helplessly. "There's less and less of us all the time."

"We barely escaped the guard just now," Trader said. "They came for us under the bridge after nightfall and our band had to scatter. We ditched the soldiers in the Copse."

"Branches everywhere," Garth said, gesturing with his hands. "They grab at you and grab."

"You've got to stay close in the Copse," Esmeralde nodded.

"Let's unsaddle these poor ponies and put them in the shed," Indigo said as it began to sprinkle once more. "They look hungry and tired, and we're getting wet."

"I'm starving," Garth said. He and Trader pulled the packs off the ponies. "I haven't eaten since midday yesterday, and then the Guard chased us all night."

"Well, then, we shall cook a big breakfast!" Esmeralde said.

"If you can concoct something without blowing up the cottage," Indigo replied, helping Garth lead the ponies into the shed.

Trader glanced up. "What happened to the chimney? What's all that green stuff?"

"Just a fire." Esmeralde shrugged. "It was supposed to be red." She eyed the packs Skye and Trader carried. "Did you bring truck to trade?"

"Did we ever!" Trader said. "I have what we think is a Possibility Bag, and Skye has . . ."

"It's a Possibles Bag," Skye interjected, flashing Trader a look. "You'll not scam Esmeralde. She has the only real Possibles Bag I've ever seen."

"Well, I've some kind of bag," Trader grumbled. They all trooped inside. Skye quickly tapped Trader's hand, brushing past as if by accident, and Trader got her message: Now was no time to mention the silver box.

"This whole thing has gotten out of hand," Esmeralde complained to Indigo, once they were all settled around the table with mugs of tea.

Indigo nodded, clearing away herb packets and broken vials to make way for plates. "The Northland Guard probably took Sierra to the Burnt Holes."

"Lavender Mae knows her way through those caves and beyond." Esmeralde cracked eggs, one by one, onto the griddle.

"Who's she?" Garth spread butter onto toast.

"Another witch, I bet," Trader said, crunching a dry crust.

"What should we do?" Skye asked. "Mother said to journey to Bordertown to find someone named Aubergine."

"They all want Aubergine," Esmeralde moaned.

"Who is she?" Garth said.

"Another witch I bet," Trader added.

"What's wrong with you?" Skye asked.

"The witches were my secret," Trader said. "Now I find out that everyone knows."

"That's because they aren't witches," Skye said. "Don't you know your yarns?"

"Get off your high horse about those stupid stories." Trader rose from the table. "Until yesterday, you didn't realize your own mother was one of the Twelve."

"She wasn't," Garth said simply. "She was just our mother. You know, she kept the house, made the meals. . . ."

"Hand-knit magic garments," Skye interjected, "that turned lies into truth and allowed the wearer to pass unseen. Garth! What other mother does that?"

Garth opened his mouth and then shut it. Indigo and Esmeralde chuckled. Ignoring them, Trader sulked at the window.

"You, too?" Garth asked the old women. "You're part of the Twelve, too?"

Esmeralde gave a wink while Indigo just nodded.

Garth shook his head, as Esmeralde plopped fried eggs onto his plate. "I thought you were just nice to me, like favorite aunts or something."

"We're something all right," Indigo said, looking around her shambles of a kitchen. Sudden bright light flooded the room.

"Come quickly!" Trader cried, beckoning from the front window overlooking the greenhouse. "Come look at the sunrise!"

Skye slid from her stool and crept over. "Heavenly hand knits," she breathed.

"What?" Garth demanded, wolfing eggs from his perch at the table.

Trader turned. The fossicker's face, like Skye's, was bathed in pink light, and their eyes glistened with wonder. "The day dawns red," Trader whispered.

Skye nodded. "Fire in the sky, like the legends said."

Esmeralde flung open the door and rosy light streamed in. She gave Indigo a triumphant look.

"We did it!" she said.

Indigo Rose's Women's-Work Fingerless Gloves

A GLOVE PATTERN

These intermediate-skill-level fingerless gloves are ideal for gardening on a cold day. The pattern is sized for an adult women's hands.

Get the pattern from PotluckYarn.com/epatterns

The first time, the world had ended in ice.

CHAPTER 10

Voices of the Ancients

AS HE STOOD AMONG THE BODIES STREWN across the river valley, Warren looked after Mae's retreating figure, dumbfounded. When she had noticed him, she abandoned her pantry sack and ran off as if she were being chased. He scooped up the sack and trailed after her through the snow. She was surprisingly agile. Granted that he was lugging the sack, but soon he could barely see her, far ahead, wending her way through the scree at the rock-strewn valley's edge. He had the unsettling thought that at times Mae lingered as she began to climb through the granite outcroppings beneath the glacier's shadow. She seemed to want him to follow her. But why?

He glanced over his shoulder, hating to leave his sled behind. But he couldn't risk losing sight of her to retrieve it. She must have a hideout nearby, perhaps a dwelling, if she used mere pantry sacks to transport her spoils. Maybe she would lead him to a fissure in the rock where she cached her stash, or to an abandoned animal lair she used for a winter camp. Wherever she was going, he was determined to find out. He was certain now that this was Lavender Mae, one of the Twelve, known as the Keeper of the Magic Crystals. His mother had told so many stories that he felt he actually knew her.

In his mother's yarns, Mae was the knitting witch who went mad and disappeared. A hermit, she wore a pouch of gemstones around her neck, and spent all her time searching for the lost crystal. As the years passed, or so his mother said, Mae had become a lone river rat who smoked too much glacier weed and wore hats and mitts she knit from bits of animal fur she found snagged in thorn bushes.

Now that he had found her, Warren did not think it would serve the Northland well if she were killed by soldiers for pilfering from the bodies of their kin. But how could he protect a crazy recluse who ran from him? He hiked up the steep slope toward the rocks. Mae's course ended at the granite face beneath the Burnt Holes. The sheer cliffs looked like a dead end.

When he reached the impenetrable wall at the foot of the glacier, her tracks through the snow ended, as he knew they must. He had passed by this bluff countless times and never found any gap in the stone at the foot of the glacier. After a moment, he thought he heard a low chuckle, although maybe it was just wind. Feeling foolish, he looked around and shouted, "Mae!"

He heard the laugh again, louder and unmistakable now. Squinting, he saw her scrawny form outlined against the glare of the alpine sun. She was standing on a narrow ledge over his head, partway up the crag.

"How did you get up there?" he called.

But almost immediately he saw a series of hand- and footholds in the weathered granite. Tying the pantry sack to his belt, he swiftly gained the defile where Mae waited. She clutched his arm with claw-like hands, pointing, and he saw why she was so agitated. A small band of Lowlanders was crossing the valley where they had just been, bent on the same activity Mae had been engaged in, scavenging the dead. His heart sank at what he saw next. Collecting their brethren, they piled Lowland body after body onto his bobsled.

"They are treating my sled like a hearse," he said.

"Mae," the scrawny old woman remarked, gravely.

He gave her a curious look. "Did you know they were coming?"

Mae patted the precious pouch hung around her neck. "Mae," she nodded.

Warren wondered if she meant something in her pouch had warned her, or if she was just reminding him of who she was. Mae pulled an odd-looking watch cap from the inside pocket of the Lowland jacket she wore. She looked at it, as if either puzzled or making up her mind, and then handed to him. It looked a little like his father's Potluck Hat, except that it appeared to be knit from wild animal fur. Warren did not know if the hat was magic, but when he put it on, it warmed his ears instantly. Mae put a finger to her puckered lips and pantomimed sneaking away. Warren nodded.

Still beckoning to him, she disappeared into a crevasse hidden in the granite face. From there, they descended toward the belly of the glacier on a steep and narrow path. The walls of the passage had been formed from yellowed ice, studded with shale and river stone that the glacier had swallowed long ago as it made its slow journey south. The air grew colder and lost its freshness. The light faded, and before long Warren could barely see the outline of the old woman in front of him.

"Mae," he whispered.

"Shh!" she hissed. And then he knew why, because he could hear it. His voice echoed and echoed and echoed back at them, getting successively fainter but still recognizable, "Mae, Mae, Mae, Mae Mae. . . ." followed by her admonishment, "Shh, shh, shh, shh, shh. . . ."

Mae halted. Reaching into the pouch around her neck, she picked out a round crystal of pink quartz half the size of her fist. She held it in front of her face and blew on it slowly. After a moment, the quartz took on a warm glow. Warren caught his breath. The stone was lit from within by a growing halo of light.

Mae flashed him another silencing glance before handing him the pink orb, which he played along the narrow passage before them. He thought he could hear the water roaring underfoot, but all the shining crystal illuminated was frozen rock.

Time seemed to stand still within the belly of the glacier. Warren did not know how long they walked, and had no idea where they were going. It got colder and colder, but with the fur cap on he barely shivered. Mae seemed oblivious to everything except moving onward. Whenever he tried to question her, she shushed him with a backward wave of her hand. He finally just gave up and followed.

At last their path leveled out and they came to a chasm that looked like an anteroom on the left side of the tunnel. The tunnel itself continued past this space, following a channel carved through the ice by an ancient river. Mae motioned for him to shove aside a stalactite that seemed to have fallen during a cave-in, but when he shouldered it aside, he discovered behind it the entrance to another room of hollowed ice.

Mae ducked through the doorway and lit four beeswax candles. What Warren had first thought was a small chamber was actually a long, low cavern, packed floor to ceiling with trash and treasure. The sweet scent of glacier weed filled the air. A small clearing in the hoard contained a fire pit and a bench, on which sat a kit for making handrolled Smokies, along with a twig basket filled with rabbit fur and sheep fleece, alpaca and musk-ox down. On top of the fiber rested a drop spindle, half filled with yarn.

Mae took the pantry sack from Warren and emptied it onto her bedroll, which lay upon dried rushes strewn across the frozen floor. With a grunt, she dropped to her haunches. Ignoring him, she began sorting the spoils, singing the same sort of mindless tune he had heard from her when she worked over the bodies. He took this as a sign that it was all right to talk.

"Mae," he asked, surveying the dim cave filled with plunder. "What is this place?"

Turning, she spread her arms wide and offered him an impish grin. "Mae's," she said. "Mae's, Mae's, Mae's." Rising, she twirled around and around and then suddenly stopped and grinned at him, gap-toothed.

"All of this is yours?" Warren asked. "Unchallenged?"

"Mmmm," Mae began, nodding. "Mine." She said the word like it was a long phrase she barely knew, savoring the sound.

"Impossible," Warren said. The cavern's rich plunder contained much more than just military articles ransacked from fallen armies. "You collected all this truck yourself?"

Mae nodded absently, watching carefully as he fingered hammered swords and jeweled daggers, dented helmets and lengths of fine chain mail. The front bobs of a sled on the floor gave him an idea of how Mae might have toted some of her salvage. Warren was amazed that Mae had been able to drag some of her stash as far as this cave. They were, indeed, deep within the glacier.

"It must have taken a decade to find all this," he blurted out. "Maybe more."

"More." She blinked in the light. "More and more."

"Why?" Warren had to ask. Fossickers like that little ferret Trader would sell relics like these to the highest bidder, but Mae looked worse for wear, not better for her riches.

"More," Mae echoed, uncomprehendingly. She rubbed her head as if it ached.

"I understand it's more," Warren persisted. "But what's it for?"

Putting her hands to her ears, Mae shrugged and turned away.

Warren stared at her. "Mae, do you have any idea what you have here? Some of this is worth a fortune. You could live a life of ease if you sold just a few of these things."

Ignoring him, Mae skipped ahead and then came back. She tugged on his arm like a little girl, urging him into the cavern's dark recesses.

With the glowing chunk of quartz held high overhead, Warren followed her deeper into the cave. Chuckling to herself, Mae lit a Smokie and led the way. She pulled him into an alcove, its walls lined with chests and traveling trunks. Some of the containers had locks, now hacked apart, while others appeared to have no lids. Several trunks remained closed, with metal-banded strongboxes arranged on top, while others had been thrown open to reveal raw crystals and semi-precious stones of every color imaginable.

As Warren picked through the unpolished bits of turquoise and garnet, star sapphire and lapis lazuli, amber and tiger-eye, Mae also sifted through them, laughing like a child. Some of the rough gem-stones were as small as peas; others were as large as quail eggs. Once or twice Mae examined a stone and compared it to one from the pouch hung around her neck, then cast it aside.

Warren thought that none of these stones had been scavenged from the dead. They were too rough, still unpolished and unset in silver or gold. He imagined that Mae, over the years, had gathered them one by one from the freshets that flowed out of the glacier each spring. If that was the case, they had to have originated in the Crystal Caves.

"Mae, are these magic crystals?" He asked, with dawning aware-ness. "All of them?"

The old woman dropped the crystals as if they burned her hands, and offered him an innocent look.

"I am not here to surrender you to the Guard," Warren assured her. "My own mother used stones to dye yarns. Do you have any idea what you have here? Does anyone else know?"

Mae began to wander farther down the passage.

"Mae," Warren called, waiting for her to turn and look at him. "Mae, there are men in my unit who have pledged to kill you for scavenging their dead. And now I fear others would kill you to steal this plunder, if they knew you had it. Let's get out of here. Let me save you."

Mae let out a hoot of laughter, followed by a long trail of smoke.

"What's so funny?"

"You." She pointed an accusing finger. "You. Save. Me." Turning, she ran back down the passage toward the clearing with the fire pit. Her voice rang down the tunnel: "Ha!"

Warren had to admit that it seemed unlikely that he could protect her, seeing as she has just saved him from Lowlanders. Or maybe the herb was making her silly. He let the semiprecious stones sift through his fingers and drop back into the chest.

"Fine," he muttered, not bothering to go after her. He shut the chest's creaky lid. "Fine."

Further into the cave lay mining gear, picks and axes, and a wooden barrow Mae must have stolen from Lowlanders who sought passage into the legendary Crystal Caves, the mythical gateway to the tombs of the ancients. Warren had seen iron tools like this, hauled north on large sledges dragged not by draft ponies or oxen but by the Lowlanders' own brute strength. Such raiding parties marched from the south, up through the Notch above Teardrop Lake, along a section of track his own father had built.

While scouting for the Northland Guard, Warren and his friend Niles had, from time to time, observed small groups of Lowlanders in the foothills below, sneaking around the backside of the glacier along a trail called the Blind Side Loop with their smudge torches. They guessed that these bands stayed small to remain undetected. Free from discovery, they could search the Blind Side of the glacier for an entrance to the Crystal Caves. Warren knew of no one—friend or foe—who had ever seen the Crystal Caves, rumored to be guarded by the graves of the ancients, known in the Northlands as the First Folk. Warren had repeatedly circled the southern base of the glacier on his bobsled, but he had never found a passageway of any kind to any cavern or tomb, real or imagined. Except for the Burnt Holes, of course, and they were nothing more than a makeshift prison used by the Northland Guard.

As Warren neared the back of Mae's lair, she appeared once again and began to trail behind him, humming loudly. He turned, annoyed at her mindless prattle, which grew in volume as she followed, watching. Her singing became an aggravating chant in which every third or fourth word seemed like it was her own name, Mae. He glared at her but she wouldn't stop. Instead she remained just out of striking distance, apparently thinking he might try to silence her with the flat of his hand. Ignoring her, he cast the light of the quartz crystal toward the back wall of the cave. What he saw there made him gasp.

"What in cracked crystal . . .!" his voice trailed off, as he strode quickly to take a closer look.

"Ha!" Mae cried out. "Ha! Ha!"

Stacked up on tattered remnants of tapestry against the back wall of the icy cavern, stood two huge earthenware vessels that looked older than anything he had ever seen, relics that could have only come from the tombs of the ancients. If he was not mistaken, the big jugs were hard-fired burial urns, hand-painted with dyes mixed from ground crystals. If he was right, the tapestry fragments were funeral drapes from the burial caves. One piece of carved limestone even looked like a broken coffin lid, chiseled in the shape of a man's body and painted with twin suns. Warren turned to Mae, who knelt in the dirt. She had not been chanting, he realized. She had been praying to the old deities, the two suns Re and Rah, which once blazed in the sky over the Tigris and the Eye, the Rivers of Life.

Of course Warren knew the childhood fairy tale of the twin suns and intertwined rivers that snaked through the valley that spawned the First Folk. Everybody did. All had heard the creation story, but, as far as he knew, none could prove that these ancestors ever existed. His mother's legends had centered on First Folk follies, and as a child the tales had fascinated him. On many cold winter nights, Sierra had knitted before the fire, spinning yarns of the ancients for her three children. Before he could cipher his letters, Warren had known the old stories by heart.

According to legend, before the age of ice, the First Folk had flourished in a fertile valley fed by the waters of the Tigris and the Eye and warmed by the twin suns. Their world never fell to darkness. The ancients worshipped both suns equally and lived in harmony with nature in the crescent-shaped bottomland between the rivers. In time, the older sun began to weaken. Fearful, the First Folk fought among themselves, and in their foolishness they lost all faith in the failing sun and quit worshipping it, turning their attention to the younger one.

Abandoned, the first sun sputtered out. Great chunks of smoldering black rock rained across the valley, causing floods and throwing the world into frigid darkness for half of each day. Instead of finding a way to cope with just one sun and the rising rivers, the ancients quarreled over the remaining warmth and light. In their folly, they let the world grow colder and colder, until the single sun could no longer sustain them and all the lands froze solid.

That first time, the world had ended in ice.

Now many said the world would end with fire, Lowland fire, unless the Dark Queen was stopped, and the Northland Glacier sealed safely away from those who would plunder once more.

Crouching beside the stone coffin, Warren ran his hand over its chiseled surface. Although the red ocher used to paint the suns' rays had faded, he could see remnants of it in the grooved limestone. That Mae possessed a carved lid such as this could only mean one thing.

"Mae," he said, trying to catch her attention.

"Tigris and Eye," she chanted. "Tiger Eye. Mae!"

"Mae!" he echoed, coming toward her.

Abruptly, she broke off her prayer, watching him warily.

"I'm starting to believe the Crystal Caves are real," he said. "Look at all these things. They look like they came from the dead."

She hesitated, peering up at him as though he asked a trick question.

"The Crystal Caves do exist, don't they?" He asked. "And the crypts within. You have been there, more than once. You brought these things back from the tombs of the ancients."

"Yes." She rose and nodded vigorously. "Oh yes, yes, yes."

"They say that if you go to the Crystal Caves, you never come back." Warren looked at her closely. She did not react. "Mae?"

"Mae," she agreed, reluctantly.

"You went there, and you came back, didn't you?"

Mae cowered and her voice quavered. "Mae. . . ."

She was terrified. Of what? For now, she seemed safe enough from the Lowland armies. And he certainly wasn't going to strike her or surrender her to the Northland Guard for supposed use of magic. He glanced past her down the long passage back to the fire pit. From what he could tell, they were alone.

"What is it, Mae?"

Mae clamped her hands over her ears and shook her head wildly.

Realization dawned as he watched Mae wag her head from side to side, as if her brain contained bees. Mae wasn't really crazy. But whatever had happened in the Crystal Caves made her behave that way. It wasn't the glacier-weed smoke or her life as a hermit that prevented her from venturing out to barter with fossickers or sell her spoils. She was trapped by something within. Although she had in her keeping priceless treasure, he wondered what it had cost her. He wondered if any of the treasures were really hers.

"These things are not yours unchallenged, are they, Mae?" he asked quietly.

Ignoring him, she cocked her head. Warren listened, too, but heard nothing.

When she nodded, as if agreeing with unseen inhabitants of the glacier rather than with his question, he finally understood. Somehow the spirits of the ancients had entered Mae, and they wrestled inside her. That was why she held her head, why she chanted and prayed, why she alternated between being mute and murmuring her name repeatedly, as if she was trying to remember who she was.

Warren took her shoulders gently. "Was it hard to come back?" he whispered.

"Mae," she shuddered. "Mae." She put both hands to her head and shook it so hard that her mane of hair slapped him in the face. "Mae, Mae, Mae, Mamie."

"It's all right," Warren soothed. "Mae, it's all right."

"Mae," she cried weakly, growing slack in his arms. She stiffened again and gave him a piercing look. "Mamie."

"Do you know how to get to the tombs?" Warren asked.

Cradled in his arms, Mae shook her head, meaning no. "Nnnn," she said, her eyes watering.

Warren persisted. "Could you find your way back again?"

"Nnnn, nnn, nnn," she uttered and finally gave up. "Yes," she said quietly.

Warren knew then that he had not come to save Mae from the soldiers of either side, or even from imprisonment in the Burnt Holes. He had come to save Mae, all right, but only from herself.

If only his mother were here, she would know what to do. But this time of year she would be in Middlemarch minding her stall at the fair. It was too risky for him to travel the main track, since he would now be wanted as a deserter. He especially could not travel with a crazy old hag like Mae, who would unavoidably call attention to herself. If he had his bobsled, he could traverse the military road back to Top Notch within three days, and wait in the Sleep Out for his mother's return. But the Lowlanders had his sled, and who knew if the Teardrop had already spilled as it did each spring? He might not be able to reach their Lavender Rill Farm at all. The chance of meeting Lowlanders on the track was high, plus he dreaded a potential encounter with his father. Warren doubted that his mother knew Kendrick for the traitor that he and Garth saw him as, although maybe she did. Glancing down at Mae, who watched him expectantly, Warren grimaced. War made strange companions, he realized, with a burst of sadness.

"You are going to have to return all this plunder to the Crystal Caves—you know that, don't you?"

Mae crossed her arms defiantly. "No."

"Whatever you took, you have to give back."

Mae shook her head and began to writhe. He grabbed her to still her quaking.

"Whatever they took, they have to give back, too," he said to soothe her, not knowing if this was true. Mae might never regain her sanity, but he felt certain that this was something his mother would have said.

"Which way are the caves?" Warren asked. "Along this tunnel? Further in?"

"And in, and in," Mae gestured, poking his arm over and over. "In, in, in."

Warren heaved a sigh. "Mae, we've got to give this back."

Mae groaned. Shaking her head, she seized an ice pick and pretended to mine. Then she pantomimed filling the wooden barrow and dumping the load.

"Lowlanders," Warren guessed. "They broke into the Crystal Caves?"

She nodded.

"I thought they didn't know how to get in. You saw them? And they took things?"

Mae nodded again. Reverently, she touched the twin suns on the broken coffin lid. When she looked at Warren her eyes glistened.

"You're not trying to steal from the ancients," Warren said. "You're trying to protect them." He looked around at the treasure. He finally got it. This cave was a safe house of all she had collected, and she was its warden.

Mae knelt in the dirt, tears streaking her cheeks. Rocking back and forth, she began to keen.

"You cannot save the world by yourself," Warren whispered, sinking to his knees beside her. She rocked harder and wailed louder, as if a storm were passing through her bones.

Warren waited until her sobs subsided.

"Who can help, Mae?" he said finally, pulling her to her feet.

Mae stared the frozen ground and began to mutter. "Ah, ah ah."

"Tell me, for I haven't a clue."

She looked up at him. "Auber," she said with a firm nod.

"Auber," he repeated, puzzled, although he began to have an idea of what she was struggling to say. "Was she one of your Twelve?"

"Auber!" she insisted with a vigorous nod. "Auber, auber, auber. . . ."

Warren frowned, trying to recall the childhood tales. His mother had a series of anecdotes she called Woolgathering, about how mere schoolgirls became the Potluck Twelve. Didn't their mistress have a peculiar name that began with A?

"Auber," he said thoughtfully.

Mae happily clutched his arm. A moment later, she sang out, "Aubergine!"

"Of course," he said, relieved. "I know who that is. Do you want to leave right now?"

With a yawn, Mae shook her head and retreated down the corridor toward her bedroll in front of the fire pit. She was spent, Warren thought, as she crawled onto the bedroll and pulled a quilt up under her chin. Here in this dark cave, he could not tell if it was late afternoon, evening, or already night. He sat down heavily on the rushes next to Mae's bedroll and unlaced his nailed boots. He was exhausted.

"Rest up," Warren said. "We'll try to leave before first light. Now what can we take so Aubergine will know where you've been?"

Mae patted the pouch around her neck sleepily.

"Of course," Warren said. "You've had something in there all along."

"Mae," she agreed. Turning to her side, she began to snore softly.

Warren's Snowflake Watch Cap

A HAT PATTERN

This advanced-beginner-skill-level cap will keep your ears warm on the coldest of days. The pattern includes sizes for women and men.

Get the pattern from PotluckYarn.com/epatterns

But what about the animal still imprisoned in the ice?

CHAPTER 11

The Dervish Awakens

THE NEW MOON CAST SILVERY LIGHT across the drifts surrounding the sleeping camp high in the foothills. Still Winter Wheat waited, as she had for hours. Huddled in her traveling cloak beneath a snow-laden fir, she was certain that no one in the Lowlander encampment could see her. More than once, passing guards had almost stepped on her. The two night watchmen shivered under thin cloaks, their biceps bare and gleaming with some kind of protective oil or wax perhaps intended to combat cold. It seemed to offer little help. At this altitude and season, and so close to the glacier, the air was thin and chilly, frost-laden. Wheat, however, was comfortable, wearing a fine lace scarf knit from rare Highland wool loosely looped around her neck. The hollow core fiber, while light and lofty, warded the weather wonderfully.

It would do nothing to protect her from bungling Lowlanders, however. Wheat snatched her foot back as a young Lowland guard almost trod on it while making his rounds. Her grunt of surprise was buried beneath the sound of his teeth chattering. The distant tinkle of a bell let her know that Tracks was afoot in the valley below. She didn't know whether her ram had been captured in a pen or was foraging with her flock.

A pulse of heat surged through her shepherd's staff. It was time to move. Hesitating, Wheat rose from her crouch, rubbing an ache in the small of her back as she straightened herself and removed the hood from the crook. The twin cabochon crystals tied to its end burned with renewed vigor, as she had hoped they would. The amber glow outlined the scarab beetles. Wheat was flooded with relief. The revival of her crystals gave her the confidence that she needed to fear no one, perhaps not even the Dark Queen, with whom she had apprenticed when they were both girls.

Although half-forgotten now, the talents that Wheat had brought to the Potluck Twelve had been useful. She understood all creatures, and they trusted her. Even as a child, she was able to gentle most wild things, whether they bore fiber or fur, feathers or fish scales. Over the years, she had become a fiber savant, and this gift served her well. She had been in demand for her expertise at the larger sheep farms and fiber festivals, or cooperatives where fleece and fur were sorted and graded for market. Yet she had less prosaic skills as well. In Wheat's eyes, crystal-dyed fibers glowed with a unique aura, no matter what the light. The magical properties of these yarns and of the resulting garments were visible to her even now, in a world bereft of magic.

Wheat possessed other lore, bits of animal husbandry she rarely had the opportunity to use. As she sat waiting in the dark for the Lowlanders in the camp to slumber, she wondered if the renewed vigor of her amber jewels was powerful enough for what she meant to do.

She looked over at the sledge, with its burden of ice encasing a barely perceptible dark form. In the past, the crystallized beetles had helped Wheat transform butterflies from their cocoons and awaken ground hogs from hibernation. She wondered if the being inside the ice, for she was sure it was not simply a shadow, might be one of the First Folk, frozen. Or perhaps it was one of the ancient dead. Alone with her thoughts in the darkness, she had come to believe the Lowlanders had stolen their heavy load from the legendary tombs of the Crystal Caves. What she feared most was that this unfortunate creature had frozen while still alive, and would slowly suffocate as the ice around it melted. If so, it would die without her help.

Creature or no creature, Wheat's first allegiance was to her sheep. She must attend to her flock and somehow see them to safety. After that, she might have the time to discover if she could do anything for the mysterious form in the ice.

The sooty stench lingering over the camp made it easy for Wheat to move swiftly, avoiding the tents of the sleeping soldiers. Their clothing smelled of burnt rags and fish oil. She could tell where they lay without looking. As she circled the tents, the bleating of her sheep grew louder, until finally she could make them out through the gloom, in a small clearing below the encampment. Wheat's heart sank as she saw the dark outlines of her little ewes cramped together in a crude enclosure fashioned from dead brush. A smudge torch thrust into a bank of snow illuminated the nearby sledge with its great chunk of ice, lashed to the sleigh bed with thick hemp ropes. Between the sled runners a Lowland boy dozed, wrapped in one of their thin capes, emblazoned with an orange sun. The painted fabric could not warm him.

Wheat threw back the hood of her cloak so that she could better assess the situation, although now she was visible to anyone who glanced her way. Quickly, she stole toward the sledge. She held her staff high, looking for Tracks in the makeshift pen. Her eyes searched the enclosure, but her ram was not among the flock. Although she could no longer hear his bell, she could sense him nearby, and so could the ewes and lambs. Restlessly, the spotted Jacobs balked and pushed against each other, threatening to trample several newborns while the sleeping guard shivered and snored.

From what Wheat could see, the sledge had never been outfitted to be drawn by horses or oxen. Maybe the parched lands of the South could no longer sustain beasts of burden or perhaps Southerners did not domesticate them, as the Middlelanders did. She had heard of cultures in which common folk worshipped cows and let them run wild in the townships, and of folk who would rather eat a horse than harness it. Maybe the Lowlanders needed to eat horsemeat for strength. It was clear that men pulled their sleds. Abandoned tethers, three to a side, lay folded on the deck above the sled runners. They were attached to the well-used harnesses that she had seen Lowland soldiers wearing.

Wheat approached the chunk of ice in silence, fighting a sudden, strange urge to sink to her knees in wonder. She tilted her staff toward what appeared to be an ice-locked face and pressed her free hand to the jagged exterior, letting the cabochons twirl freely around the crook of her staff. She felt nothing but the frozen surface at first, and she thought the being within the ice had to be dead. Then she sensed a pulse of warmth. Did that mean it was alive? Softly, the crystals of her staff clicked and clacked, until, coming together in unison, they overlapped in a circle of bright light, daring her to find out.

Wheat glanced beyond the sleigh to her bleating sheep and then behind her to the sleeping camp. Where was Tracks? She needed him to understand what had to be done, and they were running out of time. Dawn broke early in the mountains, especially this late in the spring. Steam rose from Wheat's knitted cape, and sweat ran down her back as she fought the urge to shed her traveling cloak.

She breathed once.

Twice.

And decided that she needed to crack the ice like an enormous eggshell so that the being inside would have a chance to breathe. The scarab beetles lit from within like torches, flickering as they crossed. Slowly and carefully, Wheat bent to focus the light. The hazy amber glow became a crescent of burning heat as it grew smaller and more intense. Her hand shaking with the effort, Wheat tilted the staff. She aimed the pinpoint of fire into a crack in the ice. A hiss of fog erupted. Wheat watched, hopefully, willing the dark thing inside to stir from its slumber, but nothing happened. She focused the fiery beam again and again, boring a fissure along a fault line in the ice face until she thought she felt the dark thing shrink away from the heat.

A trickle of water dripped from the icy crevasse onto the neck of the Lowland boy sleeping beneath the sledge, and he stirred. Wheat remembered that he would be able to see her, since both she and her staff had shed their hoods. His wide eyes stared at her, but he didn't move, perhaps from fear.

"Shhh," Wheat warned, as she felt the dark thing in the ice begin to shift.

The guard was no more than a youth. There was no need to harm him. Aware of the telltale warmth that accompanied the persuasive power offered by Sierra's traveling cloaks, she brought a gloved finger to her lips. The boy nodded sleepily.

Mindful that Lowlanders communicated with each other in a language of hand and eye gestures rather than one based on sound, Wheat brought the flat of her hand down in a shut-eye gesture. The guard lowered his lids obediently. Once again, he snored while the dark thing began to struggle and the sheep trapped in the brush enclosure bleated unhappily.

She sensed the small ram's approach before she saw him. "Tracks," she whispered into the dark. "Little Tracks. Finally!"

Before long, she heard his bell, a faint tinkle getting closer. She looked around to catch him poking his spotted head from a newly trod side path she had not noticed, perhaps an escape route to the lower valley. The ram took a few steps toward her and then turned and trotted briskly in the direction he had come from. As he approached her once more, she stroked his neck fondly, for she understood completely. Her flock need not become Lowland fodder, for Tracks had scouted a narrow path to safety that the Lowlanders would be unable to follow with their weaponry and the cumbersome sledge. Wheat looked over the pen, locating the twig gate that had been latched with a leather thong. With luck and some sort of diversion, she might free the whole flock.

The cabochons swirled to and fro, hitting and sparking against each other, burning random cinder holes in the snow. Wheat raised her gloved hand and caught the jewels to still them. She feared the light and the hiss caused by the bright beetles outlined in amber would awaken the camp before long. The ancient chunk of glacier had begun to give way along the fissure line, dripping freely. As the crack widened, rivulets of thawing water leaked down the frozen face. Wheat caught a scent of the dark thing.

She ran her hand along the crack and touched the wetness to her cheek. The creature was not one of the First Folk, as she had thought. It was mammal, and not from the wild. Wheat sensed that this was a domesticate of sorts, in the old tales often called a familiar. She searched her memory, trying to recall some sort of clue from Sierra's stories. Did the First Folk harbor canines or felines? In ancient times, were there aviaries filled with mimic birds? She shone the amber light into the frozen opening, trying to get a better view of the dark pelt, wet from the melting ice, the imprisoned form of an animal perhaps otherwise extinct since before the world began again. The sodden fur shivered, shrinking from the warm crystals, as Wheat felt the identity of this being come to her slowly, yet still slightly beyond her reach.

The cabochons burned radiant, signaling danger. Wheat turned to see that the camp was beginning to stir, although dawn had not broken. Several Lowlanders had noticed her and were gesturing wildly to others behind them. Wheat looked to her sheep and the fate they would face if she could not free them. Tracks' bell tinkled. It was time to run.

But what about the animal still imprisoned in the ice? It could suffocate or drown on the march south. Wheat doubted that the Lowlanders would care. Dead or alive, the creature would prove to their queen that they had found the famed Crystal Caves.

However foolish, Wheat knew what she must do. Letting the dark thing loose was rash. Her act might unleash something malicious—and certainly malodorous—from legendary times. But she could not leave it to die; and perhaps freeing it would keep the beast out of Tasman's grasp. Not least, the commotion the creature caused would create the distraction she needed to rescue her sheep. She wondered if any Lowland soldier would dare confront a familiar raised from the dead.

Summoning what powers she possessed, Wheat brought the force of the twin cabochons to bear upon the weakening ice, which spat hail-like bits at her. Soon the dark thing writhed, causing more cracks to appear. Sheep bleated in fear. The young Lowland guard had awakened, still as if in a slight trance that seemed to be fading. In a flash of heat, Wheat passed the flat of her hand before his face, but the ploy that had worked before now had no effect. As the ice melted, a torrent of icy water drenched the boy, who jumped up and ran toward his comrades, with his dripping cape dragging behind.

Wheat's time was up. She aimed the cabochons along the fault line, releasing a rush of noxious yellow liquid that pooled about her feet.

Tracks peeked from behind a drift, watching as the ice cracked and then cracked again. A group of Lowlanders, moving in silence and with pikes raised, ran toward her. Almost without thinking, Wheat sent a fire bolt toward the closest soldier, slashing his tunic as easily as she had burned holes in Ratta's dresses. The soldier went down, clutching his stomach, and the air smelled of seared flesh. Two others grabbed him by the arms and dragged him beyond the range of her staff. Wheat aimed her fire beam toward the ground, scorching a line in the snow. The Lowlanders in front fell back. Tracks trotted out of his hiding place to poke his nose into Wheat's skirts, but she would not be deterred.

The beast whirled within its icy cell. Squinting at it in the pale light of waning night, Wheat made out leathery wings flattened against sleek dark fur, wings that flexed and then beat for the first time since before the age of ice. Ancient knowledge, some odd trivial fact of forgotten animal husbandry, lurked just beyond her mind's grasp. "Tracks," she murmured. "Tracks, come here. I believe I ken this First Folk creature."

Tracks approached tentatively, watching the great piece of ice shift as the wings flexed inside, straining against the ropes that bound it—less securely every moment—to the creaking sledge. Waves of yellow water gushed from the fissure, spewing debris across the ground. Gingerly, Wheat reached into the ice with the tip of her staff. She held it to the edge of a leathery wing. The jolt of recognition that struck through the shepherd's staff flung her to the ground, sending the twin cabochons swirling like circling birds of prey. Still caught, the furred being went into hysterics at Wheat's knowing touch. The chunk of ice pitched and rocked in the tangle of hempen ropes.

Wheat scrambled back behind the drift where Tracks had taken refuge.

"It's a Watcher," she whispered. "A whirling dervish. The ancients trained them to protect their ruling class, like we would guard dogs." Crouching behind the snow bank, she held Tracks close and absent-mindedly patted his head. "Or sheepdogs."

A pike flew into the drift in front of them. Lowland soldiers with smudge torches were surrounding them, still eerily quiet. The men in front held up shields against her fiery crystals. Wheat slammed her staff hard onto the ground. The cabochons ricocheted off each other, smashing and arcing with light. As the jewels overlapped to cast burning circles, Wheat shot bolts of fire toward the row of shields and they burst into flames.

The Lowlanders threw their blazing weapons aside and scattered. Wheat stepped forth, routing them with burning beams of light.

She planted her glowing staff once more and rubbed Tracks' neck as they watched the struggling beast begin to break out of the crumbling ice.

"Nasty they are rumored to be, the dervish," she confided. "Legend has it that if they didn't know or trust you, there was a lot of biting."

Tracks gave her a questioning look. "Not to worry," she said. "This Watcher recognized my touch. He'll not bother us."

The amber beetles lit again in warning, but weaker than before. Wheat glanced at her staff. The crystals were almost spent. They would grow dark soon. She searched the edge of the woods. The Lowlanders, using snowdrifts for cover, had begun to surround the clearing, intending to block her in, along with the sledge and her sheep.

Wheat heaved herself to her feet and brushed the snow from her cloak. "Time for us to go."

With Tracks at her side, she hurried to the sheep pen. Behind them, the ice rocked, threatening to topple the sledge each time the dervish stretched its wings further. The soldiers paused at the rumbling sound of shattering shards as the ancient ice splintered along the fault line. The being still could not break free, but it would only be a matter of moments before the ice smashed to smithereens. Wheat knew she should leave quickly, but with her hand on the gate she paused and looked back over her shoulder, her face flushed with excitement. She hoped that what she would see next would be like the hatching of a great bird.

"He's wild with anger," she murmured to Tracks. "Instinct tells him to return to his First Folk Family." The Lowlanders were creeping toward the sledge. "Good thing he's mad at them, not us."

The ice was still thick in places, and the dervish was unable to fully spread its wings. The creature was laboring too hard, Wheat saw, and tiring quickly. If it stopped trying to fly, she still feared that the beast would drown. The dark wings beat desperately. Wheat raised her staff and focused the last of its waning light on the frozen shell. Almost immediately it split with a crash. The sledge tipped over backwards, taking the winged creature with it.

Lowland soldiers sprinted toward the overturned sled.

In the fray that followed, Wheat yanked open the twig gate and her sheep began to surge into freedom.

Then she pulled up the hood of her traveling cloak, and faded into the shadows as dawn threatened. She spotted Tracks waiting at the far edge of the clearing, but could not resist pausing a moment longer to see first hand if the dervish would be reborn from the ice, as legend said that fabled birds had risen from the ashes of the first dead sun.

Freed at last, the dervish whirled in place, in ever-tightening circles, flipping viscous spray over the Lowlanders who had been brave and foolhardy enough to close in. Caught in ropes of mucus, the soldiers that were able to run struggled away from the foul liquid, while others fell to the snow as the slime cooled and solidified.

Dawn began to break with a strange red light. Wheat turned as the dervish took wing, bathed in the blushing glow. The sheep bleated in terror and stampeded through the gate, knocking down sections of brush. They thundered toward the valley below in a blur of black and white. In the rosy haze, the remaining Lowlanders scattered as the dervish swooped down on the encampment. Those that dared throw pikes saw them caught in huge talons and crushed like kindling. Tracks nosed at Wheat's hand as the last ewes and lambs disappeared down the trail.

Wheat, distracted and blinking in disbelief at the reddening sky, absently rubbed the furry patch of forehead between Tracks' horns. She took an involuntary step forward, then lifted her booted foot and examined it as if it were something possessed before she let it back down. Her heart began to thump in her chest.

The dawn was too bright, its colors bloody and surreal. To make matters worse, the garish light was coming not from the east, but from the north.

Silhouetted against the lurid sky, the dervish arched high on skeletal wings. Its gray hide stretched over gaunt bone that ended in curled talons. Fine tufted ears lay flat to its head. Its opaque eyes stared out, unblinking. As fire suffused the sky, the great creature circled above the clearing with lazy, yet laser intent, as if searching for prey.

"Broken shards," Wheat swore softly, resisting the urge to step toward the light as the cold-fire crystals exploded over the mountains in spangles of scarlet and rose. It was the summons. Aubergine was calling.

The dervish flapped its wings and flew north, blind to the bloody sunrise. Soon it was a speck of black against the crimson horizon, disappearing toward the dim outline of the glacier.

Wheat stood alone at the edge of the ruined encampment. Tracks was hiding behind her, peering out in curiosity. The Lowlanders who had not fallen had either taken refuge or fled. She shook her head wearily and glanced around at the desolation. "Red sky in the morning, all take warning," she said quietly.

The sledge yawed on its side across a bed of smashed ice. The makeshift sheep pen lay flattened to the ground. Among the dead, broken pikes and smoking shields had fallen haphazardly across the dirty snow. Wheat looked up at the crook of her staff. There was no need to hood it. The spent cabochons dangled lifelessly.

Wheat scanned the rows of tents, searching for Lowlanders who might still notice her. None stirred. Even so, Wheat kept the hood of her traveling cloak up and stuck to the shadows at the edge of the clearing. She realized she would not after all be taking the easy track south, for she felt the call and could not deny it. She wished she could wing her way north, like the dervish, because that was the way she needed to go.

Picking up Tracks, she tucked him under her traveling cloak, and made her way unseen past the few stunned Lowlanders who huddled before a fire, gesturing to each other as their eyes flickered toward the sky.

Why had Aubergine waited so long to set off the cold-fire crystals? Wheat had expected to see this red dawn a decade earlier, after the Lowlanders burned out the first set of ice caves now called the Burnt Holes, or more likely a few years later, when the Northlanders banned the use of magic, or even two years ago, when the Northland Guard started rounding up conscripts.

Back at the Crossings, Wheat looked around to make sure she was not being followed. Then she let Tracks out from beneath her cloak. Once again, he refused the high northern trail, and this time Wheat did not scold him when he trotted down the southern track. She just asked, "Where are you going?" Tracks had to have his reasons.

Leaning heavily on her staff, she shrugged and began to follow. The dervish had vanished into the strange sky. The southern route was longer, but she had a chance of catching up with her flock in the lower valley. Perhaps she could convince one of the farmers in Coventry to pasture them for a while. She had a feeling that she would not be passing this way again for a long time. It was time to shed her guise as a shepherd and resume her place in the circle as one of the Twelve.

Who else among them had felt the summons, and who would give the answering call? As far as Wheat knew, Sierra Blue had last held the tinderbox. It was identical to Aubergine's seamless box, except that it contained answering fire, to let those waiting at the Potluck know that the Twelve had seen the call and were coming.

But Wheat couldn't stop wondering: Why now?

Winter Wheat's Highland-Lace Scarf

A BAG PATTERN

This intermediate-skill-level magical scarf will ward off brisk weather and more. Knit in one size approximately 6" wide by 67" long.

Get the pattern from PotluckYarn.com/epatterns

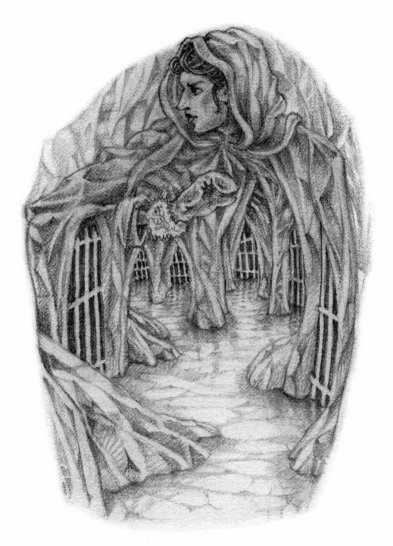

"Naught is worth saving if we do not protect what is within."

CHAPTER 12

Call of the Cold-Fire Crystal

FROM HER CELL SIERRA EYED THE guards in the antechamber, who were casting Skells by lamplight. The two were no older than her son Warren. Neither knew that their seemingly harmless children's game of cards and dice had its beginnings in magic, and that the original symbols were steeped in lore so powerful that the first cards and dice had been confiscated by the Northland Guard long ago. She remembered those painted birch-bark rectangles and carved-bone cubes. The boys played with pale imitations, but they enjoyed their game.

The round was all but over, and the burly soldier thought he was winning. He rattled the dice in his wooden cup as his companion, a skinny youth with an untrimmed beard and protruding ears, drew his card eagerly.

"Show me your money," the chunky guard said. Coppery hair covered his head, curled from the front of his jerkin, and even dusted the knuckles of his hand.

Both young men were clad in short, belted tunics with the white crest of the newly formed Glacier Guard. This meant that they were probably conscripts, taken from their families as her son had been.

The dark, skinny guard tapped his Skell card on the table. He seemed nervous. "Let them fly."

"Not so fast." The big red-haired youth looked uncomfortable in his uniform. She pictured him at a smithy in the village of Coventry, forging horseshoes and roofing nails, since she had overheard him telling the kitchen wench that he had been a blacksmith's apprentice before the war.

"Roll 'em, Hairy," said the slight and clever guard, who gave off the smoky scent of cured hide when he got close enough to hand Sierra a dipper of water. She had learned that he worked at his father's tannery in Woolen Woods before the Guard took him. Impatiently, he caught up his long black hair and pulled it back into a ponytail with the leather thong he wore around his wrist.

Hairy shook his dice cup lazily. "Let's see 'em, Raven."

Reluctantly, the thin boy produced two army-issue chits, ivory tokens that could be used in place of Northland silver at the garrison commissary and even some alehouses in Winterwatch if you knew where to go.

Hairy spit on his wrist. "For luck." He shook the cup once more and let the set of dice spill onto the table. "Tigris!" he shouted, willing the cubes to show the symbol of the ancient twined rivers.

With a smile, Raven shook his long hair. "Re." He pointed to the lidded eye carved into three of the bone dice.

Hairy looked toward Raven's unplayed card. "Ice."

Laughing, Raven turned over the Skell, showing flames. "Fire thrice. You lose."

Hairy pushed two chits toward the others and watched his companion pocket the four. "Methinks you cheat," he said sourly. Raven laughed. With a hopeful look, Hairy offered, "Another round?"

With a weary smile, Sierra shouldered her blanket and turned her face away, hoping the darkness would soothe the headache that had plagued her throughout the night. Indeed, Raven was cheating, counting combinations of cards played against the dice and marking them with fingernail strikes on his deerskin gauntlets every time he pretended to sneeze.

No matter. She found it ironic that these young men toyed with the same base magic that she was accused of using, magic she did not use—magic that instead had always used her. She gazed through the iron bars—bars that could not contain her unless she chose to make it seem that way. She was at a loss as to what she should do.

By the change of the guard, she hazarded that she had been held here little more than one day. She guessed they worked a twelve-hour shift, first these two and then two others equally young, and then back to these. Because light did not reach into the Burnt Holes, she had no other way to gauge time. Since her abduction, she had been silently watchful and listening.

Sierra had not been surprised when the soldiers had arrived at her stall in the main tent to arrest her. One among them was the surly soldier, Maynard, who had troubled her at the Middlemarch bridge. Nor had she resisted when a small detail of four Northland soldiers led her from the fairgrounds, for she felt the hands of fate guiding her, as always. For her entire life so far, Sierra had left herself to fate. She found her insights at once oddly comforting and frustrating, because she understood this: She could change nothing that was fated. People who recognized her ability to see as if with a sixth sense called that knowing look her lion eyes, since when she was perceiving in this way the gold flecks in her irises grew intense as those of a lioness watching her prey. This was especially noticeable when she sensed another of the Twelve close by. A lot of merit her unusual awareness had done her these past few days, she thought, with chagrin. She had cast her glance on those about her for direction, but had drawn a blank. Perhaps there was nothing from her mind's eye that could penetrate these walls of burnt ice.

Worst of all, her captors had confiscated her traveling cloak; so she had no way to bend any of them to her will, or to pass unseen. The soldiers in Middlemarch had taken everything from her stall, while Chloe the button vendor looked on in dismay. Sierra had watched Chloe steadily until she caught the woman's gaze. Then she let her eyes flicker ever so slightly to the bundle hidden under the table. She waited until Chloe nodded with understanding.

The only other things that Sierra had managed to salvage were her stockings, which she had been wearing when she was captured. Her feet had been hidden inside her sheepskin boots and her knee socks had gone unnoticed. She called these her Secret Socks. They looked ordinary enough, knit from fine yarn in an easy ribbed pattern that a child could master. Their similarities to normal socks ended at that. She had spun the yarn from down she had gathered one spring after arctic goats had migrated through. The fine hairs of their shaggy ruffs had caught on thorn bushes as they blew their winter coats. Sierra had never seen such loft or staple length in any fiber this fine, other than pashmina. Painstakingly, she had plucked out the guard hairs and plant matter until finally only the downy undercoat remained. This she infused with dyestuffs ground from fossilized insect shells found in glacier shards, as well as logwood and cochineal that streaked the fiber with rich plums, burnt oranges, and grays. Then she had spun and plied the yarn with the high twist levels suitable for socks. Even after they were knit, Sierra rarely wore the uncommon footwear, saving them for just the right day. For some reason, she had picked the pair of socks from a drawer and slipped them on, just before leaving Lavender Rill Farm to come to the fair. Thinking back, she must have had an inkling of what was to come, without knowing she knew. If need be, these socks might allow her to scuttle beneath these bars, snake through the walls, and roam the dark tunnels of this glacier, just as ancient insects did.

After the soldiers had marched Sierra from the fairgrounds, they had veered off the main track just outside of Middlemarch. On a secret road, waited a rolling cage, a jailhouse on wheels like gypsies might use to transport wild beasts. This one, however, had bench seats and sat empty but for her. Sierra knew the military road ran north to the glacier, for she had seen it being laid when she had ventured past the back side of Top Notch, but she had no idea it came this far south. The wide, level track had been carved out of the valley for the swift passage of many feet and heavily laden wagons. It made for quick travel, even in the rain.

The sturdy pair of draft horses hitched to the cage pulled it steadily up the wet road until the track turned into a rivulet that widened into a stream. As the day waned, the wheels mired so badly that the soldiers had to abandon the wagon in the rutted track. They tied Sierra's hands before her and perched her on a horse, which they led through the sucking mud. Only when they reached the backside of Top Notch did Sierra learn the source of the rushing water. The dam had ruptured at the top of Teardrop Lake. Hands tied and led on horseback, Sierra gazed at the deluge, hoping Kendrick and Garth were safe, although she feared otherwise. The flotsam in the churning river told of up-rooted houses, tumbled barns, and fences torn from fields. Her little Lavender Rill Farm would have been no match for this much water.

Sierra searched the roaring wreckage in silence, seeing no sign of her husband or youngest son. Maybe they escaped to higher ground.

Perhaps they had herded the goats up to the Sleep Out to wait out the spring rains, as in years past. Her lion eyes rested on the dirty water, spitting foam as it carved a new channel into the mountain and spilled over the military road. Her hopes faded as the carnage rushed by, dead chickens and bloated goats, drowned in the river.

Sierra had known she would not find her family here, for she sensed they had scattered. In her heart, she suspected that Kendrick had crossed to the side of the Dark Queen long ago. Possibly he had used the rising water as an excuse to her youngest son that they should flee south. Or possibly Tasman had been in the Middlelands all along, hiding in plain sight, as was her custom. Sierra could see the Dark Queen's hand everywhere. Even this raging river was no natural disaster. As they passed the torrent on horseback, Sierra could see the aura of dark magic rising like a fog from the angry waves.

Sierra could not guess how long they trekked. Once clear of the Notch, the broad road became passable again and they traveled swiftly through the night. She must have dozed—or maybe the soldiers put something in her tea—for when she woke, they had fresh horses and were approaching yawning caverns, charred black. Sierra knew without asking that they were approaching the Burnt Holes, in the foothills of the Northland Glacier. She had seen these dark caves before, but only in her mind's eye. The Burnt Holes had been raided by Lowlanders in the first skirmish of the Glacier Wars, and many years later were torched by the Dark Queen's minions searching for magic crystals. Now the Northland Guard used them as an outpost. Within them existed a prison from which it was said no one ever returned.

Since yesterday, Sierra had been sequestered in a holding cell near the mouth of these caverns. She had been treated with deference, segregated from the other inmates. She had seen them walking by. They were a motley assortment of dissenters and deserters, perhaps a half-dozen pretenders who claimed magical powers.

As far as she could tell, the Burnt Holes held none of the Twelve but herself, although Sierra sensed someone closer than she had imagined possible: one of her fellowship skulking through the glacier above, far beyond these walls of burnt ice. Wondering who it might be had kept her awake this evening past, bringing on a nagging head-ache. She felt the tickle in her brain like the mice she heard back at the farm, scuttling almost inaudibly in the pantry at night or in the rafters overhead. But every time she tried to cast her mind's eye, she instead heard voices, like the mutterings of the ancients over and over inside her head. Finally the voices subsided, and, glad for the respite, Sierra sought them out no more.

Instead, she turned her gaze toward Garth, fearing that, like Warren, he was lost to her. But miraculously she could sense him—oddly enough, safe with his sister. She was sure of it, because the girl's aura of raw magic was unmistakable. Thankfully, Skye was far from here, her faint trail a wispy question mark within the landscape of Sierra's watch. She glimpsed the two of them wending their way north, and hoped Skye would heed the caution Sierra had given her and would jour-ney to the Potluck in Bordertown. She concentrated on her precious bundle of magical garments, and the seamless box hidden inside, but could see nothing. She desperately hoped that Chloe had hidden them from the soldiers and that Skye had them. She hoped passionately that they had not fallen into the wrong hands.

Doors clanged down the corridor. Hairy rose from his chair to unlock the antechamber for the cook and the kitchen wench. Soon it would be time for bread and tea. Prisoners from the other cells began to stir, asking to use the latrine. Sierra watched them file by as one by one Raven led them to the lavatory near the mouth of the cave.

Was it night, or was it day? She had not slept. The guards were about to change once more. Sierra sensed that it was the dawn of an-other day as, alone in the dark, she felt Aubergine's call. The summons was so strong that Sierra found she was rising to her feet unbidden. Waves of heat washed over her and left cold sweat behind. The rough blanket slipped from her shoulders and fell to the stone floor. Feeling faint, she lurched toward the cell door. Her moose mittens gripped the iron bars for support. Her stomach churned. She tasted sour bile rising in the back of her throat. Raven, mistaking her behavior for a need to use the latrine, approached the bars with a basin of warm water and a clean rag for her toilet.

"Stand back," he ordered, unlocking the door.

Sierra swallowed hard, trying to quell her heaving stomach. Sweat slicked her face and she gripped the bars harder. "I cannot," she breathed, her eyes cast to the stone floor.

With a look of concern, Raven set the basin on her bench. "Are you not well?"

"Not at all." Shaking her head, Sierra sagged against the door, letting the cold metal bars press against her feverish face.

Shouts rang out down the corridor from the mouth of the cave. Raven turned toward the mayhem, uncertain. Sierra steadied herself, trying to regain her legs and quiet her nausea. But the call came again, this time worse. She felt as if a great hand pulled her heart from her chest. It jerked her forward like a puppet, yanked by invisible strings.

"What in cracked crystal. . . .?" Raven's voice trailed away as he watched her in alarm. Seeing that she could escape, he tried to push her back into her cell. But whatever was pulling Sierra forward was too strong for him.

"Hairy," Raven screamed down the dim corridor, unwilling to release his grip on Sierra, who did not so much struggle as drag him along.

Sierra held her hands before her face, watching herself as if from afar, staggering down the hall like an alehouse drunk. "I have been called," she whispered, with dawning realization.

"Hairy, I need some help here!" Raven yelled. The bench over-turned and the basin of water spilled across the floor. "The witch is possessed."

Sierra shrugged him off and strode past the antechamber. "Come," she hissed. "Quickly."

Keeping a safe distance, Raven scuttled behind her.

Sierra moved swiftly down the corridor. The day had not yet dawned, although the mouth of the cave was bathed in a rosy light. As she reached the opening, she saw Hairy and the two second-shift jailers standing transfixed around the cook fire with the cook and kitch-en wench. All eyes were turned skyward and mouths hung agape.

There was no sunrise.

Instead, night warred with morning in an explosion of stars. Cold-fire crystal burst into battle again and again, first to the east, then to the west, and finally directly over the glacier.

Sierra did not need to glance up to know what was happening. Why now? What had come to pass?

The turmoil in the sky crackled and popped so much that the kitchen wench cowered and covered her head as an earsplitting bang released showers of sparks and the sky glowed blood red. "It is the end of the world!" she screamed. "We shall die!"

"Fire," Raven said slowly, remembering his card game. "Fire thrice." Fearfully, he turned to the burly guard. "Hairy, the Skells fore-told this day, last night."

"Shards smashed to smithereens!" Hairy swore with a nod of his shaggy head. "Fire and ice!"

"No," Sierra let her lion eyes graze the horizon. "You know the oath you swear, cracked crystal? It really is cracked crystal."

"I'll never be married!" Sinking to the snow, the kitchen wench began to weep uncontrollably. "I'll never bear children."

"Hush," the cook soothed. "Hush up, I tell you."

"Cracked crystal is magic," Hairy said stubbornly. "It is forbidden in all the lands."

"So the story goes," Sierra murmured, her eyes on the sparks overhead. "And who knows the yarns better than me?"

"I do." The cook gave her a haughty glance. "I know my yarns."

Sierra scanned the horizon. She recognized the cold-fire crystals from Aubergine's tinderbox, freed finally to startle the heavens into ruby brightness. Even now the starbursts were lessening to spitfires whose tendrils chased each other like comets as the sky faded to a deeper red. The crystals would dull down and burn out before nightfall, mimicking the death of the paired suns. Answering fire lay inside her own seamless box, a box she had long hidden from Tasman and her subjects. It was up to her to send the answer, to let the Potluck know that the Twelve had seen the signal and would answer its call.

But she didn't have the tinderbox.

The call came again, seeming less urgent now that the crystals looked spent, although Sierra knew that was an illusion. She braced herself, barely able to resist the impulse to slip away from the guards under the shadow of the glacier. She glanced around furtively. No one had noticed the beckoning, even though she had almost lost her footing in the snow. Hairy stood at the cook fire near the mouth of the cave, yammering with the two day-shift guards. They all conjectured wildly, shrinking from the sky whenever the dying crystals spit fire. The cook set the tearful kitchen wench to work at small tasks: boiling water, steeping tea.

As Raven trudged over with a steaming mug, Sierra fought her impulse to break and run. She had to keep convincing herself that fleeing would be folly. She had no cloak. With only a small blanket, she would not get far in the cold. She could not guess how far south Bordertown was, but she had a feeling she would not arrive there alone.

"We were wondering," Raven began, handing her the mug.

The others had fallen silent, watching expectantly. Even the kitchen wench had put up her hood against the falling cinders and ceased her sobbing.

"You are one of the Twelve, are you not?" Raven asked quietly. Overhead, the sky crackled red. Ash began to drift down like dirty snow.

Sierra blew on the hot tea and took a grateful sip. Sighing, she gave a slight nod.

Raven beamed at the others, as he guided Sierra back to the cook fire. "I was right." The call pulled her forward again, and he steadied her as she stumbled. "First about the dice and then about her. She really is a witch."

Sierra raised her eyes. "You cheat at Skells," she muttered.

Raven hooted with laughter.

"I know one of your yarns," the old cook announced, looking Sierra up and down. "Once near this very spot, the world ended in ice."

Sierra smiled. "Or so the story goes."

"Aye, I had the tales of the ancients drilled into my head before I could season a stew or even boil water," the cook declared.

"What tales?" the kitchen wench asked. Wiping her reddened face, she eyed Sierra curiously. "No one tells such stories any more."

"And the world is the worse for it," Sierra sighed.

The cook nodded sagely. "Right here," she told the young kitchen girl, "at the foot of the glacier—even before there was a glacier, for in the times of the First Folk, the world was nice and warm—there was no such thing as darkness, because two suns lit the world."

Hairy stared at Sierra and crossed his arms before his chest. "Like broken shards they did."

"Oh, they did," Sierra said. "Look at the painted symbols on your Skell cards. They are steeped in this lore. They bear the lidded eye of the older sun, Re, as well as the bright halo of the smaller sun, Rah."

Raven pulled the playing cards from his coat pocket. "She's right!" He shuffled through the deck and held up the cards of each sun. He showed Hairy the lidded eye. "This is the one I beat you with last night. She's right."

Hairy nodded. "But she also says you cheat."

"Never mind the cards," the kitchen wench sniffled. "What happened to the real suns?"

Not to be outdone, the cook jumped back in. "Well, it's a sad story, I'm afraid. The pair of suns died. The one was getting old and the First Folk expected considerable too much of him. That second sun was not yet ready to warm the world alone, and he hadn't the strength to survive. Without help, I mean." She looked at Sierra anxiously. "All he needed was help, right?"

Sierra nodded.

The cook bobbed her head vigorously and slurped tea before continuing. "As the lands of the First Folk grew dark and cold, the braided rivers. . . ." She trailed off. "Did I mention there was twin rivers, too?"

"No," the kitchen wench said.

"Well, there was," the cook said, "two rivers twined together like snakes—don't query me how that happened—right here in this valley. And the First Folk lived in the fertile farmlands between, in a nice patch of bottom land shaped like a crescent moon."

"Tigris!" Raven shouted, showing all the Skell cards depicting the rivers. "And Eye."

"Tiger Eye." The kitchen wench took the painted parchments from him and examined them closely. "I've heard of that."

"I have forgot how the story ends." The cook squinted in the glare of the red sky, trying to remember.

"Ice," Sierra prompted.

"Yes, yes, of course," the cook nodded, back on track. "The Tigris and Eye froze for the first time ever," she said. "And thus began the age of ice. A deep freeze commenced to blight everything, first crops and wildlife, fish and fowl. Finally, the First Folk. It started with the elders and then the children, and they were entombed in limestone coffins decorated with the signs of the sun, here long ago. When all had died and none were left to honor the dead, this great Northland Glacier began to form, burying the whole lot." Rasping, the cook cocked her head at Sierra. "Some say the final few were laid to rest by the Guardians in a vast chamber of colored rocks."

Sierra's breath caught in her throat. "The Crystal Caves," she murmured.

"No such thing," Hairy interjected.

Sierra turned upon him. "Where do you think the cold-fire crystals came from, the ones that shade this sky? Now hush," she scolded, turning to the cook. "Go on."

"Supposedly there's lots of things left over in these caves of colored rocks," the cook whispered. "All the remains of the ancients' way of life, along with their secrets, the secrets of the days of old." She paused. "Not all of it good. For the suns did not die of old age. They died of the First Folk's poison and greed. The ancients had a foolish wish to rule all nature, human and other. These last few First Folk are buried deep inside the walls of magic crystal, where it is said they are never to be disturbed. They can't be. The Watchers see to that."

Grumbling, Hairy threw another stick of wood on the cook fire. "I hope these so-called Watchers know the Dark Queen has sent her Lowlanders to burn out the glacier."

Raven nodded, watching the cook dole out bowls of porridge from a cast-iron pot. Bits of ash floated on top. "That's what this pointless war is all about, isn't it?" he asked Sierra. "The Lowlanders fight to get in, and we fight to keep them out."

"I thought they just wanted water." The kitchen wench collected their empty teacups.

"The Dark Queen wants all," Sierra said. "She seeks to bend nature to her will as the First Folk did."

"So let me get this straight." The cook gestured with her wooden spoon. "The First Folk squeezed all goodness out of the suns and died in ice. And your Dark Queen, she will melt all the ice and make us die by fire."

"Well put," Sierra nodded, skimming flakes of ash off the top of her porridge and dipping her spoon into the comforting mush.

"That's folly!" the cook exclaimed.

"Say these Lowlanders break into this Crystal Cave, if it's even there," Hairy said, shoveling cereal into his mouth. "Then what happens? Pestilence and death?"

"Maybe it's happened already, Hairy," Raven observed, wiping soot from his shoulders. "After all, the sky's burning up. And we've been ordered to hunt down and jail all the witches."

"Why jail them witches?" the cook asked, arranging bowls of porridge on trays to take to the prisoners in the cave. "They may be the only ones who can save us."

Hairy shot Sierra a steady look. "If the world should end in fire this time, are you witch enough to save us? Or should we try to find a different one? The yarns say there are Twelve of you."

"Oh," Sierra laughed. "You are willing to heed the yarns, when it suits."

"Which witch are you?" Raven asked, refusing the bowl of ash-dotted porridge that the kitchen wench tried to hand him.

"It's just a few cinders," she said.

"It's dirt."

"Then go hungry. See if I care." She set his bowl on the tray to be taken to the jail cells.

"I am Sierra Blue. Keeper of the Tales of Old." Sierra curtsied to the cook. "And I must say, that was one of my yarns you bespoke, and you told it well."

The cook beamed with pleasure. "Ah, I would love to be a keeper of tales," she said wistfully.

"You cannot even keep house," the kitchen wench retorted, dumping sticky bowls and utensils into a bucket of hot water, but the cook was so happy she didn't hear.

Sierra turned her lion eyes to Hairy. "I am not the most powerful of the Twelve, but mayhap enough witch to save you." As she was speaking, the call came again and she took an involuntary step forward.

"What was that?" Hairy asked.

"Dunno," Raven shrugged. "She's been doing it all morning." He flashed Sierra a smile. "I'm sorry I called you a possessed witch," he said, his eyes dancing. "But I felt you trying to leave a dozen times as we stood around the fire."

"There is a summons inside me," Sierra explained, shivering in her blanket. "Even now, I find no way to bend it to my will." She looked about herself in desperation. "I am cold. Have you my traveling cloak?"

Raven exchanged glances with Hairy.

"Maynard said to keep it from her, lest she misuse it," one of the day-shift guards warned, as he returned from the mouth of the cave with an empty tray.

"But if she really is one of the Twelve, she might need it to save us," Raven argued.

"Or disappear," the day-shift guard said.

"Or run," added the other.

"Go get it," Hairy nodded. Raven sprinted back to the cave.

"Did I tell my yarn truthful?" the cook asked Sierra. "I heard that tale long ago, before magic was forbidden."

"Aye," Sierra said. "There is a companion tale, a tale of the Guardian of the Crystal Caves. I don't know it, because my mentor became too old to speak before she could tell me." She gazed up at the rippling sky. "I doubt that she has lived to see this day."

Sierra fell silent. Mamie was the key, she realized. Perhaps Aubergine was calling them for Mamie's sake, and not because of Tasman. Had Mamie died without revealing the lost tale? She watched as Raven returned, carrying her traveling cloak, and smiled. Perhaps her wrap would help her cast a clearer eye.

The others stood back, fearful, as she pulled the llama cloak around her shoulders, careful to keep the hood down, lest she disappear on them by mistake. The power of persuasion the coat offered should be enough to send her on her way. She closed her eyes as familiar heat surged through her body, infusing her with inner strength. She found she could bear the next pulse of Aubergine's call without lurching forward. She wondered how the rest of the Twelve were coping with the command. It was impossible to resist, especially for those who had been Aubergine's protégés. If she had the answering fire, she could release the grip of the call. Without that response, Aubergine would think no one was coming and would let the crystals beckon them repeatedly. The traveling cloak helped. Soon the summons became nothing more than a dull ache.

Finally the cook could bear the silence no longer. "What does your knitted magic tell you?" she asked.

"Right," Hairy added hotly. "Is it the end of the world, then, or not?"

"It is the end of the world as we know it," Sierra said, her eyes growing bright. "But you mistake the fire in the sky. It is nothing more than a sign."

"A sign," the kitchen wench mused. "Just a sign of the times."

Sierra raised her eyes and permitted a sifting of the fine ash to fall on her face. "It is a call for the Twelve to gather." Summoning the warmth of her traveling cloak, she turned her lion eyes on the guards. Flecks of gold stood out in the tawny irises. "I am destined to join them."

"Go gather," Raven agreed, waving her off. "Do whatever it is you do."

Hairy stared at the smaller guard in disbelief. "What in cracked crystal—?" he began.

"It is the knitted garment," the cook said. "It puts him under her spell."

"No, it is her stare that casts the spell," breathed the kitchen wench. "Look at her eyes!"

Sierra turned her gaze upon Hairy. "I must leave here," she said quietly. "Help me get to Bordertown. And quickly."

"Of course," Hairy said amiably. "If you can truly save us, I shall lead you to Bordertown myself."

"Save us," the cook echoed.

"Yes," the kitchen wench nodded eagerly. "I want to be saved."

She was cut short by a sudden piercing cry overhead, which had them all searching the horizon once more.

"Yet another wonder," Sierra said softly, as the guards flocked to the edge of the clearing before the Burnt Holes and prepared to draw their bows.

"This day can get no stranger," the cook said, craning her neck toward the source of the sound. She gave Sierra a conspiratorial look. "Mayhap this time I'll have my own yarn to tell."

High in the rosy sky, a creature swiftly winged its way toward them from the south, its black shape growing larger as it approached.

Hairy pulled an arrow from his quiver and turned to eye Sierra suspiciously. "What in the Lost Caves is that?"

Sierra watched the flying figure work its way closer, its movements winded and labored. Although alone, it flew as if chased. Turning her lion eyes upon it, Sierra saw nothing and she understood immediately: it was not of this world.

"Drop your arrows."

"You're daft," Hairy told her, bending his bow.

"You can't kill it. I see no aura," Sierra said. "It might be already dead."

The guards dropped their bows and ducked for cover as the great beast soared and swooped overhead, its huge wings pushing musty air down around them.

Wrinkling her nose, the kitchen wench wrapped her knitted scarf around her face. "Ugh," she spat.

"It's a monster," Raven guessed, studying the furry body and leathery wings, the dark skin stretched taunt over a framework of bones. "A great winged Lowland beast—a dragon, maybe." He flipped through his cards. "No Skells for that."

"No dragon," the cook breathed as the huge bird swooped over-head. She glimpsed ears cocked and alert behind opaque eyes. "It's blind. Blind as a bat."

The creature gave another piercing cry and the kitchen wench cowered. "I hate bats."

"Aye, it's a bat." Hairy ducked as the huge body circled the clearing once more. "A great monster bat, such as the Dark Queen would ride."

Sierra stood unmoving in the snow, staring up. She knew what the creature was, except that it was not possible. The animal she was thinking of had been dead since the world began again, or more. She scoured her memory for the tale, the tale that would explain what was happening, but nothing came to her mind except the beast's name:

"It is a dervish," she said with dismay. "The likes of which I have only heard, I'm afraid."

"A dervish?" Raven said, unconvinced. "A dervish, undead?"

"Afraid?" Hairy balked. "We gave you back your magic knits." He gestured to her traveling cloak. "You'd best not be afraid."

The dervish emitted yet another plaintive cry that sent shivers through the small group, and circled once again.

"He's lost," the cook mused. "He cannot find his way."

"Dervish." Raven fingered his Skell cards. "What kind of creature would you call dervish?"

Sierra was at a loss. She still could not summon the story, because it came from the lost yarn of the Guardian, the tale Mamie never told.

"I don't know," she said simply. "Dervishes were sacred and few. It was thought that they alone were able to guide their First Folk family from this world to the land of dreams. The First Folk treated them like royal pets."

"Like dogs?" Hairy asked. "You mean to tell me this dervish was a First Folk dog?"

"I'd hate to see what they had for cats," Raven laughed. "Big, mayhap with teeth like butchers' blades."

Finally the dervish began to wing away, disappearing around the Blind Side of the glacier.

The kitchen wench sighed with relief. "He's leaving."

"Where did it come from?" the cook asked.

"The Crystal Caves," Sierra said. "Remember the yarn you told about watchers in the cavern of colored rock? Each royal dervish was buried there along with its First Folk family."

Hairy squinted into the sky. "Well, I hate to tell you, but this one came from the South."

"No," Sierra said. "It escaped from the South." She looked at them in turn. "Someone captured it within these caves with a mind to take it to the Lowlands."

"Lowlanders," Hairy nodded shrewdly. "So where would this dervish be going now?"

"Back," Sierra said. "He's trying to find his way back to the Crystal Caves."

"Wait," Raven said. "You mean someone let that winged beast out of this glacier? On purpose?"

"Lowlanders forced it out." Sierra said angrily. "A dervish would never willingly leave its First Folk family." She eyed them all. "Someone has broken into the Crystal Caves."

Sierra finally understood the reason for Aubergine's summons. The Dark Queen's scouts had at last discovered a way into the Crystal Caves, and Aubergine knew. But did she know that the dervish had been freed? And was her summons too late?

Because Sierra had seen the dervish fly toward the glacier's Blind Side, she thought that might be where Lowlanders had excavated it.

As she pondered, the little band of guards and kitchen help packed up, preparing to flee.

What troubled Sierra most was that within her cell and even here in the clearing, she thought she could hear the mutterings of the ancients. There was no known passage between the Burnt Holes and the Crystal Caves. Sierra sensed that somehow they were connected. If she went back inside the Burnt Holes and started walking, perhaps her secret socks might help her find a way through to the crystal chambers and the tombs beyond. Sierra began to climb back toward the charred mouth of the Holes.

"Wait," Hairy called, running up behind her. "Steer clear, witch." When she didn't turn, he shouted even louder. "Hold up, I say."

"She's going the wrong way," the wench complained to the cook, who was dousing the fire.

"Bordertown's to the south," Raven called up the slope, pointing helpfully.

At the dark entrance to the Burnt Holes, Sierra turned, radiant in her cloak. "We must find the Crystal Caves," she said. "We must find them before they are plundered and the secrets lost."

"We must," Raven agreed, marching past Hairy.

"Oh, no, you don't." Hairy grabbed Raven's sleeve and spun him around. He challenged Sierra. "You'll not put him under your spell again. We gave you back that magic coat, and now you're going to save us."

"Naught is worth saving if we do not protect what is within," Sierra hissed. "The violation of the Crystal Caves must be found and resealed."

"That is certain death." Hairy shook his head. "The caves will be soon overrun by Lowlanders. We must flee to the garrison and warn the Northland Guard. They are many. We are few."

Sierra disappeared into the cave entrance. "Get her," Hairy ordered the day-shift guards. "Bring her back."

Slipping into the shadows, Sierra flipped up the hood of her traveling cloak and as the guards reached the mouth of the cave, she vanished.

Raven groped in the dark. Sierra shrank against the wall and passed down the corridor unseen, eluding them all. Once they were gone, she cleared her mind and let her feet do the walking. They seemed to know where to go.

Back in the antechamber, Raven appeared empty-handed. "She's gone. Into thin air."

"Now look what you've done," the cook scolded Hairy.

Sierra's Secret Socks

A SOCK PATTERN

*These intermediate-skill-level socks are knit from fine yarn in
an easy ribbed pattern, and will always keep you on the right path,
even if you are lost. This pattern is sized for women.*

Get the pattern from PotluckYarn.com/epatterns

After settling Mamie on a threadbare settee, Ratta tended
her animals and washed herself in Esmeralde's basin.

CHAPTER 13

Mamie's Last Message

THE BUCKBOARD WAGON THUNDERED INTO the clearing in front of Esmeralde's cottage, churning mud as the wheels splashed through puddles. Ratta slowed the sweaty mules to a halt and sat back heavily on the bench.

"For the love of the Lost Caves!" She swore loudly.

There was no need to check the house. No light shone from the windows. No smoke rose from the chimney. The flower boxes had been planted for spring, but had not been recently tended. Nobody had been home for some time, and of course she knew why.

She turned a worried glance toward Mamie, who lay wrapped in the never-ending shawl and had barely stirred since yesterday. Ratta put a roughened hand tenderly to the old woman's lined face. The skin on Mamie's cheek felt hot and papery. Donning her soft, ruffled mitts, Ratta peeled back the shawl, searching for the rhythm of breathing, which came so shallowly she could not tell if it was real or she was willing it so.

"Broken shards!" She glared at the dark house. Then she gently gathered Mamie in her arms, caressing the old woman's face with the fine Merino wool that encased her hands, begging Mamie to live. Ratta pulled on the extra-fine hand coverings when she had tender work to do, such as handling Mamie. The lanolin that had been left in the yarn softened her chapped skin, and what's more, the slightly frivolous design made her feel up to any task.

All morning long Ratta had studiously ignored the telltale red in the sky, willing the hue to be gone, to be replaced by blue or even gray-clouded rain. But the feverish color had merely faded to a rosy haze over the landscape, echoing Aubergine's words of warning when they had gathered around the table at the Potluck on that last day. Only Teal and Tasman had been missing, although traces of Teal, remained if you knew where to look.

There would be a sign, Aubergine had said, looking tired and somehow smaller without the circlet of heavy amethyst stones around her neck; and not all would heed its warning. No doubt this fire in the sky was the summons Aubergine had prophesied.

Ratta remembered that Lilac Lily had warned her that she would come, because she would have no choice. Well, Ratta told herself, she did have a choice and she wasn't going, no matter how strong the call, because she strongly suspected that Smokey Jo was behind the summons. Such a flamboyant show of fireworks smacked of Smokey Jo, who had never been able to keep her stubby hands away from a cook fire or a tinderbox. Perhaps Smokey had finally figured out how to open the seamless box and had lit the cold-fire crystals as a lark before Aubergine could stop her. Or maybe Aubergine didn't even know. There was a slight chance that Smokey Jo had prodded Aubergine into calling them all; but what was the point? The glacier burned daily, Mamie was all but dead, and the lost stone had never been found. Why would Aubergine want them to gather at the Potluck now?

In truth, the last thing Ratta wanted was to trail north to Bordertown to carry out Aubergine's bidding once more, like the underling she had been when young.

However, resisting the call was more difficult than she had expected. The sky sizzled pink, and it was nigh noon. Ratta could not deny that she felt the call, yanking at her as if she were under a spell. Mamie stirred at last, her eyelids fluttering but refusing to open, while her parched lips worked like an infant's, searching for suckle. Ratta cradled the old woman's head and shoulders, not knowing how to put her at ease.

Esmeralde's remedies or Indigo's teas and herbs might offer Mamie some relief. Ratta soaked a rag with cold honeyed tea from her flask and put it to Mamie's mouth. The puckered lips worked the cloth thirstily. Ratta raised her eyes uneasily toward the abandoned cottage. She knew it didn't make sense to drive farther in search of Esmeralde's aid. She was certain the old witch's other haunt, Indigo's greenhouse, would also be empty; for both witches would have trudged off to the Potluck together, like the good girls they were. Perhaps she did not need Esmeralde's lore, Ratta allowed herself to hope. Perhaps all she needed was a remedy or two, or maybe three, from Esmeralde's pantry. It would not hurt to look.

Ratta felt the call again, like a rosy hand reaching out toward her chest from the sky. She actually felt herself lean forward on the bench, preparing to slap the reins against the flanks of the tired mules. It took all she could muster to resist. Mamie must have felt the urge, too, for she seemed to experience a brief spasm. Ratta dipped the rag into her tea again but Mamie no longer wanted the cloth, which dripped across her lined face, leaving a sticky track like tears.

Ratta felt a prick behind her eyes and put a hand to the side rail of the wagon to steady herself. Her stomach lurched and she gave a dry swallow. She knew she was about to have a vision. It had been so long since one had come to her that the images took her by surprise. She suddenly saw a dizzying sequence: taloned fingers rifling through bodies on a killing field; a soldier boy with Sierra Blue's blond coloring and features; Lilac Lily riding beside a milk-route driver along the track toward Esmeralde's cottage; Winter Wheat as midwife, hatching a wet-winged creature from a chunk of ice; Indigo and Esmeralde standing in rain, watching green fire erupt from a fieldstone chimney. Ratta shook her head, but the pictures kept coming: children raced dun ponies through a tangled copse of trees; Sierra Blue strained to glimpse the moon through a window in what looked like a cage.

Ratta grabbed her head and tugged at her curly red hair. Where were these visions coming from? She looked suspiciously toward the vacant house and then at Mamie, who did not open her eyes or speak, although for a moment Ratta thought she could hear Mamie's inner voice, weaker than a whisper, yet coherent. Ratta shook her head in disbelief. The old woman did not have the strength for Mind Speak; and even if Mamie was trying to talk to her again Ratta did not want to admit that she was afraid to hear what the old woman might have to say after all this time.

Honestly, Ratta could not be certain of who was saying what. She had not slept in two nights, and voices in the form of whispered half-truths abounded everywhere recently. Since she had driven through Coventry last evening, she had heard talk up and down the track among folk returning from the fair. They spoke of little other than the Twelve. Rumors at the Coventry General Store had ranged from hearsay—that one of the Twelve had been captured by the Northland Guard—to conjecture that the Twelve were actually the Guard's allies, helping to gather forces in the Northlands. Fairgoers speculated that the combined power of Twelve and Guard would be First-Folk fierce. Others imagined that the Twelve would seize control of all the lands, unite the north and south, and end the glacier wars in a shower of icy sparks. The alternative, also proposed, was less optimistic—that the world was about to end, either in a burst of flames or locked again in ice.

The morning's blazing sky fueled such gossip. Resting the mules at a pull-off, Ratta had feigned disinterest when one fair follower reported that a member of the Twelve had been abducted up the military road. Others argued that the Twelve were but eight now, since one had been banished to the Burnt Holes, a second killed by a dark one who fled south, while yet a third had lost her mind in the Crystal Caves, where she wandered still. Ratta noted that their math worked no better than the logic.

While Mamie's voiceless message tumbled unintelligibly through her mind, Ratta climbed down from the wagon and tried the cottage door. It opened easily, not having been locked. Piled just inside the entry were Esmeralde's remedies, as if she had been packing or unpacking them. Ratta lifted one container after another, finding nothing that looked strong enough to sustain Mamie. All she found was basic Farmer's Market stock: strengthening teas and cough cures, salves and ointments.

What Ratta sought would surely be secreted in the pantry behind the kitchen, where it was rumored Esmeralde practiced her lore. Over the years, those dying of fever or cancerous sores sought the back room. Esmeralde had tended such folk on a broad table covered with a clean sheet, which sometimes doubled as a funeral shroud. Ratta hustled to this back room only to find the pantry ransacked, and the table bare. Not a vial or bottle remained on the shelves. No wonder the door had been unlocked. Ratta wondered if Esmeralde had been the one caught and taken up the military road. If so, then why had her vision shown her Sierra Blue behind bars?

Ratta returned to the front room and sank into one of Esmeralde's rockers, not noticing its creak of protest. It was starting to look like she would have to wend her way north to find help for Mamie. But first she would water the mules and get some sleep, and also see if she could force a little gruel into the old woman. In the jumble of ordinary remedies by the front door, she had noticed some victual syrup laced with cordial and a few other sustenance vials. They might not help much, but they couldn't hurt.

Ratta felt better as the day waned, coating the pink afternoon with the comfort of familiar dusk. After settling Mamie on a threadbare settee in the cottage, she tended her animals and washed herself in Esmeralde's basin, then dozed by the fire. Later, she slowly stirred some soup on the wood stove, all the while watching Mamie. The more she pondered her earlier visions, the more they chilled her, fleeting and unbidden as they were. It had taken her all day to come to terms with the source. She had first thought that Aubergine had sent the visions as part of the call, then that Esmeralde had used them to keep intruders from her house. Finally, she decided that it was Mamie who had cast the inner sight her way, to get her attention. Even now the old woman's lips moved, straining to form syllables that Ratta could neither hear nor interpret.

Ratta forced herself to be as still as was humanly possible, barely breathing as she tried to feel the old woman's words resonate within herself. She rested her stirring spoon in the pot and let her eyes fall shut, the better to receive the words as the images that she suspected would come. She had discovered this process when she was a girl, all those years ago as Mamie had ceased to utter sounds. Of the Twelve, only Ratta found that she could understand the old woman, who began to speak with her eyes, much like it was rumored that Lowlanders did.

For a while, she caught herself answering Mamie aloud, to the disgust of the other girls, who assumed her replies were playacting. Whenever Wheat heard Ratta responding to Mamie, she mocked Ratta by burning holes through her clothing with the crystals that swung from her staff. As time passed, inner visions began to accompany Mamie's silent words and Ratta no longer needed to look into the old woman's eyes or verbalize answers. Ratta named their private language Mind Speak, after the archaic language of the First Folk. Whenever Mamie was about to contact her, she would feel a small prick in her temples like a mosquito bite, followed by a flutter like butterfly wings as Mamie opened her mind and began paging through her memory. But that, too, had dwindled to nothing as the years passed.

The way Mamie spoke from her mind was different from the call to the Potluck, which Ratta felt even now as a foolish urge to hitch the mules and leave in the night. The summons of the cold-fire crystals was Aubergine's blatant red-sky magic trying to smother her, as it had the horizon. Ratta found it irritating, like an itch she refused to dignify with a scratch. But she knew she would succumb to it eventually, perhaps even within the hour, because as night fell the call grew plaintive.

Mamie's magic had always been more subtle and sublime than anything the rest of the Twelve could muster. Standing by the stove with her eyes closed, Ratta felt the familiar prick as the old woman began to seek her out once more. She sensed a soft flutter, a hesitant touch, and a parting of memories. Ratta felt her feet sway as her mind cleared to reveal a graveyard of crypts within a vast cavern of ice. Becoming queasy, she sank into Esmeralde's rocker. She recognized the ancient cemetery from the lost tale, the yarn Mamie had revealed only to her, a story that—if left to Ratta—Sierra Blue would never know. Ratta believed the graves were those of the First Folk, who had died in ice before the world began again. She saw ruined mausoleums housing limestone markers, stone coffins, and burial urns, some of which still bore traces of the dual suns and braided rivers. Lesser-buried dead had been stacked row upon row in catacombs that lined the corridors.

The entire cemetery was a shambles. Glacier run-off had carved out chasms and passageways, causing cave-ins that sealed over the mouths of some sections. Many of the crypts had been cracked open and the neat rows of catacombs had been twisted, whether from frost heaves or desecration by grave robbers, Ratta could not tell. Coffins lay scattered with broken lids, and ornate funeral tapestries crumpled where they had fallen.

Her vision showed the sole remaining entrance to this cemetery, by way of a serpentine passage through the Crystal Caves, where, according to legend no living person had ever set foot. Few even believed this place existed. Amethyst and onyx stalactites, resembling jeweled spears, hung from the cavern roof and pearly stalagmites rose like jagged teeth from its floor. In her mind's eye, Ratta had frequently visited these caves and the various tunnels that led to them, sometimes at Mamie's bidding, and sometimes on her own. Mamie bade her go there now.

"Watch Mae," the old woman urged in their special language, speech without words. *"Mae, Mae."*

"Mamie," Ratta answered in Mind Speak, but as soon as she repeated the name she knew she'd said it wrong, and a grimace fluttering across Mamie's face suggested the same. She caught a glimpse of light bobbing through a dark tunnel, a dull glow from a chunk of crystal held high by a scrawny arm.

"It is Mae," Mamie clarified. And then Ratta saw the yellowed fingernails and recognized the crone from her morning vision of the killing fields. It was, indeed, Lavender Mae, older than when Ratta had last seen her but still intoning tuneless ditties. As Ratta watched, the light crept along a frigid path toward the burial grounds and all around

the voices of the dead began to whisper. To combat the cacophony, Mae put her hands to her ears and chanted louder. *"Mae, Mae, Mae!"* she screeched.

"She's gone mad," Ratta quietly observed.

"Mae has the voices of the ancients inside her head," Mamie explained, with the familiar old gravelly tone beginning to tinge her silent voice. *"Do you remember the last tale?"*

"Yes, of the ancients we call the First Folk. They lived beneath the twin suns, Re and Rah, in the fertile crescent between the intertwined rivers, Tigris and Eye."

"You will tell this tale one day soon," Mamie reminded her. *"To everyone. Even Sierra Blue."*

Ratta remained stubbornly silent, watching Lavender Mae gnash her teeth and shake her head, as the voices grew unbearably loud.

"Take heed," Mamie warned. *"For this is what happens to those who enter the Crystal Caves unbidden. The First Folk find you. They inhabit your mind."*

"Mae needs to turn back," Ratta said, watching as Mae drew forward toward the crypts, like a moth seeking fire. *"Why doesn't she?"*

"She cannot, for the ancients call to her. She did not enter the caves unnoticed the first time, nor does she now. Mae has been here too often." Mamie's sadness weighed on Ratta's heart. *"The voices of the First Folk echo within her. It is too late."*

"Has the Guardian seen her?" Ratta asked.

"All the Watchers have. And scavenging Lowlanders have breached the caves from the Blind Side. The Guardian has seen them as well. Can you recall the Last Tale of the Ancients? All of it?"

"I do, but I don't know what it means."

"You were never meant to understand." Mamie paused. *"Tell Sierra Blue. She will know what to do, for she knows my fate as well as her own."*

"Why not Mae?" Ratta argued. *"I see how she is drawn to the graveyard, while crying out her own name. Perhaps the Guardian's watchers wait for her. Perhaps she knows."*

"No," Mamie said. *"She calls for me, as do the Watchers even now. The Guardian's tenure is complete. It is I who am to be the next protector of the Crystal Caves."*

With a blast of sputtering liquid, the soup began to boil over. Ratta's eyes flew open and she ran to lift the pot from the stove before turning to Mamie.

"Not you," she begged. *"Let them take her. It looks like they already have her!"*

"It is the ancients who have claimed Mae, not the Guardian. If she doesn't have my help, they will drive her crazy." The old woman's bleary eyes blinked open. Ratta gasped. Mamie's eyes were now so filmy and opaque that she knew her mistress could see nothing but the visions inside her head. *"As Guardian, I will be the only one who can free Mae from the ancients."*

"No," Ratta protested in her mind, her eyes stinging with tears. *"No!"*

"Those who watch from the tombs beyond the Crystal Caves call to Mae, but it is me they crave. Take me to the Potluck, so that Mae can lead you to them. I can free her. I can save you all."

Ratta shook her head. And then she screamed aloud. *"No!"*

"Have Smokey Jo prepare the great pot for a simmer. Then you must loose me from this shawl," Mamie continued, paying no attention to Ratta's outburst. *"In this world I am neither alive nor dead. You alone know the tale and the prophecy."*

"But I do not believe the prophecy," Ratta protested. "I never did."

"Your beliefs matter not," Mamie said gently. "It is past time that I join the Guardians."

"No," Ratta said. "Let us die together in fire as it is foretold. I do not care."

"I am dead already. There is nothing you or Esmeralde, or even Aubergine, can do but let me pass."

Ratta waited, resistant, as the thoughts tumbled in her brain. Finally, they settled and she felt resignation wrap around her, like an unending sadness. "Only if you truly will it," she said at last.

"I will it so."

"I feel the summons," Ratta admitted.

"As do I," Mamie said. "When you reach the Potluck, you will tell the entire lost tale."

"As you wish," Ratta said, as tears streamed down her face. "Is this goodbye? I always loved you."

"And I you," Mamie said, slipping away.

Wiping her face on a dishrag, Ratta went out to hitch the mules. She would go slinking back to the Potluck, but only for Mamie's sake. Lilac Lily had been right. She had no choice. Though Mamie was now lost to her, she would wait until she reached the Potluck to unwrap the precious body from the never-ending shawl. She could not bear to let the old woman pass without the support of the Potluck, even though she feared Mamie would never be able to communicate with her again.

Ratta's Muffin-Top Mitts

A MITTEN PATTERN

These advanced-beginner-skill-level mitts are quite stretchy and will fit most women's hands. The soft self-striping yarn gives them colorful rhythm and they are suitable for tender chores.

Get the pattern from PotluckYarn.com/epatterns

The back room of the Potluck bore almost
no resemblance to the hallowed space it had been
when all Twelve had circled the great pot.

CHAPTER 14

Time to Clean House

SMOKEY JO PULLED THE LACEY COWL UP over her curly head and trotted out to the dye shed once more, huffing at her exertion. Sierra had knitted the cowl in a merry colorway that Smokey Jo had dyed in a kettle long ago. The shaded reds and rust, with licks of indigo and slate, reminded Smokey Jo of a fire in the hearth, so she named it "Smoken." Unfortunately, there was no hearth-fire today. Her fingers and even the tip of her upturned nose felt numb with cold.

The back room of the Potluck bore almost no resemblance to the hallowed space it had been when all Twelve had circled the great pot. Smokey had spent part of this morning clearing a path through the heavy sacks of unskirted fleeces, the baskets of undyed yarns, and the bumps of roving that left a scent of lanolin lingering in the chill. Many of the fleeces had been graded and tagged years ago, but because fewer and fewer hand spinners made their way to Potluck Yarn these days, no one had thought to haul the bags of fiber out front to sell. Smokey had found sacks of musk-ox down and Angora rabbit fur, bricks of silk, curly kid-mohair locks, and the odd bale of carded possum. There was enough here to fill another entire shop, she mused. Too bad the shop space out front, which she managed with Aubergine, was full to bursting. They must really stop collecting so much fiber and actually start spinning and dyeing it again, or at least prepare it for sale.

Smokey's breath came in ragged gasps as she attempted to drag the dye pot over to the fire pit, wresting it one way and then another. What she wanted was for it to sit squarely on the stones, ready to be lit. But the huge iron cauldron was heavy, and the floor over which she needed to haul it wasn't clear. Cartons of dyestuffs had been scattered about. Squirrels had upended some crates, while mice had eaten through the wooden slats on others. Smokey tugged on her cowl, which had fallen down over her eyes. It was discouraging. She needed help.

As if on cue, the bell tinkled over the front door signaling a customer. But when Smokey bustled through the narrow hall connecting the dye shed to the yarn shop, it was just Aubergine returning with their midday meal. With just the two of them here, they rarely laid a fire in the hearth or used the bread oven anymore. Instead, they bought food from the row of stalls on the next street over, closer to the city center. There, just a few coppers could bring them spiced meat pies and hot honeyed teas, as well as Smokey Jo's favorite snack, kettle corn from the street-cart vendor, who popped the kernels in an oiled iron pot. She loved it drizzled with cinnamon icing or caramel, or sometimes buttered with a generous sprinkling of maple sugar.

Today Aubergine's market bag held no rolled cone of hot buttered corn. She began to unpack just meat pies and a pot of lemon tea with sugar cookies.

"No kettle corn?" Smokey Jo cleared a space for their lunch on the cluttered table. She threw her knitting into a twig basket beside her chair and pushed a few knitted swatches into a heap in the middle of the table.

"It seems your kettle corn vendor is still not back from the fair," Aubergine said. "The others told me he has a stand along the main track beyond Banebridge and won't be back before midweek."

Smokey sank heavily into the soft cushions of her chair, and, reaching across her meat pie, bit dejectedly into a cookie. She kicked at a few balls of yarn that had rolled across the dusty floor.

"I wish Lily was here," she said. "The back room is a mess and we've no one to cook for us or ready the house, with all of them coming."

"The Potluck could use some spring cleaning." Aubergine assessed the streaked windows and cluttered counters.

Smokey raised her brows. "Unless you think none of them are coming? It's been two days."

"Oh, they're coming." Aubergine smiled, pouring the tea. "Just not all."

"There's been no answering fire."

"Perhaps the other box is lost," Aubergine replied. "As ours was, all those years."

"I know who's not coming. I can guess," Smokey crunched up her cookie and brushed the crumbs to the floor before reaching for her teacup. "Tell me if you think I'm right. Teal isn't coming."

"Since we've seen nothing of her for twenty years but the odd wisp of smoke, that's a reasonable wager. But I've a feeling she'll send someone in her place."

Smokey Jo nodded shrewdly, gesturing with another cookie. "And Tasman."

"The Dark Queen." Aubergine's gaze seemed to focus far away and her eyes grew violet. "That is what they call her now. She is nowhere and everywhere." Aubergine considered before she spoke. "No, she will not arrive like the others, although I am certain she will be among us."

"Locking the doors won't help?"

"No, little one," Aubergine gave a tired smile. "Besides, I thought you lost the key."

Smokey glanced around the untidy shop, at the shelves and baskets overflowing with yarns and rovings, needles and notions. A tippy pile of unanswered posts littered the counter next to a sleeping cat. "It's here somewhere, probably," she said. She rummaged in the cookie sack. "Esmeralde and Indigo will come."

"Perhaps they will be the first ones here." Aubergine unwrapped her meat pie. "No doubt they have convinced each other that they can run the Potluck better than we."

"They've been sharing their visions again, have they?" Smokey asked anxiously.

Aubergine nodded. "They are under the impression that I don't know. Their so-called visions laced with Crystal Cordial and glacier weed come to me unwanted, like indigestion."

"What are they looking for? Something we have?"

"They don't agree. One says an intruder, while the other thinks an interloper." Aubergine smiled. "As we do, they seek the lost crystal. Yet they erroneously believe that Lavender Mae has it, or another that will substitute."

"Lavender Mae has many crystals."

"But neither that one nor a twin."

"Do you think it isn't lost after all? Perhaps around here some-where, misplaced like the keys?"

"It is no more lost than Teal is dead," Aubergine said, laying aside her pie. "Greasy, that," she complained, reaching into the sack for a cookie. "If Lily shows up and we ask the right questions, we'll find both Teal and the crystal hiding in plain sight."

"Wheat will be here." Smokey slurped tea. "And Sierra."

"I am not certain of Wheat," Aubergine admitted. "She may have been delayed in the Western Highlands. And I've a bad feeling about Sierra Blue. There's something amiss with her."

"Have you been conjuring visions over the dye pot, too?" Smokey demanded, searching in the clutter for the honey pot. She finally found it, stuck to the table, under a sheaf of patterns. "Without me?"

"No," Aubergine shook her head wearily.

"I dislike it when you retire to your room so early in the day," Smokey objected, stirring more honey into her tea.

"I just need an afternoon nap now and again," Aubergine said gently. "I have much to consider for an old woman who runs a yarn shop."

"It is I who runs the yarn shop," Smokey said. "I'm right down here most days."

Aubergine began to laugh. "Why do you protest so?"

"Because the Twelve are coming!" Smokey explained, swiping a napkin across her face. "And we've much to do!"

"Surely it can wait until after lunch. Don't you want your meat pie? It's bear sausage with anise."

Smokey shook her head and crunched another cookie. "I don't have time for meals. Plus sweets give me energy. Have you seen the condition of the back room?"

"Not since last summer. I am sure you will put it to rights."

"Not without help." Smokey shook the bag, but the cookies were gone. "What about Lavender Mae? Is she coming?" She answered her own question. "Hard to say."

"Perhaps if we went and got her," Aubergine suggested. "She might need persuasion."

"Don't look at me. I hate the cold. That leaves Mamie and Ratta. Do you think Mamie passed?"

"Perhaps." Aubergine sipped her tea. "As well she should have, by now. If she did not, she's no longer the Mamie we know. Her presence will bring more harm than good."

"Her red-haired henchmaid Ratta will see to that." Smokey gave Aubergine a defiant look. "I cannot stand her."

"Nor can anyone else, it would seem." Aubergine emptied the last of the tea into their cups and reached for her knitting.

"Well, why would they? You know, at the end of it she would not even listen to Sierra's yarns, and you know we all loved Sierra's stories."

"Yes we did." Aubergine began to count stitches.

Smokey squirmed in her chair. "I'm most wary of Lily. Not of her exactly, but of what she knows." She looked Aubergine in the eye. "Lilac Lily knows a lot about me."

"She knows a lot about everyone," Aubergine said complacently and slipped a marker between two stitches. "That's her gift."

"Well, she'd better not tell everything."

"I think she will be more careful this time," Aubergine said, straightening her row. "We all will."

"I know I said I forgave her for breaking up the Potluck, but I didn't," Smokey picked at her pie. "I couldn't."

"It wasn't wholly her fault." Aubergine pinched the stitches she was counting between her fingers to hold her place and looked up.

"It was Tasman's fault for running off, or maybe it was my fault for believing Tasman only wanted to try on the necklace."

"It was Sierra's for letting Tasman take her place," Smokey said darkly. "Sierra never would have stolen the necklace of the Twelve."

Aubergine resumed her work. "We all had a part in what happened."

"What was mine?" Smokey asked, watching Aubergine knit. Her stitches were so small and even that she never had to glance at her work. Smokey had to watch her knitting constantly, because her loops were so big that the knitting refused to stay on her needles. She might be better off taking a beginner knitter class rather than trying to teach one.

Aubergine's birch needles clicked and clacked. "You, little one, should have pestered me to summon the Twelve last year or the year before, before the Lowlanders started coming up beyond Top Notch."

"I was thinking we should, except I couldn't remember where we hid the tinderbox." Smokey admitted. "Come to find out, it was on a high, high shelf. And you know I am vertically challenged. Plus I fear ladders."

"I have a feeling Tasman's lackeys have broken into the Crystal Caves." Aubergine paused for a moment before she continued. "I'm afraid we shall have to get out the big pot and have a simmer, to see."

"The pot is full of old dyestuffs, none of them good any more." Smokey began to pile the remains of their lunch on a tray. "And it feels heavier than it used to. I can't push it to the fire pit."

"It might be worse." Aubergine handed Smokey her empty cup. "The Crystal Caves are a treasure, but the real prize for Tasman would be the tombs of the ancients."

"What would the Dark Queen want with the graves of the First Folk?" Smokey struggled to keep the pile of crockery from tipping over.

"There is no telling without seeing," Aubergine said, rummaging in her knitting bag for her magnifiers. "Thus we need to circle the pot."

"What we need is help!" Smokey said, setting the tea tray back on the table. First the teaspoons and then the saucers clattered to the floor. She bent to pick up the broken dishes. "Is there no other way to gain the knowledge of the Crystal Caves?"

"Sierra Blue cannot tell us. She doesn't know." Aubergine settled her half-moon spectacles across her nose. "The one yarn Mamie never spoke aloud was the lost tale of the First Folk buried beyond the Crystal Caves."

"I shall wring the story from Ratta's throat myself if I have to," Smokey said fiercely. "You watch."

"She may know nothing," Aubergine soothed, looking up from her pattern. "Or even if she can recite the tale, she may not understand it. To derive the meaning of a legend, you have to understand it."

"I doubt she can tell the time of day, let alone an ancient yarn," Smokey climbed under the table to retrieve her knitting basket.

"What about the stable boy?"

Smokey's voice was muffled. "What?"

"He can move the dye pot to the fire pit," Aubergine suggested. "We must have a simmer."

Smokey straightened up so quickly that she hit her head on the underside of the table. "Aubergine, we let him go last winter after the horse died. Don't you remember?"

Aubergine nodded. "I remember the horse. Dapple-gray draft, wasn't he? And the stable boy was big and brawny." She watched Smokey paw through her untidy basket of half-knit scarves and mittens. She sighed at all the dropped stitches. "He smoked glacier weed in the stable, though, and I won't tolerate that. The horse is dead?"

"Of old age. The boy is gone." Smokey abandoned her knitting and gave Aubergine a quizzical look. "And we have no cook or gardener or housekeeper. There are just you and me to ready all."

"We shall have to hire help, then."

"That's what I've been trying to tell you!" Smokey sat back down, exasperated. "The Twelve can show up here at any time, and none of the beds have linens and none of the rooms have been aired. No fires have been laid, and there is no heat at all upstairs."

"I don't care for stairs." Aubergine pointed a needle toward the narrow staircase in the front hall. "I prefer to sleep downstairs." Yawning, she set her knitting aside. "Go hire your help, if you must."

"I shall run down to the farmer's market and post a notice," Smokey said, climbing down from her chair before Aubergine could change her mind. "I shall post two notices, one for a housekeeper and one for a handyman. That should do to start."

Before Smokey could fasten her cloak, the bell tinkled and the door swung open. She stopped in her tracks. The lined face looked familiar, but she wasn't certain of who it was until she noticed the market bag. "Lilac Lily?" she asked. Then, "Lily! Am I glad to see you!"

"And I you," Lily laughed, setting down her bag and shedding her cloak.

Smokey clasped her hands and did a little jig. "We were just speaking of you!"

Lily glanced toward the table and the smile left her face. "Meat pies from a street vendor for lunch?" She looked to Aubergine in alarm. "Weak tea, and store-bought cookies! Does the oven no longer work?"

"To tell you the truth, I don't know," Aubergine replied, rising to give Lily a hug. "We have not lit it in months. How are you, dear?"

Lily held her close. "I have weathered better than you, I fear," she murmured into Aubergine's neck, before releasing her. "What a sorry state of affairs. Look at this place!"

"We've kind of let it go," Smokey admitted, watching as Lily took in the overflowing baskets of half-knit socks, bins of tangled yarn, and dusty spinning wheels, surrounded by sacks of jumbled roving. "I was just now going out to post a work-for-hire bill in the market."

"You will do no such thing." Lily began to clear the lunch tray from the table.

"The dust and dirt are worse upstairs," Aubergine said, as she and Smokey followed Lily into the neglected kitchen. "Some of the doors to those rooms have not been opened in years."

Lily stood in the dim space, taking in the littered countertops and the small round table piled high with take-away sacks and with hot pots rimmed with old tea leaves. Forgotten market bags half full of sprouted potatoes and rotting vegetables sat on chairs and the floor. The air smelled of rancid cream. Lily opened the icebox and shut it quickly.

"How long has it been since the ice man came?"

"Quite awhile," Smokey said. "He stopped coming when no one shoveled the snow from the garden path."

"What about the stable boy?"

Aubergine nodded toward Smokey Jo. "She let him go."

"Well, the horse died," Smokey Jo put up both hands.

Lily shook her head. "I cannot believe this," she said, opening a window.

"Don't go upstairs," Aubergine warned, as Lily turned away.

"Did you see our fire in the sky?" Smokey asked hopefully, trailing Lily down the hall. "Is that why you came?"

"I did see it, yesterday morning, but I was already halfway here, in Woolen Woods." Lily was heading for the staircase. "I set out after I saw Sierra Blue at the fair, three days ago."

"Is she coming?" Smokey's eyes gleamed. "I guessed she was coming."

"I don't know if she will come." Lily paused, her hand on the banister. "I was afraid to talk to her."

"Afraid?" Aubergine asked. "Of Sierra Blue? Why in the world, when all fear you? Child, what has come to pass?"

Lily's eyes dropped. "Aubergine, I did what you asked," she said, quietly. "For twenty years I have practiced my lore. You have only to ask me the questions and I can answer." She gave a cursory glance up to the second floor. "Where is that red-haired scullery girl, Ratta? I've a few questions I want her to ask."

"We don't know," Smokey said. "You're the first to arrive." She trudged up the stairs after Lily. "We haven't even seen Indigo or Esmeralde, and we thought they would be here first."

"I wouldn't count on Esmeralde," Lily said. "Her booth at the fair was empty. The Northland Guard was everywhere."

"Do you think they arrested her?" Smokey asked, breathing heavily.

"Maybe," Lily said. "The milk-route driver I was riding with dropped me at her cottage two nights ago." She began opening doors along the upstairs hallway. "Ugh!" She swiped at dust motes that swirled around her head. "I stopped there wanting to find out why Esmeralde missed the fair, and perhaps to spend the night."

"I dislike climbing stairs!" Aubergine called from the hall.

Lily opened the shades in all the rooms. "No linens?"

"In the closet. What about Esmeralde?"

"She wasn't home," Lily said, heading back downstairs. Smokey had to trot to keep up. "The remedies that she sells in her booth were by the door—in fact, I gladly found my headache medicine—but the pantry where she keeps her Possibles was empty." She opened the door to the linen closet. "All the glass vials and stoppered bottles, everything, was gone."

"What did you hear along the track?" Smokey Jo asked, holding her arms out for Lily to pile high with old sheets and pillowcases.

"Some said soldiers had taken one of the Twelve up the military road, but that could have meant any of us, or an impostor." Lily, too, carried a load of linens into the deserted dining room, where she began sorting bedding onto the table. "Everyone saw red the other morning, and you know how people talk."

"If Esmeralde was captured, the Guard would have imprisoned her in the Burnt Holes." Aubergine had joined them and was pulling out one of the twelve chairs. "It will be difficult to find her, but nowhere near impossible." Sighing, she sat. "Freeing her will be the hard part."

"Maybe she will put a pox on the lot of them and free herself," Smokey said gleefully.

"Perhaps," Aubergine said.

"I need help getting out the big pot," Smokey told Lily.

"Don't you have a kitchen boy, a gardener, anyone?" Lily asked. Pausing, she looked around the dusty dining room and threw up her hands with a laugh. "Of course not!"

Aubergine took the lid off a serving dish and spilled coins onto the scarred oak table. "We have newly minted Northland silver," she said. "Lots of it."

"Where did you get all that?" Smokey gave Aubergine a shocked look. "You didn't."

Aubergine shook her head with a glance to Lily.

"Never mind, we're going to need lots of silver to put this place to rights," Lily said, pretending not to notice. She scooped the bright coins into her market bag.

Happy once more, Smokey took Lily's arm. "We'll be back," she said to Aubergine. "Why don't you have a lie-down?"

"Gladly." Aubergine waved them off.

As Smokey scuttled down the hallway after their cloaks, Lily paused in the dining room doorway. "Don't forget, I know everything," she told Aubergine gently. "Ask the question."

"Will they hate me?" Aubergine whispered, her eyes shining with unshed tears.

Lily shook her head. "Aubergine, we all do what we must. No one will blame you. Everyone here will bring regrets." She considered what she had said. "Well, almost everyone."

Smokey Jo's Smoken Cowl

A COWL PATTERN

Wear this intermediate-skill-level cowl as a neck warmer,
or pull it up higher for more protection. It measures
a 23" circumference by 14" length (adjustable with blocking).

Get the pattern from PotluckYarn.com/epatterns

"I'm afraid we have a dangerous road ahead."

CHAPTER 15

Journey to the Border

ESMERALDE LURCHED FORWARD. "The call is strong," she breathed, gripping the edge of the kitchen table for support.

"It's the cold-fire crystal." Indigo braced her hands against the doorway, fighting the urge to leave her cottage. "As long as it burns in the sky, we won't be able to resist the summons."

"Well, we can't leave yet." In the awful pink light, Esmeralde surveyed the ruined kitchen and the bedraggled youths, half asleep at the table. "These children rode through the night and we've barely slept in two days."

Garth yawned. "I could sleep all morning."

Trader gave the witches a resigned look. "I bet there are chores to do."

Indigo nodded to Esmeralde. "We don't have to heed the call just yet."

The two witches needed to make arrangements before they could leave the greenhouse garden behind. Esmeralde asked Skye to help her set the cottage to rights, while Indigo took Trader out to water the greenhouse plants. Garth was sent to the barn to feed Indigo's laying hens and her pair of oxen, and to muck out the pony stalls. As soon as Indigo's hired girl arrived, Indigo offered to let the young woman stay at the cottage if she would take care of the plants and animals while they were gone. "Just a week," she told the girl.

"Maybe two." Esmeralde adjusted the beret that never seemed to leave her head.

"Or three or four," Indigo admitted, with a swing of her gray braids beneath her bandana. "Actually, we don't know."

Watching their banter, Skye felt restless and irritated. It seemed to her that the five of them should have left by now, if they were to have any hope of catching up with Sierra's captors. Yet no one had yet packed anything for the journey, and they were all tired. The excitement of the night before had yielded no time for sleep.

After morning chores, Trader spread out the bedrolls in the loft, and soon she and Garth were snoring softly among the fragrant bales of hay.

Skye wandered back to the cottage, where Esmeralde and Indigo were planning the trip to Bordertown. Just listening to them made her more anxious. She also felt an unpleasant tightness in her chest that made her heart pound.

"I can't sleep," she said, slumping into a kitchen chair near the window.

"What's wrong?" Esmeralde asked.

"I'm too worried about everything. The Northland soldiers took my mother away, for no reason. And now, just listening to you, I'm afraid we have a dangerous road ahead. How will we ever find my mother without being caught ourselves?"

Indigo brought Skye a cup of chamomile tea. "To soothe your nerves," she said. "We're witches. You don't have to worry."

Skye nodded, but she was unconvinced. "I am glad that Garth is safe," she continued. "When we escaped the Guard in the Copse last night, I could scarcely believe our luck. Those armed soldiers were afraid to follow us through the forest. If it wasn't for Trader, we would still be lost in the woods." Skye shivered. She had been so relieved when Trader had known the way to Indigo's cottage after they galloped out of the pitch-dark Copse. "We barely made it here," she said, blinking back tears.

"Sip the tea," Esmeralde said. "Take slow, deep breaths."

Skye held the warm cup close to her face, trying to quell her anxiety as she listened to Esmeralde and Indigo squabble over packing for the trip. Esmeralde thought she had to take everything she owned, because there was no way to tell how long they would be gone. Indigo kept reminding her that they would be guests at their childhood home, where there had always been plenty of pillows and bed linens, crockery and cutlery, and wash basins with soap and towels.

"I doubt they have thrown out that big bathtub in the washroom downstairs," Indigo remarked, examining her smoke-stained hands, and her fingernails rimmed with potting soil. "I could use a hard scrub with plenty of hot water." She wrinkled her nose at Esmeralde. "So could you."

"I bet they don't do laundry," Esmeralde said darkly, stuffing two shifts into a pantry sack already overflowing.

"It won't even take one shiny piece of Northland silver to get a washerwoman to come by the back alley and do all of our laundry."

"Fine." Esmeralde tied the pantry sack, grumbling. "I guess I'm packed."

"We'll take my produce wagon," Indigo decided.

"With us on the ponies behind?" Skye asked.

"No, all five of us should ride together," Esmeralde said. "If we run into soldiers or checkpoints, we can pose as a farm family returning from the fair."

"Do you think that would work?" Indigo asked. "Magic is easier."

"Magic is exhausting, and calls attention to itself," Esmeralde argued. "The fair just ended. There will be plenty of carts returning north today and tomorrow."

Indigo nodded. "It will be easier to lose ourselves in the throng than to use magic to try to pass unseen."

"We could always make the journey separately," Skye suggested.

Esmeralde dismissed this idea with a wave of her hand. "Traveling apart, we're two witches and three children, all easy prey for soldiers looking for any of the Twelve or for new recruits. We will fare better together."

Skye knew that the Northland Guard was already searching for her and Esmeralde and Indigo. Getting what they thought were two teenage boys into the bargain would just sweeten the pot.

Though the wagon was just a rough flatbed, with removable sides for loading baskets of vegetables and sacks of potatoes, it was large. Garth thought he could easily hitch Shep and Chuffer to it in place of Indigo's oxen. The fact that soldiers might take Garth and Trader as conscripts could not be helped. If it came to that, Esmeralde and Indigo planned to don their traveling cloaks and plead like old farm wives. They would use their powers of persuasion, coupled with copious tears, to argue that, as their husbands and older sons had already gone off to war, they needed their younger boys on the farm. If that did not work, they could take stronger measures. Esmeralde stowed these in moss-wrapped glass vials within her Possibles Bag. Although Trader remained silent, Skye wondered how much longer she planned to masquerade as a boy. Skye bet the disguise would not suit Trader for much longer, especially if the Guard tried to detain her.

When Indigo paused from packing to enjoy a smoke and Esmeralde poured herself a cup of cordial, they questioned Skye closely about the events of the past few days. It did not take Skye long to relate what had happened since she and her mother had left Top Notch, although the three days felt like a lifetime. Neither witch appeared surprised that her mother had been abducted or that her father had gone missing. Skye wondered whether they had seen the events foreshadowed in one of Esmeralde's portents or illuminated in Indigo's visions above her dye pot.

What did astound the two witches was the fact that Skye and Garth had chosen a fossicker as a traveling companion, especially a ruffian like Trader. Esmeralde had taken a cursory glance at the ruined medicine bag Trader had thought so valuable. She declared it nothing more than a glorified first-aid kit, lost off a military wagon. A few of Trader's riverbed finds had interested her, however, and Skye had seen Northland silver change hands over what looked to her like a handful of dead leaves and fishing line tied to a bit of burnt wood. Skye had seen Trader look longingly at her mother's rucksack of knitwear; but they both knew that there was no way Trader could sell, nor Esmeralde and Indigo buy, any of that truck, knowing it was Sierra's—even the curious silver box. No one would want to challenge Sierra's ownership, even though she was not there to defend it. The witches would consider the magic hats and bottomless bags and traveling cloak stolen.

Besides, it became evident that they already owned garments like these. Each witch had laid out for the trip a traveling cloak identical to those owned by Sierra and Skye, along with Potluck Hats in shades of pink, blue and green. The children had watched Indigo load a felted market bag full to bursting with dried fruit, shelled nuts, and beef jerky, and still be able to wedge in half a wheel of cheese and a dozen hard-boiled eggs.

"Of course I wanted to mind my booth at the fair," Esmeralde explained to Skye as she finished packing her Possibles Bag. "But all signs pointed north, and now the red sky above the glacier confirms it." She lurched forward.

"What's wrong?" Skye said.

"Did you feel that?" Esmeralde asked Indigo.

"Aye," Indigo replied. "It's like a hand coming down from the clouds, beckoning me. It makes me act like a puppet."

"Well, it's not going to stop until we either show up at the Potluck or someone sends the answering fire, to let Aubergine know we're coming."

"Fat chance of that." Indigo handed Esmeralde a basket of apples.

"Are some of the Twelve not coming?" Skye asked.

"Who knows? Everyone's supposed to," Indigo said. "We've all been called." She gave Skye a quizzical look. "Do you feel anything? It's like rosy fingers; they reach in and pull you."

Skye shrugged. "My chest hurts. She touched a hand to her breastbone. "Here."

Esmeralde nodded. "There's nothing to take for it. Believe me."

Indigo set her market bag by the door. "I doubt we'll see your mother," she said. "The chances are slim to none that she can escape the Guard without her traveling cloak, or these garments of hers you managed to save." She gave Skye a shrewd glance. "Don't let them out of your sight. Or let that no-good Trader talk you into bartering them or selling them for silver."

"I won't," Skye said. "They are worth far more to me than you know."

Esmeralde glared at Indigo. "Indy, why do you badmouth Trader so much? You like the odd thing he brings you. Especially if those things happen to include pipe weed."

"He'd sell his own mother for a copper," Indigo said.

"I don't think Trader has a mother," Skye said. "Mayhap he's an orphan."

"A runaway's more like it," Esmeralde observed, and Indigo laughed.

"He's neither one of the Twelve, nor one of our own," Indigo said. "I don't see why we're taking him. The Potluck is no place for such boys, unless you need the firebox filled or the walkway shoveled."

"I felt the same at first," Skye said, in a small voice. "But Trader saved Garth from the flood, and all of us from the Guard as well. He is not mean spirited, and he is not who he seems to be."

"He is just a lost boy." Esmeralde narrowed her eyes at Indigo. "You should take pity."

"There is someone he wants to find," Skye decided to tell them. "That's why he left his band. He thinks this person might be a prisoner of the Burnt Holes, along with my mother."

Esmeralde adjusted her beret over her unruly curls. The fine merino was dyed jet-black shot through with bits of fuchsia, emerald, and amethyst crystal powder in a colorway she had named The Northern Lights, and it suited her perfectly. Whenever she wore the simple beret, she felt fine about traveling alone or in the dark or on a track she did not know. "Indy, let Trader alone," she said quietly.

Indigo sighed and waved her hand. "Go tell the boys to hitch up the wagon and bring it around front," she said to Skye.

Just then, Esmeralde took another involuntary step forward, Skye put a hand to her chest, and Indigo grabbed onto the table.

"We're coming, already!" Esmeralde yelled at the sky.

Skye roused Garth and Trader from the haymow and helped Garth harness the ponies to the single pole. Garth drove Shep and Chuffer around to the front of the cottage with the wagon. They quickly stowed their belongings in the bed under a piece of oiled canvas, to keep everything dry if it rained.

Indigo settled herself on the wide plank bench, lifted the two sets of reins, and peered up at the sun, an orange disc in the pink sky. "We're more than a day away," she said to no one in particular as she urged the ponies into a trot.

"Hopefully we'll make it to Woolen Woods tonight." Esmeralde said. "Remember that little mead hall there, where they brew their own beer and hard cider?"

"That was years ago," Indigo replied. "I've heard Woolen Woods has turned into a tannery town, full of the stink of sheep dung."

"The smell is the urine they cure the hides with," Esmeralde said.

"Whatever it is, it reeks," Indigo said. "I hope we can make it farther."

Sitting just behind the two, Garth had been following their conversation with great interest. His head bobbed between them, drinking in every word. "I can't wait to see and smell it all," he exclaimed, gripping the wagon's low sideboards. "Indy, I've never been farther north than Banebridge."

"Nor have I," Skye said, watching the scenery go by. She sat comfortably propped against the rails of the wagon behind Indigo, cushioned by her mother's rucksack. The light of this strange day dressed everything around them in a pink haze, as if it had been dusted with colored sugar.

Trader lay sprawled in the back, head resting on a bedroll at the foot of the wagon, chewing on a piece of dried sweetgrass. "Woolen Woods is nothing more than a tannery with a few hired-men's houses surrounding it. It isn't much."

"There's not much to this town, either," Garth said, as the wagon rumbled down the hill and onto the flats toward Banebridge. "But I always liked coming here."

Soon they were at the Trading Post, where Indigo turned the team of ponies toward the high trestle bridge that crossed the River Runne.

"There's Ozzie," Skye said, and they all waved at him.

The storekeeper waved back, looking a little bewildered. They saw him take off his spectacles to rub the lenses clean with his apron.

"He didn't know we all knew each other," Garth smiled. "He can't believe his eyes, even with his magnifiers."

On the main track, they joined the cartloads of folk going home from the fair. There were farmers and craftsmen, food vendors and artisans. Even in this strange light, the atmosphere was more merry than fearful, because most of the wagons contained nothing but folding tables and empty baskets. Even in these hard times, the fair had been prosperous. Many farm families had been able to sell their surplus winter stores of root vegetables and animals for slaughter, exchanging their goods for Northland silver, which almost overnight was becoming the coin of the realm.

The witches decided to rest Chuffer and Shep at the Forks, a well-known bend in the River Runne, where the water flowed east but the main track followed a smaller tributary, called the Trickle, which flowed down from the north through Bordertown. The Trickle was pure glacier run-off, and popular with fossickers. In cold weather, the water did not run at all, Trader explained. Even during some springs the riverbed was dry or just a tiny flow, thus the stream's name. Today the Trickle thundered into the Runne, spewing foul water. A huge wooden sign posted at the entrance to the Forks campground warned, Don't Drink the Water.

"The water is unsafe to drink," Skye said in disbelief, recalling the prediction offered by the hoary-eyed judge's prediction when she had tried to enter her shawl in the Always Alpaca competition. "Would you look at that?"

"That's why I always carry plenty of my own drink," Esmeralde nodded, patting the flask of cordial at her side.

Indigo cleared her throat loudly, as she swung the wagon off the track and into the Forks. She pulled up alongside several other carts. Travelers on horseback or foot had also stopped for a bite to eat or a rest. She nodded toward an old man dipping buckets into the Runne just before the bend in the river. "Only the Trickle is fouled," she noticed. "The water upriver seems fine."

Garth hopped down and Skye handed him the ponies' water buckets. Across the way, she saw an old woman pouring cups of sweet tea from the tailgate of a tiny pony cart, and a young family hunkered over cold roast chicken in a large covered wagon, pulled by a mismatched pair of draft horses. There was even a vendor popping kettle corn in an oiled pot over a small blaze, offering rolled paper cones and sprinkles of sugar to anyone with a few coppers.

Small children and farm dogs frolicked through the new grass and budding flowers along the riverbank, but little frivolity disturbed the group of men smoking around the fire pit. Skye guessed that they were talking about the bloody sky and what it might mean.

Indigo wasted no time to get in on the gossip. As soon as the wagon rolled to a stop, she handed the ponies' reins back to Skye and pulled out one of her foul-smelling, hand-rolled Smokies. Soon she was striding across the clearing to join the travelers smoking at the edge of the fire pit. Esmeralde hopped down from the bench and took a nip from her flask before rummaging under the canvas tarp for mead cups. She handed the heavy market bag of food up to Skye.

"Break out something for your lunch," she said, collecting two crockery cups and her Possibles bag. She nodded toward Indigo. "I'll be back in a few."

It wasn't until Skye began laying out their places for lunch that it occurred to her that Trader had disappeared. She had slept the whole way to the Forks, but now she was gone, and so was her knapsack.

Skye scanned the folk along the riverbank. Trader wasn't with Garth, who was dipping water for the ponies, and she hadn't joined Indigo and Esmeralde, palavering with the group around the ring of blackened stones. She wasn't hanging around the corn vendor or the tea seller. Skye was about to give up looking when she caught sight of a new group from the corner of her eye. There was Trader, with her packsack of odds and ends spread out on the ground in front of a few old men gathered around a string of riding horses at a hitching post. Whatever she had, it looked like the men wanted it. They picked through her items with interest. Skye was so mad that her face flushed red. What if Trader called attention to herself? What if she got them all in trouble just to make a few coppers? Holding the ponies, Skye watched helplessly, waiting for Garth to return with the water, while the two witches chatted away and Trader hawked her treasures. At last Garth returned, slopping water over the rims of the buckets.

"Look to Trader!" Skye hissed.

Garth squinted in the weird light as the ponies nosed at the water. "What's he doing?"

"Selling stuff," Skye said. "Or getting in trouble. I don't know which." She handed the ponies' ropes to Garth.

"Skye, don't go over there," Garth said, steadying her arm, his eyes on the men surrounding Trader.

As they watched, Trader finished her transactions. She packed her wares and turned toward them with a smile and a wink and a fistful of coins. She stopped at the kettle corn stand and moseyed back to the wagon with a cone of sugared treats.

"That was slick," she said, munching popcorn and offering the rolled cone to Skye and Garth. "I don't care what your witches say. I knew that fossick was worth something."

"What did you sell them?" Garth took a handful of popcorn.

"It was all that military stuff I showed you. There was that medicine bag, and the Skell dice, a road pass, and it turns out those bits of ivory were commissary chits. I guess chits are as good as money in Bordertown, better in some of the alehouses."

"It's illegal to sell such items," Skye said. "If you find chits or passes, you're supposed to turn them in."

"Oh, like anybody does," Trader said, with a wave of her hand. "Really."

As they watched, the group around the fire broke up abruptly. Indigo and Esmeralde hurried back to the wagon.

"Time to go," Indigo said, dumping the water the ponies hadn't drunk out on the ground. She took the leads from Skye. "Hop in."

"We haven't eaten yet," Garth said, stacking the water buckets into the back of the wagon.

"Eat on the road," Esmeralde replied, mounting the bench beside Indigo. "There's a checkpoint up ahead at Woolen Woods, and we've got to get around it before dark."

"Can't we just pretend to be a family?' Trader asked. "I can be a girl."

"Apparently the Guard knows that the reason for the red sky is that the Twelve have been called," Indigo said. "They're looking for us, not you."

"I told you there was an interloper," Esmeralde muttered.

"Or an intruder." Indigo turned to Trader. "I saw you talking to those men," she said fiercely.

Esmeralde glowered. "If we find out you're the one who's been selling secrets, I'll put a pox on you so harsh that you'll lie in bed sweating in your sheets all summer."

"I've done nothing, truly." Trader raised her hands to show open, innocent palms.

Indigo slapped the reins and the wagon lurched forward. "You'd better be right."

Esmeralde pointed at a lone rider up ahead, wearing a brimmed hat. "Follow him, on the bay gelding. He knows the way around."

"Are you sure?" Skye asked.

Esmeralde nodded. "I put a pinch of truth powder in the glass of cordial I gave him." She smiled craftily. "No one can resist my cordial. It works every time."

"What's the damage?" Indigo asked.

"Five pieces of Northland silver. One for each of us," Esmeralde replied.

"Before or after?" Trader asked.

"After we make it through." Esmeralde smiled knowingly at Trader. "If we are caught, he gets nothing."

Trader gave a nod of approval. "Good deal," she said.

The route around the checkpoint turned out to be a game trail, muddy and meandering. Even with a guide, it took them most of the afternoon. The wagon got mired in a rivulet that ran along the path and they all had to climb out. While Garth splashed around to the ponies' heads and urged them through the icy water, the others pushed the wagon from behind.

The old man on the bay gelding was true to his word. Wet and tired, the group and their mud-spattered wagon finally emerged into a pasture where dairy goats were cropping new grass. Shep and Chuffer were used to such animals and paid them no mind. After the ponies were unhitched, all they wanted were the tender shoots of green timothy. The three young people watched as Esmeralde counted out five pieces of shiny Northland silver and handed them to Indigo, who lit a smoke and walked to the pasture gate with their guide. After a short discussion, the man tipped his hat and bid them farewell.

Indigo came back with directions. "He said Woolen Woods is just up the track," Indigo pointed. "We get to the fork, and then bear left past the sheepskin tannery into town."

Esmeralde shaded her eyes against the glare of the sun beginning to set in the dusky pink sky. "We should either stop for the night or drive straight through."

Nodding, Indigo blew a stream of smoke. "Woolen Woods is no place to be after dark, when the mills close down and the alehouses open," she agreed, eyeing Trader and Garth. "Not for boys, anyway."

"I can take care of myself." Trader shrugged. "Stop if you want, I'm game."

"As can I," Garth chimed in, grinning at Trader. His eyes sparkled with excitement. "I'm game, too."

"It's not a game," Skye said. "So stop acting foolish."

"What are you so mad about?" Trader asked.

"Soldiers are looking for boys," Skye shot Trader a warning glance. "Like my brother." She turned to Garth. "Do you want to get taken away in a rolling cage by the Guard, like Warren did?"

Garth looked at the ground. "No," he said, under his breath.

"Come on, then," Skye yanked him up by his elbow, and glared at Trader. "It's time that you boys saw to the ponies."

As Skye stalked away, Indigo glanced at Trader. Esmeralde uncorked her flask and took a nip before pulling the mead cups from her pack. "Indy, let's relax for a bit and then move on after the horses are rested."

"My, your call is strong," Indigo joked.

Esmeralde poured cordial and handed a cup to Indigo. "We could be at the Southern Gate of Bordertown by tomorrow evening," she said. "I doubt any of the others will get to Riverwalk as quickly."

"Barring anything unforeseen," Indigo agreed, clinking her cup against Esmeralde's. "Like checkpoints and muddy rivers."

"Once we step inside the city walls, you have no worries," Trader said airily, watching the witches drink the liquor. "I know every nook and cranny in the Seven Boroughs."

"Do you, now?" Indigo said, blowing glacier weed smoke into the air.

"Ugh." Esmeralde waved it away.

"It's no worse than the stink of the tannery," Indigo said, holding her cup high. "Bottoms up!"

"I know Riverwalk, Winter Watch, Merchant's Pass, and Artisan's Hand like the back of my own hand," Trader boasted. She waved her hand toward Skye and Garth. "I'm not like these country bumpkins. I was born on the streets."

"It's been twenty years since we've been inside the city walls," Esmeralde reminded Indigo, as she wiped her mouth.

"There's the Guard, and who knows what else, looking for us," Indigo agreed.

Esmeralde gave Trader a crafty look. "Can you sneak us into Merchants' Row quickly, without attracting notice?"

"Not with horses that look like that," Trader said, pointing to the ponies being brushed by Skye and Garth.

"Forget about the mountain ponies," Indigo threw down her smoke and stamped it out. Finding her cup empty, she reached for Esmeralde's flask. "We'll stable them elsewhere."

"We have a plan," Esmeralde's face was flushed with cordial. "And it's not a nice one, I'm afraid," she said, with a tipsy smile.

"It would upset Skye," Indigo agreed, wagging her finger, "For she is her mother's daughter." She let her voice drop to a whisper. "Our plan is not nice," she told Trader. "Not nice at all."

Trader laughed. "Well, that could be almost any plan that I've ever heard of. What is yours, exactly?"

Esmeralde eyed Indigo. "What's the harm in speaking freely? He is just a boy."

"No," Indigo disagreed, with a shake of her head. "He is a turncoat and crafty. They don't call him Traitor for nothing."

Trader got up, climbed into the wagon, and disappeared into the bed. "Suit yourself," she called, feigning disinterest.

Esmeralde cupped her hand and put her lips to Indigo's ear. "There is no harm in telling him that we are going to take over the Potluck," she hissed, her breath laced with sweet wine. "It's the truth."

"I know it's true," Indigo conceded, draining Esmeralde's flask. "I was there when we concocted the plan."

"We saw ourselves in a true vision. Everyone will know soon enough."

Trader's unruly head popped up over the sideboard of the wagon. "What kind of vision? Are you two having one right now?"

"No," Indigo said. "We're having drinks. You can only have a vision over a proper simmer."

Trader turned to Esmeralde. "What's a simmer?"

"It's a crystal-boil where you see the future," she explained. "You search for clues to your destiny in the steam over a dye pot."

"We saw ourselves, and we were ruling the Potluck better than Aubergine ever did," Indigo could not hold her tongue. "Two heads are better than one."

"Did you notice?" Esmeralde plucked at Indigo's sleeve. "When we conjured up our destiny, there was no need to summon all Twelve.

Smokey Jo was wrong. You can have a true vision over a simmer, even with just two of us."

"And without Aubergine's great pot," Indigo added. "We used my little soup kettle and it worked just fine."

Trader laughed out loud. "What did you see yourselves doing in the soup pot? Did you just throw on some magic knits and take over?" She pointed to Esmeralde's Possibles Bag. "Or make them drink one of your strange potions cut with wine? Do you forget that they are witches, too?"

"Our vision was true and good," Indigo said irritably. "All we need to do is make them our offer."

"They will all see reason," Esmeralde assured her. "Especially if we reach the Potluck first and assume our new roles. Aubergine is old and forgetful, and Smokey Jo is nothing more than an impish pyromaniac."

"I thought she was born a gypsy child," Indigo interrupted, bleary-eyed. "Or a changeling, perhaps."

"You remember. She's a gnome," Esmeralde explained. "They are small, like imps. Pyromaniacs play with fire."

"Well, she does do that." Indigo eyed Trader. "Did you know that girl always smelled liked bacon? She could disappear into smoke."

"And that is not someone fit to rule the Potluck when it is time for Aubergine to step down," Esmeralde declared.

"It is time," Indigo said solemnly.

"Past time. Thus our plan, remember?"

The wobbly witches watched Skye and Garth make their way back across the goat pasture to the wagon, leading the ponies.

"Pack up. We're riding through, just as you wished," Esmeralde told Skye, who smiled.

Indigo tapped Trader on the chest. "Not a word of this yet," she warned.

Trader shrugged. "What's in it for me?"

Indigo sized him up. "Treat the two of us well and we'll see what's in it for you, fossicker boy."

Esmeralde's Jaunty Beret

A BERET PATTERN

Knit this advanced-beginner-skill-level adult beret to protect you when you're traveling alone. This pattern comes in one size only.

Get the pattern from PotluckYarn.com/epatterns

Mae shone the blazing beam straight into his eyes,
then turned and fled.

CHAPTER 16

A Rude Awakening

WARREN AWOKE WITH A START IN PITCH DARK, with no recollection of where he was, unsure if it was day or night. He lay wrapped in unfamiliar blankets, atop rushes rancid with age. At his feet, the fire had died to embers in an untended hearth, and all around him the air was frosty. Even beneath the musty blankets, his back felt frozen. He burrowed his fingers into the thin padding beneath his bedroll and touched ice. The day's events came back to him and he remembered he was in Lavender Mae's lair, a cavern deep in the Northland Glacier.

With a yawn, Warren wiped the sleep from his eyes. It seemed to him that the years had not treated Mae as well as they had his mother. At some point, maybe not so long ago, Mae had clearly lost her mind. He assumed that she had been affected gradually, beginning when she had stumbled upon the legendary Crystal Caves while searching for the lost crystal. Warren put together scraps of information from his mother's stories. Perhaps the familiars called Watchers or even the ancients themselves had cursed Mae for trespassing, plaguing her mind with their reawakened voices. He imagined that eventually their incessant murmurings had overpowered Mae's sense of herself and driven her crazy.

From the legends his mother had told, Warren knew of the First Folk, who lay entombed in a vast chamber beyond the enchanted caves of colored rock. According to legend, they had perished in an age of ice, taking the remnants of their civilization and the secrets of the magic crystals with them. For years, fossickers and adventurers from all the lands had searched for the entrance to the mystical Crystal Caves. Most did not return. Those who did had failed to find a way in. As far as Warren knew, no one but Mae had come back from the frozen caverns alive, if he could call her madness living.

As he recalled where he was, Warren remembered that he had made a promise generated by what now seemed like shortsighted chivalry. He had promised Mae that he would safeguard her back to the only one he believed could help her, and that was the Potluck witch, Aubergine. Even though practical magic was now a lost art, and using it was an offense that would get a person jailed, during his training at the garrison Warren had learned that many still called Aubergine the Potluck Queen—usually derisively, and never to her face. At the garrison, the recruits' whispered joke in the barracks at night was that the Dark Queen sought to rule everything that the Potluck Queen and her half-pint sidekick had not already lost or misplaced over the years.

However, Warren had also learned that there was a strange connection between Aubergine and the Northland Guard, because the old knitting witch had been seen entering the garrison late at night. Rumors abounded that she secretly ruled the last magical stronghold in the Middlelands; although most folk believed she only ran a yarn shop.

Warren threw off his dank covers and sat up, as his eyes adjusted to the layers of gloom in the cave. He recalled that he had intended to take a short afternoon nap, before beginning the southern trek to Bordertown with Mae under the cover of darkness. The fact that he was hungry and had to empty his bladder led him to believe exhaustion had taken over, and that he had slept much longer than he intended. He groped for the glowing rock that Mae had given him to light their path through the winding tunnels of the glacier. The chunk of pink quartz was gone. So, he feared, was Mae.

"Mae," he called, crouching on all fours as he slapped around blindly for her bedroll. When he reached it, he found the rumpled blankets empty and the sheets without any trace of warmth. His hand closed around Mae's wool afghan, a curious knit patchwork of mitered squares constructed in garter stitch from odd balls of yarn that Mae had collected over the years. When she had taken the blanket from the chair by the fire it had looked smaller than a lap robe, but when she lay down to sleep, it covered her entire body.

The base magic within simple household things knit from crystal-dyed yarn had always amazed Warren. Mae was not a talented fiber artist—that was obvious. A child could have patched together the afghan. But she had apparently colored the wool with ground crystal mixed with boiling glacier water, something he had seen his mother do many times, and which he knew gave the patchwork piece a little power. Now that the afghan was unneeded, it had become no bigger than a baby's blanket.

Warren realized that his offer to guide Mae, although gallant, might turn into complete folly if he tried to carry it out. He was branded a deserter, with a price on his head. Besides, how could he protect Mae when he couldn't even keep track of her in the ice caves? He had never met Aubergine, nor did he know his way around Bordertown. That settlement was huge, divided into boroughs that ran from the town center like wagon spokes. He had no clue which of the seven pie-shaped districts housed Aubergine's shop. In Bordertown, he was only familiar with the borough of Winter Watch, which was closest to the garrison. Wandering unfamiliar neighborhoods with a cackling crone, while searching for a knitting witch who lived behind a defunct yarn shop, would shift more than a few glances his way. Warren heaved a sigh. He would have to come up with a different way to save Mae.

But first he had to find her.

His fingers strayed across the abandoned pile of coats and tunics that Mae had worn on the battlefield—was that earlier today, or already yesterday? He felt a uniform sleeve, festooned with pins and emblems. What if Mae was scavenging again? Worse yet, what if she had been lured off toward the Crystal Caves by the voices of the dead?

How could he find Mae without losing himself? He needed the old witch as much as she needed him, and perhaps more. Alone, he couldn't even retrace his steps and get out of here.

If she had ventured into the Crystal Caves, he could do nothing for her. Even if he could find her, he had no defense against the Watchers or the dead who lightly slumbered. What if he disturbed some of the ancients and they invaded his mind as well? The only knitted thing that might ward off danger was the furry watch cap Mae had given him. But he didn't know if it contained any crystalline magic at all.

Warren stood and felt his way to the mouth of the cave. "Mae!" he called, but the only answer was his own voice echoing, "Mae, Mae, Mae, Mae, Mae," in lessening waves until her name was only a dark whisper.

"Fire and ice," he swore softly. After relieving himself in the tunnel, he crept back into the low cave, where he stumbled across his gear. He laced his heavy, nailed glacier boots and shrugged into the outer tunic of his Guard uniform, securing it with his oiled climbing belt. From his rucksack, he broke out a ration of deer jerky and chewed slowly. The idea of waiting here, hoping Mae would return, made him uneasy. The solitary witch might have several hideouts in this glacier, or maybe she spent more time roaming the Crystal Caves than she had let on.

Warren counted up what he knew. Quite by accident, Mae had found the forbidden caves and inadvertently awakened the ancients. A scouting party of Lowlanders had broken into the chasms as well and begun to plunder the graves of the First Folk. He added his fear that soon the Dark Queen would amass enough troops to return and ravage the ancient tombs in search of powerful crystals and secrets of old to conquer all.

As a sledder in his youth and later as a scout in the Guard, Warren had witnessed bands of Lowlanders on the move. Many of them were masters of infiltration, able to move quietly and quickly as a group, because they talked with their eyes. There were thousands of them, and he suspected they would return in full force in a matter of weeks. What chance did Mae have to save the First Folk from desecration? What chance did any of them have to protect the ancient secrets?

Warren swallowed the last of his jerky and took a swig from his water skin. Somehow, he would have to escape this glacial maze and get word back to the garrison in Bordertown without attracting notice. He had no delusions about tracking Mae. He knew he would find her only if she wanted him to. Even if he did manage to get back to daylight without Mae's help, who would pay attention to his warning? Certainly not his company commander, a surly man called Tanner who would sooner jail him than listen to him. During his short stay at the garrison, he had made few friends. Many of the other conscripts were frightened farm boys from the Western Highlands or deckhands from the fisheries of the Far East, slow to learn sled craft. They had little appreciation for a trainer barely older than themselves who had won the Winter Games. He had only found one real friend, Niles, a Northland youth who was almost as skilled with a bobsled as he was. Niles was probably the only recruit from his unit who would not report him on sight.

Warren shoved what little gear he had into his rucksack. The Lowlanders had his sled. He might never see it again. As an afterthought, Warren went into the back of the cave and rummaged around until he had a good-sized handful of crystals from one of Mae's lidless trunks. He might need them for barter, a bribe, or simply to prove the truth of his story.

Outside Mae's cave, he hastily disguised the opening with the fallen stalactite and turned to the right, going up the icy passageway toward what he hoped would be the outer world. Though his eyes had adjusted to the dark as much as they could, he had to move slowly in the gloom. Even with his hands stretched out in front of him, he kept hitting his head against outcroppings of ice or stone. He couldn't even tell where the walls were. Warren climbed, keeping the sound of rushing water underfoot and to his right, remembering the unnerving vibration of the hidden river below and to his left when he descended through the tunnels behind Mae.

For a while, Warren felt hopeful. As he moved through chasm after chasm, he sensed that he was rising steadily. He thought he felt fresh air stirring through a side passage, so he turned in that direction. The tunnel grew lighter, and the icy walls began to stand out from their dusky surroundings. He no longer had to reach out his hands to keep from hitting his head. A chilly breeze began to whistle through the cave, ruffling the hair that stuck out beneath his snowflake watch cap. Encouraged, he climbed faster, relishing the rush of cold air and the light, which seemed to grow brighter with each step.

Suddenly the passage dead-ended in a cavern filled with wind and alive with blood-colored light. In the ceiling far above he saw a hole, a natural skylight intensely illuminated with an eerie red glow. Warren thought the light came from outside the glacier, but it was so strange he could not tell if it shone with daybreak or sunset. Behind the wailing wind he heard a distant hiss and pop, as if there were an enormous bonfire, perhaps consuming everything beyond this barren place from which it seemed he could not escape.

As Warren gazed upward and wondered if he would find his way out to discover he was the only being left alive, soot began to sift through the shaft, coating the ice around his feet in fine ash. As a child, he had watched fireworks displays on the eve of each New Year. Before the war, the Trading Post would bring in wagonloads of sparklers and bottle rockets that the Banebridge townsfolk would set off from the trestle bridge over the River Runne. Those fireworks welcomed the New Year with a festive rainbow of colors. This burning red light looked more like warning than welcome.

Suddenly, he remembered an old nursery rhyme, from a fishwives' ditty: Red sky at night, sailors' delight. Red sky in morning, sailors take warning. Shivering, Warren gazed at the blazing sky beyond the icy vault, realizing that whether it was night or morning didn't matter, because he was miserably lost.

Even though time seemed to stand still within the glacier, Warren bet it took him the better part of an hour to get back to the dark passage from which he had turned into the dead-end tunnel. He again turned right and started climbing. Before long it became obvious that someone was on the path behind him. First he heard the sound of booted feet tripping drunkenly up the incline. Then an orb of light bobbed past his head to flick across the contours of the passage in front of him.

When he heard a cackle of laughter, he turned. "Mae," he said, his voice flooded with relief, followed by anger. "Where were you?"

"Were you, were you, were you," his echo mimicked.

Mae stopped, holding her pink quartz high over her head. She looked more agitated than usual, if that was possible. Although her face was hidden by shadows, he could see that her free hand kept straying to her breast, as if she were suffering from heartburn or indigestion. She lurched toward him for no apparent reason, and then, scowling to herself, scuttled back.

"Mae, what's wrong?" He said, starting toward her.

She shone the blazing beam straight into his eyes, then turned and fled.

Staggering back, Warren put his hands to his face. "You crazy witch!" In her lair, she'd left him sightless as a bat, and now she'd tried to blind him.

When he opened his eyes all that remained of Mae's presence was a trace of light flickering far down the corridor. In a moment, he would both lose her and be in the dark again.

"No, you don't," he growled.

He began to run as fast as his nailed boots would permit, the sound of steel on ice ringing down the passage with each step. Mae stayed just out of sight, skittering around a slippery corner or ducking into a crevice. More than once he had to retrace his steps to pick up her trail. Following her bobbing light, he chased her through cave after cave until they were both exhausted. Finally Mae skidded to a stop within the entrance to a large cavern. Warren had no idea where they were. Pausing to catch his breath, he watched Mae turn toward him abruptly, as if pulled by an unseen force. Her movement reminded him of metal filings drawn to a magnet.

"Nooooooo!" Mae howled, clutching at her breast.

She wore a tattered lace-up jacket that looked as if it had been salvaged from an old Guard uniform. It hung to her knees, as big as an overcoat. She tore at the rotted laces, ripping them savagely.

"No, no, no," she muttered.

"Mae." Warren held out his palms to her. He edged closer. "Mae, look at me."

Mae fixed him with a glare of hate. "No," she spat.

As she turned to escape into the dark void, Warren tackled her from behind. The glowing crystal flew from her hand and skittered away, leaving them in shadows. Mae's breath collapsed with a whoosh and she fell over like a rag doll. Fearing that she was faking but also worried that he had hurt her, Warren pulled the thin length of braided rope off his climbing belt and secured it around her waist, so they were bound at the hip.

"Try to get away now," he taunted, stepping back so that the line pulled tight. Instead of scrambling to her feet, Mae lay flat on the ice and bit at her tether, snarling like a cornered animal.

Inside the lip of the immense ice cavern, the pink quartz rose from where it had fallen and bathed them in its eerie light. Holding out his hand to shield his eyes from the glow, Warren watched the orb begin to bob toward them. It moved slowly, while Mae whimpered like a puppy, refusing to rise, even slapping away his hand when he offered it.

He prodded her with the toe of his boot. "Mae, get up," he said.

Instead she moaned and twitched further from him. Her involuntary lurch jerked the cord so tight that Warren was surprised she could still breathe.

As the beacon floated closer, he began to panic. Why wouldn't Mae get up? He tried to lift her, but that only led to more biting. He cursed his own stupidity for binding them together, for she had become a human anchor. He didn't have time to undo the knots and leave her. Hesitantly, he unsheathed his climbing pick. It was against sledding lore to cut good, braided rope. With the other athletes at the Winter Games, he had even sworn an oath against it. But this was no game and it was time to run.

As he bent to hack the rope, the magic crystal blazed just inches away. Fierce light flooded over him into to the corridor beyond, toward which Mae kept jerking in fits and starts. She blinked in the brightness, a secret smile on her dazed face.

"Mae," she said, closing her eyes to bask in the rosy glow. "Oh, yes."

"What in cracked crystal?" Warren swore angrily, tightening his grip on the ice pick. He would use it as a weapon if he must. "What now?"

The air behind the shining quartz began to ripple. Warren raised the pick overhead and stopped in shock as he watched his mother, or a ghost that looked like her, appear in front of them.

"That's no way to greet your kin," Sierra said, pulling down the hood of her traveling cloak and stepping forward to embrace her son.

"Mother!" The pick clattered to the ice. "What did you . . .?" His voice trailed away as his eyes took in the crystal in her hand and the familiar multicolored mantle she wore. "How did you . . . .?" Then he made the connection. "Your traveling knits harbor magic," he accused.

Sierra laughed. "They always did."

"What about this hat?" Warren touched the snowflake fur cap Mae had given him. "All it's really done is keep my head warm."

"If that's what you think," Sierra said, as Mae scrambled to her feet to hug Sierra, pulling so hard on the rope that Warren almost fell over.

"Mae!" She hung her skinny arms around Sierra's neck and squeezed tight. "Mae, Mae, Mae!"

"I'm glad to see you again, too, Mae," Sierra said, trying to pry her off gently.

As Mae loosened her grip and lurched away, Sierra took a deep breath and put a hand to her chest. "She's acting a little stranger than I remembered," she admitted.

"She's no more crazy than usual," Warren replied, tugging on the cord around Mae's waist to keep her from wandering farther. "Of course, now she's got the voices of the First Folk in her head. But she's used to it." He turned to Sierra, unable to prevent anger from creeping into his voice. "I guess you know all about that."

"Untie her." Sierra searched his face. It wasn't just the stubble on his chin or the look in his steely eyes that made him look older. Truth could age a person. "I don't know how much you've gleaned in the few months you've been gone," she began.

"More than I ever thought possible," Warren answered, his blue eyes flashing. "You should have told us who you were. You are The Keeper of the Tales, aren't you? The only knitting witch alive entrusted with all of the yarns?"

"So they say." Sierra felt her cheeks burning.

"Well, I should not have had to hear your own tale told by a toothless trustee passing out washrags in the garrison," he said. "I didn't know whether to believe him or not until I heard a similar story from a barmaid at an alehouse, and then an old Guardsman visiting his son in the infirmary. They all say the same thing, Sierra Blue."

Still tethered by the climbing rope, Mae began to worm her way between them. As they argued, her face began to crumple, as if she fought tears.

"I have had no choice but to live my life as it was fated," Sierra began, already aware that her son would not understand, for she saw his path as clearly as her own. His time had not yet come to decide if he dared to tempt fate or not.

"I am your son, not a pawn." Warren interrupted. "First father used me, to guide the Dark Queen's Lowlanders. Then, after I got caught on the military road, you let the Guard take me away in a rolling cage."

Sierra shook her head slowly. "I have no power over the Guard."

"You are the next witch in line!" Warren shot back. "That is what they all say."

"I was next in line," Sierra said. "There's a difference."

"Your Northland Guard trained me," Warren thumped his chest. "They trained me well. Do you know what they trained me for? To become Lowland fodder. They trained me to die." He threw up his hands. "Now here I am, lost, with a crazy old witch, a mother I don't know, and a price on my head."

Sierra eyed him silently. Flecks of gold stood out in her irises and her face took on the long-range look Warren had learned to fear as a child. Sierra turned her gaze on Warren and wrapped her traveling cloak tight. "Are you through?" she said. "Because there are a few things I would have you know. Then we must leave this place. Time is short."

Afraid he had already said too much, Warren looked away from her.

"The soldiers of the Guard are not my allies. They arrested me," Sierra told him quietly. "They took me away in a rolling cage, the same as they took you. Until this morning, I was imprisoned in the Burnt Holes."

Warren raised his eyes. "No one ever escapes from the Burnt Holes," he whispered.

"So they say." Sierra's voice was hard. "I see that you are now a man, no longer a boy. So do not whine to me like a spoiled youth about your troubles, for everything that happens does so for a reason. We all have plenty of misfortune," she said, laying her hand on Mae's shoulder. "Some more than others."

The slight figure swayed between them with her hands over her ears, her eyes bright with unshed tears.

"I'm sorry," he said.

"Free her, then." Sierra said, more gently. "Let her off your leash. She's one of the Twelve, not a dog."

"As you say." Warren bent to untie the rope. "But she'll try to get away. She always does." Mae twitched a step toward the corridor, pulling the line tight again. "See?" He said grimly.

Sierra put her arm around Mae and smoothed her ragged hair. "She's not trying to run off."

"Mae," Mae purred, settling her head against Sierra's chest.

"Lavender Mae has been called," Sierra explained. "All twelve of us have. When the summons calls you, it feels like a hand reaching for your heart, pulling you forward." She peered past him into the gloom. "I hazard that you did not see the fire in the sky this morning?"

"Was that what I glimpsed through an air shaft? A blood-red light filled the cavern."

As Warren freed her, Mae jerked away, only to scramble back and clutch at Sierra's skirt.

Warren looped the rope back around his climbing belt.

"The red dawn is Aubergine's doing," Sierra said. "She is calling the Twelve to the Potluck. All these years, Smokey Jo saved cold-fire crystals, smoldering in a box, to use as a signal if Aubergine needed to bring us together." She gazed at Mae, who clung to her leg. "That's what you saw in the sky. The lure is involuntary unless someone sends the answering fire."

"You can't stop yourself from going?" Warren asked in alarm. "None of you?"

"Only if one of us sends the crystals from a corresponding box skyward. The answering fire releases us from the call, by letting Aubergine know we are coming."

"Who has the other crystals?" Warren asked. "The Dark Queen? Or does Aubergine herself keep them somewhere safe?"

"Until a few days ago, the answering fire was in my care," Sierra said. She seemed painfully tired.

"You?" Warren asked, dumbfounded. "Why you? You lived as a farm wife, not a witch."

"If that's how it looked to you, then I did a good job."

Peering up at her, Mae nodded vigorously. "Mae," she agreed. "Mae."

Sierra eyed Warren coolly. "I harbored that box of cold-fire crystals until I was arrested at the fair."

"The Guard arrested you in Middlemarch?" Warren snorted in disdain. "Why? Did you give someone wrong change, or something?"

"I wish," Sierra laughed without humor. "No, I was accused of using magic, what else?"

"Well, were you? Magic has been forbidden. That includes at the fairgrounds."

"Of course I was," Sierra said, with irritation. "I do it every day. But not in a way mere soldiers could discern."

As Mae began to cackle, Sierra paused and spoke directly to her. "Someone has betrayed us, dear."

Then she turned back to her son. "The Northland Guard is hunting down the Twelve. Before they forced me from my stall, the soldiers were watching Esmeralde's stand as well. Fortunately, she never showed." She looked at him grimly. "The men who led me away knew who I was. They know who all of us are."

"I have heard it said that the Guard is on the hunt for knitting witches," her son confirmed. "But I don't know why. What happened to the crystals? Did the soldiers take them?"

Sierra shook her head. "I hid the box from them. I think your sister wards it now."

"Skye?" Warren asked with a frown. "She seems too young. She prefers hair ribbons to magic." Fingering the scrap of bloody silk in his mitt, Warren did not mention that he had found Averill.

Sierra shrugged. "Skye has no power to use cold-fire crystals. She has not learned the lore. Not yet, anyway."

"Yet? What do you mean, yet?"

"I expect you will see your sister when we reach Bordertown," Sierra sighed. "I have seen her, and your brother Garth, in my mind's eye. They have been wending their way north in the company of Esmeralde and Indigo Rose."

"My sister is a knitting witch?" Warren asked. "My baby brother, too?"

Sierra shook her head. "The power of the Twelve passes only from mother to daughter, or aunt to niece."

"What about someone like Mae?"

"If there is no female heir, the dye mistress is free to appoint a girl child as a ward," Sierra replied, unsurprised at his ignorance. "Your sister is not ready to become one of the Twelve, but she may have to act as one." She gave Warren a wry smile, indicating herself and Mae. "Some of us are missing."

Mae twitched away once more, with an exhausted cry of discomfort. Sierra gave her shoulder a gentle squeeze.

"I know," she murmured to Mae. "I feel it too, but less so in my cloak." Holding the glowing crystal before her, she turned toward the cavern from which she had come. "You will feel better if we start walking in the right direction. Come this way."

"Wait," Warren warned, recalling the rumor that Aubergine was in league with the Guard. "What if this summons is a trap? Do you know why you are called?"

"At this late date, I can barely hazard a guess," Sierra admitted. "We expected to be summoned long ago."

"I may know why," Warren said, recalling the stones he had pilfered from Mae's lair. "Perhaps Aubergine has called you because she has learned what I just found out from Mae."

"Mae?" Sierra asked.

Frightened, Mae buried her face in Sierra's skirt. "Mae," she squeaked.

Stroking Mae's head, Sierra asked, "What is it?"

"The Lowlanders have discovered the passage to the ancients." Warren's eyes blazed. "Mother, the Crystal Caves are real. The Dark Queen's toadies are grave robbers who desecrate and plunder First Folk tombs. I have proof in my rucksack. And Mae has seen the broken coffin lids with her own eyes."

"Oh, I know the Caves have been breached." Sierra gave Mae a sidelong glance. "They've been breached for a long time, haven't they, dear?"

Mae hung her head. "Mae," she quavered.

"I saw a First Folk dervish circling the glacier outside the Burnt Holes this morning," Sierra continued. "The Lowland raiders you mention must have stolen it from an ancient's tomb to offer as a prize to Tasman." She smiled with satisfaction. "But it escaped somehow. A dervish is will always seek out its First Folk family."

"What's a dervish?"

"According to legend, the dervish was a winged beast raised by ancient royalty. Every family of royal lineage harbored one for protection. Common folk called such familiars Watchers. When the last descendant of a line died with no heir, the dervish was buried along with its family, to watch over its members as they slipped into the land of dreams."

"Dervish," Mae nodded.

"That's right," Sierra said. "One does not see one every day."

Mae took another involuntary step toward the corridor and Sierra grabbed her arm to pull her back into the cavern. "The call grows stronger," she said, leading Mae along. "Come, we have to go."

"How will we ever find our way out?" Warren asked, trailing behind. He pointed back toward the corridor. "She wants to go that way," he lifted his chin. "You lead us this way."

Mae gave him a blank stare and patted her pouch.

"Mae's got her crystals, to guide her through the glacier," Sierra explained. She hiked up her long skirt to reveal the knee socks that barely showed above her boots. "My secret socks know another way through the caves." She whispered to Mae, "My path is faster."

Warren hooted with laughter. "Her shards of broken rock and your magic knits argue with each other?"

Sierra shrugged. "My socks are knit from fiber spun from the ruff of the alpine musk ox, then dyed with ground crystals and the shells of glacier insects. The combination of red ocher and cochineal will never steer you wrong."

"Sorry I asked." Warren took the crystal his mother handed him.

"There's our path." She pointed toward the cavern from which she had come. "We'll leave through the Burnt Holes. It's quicker."

Warren stopped short. "Mother, the Burnt Holes are a prison. You escaped only hours ago, and I'm a wanted man. Maybe we should heed the advice of Mae's crystals."

"This passage is faster," Sierra said. "And we are short on time."

"It's dangerous," Warren countered.

"Not now, for after they saw the dervish all the soldiers fled back to Bordertown." Sierra fingered the hood of her traveling cloak. Mae cackled and patted the bulging pouch hanging from her neck.

Warren backed away. "Do not use your magic knits on me, either of you," he warned. "I will follow on my own."

Sierra waited until they had safely picked their way through the cavern before she released Mae's arm. To her relief, Mae skipped ahead happily. "You keep saying you are wanted," she mentioned to her son. "What did you do?"

"I deserted my unit," Warren replied. "A few of the other scouts saw Mae scavenging their dead in a valley and vowed to kill her. I guessed who she was, so I slipped away to warn her."

"No soldier can kill her," Sierra said gravely, watching Mae.

"I wish I'd known that."

"I suspect that Aubergine is not calling us to the Potluck because the Lowlanders have gotten into the Caves," Sierra said. "Although that surely has something to do with why she summoned us. I'm not sure, but perhaps Mae holds the key."

Mae skipped back. "No, no, no," she sang. "Mae Mae, Mamie."

"And Mamie as well," Sierra agreed.

"For the longest time, I thought she was just repeating her own name," Warren said, as they picked their way along a narrow ledge and began to climb a set of stairs cut into yellowed ice.

"No," Sierra shook her head. "She calls for Mamie Verde, just as the First Folk do inside her head."

"Why?" Warren asked. "What would the ancients want with Mae or Mamie, or any of you?"

"I don't know," Sierra replied. "Mamie Verde was The Keeper of the Tales before me, and those at the Potluck believed that she revealed all for safekeeping. As it turned out, there was a Lost Tale that Mamie never uttered aloud. It's called The Guardian of the Crystal Caves."

"Who else knows this tale?"

"Supposedly Mamie related it to her maid, Ratta, in the same language the ancients use." They mounted yet another narrow set of stairs. "I believe it is called Mind Speak."

"The Lowlanders talk that way as well," Warren said. "I've seen them. They move their eyes, and gesture with their hands, but don't make a sound."

"I hope that Aubergine summoned us all to force Ratta to reveal the tale—if she remembers it." Sierra glanced at Warren. "Maybe then we'll know what to do."

Ahead of them Mae pitched forward with a yelp. Sierra closed her eyes and put a hand to her heart.

"Let's keep moving," Warren said.

Mae's Mitered Afghan

AN AFGHAN PATTERN

This intermediate-skill-level afghan is a patchwork of mitered squares constructed in garter stitch. Approximate finished size is 45" by 50"—8 blocks across and 17 blocks up.

Get the pattern from PotluckYarn.com/epatterns

"Hello, and welcome. I'm Miles from nowhere."

CHAPTER 17

Stories too Close to True

AFTER LEAVING ESMERALDE'S COTTAGE, RATTA drove the mules to the main track and turned them north toward Banebridge. But soon she found herself swinging the wagon wide and slowing it to a stop in the first turnout not swamped with rainwater. Just ahead loomed a thicket of fir trees. She put a hand to her heart. Although the most direct route to Bordertown led north through the western edge of the Copse, she felt Aubergine's call pulling her farther toward the west, perhaps by way of Coventry. That was an odd way to go, although something felt altogether wrong about taking the main route.

Ratta had heard unsavory things about the woods. Travelers, familiar with the adage keep close in the Copse, often formed caravans to pass through the tangled forest together, for protection. Rumor had it that the Copse was a living thing, quick to close its roving branches and thorny brambles around those who could not defend themselves. Ratta worried that snarls of roots and vines might foul the spokes of the wagon's wheels and rip at the mules' leather harnesses. Worse yet, what if tree limbs tore at Mamie, who lay helplessly in the bed of the wagon?

Even if she got through the Copse with mere scratches, Ratta did not trust the road beyond. It had been years since she had traveled the main track along the River Runne. It led past Banebridge and through the Forks to the rough town of Woolen Woods before it reached the Southern Gate. Who knew what she would find there?

She preferred the lesser-trafficked Coventry road to the northwest. She knew that way well. It wound through the foothills below her cabin. Lesser trails leading down from the Western Highlands joined the track, which broadened into a thoroughfare that eventually led to the Western Gate of Bordertown and stockyards beyond in the borough of Butchers Block. Was the preference she was feeling for that route only a matter of comfort and familiarity? Was she simply kidding herself, wanting to take the easy way out? Ratta put a hand to her heart as the call came again, and this time she was sure. Clicking her tongue to the mules, she swung the wagon around and doubled back.

Almost immediately, her spirits lifted. This far south, the highland route was not much more than a trail that snaked through the river valley, but she would be able to avoid the Copse. Now that she was moving in the right direction, Ratta found that she was less irritated by Aubergine's summons. The wagon rumbled pleasantly along the two-wheeled track, while the sun arced across the sky, trying to burn through the pink haze. Mamie, however, did not stir, even when Ratta held the rag dipped in sweet tea to the old woman's lips. Ratta blinked back tears, afraid that Mamie had already drawn her last breath. But what was she to do?

In the middle of the afternoon, Ratta paused at the turnoff to Coventry, which led to her log cabin in the foothills. Perhaps she should just take Mamie home and lay her to rest her in the old family plot behind the boarded-up farmhouse. She knew she could bury Mamie properly, because she had taken a ceremonial scarf from Esmeralde's cottage. Hidden among the glass vials of herbs and tinctures that Esmeralde had abandoned just inside the front door, Ratta had found the Land-of-Dreams scarf, sparkly with stars. Ratta had seen such magical raiment before, scarves or shawlettes knit with stars or sometimes with leaf motifs. But she had encountered them only at sick houses, or in the possession of remedy women like Esmeralde.

The glittery hand knits, patterned with symbols from nature, were used to celebrate passages: from childhood to adulthood, joining in marriage or passing into death. These rare, expensive scarves were dyed with shards of ruby garnet, painstakingly picked from the Trickle by fossickers. The crystals ranged in color from burgundy to deep plum, and resembled drops of dried blood. Heavier than more common pebbles of the same size, these special stones washed up along the banks of the Trickle each spring. According to one of Mamie's tales, they were carried out of the glacier by an underground river that began deep within the Crystal Caves, beneath the tombs of the ancients.

Garnet-dyed funeral scarves shimmered in daylight only if they had not yet honored the dead. The glitter vanished as it lofted the departing spirit into the land of dreams. Ratta had witnessed this transformation from death to afterlife more than once. When the knitted garment had fulfilled its ceremonial function, the scarf remained behind, minus its sparkle.

Ratta had plucked the scarf from Esmeralde's belongings, hoping that it might ease Mamie into the land of dreams. It winked vividly. She guessed that Esmeralde must have crafted it recently, for folk she planned to meet in Middlemarch. Ratta was tempted to drive home, drape the alpaca scarf around Mamie's neck, and perform the funeral ceremony herself without involving the Twelve.

It sounded like a good idea. But as she picked up the reins to turn onto the Coventry Road, the call came abruptly. Instead of pulling at her heart, it slapped her in the face. Ratta shook her head to lessen the sting. "All right," she growled. "I'll bring her to you. But you will not like what I have to say."

Heaving a sigh, she slapped the reins and continued up the western track. The mules pulled steadily, hauling the wagon gradually upward into the foothills in the strange afternoon light.

As Ratta had guessed, traffic was thin along this high route. In spring, she had often watched shepherds descending the mountainsides with the flocks they herded back from their winter breeding grounds. The ewes would waddle along, heavy with the lambs that would soon be born in the mild climate of the river valley.

Riders on horseback or driving wagons were uncommon on this track, because no one wanted to be delayed behind a slow-moving flock of sheep or goats. Luck was with her today. There were no herds clogging the trail. Although this passage was longer than the route through the Forks and up the Trickle, Ratta made good time. At nightfall, she halted at a stagecoach inn, just south of the juncture with the migratory trail from the Western Highlands, and carried Mamie inside.

The inn's main room was half filled with fairgoers returning from Middlemarch. Because most of the travelers had stopped for a cold drink or a quick meal before continuing north, Ratta had an easy time renting a room for the night at the top of the stairs. After settling Mamie on a pallet under the eaves, she went downstairs in search of a mug of mulled cider and a bowl of stew.

At the bar, she found an empty stool along the counter. A fire blazed in the stone hearth, and the lively talk filled the room. Just after her beef barley soup arrived with a heel of rye bread, a slight man in a bright vest rose from the end of the bar to parade before the fireplace. He pulled a penny whistle from his pocket and played a few discordant notes to get their attention.

"Hello, and welcome. I'm Miles from nowhere," he boasted, with a flourish. "Neither the Northlands nor the South, the Western Highlands nor the Fisheries of the Far East do I call home. I hail from no place and all places, collecting tales in the way that others gather ripe chestnuts. I am just returned from the Middlemarch Fair with fresh yarns to tell. Folk of the Middlelands, what would you hear?" He took off his hat and held it out. "I'll regale you with any story for a copper, or two or three."

"Sadly, I tire of tall tales," said a heavyset man hunkered over the bar and holding up a newly minted coin. He wore the garb of the merchant class, a surcoat woven from black cashmere over a dove-colored tunic. His wool leggings, which matched the coat, were tucked into tooled kidskin boots. "Tell a yarn and tell it true."

Ratta's eyes went wide at the southern silver, because coins of the Lowlands were seldom seen this far north. The thin disc of precious metal bore the engraved visage of the Dark Queen. The bard smiled and held out his hand for the coin. The smile revealed rotted teeth, and stretched into a grin that resembled a grimace.

"My yarns always ring true," Miles said. "What would you hear? Stories of the Lowlands? Yarns of the Far North?"

Ratta stared at the coin. Now she could discern a thinly veiled aura of magic hovering over it. "Have you any new tales of the Twelve?" She heard herself ask.

Taking a sip from his pint of beer, the large man peered down the bar, to see who had spoken. His black beard hid a smile.

"Funny you should mention the knitting witches," the bard nodded eagerly, looking from Ratta to the big man. "The main track buzzes with talk of the Twelve. I've a new cycle of stories I call Woolgathering. Would you hear one? Or several, perhaps?"

"I've no mood for bedtime stories," the large man grumbled, his black eyes glittering.

"No, no, no, it's all true, every bit of it," Miles said, with a shake of his head. "Except for the trifles I made up."

Satisfied, the large man flipped the storyteller his piece of silver. As the coin arced through the air, Ratta watched a mysterious dark aura chase after it. The bard caught it deftly and slid it into a pocket inside his vest.

"And so we begin." Miles cleared his throat and played a merry introduction on his pennywhistle. "This yarn I call "How the Twelve became Twelve.'"

"Because they were more than eleven," heckled a tipsy man slouched at a table near the fire.

The bard ignored him. "There was a time when the Twelve were not yet twelve." He paused to play a short refrain. "Just novices full of girlish mischief. They came of age at the Potluck during its heyday and desired nothing more than to revel in its colorful glory. Their mistress was none other than the Potluck Queen, Aubergine." He blew a few high notes. "She wielded the powers of the ancient dye crystals freely, for magic was not yet forbidden in all the lands. As word of her fanciful fiber shop spread, Potluck Yarn became a haven for dyed-in-the-wool believers. Initiates flocked to her like sheep."

Here the storyteller paused to improvise a melody. Ratta felt the dark eyes of the large man with the raven beard studying her. There was something familiar and unsettling about him, although Ratta was certain she had never met him. Had he been sitting at the bar when she paid for her room?

"Many girls desired only to possess whimsical coats and capes that could make the wearer serene, or able to pass unseen or to survive the harshest blizzard, no matter how cold and blinding," Miles went on, piping on his whistle now and again for emphasis. "Others sought fine work of the hand, or to master the art of melding dye crystal to fiber. Still fewer arrived to apprentice with Aubergine and learn her lore. All were admitted, but only a handful was chosen. This is their story."

Finishing her stew, Ratta wiped the bowl clean with the bread. She chewed the hunk of dark rye slowly, disliking the probing she felt from the large man's eyes. Why had she asked the storyteller for tales of the Twelve? She had no desire to call attention to herself or Mamie.

The large man bought the bard a pint of ale. Miles thanked his benefactor with a bob of his head, took the tankard from the barmaid, and quaffed half of it quickly. He set the foaming mug on the mantelpiece and continued.

"As Aubergine's lore spread, the Potluck became an arcane collection: a studio center, a company store, and a boarding school, all in one," he explained, with large, theatrical gestures. "The structure was a two-story, timber-framed building of stone and wood, fronting a well-trafficked thoroughfare in the market district of a bustling border town. To the side, a walled kitchen garden stood between the Potluck and a pottery next door, where greenware awaited the kiln. Behind, an arched breezeway connected the main house to a long, low dye shed. Few customers knew of the secret entrance to the dye shed from the alley, a door built to look like an unbroken piece of the fence.

"Customers entered the shop from the winding cobbles of a merchant street lined with storefronts displaying work of the artisans' hands. Whenever the door opened, a bell affixed to the handle jingled merrily, announcing the arrival of visitors. Newcomers immediately noticed the rarefied air, swirling with sparking motes that danced in the light. Their ears became assaulted by, but quickly adjusted to, the rhythmic clack of spinning wheels, knitting needles, and looms. The magical multicolored fibers offered a feast for their eyes."

Here he paused for effect. As she watched, Ratta wondered where the bard had sourced his story, because so far almost everything he said was rooted in truth.

"In the front room, spinning wheels revolved as a group of girls learned to treadle, draft the fibers evenly, then spin and ply," Miles continued, gesticulating wildly as he pantomimed students learning to spin, eliciting laughs from the crowd. "Other interns gathered around the shop's table, heads bent over knitting needles, learning to finish sweaters with invisible bind-offs and duplicate-stitching techniques that would someday have specialized names. Magical auras floated over garments for sale in the showroom, while the air within the shop mixed the aromas of lanolin, the lavender soap, birch knitting needles, and drying herbs, hung from the rafters."

What if this was a trap? Ratta's eyes flitted between the bard and the merchant. What if the storyteller was in league with the big man, and both were bounty hunters, with a plan to round up the witches? She finished her cider and slid quietly from her stool.

"Initiates in dye-splotched aprons appeared at intervals from the dye shed with dripping fleeces to spread across the drying racks," the bard continued blithely. "The wools were the finest Merino and Corriedale, spotted Jacob and Bluefaced Leicester. Other apprentices bent over the rows in the garden, harvesting dye plants. Carefully they separated the flowers and leaves and spread them out to dry on old sheets along the sunny path."

As Miles blew a short tune on his pennywhistle, Ratta gazed at the bard intently, wondering if he would dare identify the Twelve. If she heard her name or Mamie's, she resolved to pack up and leave immediately, whatever the hour. She pulled out her change purse. The barmaid ignored her. The storyteller played another short melody and went on.

"In the back of the dye shed, the great pot balanced on a circlet of blackened hearthstones. It was cast iron, darkened by the flames of a thousand fires. The soot-stained lip stood so tall that some of the younger girls could not see over the edge. From morning until late afternoon and sometimes into the night, the great pot simmered, infusing fleece and roving with magical shades, hues that refused to fade. Burlap sacks of marigold and cochineal, logwood and indigo sat ready near casks of clear vinegar, boxes of sea salt, and a barrel of spring water. Behind, tucked in the darkened pantry were the rarest dyestuffs, as well as those that were perishable, light sensitive, or for some other reason hidden from sight. Sealed in seamless boxes that only Aubergine could open, were magic dye crystals, gleaned from the freshets that coursed from the Crystal Caves deep within the Northland Glacier. These fragments of ancient rock and cold-fire crystal had accompanied Aubergine when she moved south to the safety of the town on the Border. She used them sparingly, and alone. But that would not be for long, she hoped."

Ratta stared at the brightly dressed storyteller in shock. There was no way he could know these things, she realized, unless he was one of the Twelve himself. But that was impossible. Men were not allowed in the dye shed, or in the backroom of the Potluck. She searched the bard's face for signs of recognition. She found nothing. He could not be anything more than a traveling gypsy. But how did he know so much?

"Sprinkled throughout the novices and teachers were eleven that Aubergine had chosen to join her, eleven that showed more promise than the others," Miles continued. "One of them was an unlikely student. She sat dejectedly on her stool before the spinning wheel, kicking at air, for her stubby legs did not reach the treadles. Even when she could spin a yarn, her lumpy roving would not strip evenly. The other girls were wont to pick plant matter out of the silk batts she prepared. So small that she was easy to dismiss, outside of the yarn shop many mistook her for a baby. Ah, until they saw her scamper off quick as a whip down a side street, or squirm under the garden gate to beat the other girls home. She was a gnome named Josephine. All called her Smokey Jo."

When Ratta tried to pay her bill, the barmaid refused her coin, inclining her head toward the large man still sitting at the bar. Ratta could stand it no more. She walked over to him and met his unnerving eyes. "No one pays for my meals unbidden," she said, slapping a handful of coins on the bar. "Do I know you?"

The large man shrugged. "Take care of your mistress, Ratta. Take care on the road." His mouth curled into a cruel smile and his eyes sparkled as they held hers. "We'll meet again, in the most unlikely of places."

He rose and left the bar. Ratta turned to question the storyteller, but Miles had vanished without finishing his beer. The tankard sat half full on the mantelpiece.

Her heart pounding, Ratta ran up the stairs. The door to her room was still locked. When she opened it she could see that nothing had been disturbed, least of all Mamie. Relieved, she bolted the door and fell onto the bed, without bothering to undress. Thanks to fatigue, she slept. Thanks to the man at the bar and the storyteller, her sleep was restless.

The next morning, with Mamie no better or worse as far as she could tell, Ratta got an early start. By midday she could see the stone walls of Bordertown, under the shadow of the glacier. As she feared, there was a checkpoint at some distance from the city, but she got through it easily in her traveling cloak. The yarn she told was one she had practiced all morning: Her mother had just died, and her final wish was to be laid to rest in the family crypt within the borough of Merchant's Row. In preparation for the lie, Ratta had covered Mamie, still wrapped in the never-ending shawl, with a light sheet she had taken from the inn. None of the young soldiers chose to lift the sheet, for fear of imagined sickness or plague.

The afternoon sky was the color of a dusty rose. The air smelled of smoke, a distasteful odor that grew stronger as the mules pulled the wagon along the broad thoroughfare toward the Western Gate. Just a mile or so from the city, Ratta happened upon a curious sight. A shepherd with a large staff strode alongside the track ahead of her, driving a single sheep. Ratta wondered if the tall figure was a farmer returning from the Middlemarch Fair, perhaps having purchased a rare breeding ram. She had never seen anything like this animal, which was spotted black and white, small like a dog, and bore what looked like a crown of thorns protruding from its head. As she approached, she saw that the creature was a sheep with a peculiar double set of horns and that it was limping. The stout shepherd picked up the ram and began to carry it like a child.

Ratta slowed the wagon. "Hold up there," she hailed the shepherd.

Even with Mamie lying in the back of the wagon, she certainly had plenty of room on the buckboard for a shepherd forced to carry a lame sheep.

"You, with the sheep," Ratta called again, catching the shepherd's attention. "Do you need a ride?"

The shepherd turned, and Ratta could see that the voluminous figure was no man, but an older woman. "Thank you. My ram has a stone bruise," she called, waiting for Ratta to catch up.

As she halted the mules, Ratta felt a prick of recognition that made her hesitate. There was something odd about the shepherdess, as well as the sheep. Over her oiled canvas cloak, the older woman carried a large felted backpack, dyed in the colors of winter grasses. Her hand gripped a staff, its crook hooded with felt in the same color.

The shepherdess lifted her eyes from the sheep to Ratta. "If you could carry us as far as the Western Gate?" The words died in her throat.

"You," Ratta hissed.

"Well met on the road," Winter Wheat said grimly. "I feared I might find you on this track. You have been called, haven't you?"

"Like moth to flame." Ratta gave her a hard look.

Wheat's eyes flickered to the empty bench beside the red-haired woman. "Or perhaps you are answering the summons in Mamie's stead?"

"I feel the call myself," Ratta retorted, her hands grasping the mules' reins fiercely. "I am one of the Twelve, like you. Yet even now you would deny me."

Cradling the small ram under one arm, Winter Wheat slid her free hand up along her staff to uncover the crystals tied at its crook. "Where is Mamie?" she asked casually. "Has she passed?"

Ignoring her, Ratta stood and backed the wagon beyond the range of the amber cabochons. "I will not be burned," she cautioned. "Keep that staff hooded if you want a ride."

Wheat's fingers fumbled at the felted hood, unable to uncover the crystals while holding Tracks. "If you will just carry my sheep," she said, "I will hike alongside."

Ratta looked at the ailing ram, whose bright eyes gazed at her innocently. "As you wish," she agreed. Laying the reins aside, she reached down. "You can put him up front with me."

"There is no need for that," Wheat grumbled, carrying Tracks around to the bed of the covered wagon. "He's a sheep, not a dog. He will be fine in the back."

Ratta turned, her frizzy hair flying. "Stay away from there," she warned, afraid of what accusations would fly from Wheat's mouth if she saw Mamie. But it was already too late.

"What is under here?" Wheat asked, lifting Tracks carefully into the wagon. She pulled back the sheet and her eyes went wide.

"Mamie Verde," Ratta said quietly. "Don't you say anything about her. I did all I could."

Wheat gazed speechlessly at the shrunken form. Translucent skin, mottled with liver spots, stretched tightly across bone and sinew. Wheat dropped the edge of the cloth and stared at Ratta. "Is she dead?"

Ratta let her breath out slowly. "Truly, I cannot hazard a guess," she admitted. She watched Wheat place a practiced hand against the lined skin of the old woman's face, gently touching the blue-veined eyelids. Ratta gave Wheat a hopeful look. "What do you think?"

"I can tell whether animals still hold their spirits." Wheat shook her head. "Not people."

"I have just been trying to get Mamie to Bordertown before she died. It was her final wish." Ratta's eyes filled with tears and she wiped them away angrily. She glared at Wheat with defiance. "I want to go home. I swore I would never return to that miserable Potluck. If Mamie has truly passed, then I will not. I was only doing it for her."

"That is untrue." Wheat laid aside her staff. She clambered into the back of the wagon next to Tracks and knelt before Mamie. "If you are one of us, as you say, you were doing it for all of us." Putting a hand to Mae's cheek, Wheat traced a vein down her neck, feeling for pulse. "We have no choice but to go, for we have been called."

"The summons is a hand leading me by the heart," Ratta admitted. "Once it slapped my face."

Wheat nodded, suppressing a smile. Leaning over Mamie, she brushed the back of her hand against the old woman's delicate neck. "This is strange." She raised her head and looked across the wagon at Ratta. "I sense that she is neither part of this world nor the next." Her hand fingered the never-ending shawl. "This old shawl you knit so long ago. What did you fashion it to do?"

"I dyed the Merino bouclé yarn myself in a single hank, using malachite I found in Mamie's jewelry box mixed with blush wine from the cellar. I called the new colorway Old Rose. To you, Mamie was a wilted flower past her prime, but even in her last years she was still a rose to me. The pattern is called never-ending shawl; for as I knit, it grew into a triangular wrap and then an afghan, and still the ball of yarn did not run out. I thought that, wrapped in such a garment, Mamie would be safe with me forever." Ratta's voice dropped to a hoarse whisper. "Now I see it only kept her in limbo, like a caterpillar trapped in a cocoon. It did more harm than good."

The bell around Tracks' neck tinkled as he stood to peer with interest into Mamie's wizened face. With a questioning look to Wheat, the little ram began to sniff at the colorful shawl.

"Mamie was never supposed to become the butterfly you envisioned," Wheat said gently, stroking Tracks' back. She paused. "You will have to release her from the magic knits that tie her to this world, so that she may pass to the next. You know that, don't you?"

Ratta nodded. Her words came slowly. "I should have let Aubergine release Mamie Verde to the land of dreams twenty years ago," she said. "She would have performed the ceremony gladly, had I asked. But I could not. I did not want to be alone."

Wheat pulled the little ram back as he began to sniff at Mamie's face. "No, Tracks."

Ratta gave her a hard look. "I don't care what you or the others say. She really did talk to me, even after she ceased to speak. And I could talk back."

"I believe you," Wheat said, raising her palm. "I have seen Lowlanders communicate. They do not utter words."

"They talk with their eyes." Ratta scoffed. "Mamie never did that. She used Mind Speak."

"What is that?" Wheat gave her a sharp look. "Something you made up?"

"I thought so, for a time. But then Mamie told me that it had been the language of the ancients." She gazed at Wheat. "Do not forget that what you all feared is true. I alone know the Lost Tale."

"I expect we will all will hear it soon enough," Wheat said evenly.

"We had best get on then. I would like to be in Merchants' Row before nightfall." She held out her arms for the sheep. "Give him here."

"His name is Tracks," Wheat said, handing him to Ratta. Tracks sniffed Ratta as Wheat began to clamber down from the back of the wagon, then relaxed in the young woman's arms. "I call him Tracksie."

"You can ride on the bench," Ratta said gruffly. "Both you and Tracks." She pointed at Winter Wheat's staff, which lay forgotten next to Mamie. "But leave the hood over that thing."

Their differences settled for now, the childhood adversaries sat side by side as the wagon rumbled beneath the Western Gate and through the stockyards that edged the borough of Butcher's Block.

Land-of Dreams Scarves

SCARF PATTERNS

These intermediate-skill-level alpaca scarves have a sparkly mesh finish to be worn for special occasions. They measure 8" by 50" after blocking.

Get the pattern from PotluckYarn.com/epatterns

Smokey felt the jacket being ripped from her shoulders.

CHAPTER 18

The Gathering

AS SOON AS LILY LEFT THE KITCHEN, Smokey Jo hopped down from her stool at the counter, where she had been sprinkling cinnamon sugar over the mountain of apples the new kitchen girl had sliced for pie. The stool's wooden legs screeched as she pulled it across the uneven stone floor to the cook stove.

After checking to be sure that no one could see her, Smokey climbed the stool, slipped on the giant kitchen mitts, and thrust the bubbling pot of sweet potatoes aside. Water slopped across the newly blacked cook top, and the fragrant hiss of steam made Smokey smile. Taking a griddle handle from its hook on the wall, Smokey pried the hot disc of iron from the top of the wood-stove and peered into the lively blaze. She pulled a strip of birch bark from her apron pocket and

293

touched it to the coals. The translucent white bark began to curl as it smoldered, releasing a delicate aroma in the instant before it ignited in blue flames. Smokey breathed deeply. The burnt wood smelled like roasted almonds.

"Smokey Jo, leave that griddle alone," Lily reminded her for the third time, as she swept into the kitchen with the butter and cream she had put to cool in the cellar.

Because the icebox in the summer kitchen had been too damaged to repair, Lily had ordered a new one from a cabinetmaker. The oak chest would arrive on a flatbed wagon from the borough of Artisan's Hand, but had not yet been delivered.

This morning, Lily had begun to overhaul the neglected kitchen. She had cleaned the ashes from the stove, filled the wood box, and scoured the griddle. It helped that on their outing the day before they had hired a scullery maid, plus a grounds man; and a stable boy had started work this morning. It was spring, and it had been years since anyone had opened the windows upstairs or turned the earth for a kitchen garden.

Now the brick oven above the fireplace had been fitted with a new baking rack, and Lily had laid in enough supplies to feed the Twelve. She had gathered a basket of apples, burlap sacks of onions and potatoes, and sent the stable boy to Butcher's Block for a fresh turkey and a side of bacon. Lily and Smokey had spent over an hour in the sundries tent at the farmers' market and had returned to the Potluck with paper twists full of herbs and spices.

"If you keep moving the pots off the burner, we'll never have dinner ready for our guests," Lily scolded.

"But we haven't had a nice warm fire in the kitchen stove in months," Smokey protested, her eyes dancing. "It's so pretty." Reluctantly, she replaced the iron disc and slid the sweet potatoes back over the heat, where they resumed their boil. She gazed up at Lily. "Besides, there's just the three of us. We have no guests."

Lily looked at her and said nothing.

"Oh, I know," Smokey sighed. "We have to ask or else you won't tell us anything. How tedious. Do you mean I have to ask a question even for something as small as this?"

"Yes."

"Well, are they coming today?"

"Of course! Why else would we be roasting such a large turkey, and baking not one but two apple pies?"

"Who will come? Everyone?"

"You know better than that." Lily nodded toward the summer kitchen, which opened into a low-walled yard where they used to plant a kitchen garden. The wooden gate led to the alley between the Potluck and the pottery next door. "I think I hear a cart. Why don't you see if there's someone at the gate?" Lily had begun rolling out pie crusts.

"Do you think it's the icebox?"

"Go see," Lily said, as she cut pretty diagonal slashes in the top of each crust and dabbed the pies with butter.

Smokey Jo needed no more encouragement.

Smokey jumped down from her stool and hustled through the doorway into the summer kitchen. She needed to go outside to check the alley, because she could see nothing through the window. The side gate was closed, and she was too short to see over the wall. All the deliveries came to this side of the property. Just this morning a new cutting board had been dropped off to replace their scarred wooden block, and sacks of flour had come from the grain mill. Now they had corn meal and stone-ground wheat flour for baking, as well as steel-cut oats for porridge.

Finding none of her own outerwear near the door, Smokey threw on the old patchwork kimono that had hung from a hook by this door almost as long as she could remember. Before she disappeared, Tracery Teal had knit the motley garment from scrap sock yarn. Since Teal had evaporated into a cloud of green haze, the bright jacket had belonged to no one, but neither Aubergine nor Smokey Jo could bear to get rid of it. Not only did the kimono keep the memory of Teal present in their minds, it was also handy. They both wore it at one time or another, as a barn coat or to walk to the market on cool days.

The jacket hung to Smokey's knees and its bell sleeves covered her fingertips. She ran out the door, letting it bang shut behind her, and skipped across the garden path.

She unlatched the wooden gate and flung it open. A pair of gray mules pulling a covered wagon was approaching the side entrance. Two women sat side by side on the bench seat. Smokey tried to figure out who they were, and thought she recognized the driver.

"Ratta, is that you?" Mamie Verde's servant girl had become a middle-aged woman, but the frizzy red hair that threatened to escape her bun gave her away.

"That it is." Ratta pulled the mules to a halt. "You look the same, Smokey Jo."

"Well, you don't," Smokey said. "I could only tell you by your hair."

"Then who am I, little one?" The stout woman sitting beside Ratta shook out her bun to reveal blonde hair beginning to gray, which did not help Smokey identify her one bit. Smokey examined her clothing. Over sun-bleached pantaloons tucked into hiking boots, the woman wore an oilskin mantle of the type favored by migratory trekkers from the Western Highlands.

"One of the Twelve, surely, but not Mamie Verde, for you are not that old and you have no wheeled chair."

The Highlander smiled. Smokey noticed the large felted backpack stowed between her trekking boots. On her lap she held what looked like a spotted dog, except it had horns. The animal looked at her and let out a baa. Then Smokey could guess, although she could barely believe her eyes.

"Winter Wheat?" Smokey asked in a timid voice, hard-put to believe that Ratta and Wheat would be traveling together, since they'd never gotten along.

Smiling broadly, Wheat nodded.

"The sheep gave you away." Smokey reached up to pat the little ram. He arched his neck so that she could scratch under his chin.

Wheat handed him down to Smokey. "This is Tracks. Watch that front foot; he's lame." Shouldering her backpack, she clambered from the wagon.

"You two always disliked each other," Smokey commented.

Ratta shrugged and laid aside the mules' reins to lean back and check the wagon. "We have a common cause," she said, distracted.

As the gnome watched, Wheat rummaged behind the bench seat, and lifted out her shepherd's staff. Smokey's eyes lit with delight when she saw the hooded crook. "Wheat, you used to zap her with that thing, remember?"

"It is I who remember," Ratta said. "She burned holes in my sleeves and my skirts. I did not own one article of clothing without singe marks."

"Nothing my staff burned through your garments was as fiery as your tongue toward me," Wheat said. "You forget that Lilac Lily made me mend all of your clothes. I went through entire spools of thread."

Ratta stepped down from the wagon. "Lily must be here."

Smokey nodded. "She arrived yesterday. She's in the kitchen, baking pies."

"Anyone else?" Ratta asked.

Smokey shook her head. "Just me and Aubergine, same as always." She paused. "Aubergine is napping. She does that now, most afternoons."

Ratta eyed Wheat. "Let's get this done with before anyone else shows up. Will you help me?"

Smokey reached up for Wheat's staff. "Can I hold it?"

With a laugh, Wheat surrendered her crook and followed Ratta to the back of the wagon. Together they let down the tailgate and reached inside. Filled with glee, Smokey regarded the crook no differently than she had as a child. With a secret smile, Wheat nodded her permission.

Smokey leaned the tall staff against the garden wall and snatched off the hood.

Freed, the crystals began to swirl on their tethers. They hit and sparked. Inside each golden orb Smokey saw what she fondly remembered: the outline of a scarab beetle, encased in amber, more beautiful than it had been when alive.

"Ooooh," Smokey whispered, mesmerized. "Can I practice with them?" she asked, but no one was paying attention. Wheat was carrying the lame sheep and Ratta had hefted a large bundle wrapped in a shawl.

The grounds man arrived to unload their bags, followed by the barn boy. As the stable hand led the mules and wagon away, Smokey escaped down the alley with Wheat's staff and trotted around back to the hidden entrance to the dye shed. As a child, she had often stolen this same staff from the hall tree in the summer kitchen and snuck back here to practice burning holes in the snow banks. Now, even though the snow was almost gone, she could not help herself. Standing near the secret door to the dye shed, she pointed the staff across the alley. As the cabochon crystals crossed each other in a circle of light, Smokey focused the beam on a lump of dirty snow. Her heart began to pound, anticipating the delightful hiss of melting ice, but that did not happen. Instead Smokey found herself dissipating into the air. She would have clapped with glee, except she had no hands. She was unseen vapor, drifting anywhere she wanted to go. Smokey hoped that whatever spell she had somehow cast over herself would last all day.

It had been many years since Smokey Jo had disappeared into smoke. The last time it happened seemed like a half-forgotten dream. She had been a young girl playing with Wheat's staff in this same alley, wearing this same patchwork coat of Teal's. Early one morning, Smokey had nicked both the staff and the kimono and run out to the garden before anyone but the cook had stirred from bed. Smokey had begun by melting a pretty pattern of holes in the snowdrifts with pin-pricks of light. Except then the cabochons had swirled back and hit behind the staff, sending a shower of sparks over her. Fearful that she had burned Teal's jacket, or singed her own hair, Smokey had put a hand to her head but saw no hand. Then she had peered into an icy puddle and seen no reflection. That had made Smokey grin, for no matter how hard she tried to make herself disappear on her own, it never happened.

Smokey recalled the wonderful day she had spent drifting about the marketplace. She hovered above the food tents, drinking in the sights and smells. She watched sausage sputtering over an open fire, while next door licks of flame from a brazier sent corn popping inside a covered iron kettle. At another stand, she observed chestnuts roasting among glowing embers, while on the rack above peanuts boiled in brine. When the spell finally wore off in the late afternoon, Smokey had reappeared, hungry and tired. She had walked home dejectedly, the kimono tied around her waist and the staff resting over her shoulder. Even though she had only borrowed them, Teal and Wheat would be angry. She had no doubt that she would be punished with a week's worth of kitchen chores. How she hated peeling potatoes.

Today, Smokey Jo did not want to waste precious time at the food stalls in the marketplace. Almost without thinking, she seeped through the back fence and slid under the doorway of the secret entrance to the dye shed. Soon she was in the room that housed the great pot. She noticed with satisfaction that Aubergine had been busy preparing for a simmer. The dye pot had been cleaned and set on a platform over a freshly laid fire that had not yet been lit. The huge iron cauldron was half filled with clear spring water, and a jug of white vinegar stood ready on a side table, next to a pillar of sea salt. Places for all Twelve of them had been cleared in a circle around the great pot, and behind Aubergine's chair, dyestuffs had been laid out carefully. There were logwood and cochineal, indigo and madder, rosewood, marigold and jet. Smokey looked around for the little milk-glass jars of ground crystal, but saw none. The mortar and pestle stood off to the side, empty. The pantry door was closed and locked as usual, but it only took Smokey a few seconds to find the keyhole and push her way through.

What she saw in the dark closet disturbed her. The shelves meant for dye crystals and other rare stones lay bare. There was no shard of amethyst or fire opal, no nugget of turquoise or malachite, crystallized amber, raw ruby garnet. Not even a chunk of common rose quartz sitting on a shelf glowing in the dark. What was worse, a mossy haze hovered high in the back corner of the pantry. As Smokey watched, the fog began to collect, like cream rising to the top of fresh milk. Soon it became an angry green cloud and Smokey, no more than vapor herself, understood who it was.

"Teal?" She asked, thinking it might be best to offer up the kimono. "I did not mean to take your coat unchallenged."

In answer, the storm cloud engulfed her like a sudden squall whipping across a glacier pond. The harder she fought to break free, the more the swirling mist obscured her vision. Smokey felt the jacket being ripped from her shoulders. All around her it began to rain.

"I was just borrowing it!" Smokey protested.

The cloud released her suddenly and she tumbled in a wet heap to the floor. Seconds later, Wheat's staff clattered down beside her.

Smokey held a grubby hand in front of her face and grimaced. She was no longer smoke. Even in the gloom she could make out all five fingers. She hugged her damp sleeves, shivering, because the kimono had vanished. Wiping her eyes, she peered upward, searching for the teal-colored mist, but whatever had taken the jacket had evaporated. Rising, Smokey snatched up the staff. The cabochons had gone dark. She always hated it when that happened. The spent crystals would have to rest, perhaps for hours. She tried the door. It was still locked. Its only key hung from a metal ring that Aubergine kept in her knitting bag. Smokey was not supposed to touch the key, although she sometimes did when Aubergine was napping.

Alone in the dark, Smokey sat against the door and pulled an apple from her apron pocket. What to do? She bit into the crisp fruit. What to do? She listened at the keyhole. If she heard anyone in the dye shed, she would call out and kick the door until someone unlocked it, for the last thing she wanted was to miss pie for dinner.

Lily waited in the open doorway of the summer kitchen with a bright smile, wiping her hands on her apron.

"Who have we here?" she called to the two road-weary women who made their way slowly up the path. She stepped aside so that they could enter with their bundles and bags. "Ratta?" She took the carpetbag from Ratta's arm.

"Lily," Ratta said. "Well met."

"Who is that behind you—Winter Wheat?" Lily looked at Ratta in alarm. "Did you arrive together?"

"We did," Ratta said. "And we brought Mamie Verde too." She dipped her chin toward the quiet, shawl-wrapped form. "Lily, you seem surprised."

"Imagining you and Wheat as traveling companions is difficult."

"You haven't seen anything yet." Ratta rolled her eyes toward the shepherdess behind her. "Wheat has a sheep that she pampers like a lap dog. She means to keep it in the house."

"A pet sheep?" Lily's smile began to fade. "In the house?"

"Hallo, Lily," Wheat clapped Lily on the shoulder and held out her backpack. "Meet Tracks. He's a purebred Jacob ram."

Lily took the felted bag from Wheat's shoulder and glanced at the animal cradled in her arms. "He is a sheep," she said. "He belongs in the barn."

"Not Tracksie," Wheat countered. "Lily, the Lowlanders scattered my flock. Tracks is all I have left. And he is lame."

"He is a barnyard animal," Lily said firmly. "Fix him a pen in the stable."

"It won't be as it was before," Wheat promised, brushing by Lily. "There's just the one animal and I'll confine him to my room, until he is healed enough to walk freely."

"Here we go again," Ratta snorted. Still bearing Mamie, she trailed Wheat into the kitchen. She looked around for a good place to rest the old woman. The only clear space was the small round table near the wood stove. Gently, she laid her bundle on its surface, keeping her hand possessively on the shawl-wrapped body. She would move the old woman to a comfortable bed as soon as possible. She eyed Lily. "No one will want to room with Wheat."

"No one has to room with me. There are so few of us left that we shall all get our own rooms. Right, Lily?"

Lily looked at her blankly.

"You are bound to answer true if she asks," Ratta said.

"I simply don't know," Lily replied. Peeling back the shawl covering Mamie, she gazed thoughtfully at the wrinkled face with the closed, sunken eyes. She gave Ratta a brief glance. "I suppose you want the downstairs room again?" Turning, she led them through the kitchen. "Well, you are going to have to fight Aubergine for it."

Ratta lifted Mamie's body and followed the others into the front hall. "Aubergine sleeps down here?" She glanced at the closed bedroom door. "When she has that upstairs suite, overlooking the city center?"

"Aubergine is old," Lily said. "She does not care for stairs."

"Can I have my childhood cell with the dormered window?" Wheat asked.

"There are fresh sheets on the bed and the room has been aired." Lily looked at the sheep and sighed. "Let the barn boy know if you need a forkful of straw."

"Thanks, Lily." Wheat made her way toward the front staircase. "It's really good to see you again." She clumped up the stairs in her hiking boots.

"If Aubergine has Mamie's room, where are we to sleep?" Ratta asked. She peered past the kitchen pantry to the tiny maid's quarters. "I once slept back there."

Lily shook her head. "We hired a scullery girl to mind the kitchen. She sleeps there." She looked Ratta over carefully. "You need not do chores any longer, for you are one of us. It will be your folly to forget that."

"It seems that no one else remembers," Ratta said. "When I met Wheat on the road this morning, she asked if I was coming here in Mamie's stead. I came in my own stead." She narrowed her eyes at Lily. "If you know any of my secrets, then you must know that."

"I do," Lily said. "And I know you will do what you must to save us."

"I am bound by Mamie to voice the Lost Tale. But only if Sierra answers the call." Ratta looked down at the still form in the sparkling shawl. "There are rumors on the track that the Guard has arrested members of the Twelve. I don't believe we will be seeing Sierra any time soon."

Lily opened her mouth, but then thought better of speaking.

"I did not ask." Ratta warned. A harsh laugh escaped her lips. "Don't tell me what I don't want to know."

"Suit yourself." With a sweep of her skirts, Lily turned back down the hall toward the kitchen. "I need to see to our supper. Take any room on the second floor."

"What about Mamie?" Ratta called after her. "I have little desire to traipse with her up and down the stairs, day in and day out."

From the kitchen doorway, Lily looked at Ratta steadily.

"What?" Ratta implored her, in the silence that followed. "I would know," she admitted angrily.

"There is no need to carry Mamie upstairs," Lily said at last. "The parlor is prepared."

"We do not know if she has passed," Ratta protested, as fear crept into her voice. "She may still live. Wheat said so herself."

"Wheat sees to the ailments of sheep." Lily stepped forward and put her hand to Ratta's heart. "You know. Right here you do."

Instead of pointing Ratta up the stairs, Lily brushed past her to thrust apart the pocket doors of the parlor. The formal room had been dusted, and the floor mopped. The furniture gleamed with lemon oil. Chairs were positioned around three of the four walls, among urns filled with cut lilies and fern fronds. The front of the room held a long, narrow table covered with a freshly ironed cream-colored cloth edged with lace. Nothing sat on the tablecloth except for unlit tapers in bronze candlesticks at either end.

"No," Ratta quavered. Her arms, holding Mamie's body, began to shake.

Lily took her elbow. "You must."

"I can't bear it." Ratta blinked back tears.

"Come, I will help you." Lily guided Ratta to the front of the room, where they stood before the viewing table.

"I do not want to be alone," Ratta cried hoarsely.

"You are not alone." Lily gently lifted the bottom of the shawl, which held Mamie's feet. "You have us. Now lay her down."

"I can't," Ratta protested, although she took Mamie's shoulders and did as Lily told her. Carefully, they positioned Mamie's body on the table with her head facing north, toward the glacier, and her feet pointing south toward the Lowlands.

"You can keep her body wrapped in the shawl for now, if you like."

Ratta nodded mutely as tears streaked her face. Lily rearranged the knitted opening to reveal Mamie's face and lit the candles at her head and feet.

"Aubergine has planned a simmer as soon as everyone arrives," Lily said. "Then we must free Mamie from this shawl so that she may pass into the land of dreams."

"Mamie is not going to the land of dreams," Ratta murmured.

Lily looked at her sharply. "No?"

"Not according to the Lost Tale of the Guardian." Ratta met Lily's gaze. "I have seen it in my mind's eye countless times, but I never believed. I even took a funeral scarf from Esmeralde's cottage, thinking that might change things." Ratta shook her head and laughed with chagrin. "Mamie is the next Guardian of the Crystal Caves. She was due to commence her watch years ago—and she would have, but for this shawl. Who knows what will happen now?"

"When the time comes, you must ask the question," Lily urged Ratta. "Promise me. I think I may have the answer."

"If Sierra shows, then I will."

Lily smiled. "Take the room next to Wheat. Unpack your belongings and settle in. I'll call you when it's time for dinner."

A few hours later, Lily passed swiftly through the butler's pantry, nodding to the dark-haired kitchen girl who waited with the serving cart. She strode into the dining room and approached her mistress. Aubergine sat in the armchair at the head of the table. The high chair next to her place stood empty. The only other two people at the table were Wheat and Ratta.

"We can't wait dinner any longer, I'm afraid," she apologized.

Aubergine nodded. "Very well. But I wonder what has happened to Smokey Jo. It isn't like her to miss dinner, especially when there is pie."

Lily gestured to the kitchen girl and settled herself into the armchair at the far end of the table, opposite Aubergine. The serving girl, a young thing with dark hair and a delicate complexion, pushed in a cart laden with a large pot of tea and pitchers of cream and sugar. She poured first for Aubergine, and then for the others.

"I let Smokey play with my staff," Wheat said. "Has anyone checked the alley?

"Jo will come in when she's ready." Ratta added sugar to her cup. "Finish telling us about the dervish."

"As I said, I believe it was not dead," Wheat said. "I thought it might have been frozen while still alive."

"That is entirely possible. The age of ice took everyone unaware," Aubergine said. "Even the First Folk."

"While the Lowlanders slept, I melted the dervish from the ice with my staff," Wheat continued. "Once freed, it circled the camp a few times and then winged north. I assume it was flying back to the glacier. In ancient times, weren't the dervish Watchers sworn to protect their First Folk families?"

The kitchen girl began to serve cups of onion soup. As she set the steaming broth in front of Wheat, the shepherd felt a strange tingling that she attributed to how long it had been since she'd sat to a nourishing meal.

"At all costs," Aubergine said, taking up her spoon. "And only the ruling class was permitted the dervish as a familiar. If you really saw a Watcher outside the glacier walls that means that the tombs of the ancients have been desecrated."

"Well, I did," Wheat said. "I have no doubt."

Lily frowned and pinched pepper into her soup. "According to Mamie's tales, the only way into the First Folk graveyard was through the Crystal Caves."

Aubergine nodded grimly. "So now it must be that both the Caves and the tombs of the ancients have been discovered. But how? Supposedly a Guardian protects the graves."

"Surely this Guardian would not let anyone pass into the mausoleum, let alone rob it," Wheat said.

Ratta sopped up her soup with fresh sourdough bread and took a big bite. She felt Lily's eyes on her and avoided meeting them.

"I wish Sierra was here." Lily pushed her unfinished soup away as the servant wheeled out a cart bearing platters of stuffed turkey and boiled sweet potatoes.

Wheat reached for a plate and helped herself to the gravy boat. "Sierra would know which tale holds the answer."

"I think not," Ratta said, exchanging her empty soup bowl for a serving of turkey as the cart passed by her chair.

"What do you mean?" Wheat said.

Refusing to answer, Ratta cut her sweet potato in half and slathered both sides with butter. Wheat turned to Lily, who was steadfastly cutting her meat into bites.

Lily looked up. "Are you asking me?"

Since her mouth was full, Wheat could only nod and gesture with her fork.

Lily glanced at Aubergine, who paused with a forkful of stuffing to give her a slight nod. Lily took a deep breath.

"There is another yarn untold," she explained. "It is called the Lost Tale of the Guardian. Sierra does not know the story, for Mamie never voiced it before she ceased to speak aloud."

"I assume you alone can recite the tale," Wheat said, pointing her butter knife at Ratta.

"That's the only reason I'm here." Ratta reached for the gravy. "I swore to Mamie I would reveal the Lost Tale to Sierra. But because she has not heeded the call, there is no need to say anything." She gave Lily a fierce look. "Is there, Lily?"

"I thought you summoned us all that we might save the Middlelands," Wheat complained to Aubergine. "I did not come all this way just to hear an old yarn told by a kitchen wench."

"Watch your mouth," Ratta said.

"Watch yours." Wheat reached for her staff, only to find it missing. Ratta laughed.

Lily smacked the flat of her hand on the table so hard that her water glass jumped. "Ladies!"

Aubergine laid down her utensils. She wiped her lips on a cloth napkin and set it aside. "I called you all here for several reasons," she said, after the others quieted. "Reasons that hinge on the revelation of the Lost Tale."

The kitchen girl cleared their dinner plates, then set a browned apple pie before Lily and handed her the silver server. Lily felt a shock of familiarity as their fingers touched. With a wary glance at the serving maid, she cut into the piecrust. The servant gave her an innocent smile, and Lily averted her eyes. She sensed a migraine coming on. The pie was still warm, and the aroma of cinnamon apples filled the room.

Lily nodded, satisfied with the pie. "Serve it with cream," she directed the maid whose eyes danced in a peculiar way. Lily had the sense they had met before. Yet she had just hired the young woman in the marketplace yesterday.

"The impossible has come to pass, it seems," Aubergine continued. "The secret passage to the Crystal Caves has been found, and the tombs of the ancients have been plundered. Our own Mamie lies in the parlor, suspended between this world and the next, unable to pass into the land of dreams. Who knows what has happened to the Guardian of the Crystal Caves, or the Secrets of Old?"

"Are such secrets safe from the Dark Queen?" Lily asked, waving away the plate that the serving girl offered her, with its wedge of pie and dollop of cream. "If Lowlanders have ransacked the tombs, they could have discovered its secrets."

Aubergine pursed her lips. "Tasman may have found some secrets, but she can't unlock them without my amethyst necklace."

"I thought she had your necklace," Ratta said, licking cream from her lips.

"She stole a broken string of eleven stones twenty years ago." Aubergine stabbed a fork into her piece of the steaming pie. She shook her head. "The circle is far from complete."

"Hasn't anyone ever found the lost gem?" Wheat looked from Aubergine to Lily. "Are you sure?"

"No one," Lily confirmed. She felt uneasy. The maid seemed to be lingering unnecessarily over the dessert plates.

Aubergine gave Lily a strange look. "That may not be entirely true. For a while, I believed that Lavender Mae had come across the crystal and hidden it among lesser stones in the pouch she wears. Then I thought that perhaps Esmeralde had discovered it in one of her fossickers' spoils, among shards foraged from the Trickle. Now I think someone else has it."

"I assumed it disappeared with Teal." Ratta shrugged.

Wheat eyed Aubergine curiously. "I thought for certain Aubergine had it." She turned to Lily, who sat strangely silent and had turned away the pie.

The serving girl scraped their plates noisily.

"Let's leave this for another time," Lily said through gritted teeth as her head began to pound.

"You mean you know where the lost stone is?" Ratta asked her in disbelief. "Who has it? Aubergine?"

Lily pressed her fingers to her throbbing temples. "No," she grimaced.

Ratta took another wild guess. "The Dark Queen?"

"If the Dark Queen harbored the lost stone, we would all be enduring her wrath right now," Aubergine intoned.

"That's right," Lily agreed. "Now ask a proper question."

"I see what she means." Wheat smiled. "She wants a more general question." She eyed Lily. "Where is the stone?"

"Finally!" Lily sighed. "You must learn how to ask questions, all of you." She looked at each of them in turn. The serving girl hid a smile. "The lost stone is not lost. It is hiding in plain sight. We will see it sooner, rather than later."

Aubergine nodded with satisfaction and turned to Ratta. "We will hear your lost tale when we have our simmer over the great pot tomorrow night," she decided. "Then will we see what to do."

From the dye shed came the muffled sounds of scuffling. A door banged open. Wheat and Ratta looked toward the hall in alarm. Recognizing familiar crows of delight, Aubergine tried not to laugh. Lily suppressed a smile and held up her forefinger. They all heard a clatter of booted feet coming up the hall toward the main house.

"Shhh!" Someone kept whispering, while other voices giggled. "Shhh!"

The dining room door burst open and Smokey Jo skipped in, flanked by Esmeralde and Indigo Rose and followed by several young strangers.

Smokey's eyes lit up. "Pie!" she shouted.

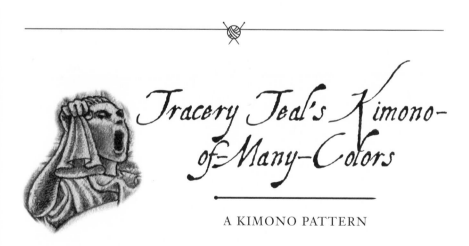

Tracery Teal's Kimono-of-Many-Colors

A KIMONO PATTERN

Knit this experienced-skill-level kimono as a barn coat or to walk to the market on cool days. Finished sizes for women are small to extra-large.

Get the pattern from PotluckYarn.com/epatterns

Lily felt a shock of familiarity as their fingers touched.

CHAPTER 19

LILY ROSE FROM HER CHAIR IN GREETING. "Welcome. Who have we here?"

Ratta turned from her pie plate "Esmeralde, you look so old," she said to the herbalist. "And Indigo Rose, is that you? Your braids have gone gray."

"You're full of compliments as usual, Ratta." Esmeralde limped through the doorway with her heavy Possibles Bag smacking against her hip. "Aubergine, we apologize for interrupting your dinner."

"Sorry we're so late." Indigo glared at Trader. "We had unforeseen trouble getting into the city."

"Nonsense. You're just in time to eat." Aubergine waved them in. "Everyone, come sit."

Lily beckoned to the serving girl, who was wheeling the cart back to the pantry. "Bring more plates and silver," she said, rounding the table to hug Esmeralde and Indigo Rose.

"You must be Sierra's daughter," Lily said to Skye, holding her at arm's length. "You are the spitting image of your mother."

"I am Skye Blue," the tall blond girl said, blushing. "And this is my brother, Garth."

"Hello," Garth grinned. "Are you all knitting witches?"

"We are," Lily smiled. "I am Lilac Lily, and this is Winter Wheat, and Ratta. I see you have met Smokey Jo, and you know Esmeralde and Indigo Rose. At the head of the table is our dye mistress, Aubergine."

"The Potluck Queen?" Skye's eyes shone as she took in the violet eyes and long gray hair. She turned to her companions and lowered her voice. "In truth?"

"None other," Esmeralde said.

"Boys," Ratta complained to Aubergine as the travelers settled themselves noisily into the empty chairs. "I thought we allowed no boys at the table of the Twelve." She watched sullenly as the serving girl set out steaming plates of food before the new arrivals. She narrowed her eyes at Trader. "Who might you be?"

Trader shrugged and gave Aubergine an impish grin.

Aubergine's eyes glinted with a spark of recognition. "Do I know you?"

"Mayhap."

"Little Teal?" Nodding, Trader rose to stand with a broad smile before the Potluck Queen. Aubergine took the fossicker's hands. "I set these weary eyes on you again at last," she whispered. "Does anyone else know you have returned here safe?"

Trader shrugged. "No one but you, I hope—and now a few others in this room."

"She looks just like a boy—a ruffian, even!" Smokey cried from her tall chair, clapping her hands. "What a clever disguise!"

"You are mistaken. His name is Trader," Garth insisted, popping a chunk of potato into his mouth. He chewed busily. "Only some folk call him Traitor. He is a fossick boy, and you're right that he's a ruffian, too."

Skye burst out laughing. "It is you who are mistaken," she told her brother.

"Well, he got us into a lot of trouble this morning," Garth said. "We passed through the Southern Gate all right, but then a gang of youths dicing at the River Walk moorings recognized him. He had to split and run. It took forever for us to find him."

"We should have left him in that alley in Winter Watch," Indigo muttered.

"We had to rescue him," Esmeralde reminded her. She pulled out her flask of Crystal Cordial. "We were hopelessly lost."

"Trader?" Aubergine asked. "Is that your moniker now?"

"Yes," The scrappy-looking girl returned to her seat. "To tell you the truth, after all these years, I prefer it. In my eyes, there was only one Tracery Teal."

"Teal was one of our own," Ratta huffed. "And a woman."

"As am I," Trader said. "Well, a girl, anyway."

Indigo Rose threw down her napkin. "A girl? You little imposter!"

"I swear I did not know it, Indy," Esmeralde said. She quickly dumped two glasses of water into a pitcher containing fresh flowers, and refilled the cups with measures of cordial. "Here, have a drink."

Garth gaped at Trader. "It is not possible that you are a maid," he protested, looking her up and down. "You lead a band of fossick boys. We're comrades. We've shared meals and a tent." He grimaced. "I don't camp with girls."

"Why would you pose as a boy, anyway?" Ratta eyed Trader suspiciously. The fine red frizz that had escaped her bun haloed around her head. "The Northland Guard collects youths."

"For me, being mistaken for a boy is less dangerous than being seen as a girl," Trader replied, helping herself to bread and butter. "I'm trying to avoid notice by blending in with the scenery. I'm trying to recall how you say it." She took a bite of her roll. "Oh, I remember. You call it hiding in plain sight."

"I know what we call it," Ratta retorted.

"You seem to know an awful lot about our ways." Indigo pointed her meat knife at Trader. "Who are you, really? What are you hiding from? I would like to know. You almost got us killed this afternoon."

"Those boys just wanted money I owed them from dicing." Trader finished the roll and began to slice turkey. "It was nothing."

"It was ten pieces of Northland silver," Esmeralde reminded her.

"I'll pay you back in kind," Trader said.

"Would anyone like another cup of tea?" Lily asked brightly. "Who is ready for pie?"

Smokey raised her hand. "Me!"

Lily watched the kitchen maid bring dessert for the second round of diners. The girl seemed humorless. Well, an inability to be cheerful wasn't a character flaw, and she was efficient and quiet in her work.

As the others chatted over dessert, Aubergine put her arm around the little gnome. "Smokey Jo, where were you? You had me worried."

"Locked in the dye shed storeroom," the gnome said, in a small voice.

"Locked in the storeroom?" Aubergine frowned. "It was locked to begin with. How did you get in?"

"Through the keyhole," Smokey answered, licking her lips. "Can I have more clotted cream on my pie?"

"Never mind that." Finished with all but her crust, Wheat noticed the quiet conversation near the head of the table. "Smokey, where is my crook?"

Smokey glanced around her chair and peeked under the table. "I must have left it in the storeroom," she quavered.

Wheat pushed back her chair and jumped up from the table. "What?"

"The amber crystals went out and it got dark," Smokey tried to explain.

"I hope it's still there." Wheat stalked out of the dining room. "Don't ask to use it again."

"I almost never ask," Smokey said, looking down. "I just take it."

Trader laughed. "How did you get in through the keyhole? I had to pick the lock to get you out."

"I was smoke," Smokey said. "Wheat's staff does that to me sometimes." She turned to Aubergine. "You know what else? Teal was in there, and she was smoke, too. Only I was gray and she was green."

"You saw Tracery Teal in the storeroom?" Lily asked. "I've not laid eyes on her in twenty years."

"She wasn't really Teal," Smokey replied. "She was just green fog."

Indigo Rose shook her gray braids and adjusted her bandana, before turning to Aubergine. "Do you believe any of this?"

"I do," Aubergine confirmed. "All of us who live here have seen Teal's ghost behaving fretfully from time to time. She appears as a wispy cloud floating in the hallways, or as green haze hovering over the kitchen stove."

"I assumed that was merely smoke from burnt toast, or Smokey Jo playing with the cook stove," Lily said. "She is forever putting bits of bark and moss into the fire to watch them smolder."

"A trail of mossy mist is all we have left of Teal. She is a restless spirit and almost impossible to contain." Aubergine placed her hands on the table. "It was I who lured Teal into the storeroom."

"Why?" Trader asked. "You can't confine a ghost."

Aubergine shook her head wearily. "Little Teal."

"Trader," the fossicker corrected her.

Aubergine shut her eyes and smiled. "Trader," she began again. "If you only knew. The Teal who came before you constantly reminds us of her presence. She can be tiresome and unnecessary."

"She takes things to get attention," Smokey said. "Things she doesn't need."

"I'm missing a few utensils," Lily added. "Has anyone seen the new soup ladle I bought in the marketplace, or my fine-bristled bottle brush?"

"One day you will rummage around in a closet or open an armoire and your misplaced items will tumble down on your head," Aubergine predicted with a rueful smile. "It has happened to me more than once."

Smokey plucked Aubergine's sleeve. "Teal was mean to me. She took my sweater. Then she left me locked in the dye closet." Smokey turned to the rest seated around the table. "All I had to eat all afternoon was an apple."

Wheat stomped back into the dining room carrying her staff. "The lock is broken on the storeroom door," she reported. "And all the dyestuffs are missing." She pointed her staff at Smokey, letting the amber crystals hit and spark. "Lucky for you, no one took my crook."

"Did you see any green smoke in the air?" Aubergine asked.

"There was steam over the dye pot." Wheat acknowledged. "But the fire wasn't even lit."

"I shall have to find a new way to coax Teal into a different sort of enclosure—perhaps my seamless box." Aubergine eyed Trader. "Teal has not been in your presence since you were a babe. Come help me catch her."

Trader rose and grabbed her belongings. She picked up her walking stick from behind her chair.

"Wait, what are you saying?" Ratta handed her empty pie plate to the maid, who added it to the stack on the cart. "That our Tracery Teal knows of this Trader who runs around in rags masquerading as a boy?"

Trader rapped her stick on the floor. "Tracery Teal was my aunt, my mother's sister. I am her namesake. But I have never met Teal in person, obviously. She disappeared before I was born."

"Trader, is that why you offered to take me to the Burnt Holes to find my mother?" Skye asked. "Did you really want to look for Tracery Teal?"

Trader nodded. "I thought she might have been imprisoned. But now I have learned that she's here."

Aubergine rose slowly from her seat. "No, child, Teal is not here," she said softly.

A delicate Merino lace wrap lay folded over the back of Aubergine's chair. She reached back, picked it up, and settled it around her neck. Hand knit in an allover lattice pattern, it hung like a mantle over her shoulders. Only Smokey Jo was familiar with the garment, a ceremonial piece dyed in shades of purple and black. Aubergine only wore it when she was preparing for a vision over the great pot. Standing at the head of the table, Aubergine gripped the edge of the table. Like most Northlanders, she was exceptionally tall. Unlike many, she appeared exceptionally regal, with the shawl over a deep eggplant gown and her violet eyes, shining from a careworn face framed by a mane of silver hair. She seemed not only regal but imposing.

"You witness mere wisps and trails of the Teal that was." Aubergine explained, in a grim voice. "She can never appear to us in her solid form again, because Tasman destroyed her. Only traces remain." Her dark eyes pierced Trader. "Thus your given name, Traces of Teal."

"What happened to your aunt was my fault," Lily admitted, her face burning with shame. "It was I who put Teal in Tasman's path that terrible night."

"The Dark Queen destroyed Teal, yet still seems to seek her." Aubergine looked to Lily. "Can you tell us why?"

"Tasman believes that Teal's ghost saw what happened to the lost jewel," Lily said. "When the necklace broke, that stone disappeared along with Teal."

"Maybe it's in an upstairs closet or armoire, like Aubergine said." Garth whispered to Skye. "I want to go look."

"Hush," Skye held out a hand to still him.

"I can't ascertain what the remaining traces of our Teal may know about the missing amethyst." Lily shook her head. "It isn't possible to read the mind of a person whose essence has evaporated."

"Teal is nothing more than morning mist," Aubergine agreed. "Whatever her spirit knows, it has no way to tell us."

"Fair enough, but we all name successors," Wheat said. "Who stood to inherit Teal's lore?"

Indigo turned to Lily. "Her sister, perhaps?"

Esmeralde nodded in quick agreement. "Surely whoever was chosen to take Tracery Teal's place in the circle of Twelve would have knowledge of the lost stone." She looked at Lily expectantly. "Who is it?"

"Her namesake niece here, Traces of Teal," Lily revealed with a smile.

"Who prefers to be called Trader," Aubergine added. "If the Dark Queen seeks any of us more than the others, it is she." She glanced at the girl. "We must all protect Trader, as I have sought to do by hiding her as a boy in the Middlelands all these years."

"Why?" Indigo Rose wanted to know. "She isn't Teal, really."

"No, but she is the embodiment of all that remains of the Teal you once knew," Aubergine said. "Trader stands to inherit Teal's lore, as well as her place in our circle of Twelve. If Teal ever did know what happened to the lost stone, Trader may yet help us find it."

"First I find out that you're a girl, and now I find out you're a knitting witch," Garth complained. "Have you seen this lost stone? Is it hiding in a closet, upstairs, perchance?"

"How would I know?" Trader said.

Garth persisted. "Is it among the fossicks you keep in your pack?" He laid a hand on Trader's shoulder. "You didn't sell it to those men at the Forks for a few coppers' worth of kettle corn, did you?"

"Of course not." Trader shrugged him off.

"She is not one of us," Ratta scoffed. "I doubt she has even heard of the lost stone. And she's just a girl, too young to be of any use. "

"We all were girls once," Indigo said, draining her cup of cordial.

Aubergine was not listening. Her eyes had grown dark as a distant storm. First the table under her hands began to vibrate, and then air buzzed with a charge of electricity. The rest of them startled, expecting a clap of thunder. Instead, the dye shed door banged open and cold air rushed out of the night and up the hall. It blasted into the dining room, scattering napkins, swirling salt, and knocking the pepper mill onto the floor. Aubergine's silver hair tumbled wildly around her face.

"What is it, Aubergine?" Lily cried.

"Tasman is close, as is the stone." Aubergine's voice dropped to a whisper. She put up a hand to shield her face from the stinging squall. Her breath grew shallow as she focused her sight inward. "I can see them both in my mind's eye. But not together."

The wind died as quickly as it had started. Blinking, Aubergine's eyes examined each of them in turn, coming to rest on Trader. "We must start a simmer," she said at last. "Ready or not, even if the others aren't here, we begin tomorrow. We can't wait."

"What about Skye?" Garth asked. "And me? Can't we be witches, too, and help make the Twelve?"

"The lines of the Twelve are matriarchal," Lily said. "You may not."

"May-tree what?" Garth asked.

"It means no boys," Ratta growled.

"Our power passes from mother to daughter, aunt to niece, or mistress to ward," Aubergine said. "If we cannot hold Teal captive, Trader must take her place when we circle the great pot." She looked down the table. "And it's true, Skye, you may have to stand in for your mother."

"You're not expecting her?" Skye asked, blinking back tears. She searched Aubergine's face, and then Lily's.

"Not Sierra," Lily replied, with a glance at Aubergine. "Not in time."

"Even if she does heed the call, Sierra cannot assume her previous place in our circle, for she is no longer my successor," Aubergine explained. "If everything goes as planned, Sierra will be named The Keeper of the Tales."

"Sierra will inherit Mamie's lore?" Wheat gasped. "We all thought Sierra would one day wear your mantle. Then who is your rightful heir now?"

Indigo smiled at Esmeralde, who smiled in return and topped off their glasses with a celebratory measure of cordial. Indigo caught Trader's attention and put a finger to her lips. All Trader could do was shake her head and roll her eyes.

"Ratta knows all of the tales," Wheat said, ignoring their antics. "We thought Mamie's role would pass to her."

"I keep telling you, I am here in my own stead," Ratta said. "Will you get that through your head?"

Wheat reached for her staff, letting the glowing crystals click together. "What does Ratta offer?" She asked Aubergine. "She possesses no more arcane lore than this boy." Wheat pointed her crook at Garth.

Aubergine wrapped the ceremonial shawl around her shoulders. She fixed Wheat with a stare so frigid that the crystals on the shepherd's crook went dark. "How many of you speak the silent tongue of the ancients?" Aubergine surveyed them all. "Who here but Ratta understands First Folk Mind Speak?"

The table was silent.

"As I thought," Ratta said, looking smug.

Unable to hold back any longer, Indigo nudged Esmeralde. Together, they stood and toasted each other with freshened glasses. To make herself taller, Indigo stood on her chair seat. She held both glasses as Esmeralde climbed aloft, too.

"Here's to us," Esmeralde announced, as they stood above the others. She smiled at Indigo. "Two heads are better than one."

"What in cracked crystal . . .?" Wheat began.

"Indy and I are trading places as well," Esmeralde told the group.

"With who?" Ratta snorted. "Each other?"

Trader could contain herself no longer. "No one wants to succeed either of you," she laughed.

"No matter." Esmeralde raised her cup. "We're taking over."

"Taking over what?" Wheat asked.

"The Potluck," Indigo said. She clicked cups with Esmeralde and took a big gulp of cordial. "It's our turn to run it."

"Whatever gave you that idea?" Lily asked mildly.

"The Potluck is not a game of musical chairs," Aubergine said.

"We saw it in a vision," Esmeralde replied. "Over the pot in Indy's fireplace."

"You need all Twelve to have a simmer," Smokey said. "Everyone knows that."

"There was only the two of us," Indigo argued. "But we saw everything just fine. Esmeralde and I were sitting here and here," she pointed, indicating Aubergine's and Smokey Jo's chairs at the head of the table. "Presiding over dinner."

"Had you been drinking? Or smoking?" Wheat asked.

Esmeralde looked at Indigo, who shrugged. "Not more than usual."

"Are you certain that what you saw was over a dye pot?" Lily chimed in.

"It was just a soup kettle," Indigo admitted. "But it was a large one."

"You did not have a vision," Aubergine told them. "You had a hallucination. As did I, when you undertook this farce, because your show of hissing flames and that shower of green sparks popping from the chimney came to me unwanted, like a headache after sour wine. Now sit down."

"We were just trying to help," Indigo argued peevishly. She swallowed more wine.

"That's right. We were just making an offer," Esmeralde said, jovially raising her cordial cup in Aubergine's direction.

Suddenly the glasses flew from Esmeralde's and Indigo's hands and upended, pouring dregs of sticky liquor over their heads. Then the empty cups crashed to the table where they exploded into bits.

Aubergine's eyes blazed purple. "Sit down."

Esmeralde and Indigo jumped to the floor and took their chairs in haste.

"Aubergine, you're getting old," Indigo could not help pointing out, a bit shaky. She wrung out her sopping braids one by one as

Esmeralde scooped together the pieces of broken crockery. "We all know Smokey Jo spends most days playing with fire." She picked up her napkin and absentmindedly wiped the wine from her face. "Who will head the Potluck when you're gone?"

"Who said I am going anywhere?" Aubergine's eyes blazed dark and terrible. Indigo opened her mouth, but no sound came out, so she shut it again.

"As we've had no answering fire, we shall wait one more night for the others." Aubergine spoke into the silence that saturated the room. "At daybreak, Smokey Jo will light the fire under the great pot."

As soon as Aubergine had made her pronouncement, the others began to chatter.

"Once the blaze is started, we mustn't let it go out," Smokey Jo said.

Lily nodded. "I'll have the stable boy bring in more wood. Garth, you can help with that."

"The water and the iron pot are both so cold," Smokey said. "Aubergine, it will take a long time before something that big can come to a boil."

"The pot should start to simmer by mid-afternoon," Aubergine calculated. "Then we will add the crystals. It's a pity that Lavender Mae isn't here to grind them. Indigo Rose, I ask you to do the honors." Aubergine turned to Wheat. "Prepare your best fleece for the dye pot."

"I have no fleeces," Wheat said. "My flock was scattered by Lowlanders. I have just the one lame sheep."

"This is folly," Ratta said. "Half of us are missing. The crystals are gone."

Esmeralde raised her eyebrows. "Indy and I think there is an interloper."

"Or an intruder, perhaps," Indigo added.

"It was probably just Teal." Smokey bent her head and counted on her fingers. "There are but nine of us," she announced at last, holding out both hands with one thumb bent over for the rest of them to see. "Ten if you include Mamie." She gave Lily an anxious look. "Can we count her?"

"I'm afraid not, for she is neither part of this world nor the next."

Aubergine nodded to Ratta. "Recite the lost yarn and we can let Mamie pass."

"I will tell nothing without Sierra's blessing." Ratta was stubborn. "Only she can decipher the meaning of the Lost Tale."

"Get some sleep, all of you," Aubergine ordered, ignoring their objections. "Lily will show the newcomers where to sleep. After dinner tomorrow, we shall assemble around the great pot." She beckoned to Trader. "Let's try one last time to catch Teal."

Aubergine's Simmer Shawl

A SHAWL PATTERN

This experienced-skill-level shawl is knit in an allover lattice pattern and helps with composure when you must preside over events. Finished in two sizes: 18" by 54" and 32" by 60".

Get the pattern from PotluckYarn.com/epatterns

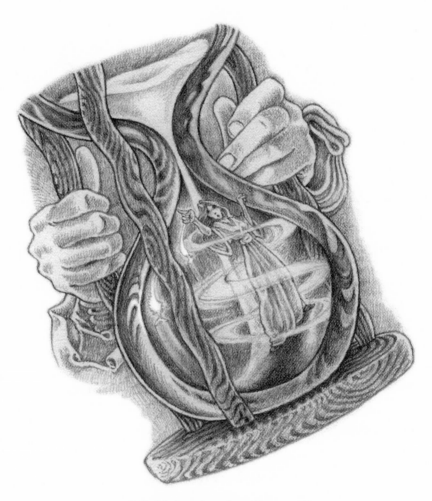

"Hold the glass for all to see."

CHAPTER 20

The Lost Tale

LATE THE FOLLOWING AFTERNOON, the chosen women filed quietly down the hall and into the dye shed. They formed a silent circle around the great pot, which had been gradually approaching a boil all day. Those who knew their places around the black iron cauldron took them quickly. Smokey Jo nudged her stepstool to Aubergine's left, and Lilac Lily swept in on Aubergine's right, followed by Winter Wheat, trying to tread lightly in her heavy boots. Indigo and Esmeralde crowded in on the far side of Smokey Jo, while Trader crept up the other half of the circle to take Teal's place next to Wheat, because they had failed to catch the wayward spirit. Ratta dragged herself into the circle reluctantly, unable to keep from looking toward the back of the room every few seconds. Mamie's body, still wrapped in the never-ending shawl, lay in repose on the viewing table Lily had helped Ratta carry in from the front parlor.

Across from Smokey Jo, Skye trembled, fearing that she would dishonor her mother's place in the circle. She stood alone. To her right was a space reserved for Lavender Mae, and to her left was the vacancy created by Tasman the night she broke the necklace and fled. Garth had been banished to the main house, and no amount of pleading had gotten him any closer than the summer kitchen, even when he offered to stoke the fire.

"We allow no boys," Ratta had explained, not unkindly. "Besides, fire-tending is the kitchen maid's chore."

The humid air was suffused with the aroma of fleece freshly scoured with lavender soap. Beeswax candles flickered around the gathering, providing the only light other than an oil lamp that glowed on a small stand near the door.

As the others joined her, Aubergine gazed intently into the pot that bubbled over the fire pit, her back to the broken lock on the storage room door. Draped across her shoulders was the ceremonial shawl, its patterned purples and blacks so dark that they seemed to melt into the surrounding shadows. As the iron pot steamed, Smokey climbed onto her stepstool she had used to peer into the cauldron earlier and counted the figures in the dim light of the broken circle. "We are but nine," she announced. "Aubergine, nothing works with nine."

"Never mind that now." Aubergine turned her violet eyes toward Ratta. "Are you ready?"

"First the crystals," Ratta countered. "Then we wait for Sierra."

Aubergine sighed. "The storeroom is as bare as Wheat reported. There are no more crystals to speak of."

"No crystals?" Smokey Jo asked, in a worried voice. "Aubergine, surely you haven't used them all. We haven't had a simmer in years."

"No, I have not used them all." Aubergine's voice sounded weary.

"Did you take some to your room, maybe?" Smokey asked. "Are they out of reach, perchance? What about that high, high shelf?"

Aubergine shook her head. "I did not misplace them."

"Does Teal have them, then?" Smokey said. "Has she hidden them, along with my sweater?"

When Aubergine just pursed her lips, Ratta let loose. "Don't tell us you have squandered our crystals," she lashed out. "We didn't travel all this way to find that you wasted them on foolish visions or ground them into dye for whimsy."

Aubergine's eyes grew dark and thunderous. "You seem to have forgotten that the magic crystals were mine," she reminded them all. "They came with me from the shores of the Crystal Lakes when I migrated to Bordertown more than forty years ago. I carried an entire sack of them here, and I gleaned a few more over the years from fossickers who frequent a certain rock shop in Artisan's Hand. But for the most part, the crystals were never replenished." She held her head high. "They were mine unchallenged, and I used them as I wished."

"Is that where all our Northland coins came from?" Smokey Jo whispered. "Have you been trading crystals for silver?"

"You can't sell crystals," Skye said. "Crystals harbor magic, and buying or selling them is against the law."

"Then we all belong in jail," Indigo said.

"Magic is forbidden by those who desire it most," Aubergine replied. "Only those who do not understand how to use crystals fear them."

"Such as men," Ratta added with a firm nod.

"I did sell some of the crystals," Aubergine admitted. "Shards and slivers, lesser bits."

"To whom?" Wheat demanded.

"The Northland Guard," Smokey Jo guessed. "That's why you've been retiring to your room to nap. You've been frequenting the garrison at night."

Indigo turned to Esmeralde. "You see, I knew there was an interloper."

"You are our intruder?" Esmeralde stared at Aubergine. "You are the one who has spread rumors of the Twelve along the main track?"

Aubergine shook her head. "No, the Guard has done all of that. I just made them a little more aware of you, I'm afraid."

"Well, whatever you did," Indigo said, "it tipped them off nicely. We were sought at every checkpoint."

"There were even soldiers watching for us at the fair," Esmeralde said. "At least most of us knew better than to show our faces there. Only Sierra got caught."

"For that I am sorry," Aubergine said. "The garrison commander and his council saw you briefly in a passing vision. It could not be helped."

"You sold the last of our crystals to the men who outlawed them?" Indigo asked, incredulous. "And then revealed us in a vision?"

"You knew the Guard would seek us out!" Ratta raged, her face growing red. Her hair came loose from its bun and fell around her shoulders. "You knew we might get caught! Why in cracked crystal would you do that to people you call your own?"

When Aubergine remained mute, Ratta whirled on Lily. "Why?" she demanded.

"The question has been asked," Lily warned Aubergine. "It will be answered."

Aubergine met her eyes steadfastly. "As you must."

Lily stepped forward into a beam of candlelight and faced them all. "Aubergine did trade the last of the crystals to the Northland Guard for newly minted silver."

"Enough silver to live out her days, I am sure," Ratta spat.

Lily held up a hand to silence her. "Enough silver to mount an expedition to the Crystal Caves," she replied sternly. "War is expensive, and without the lost gem we are defenseless. But that is not the reason she offered the Guard crystals." She paused to exchange looks with Aubergine. "As you all are aware, magic stones are useless to the Guard without our guidance and interpretation."

"A simmer without the Twelve? True, it can't be done," Smokey said.

"Exactly," Aubergine agreed, with a satisfied look. "I'll continue," she told Lily.

With a nod, Lily stepped back into the shadows.

"The garrison commander and his council wanted to experience a vision, so I created one for them," Aubergine said, her eyes flickering in the light. "Over a false pot simmering in their chambers, I showed those men of war a future they wanted so badly that they could not help but believe it."

"What did you reveal to them?" Trader asked.

A crafty look came over Esmeralde's face. "Tell us," she said.

Aubergine smiled, remembering. "The commander and his war council saw the Twelve detained within the Burnt Holes, and the Dark Queen imprisoned in a rolling cage while they went about their war. They witnessed a Northland Army tens of thousands strong, taking the Lowland forces by surprise in the icy Out Crops of the Far North. They saw their captains subduing the South by brute force and marching the remains of the Lowland Army back to the garrison in surrender. It pleased them that they appeared to have no need of any witches or magic or crystals. Finally, I showed them the secret entrance to the famed Crystal Caves. Once inside, they all saw that the caverns were just pretty rooms of ice fit for tourists. The crystals sparkled in the light, but none of them exuded magic." Aubergine paused. "Everything I showed them was a lie."

"You used our crystals to spread lies among the Guard?" Ratta asked, warming to the idea.

"I aimed to busy them with their war, so that we would have an opportunity to secure the Crystal Caves against the Dark Queen without interference," Aubergine said. Her brow furrowed and she looked troubled. "I sought to make us look harmless. Little did I realize that the council would take the part about detaining the Twelve so seriously." Her face cleared and she continued. "They will soon be mounting an expedition to the Out Crops of the Far North, because that is where they think the Dark Queen's armies are massing. That should keep them occupied. The going is slow around the top of the glacier, and there is nothing up there but windswept ice."

"Fine and dandy," Ratta said. "But how can we to have a simmer without crystals?"

Aubergine frowned. "I thought Mae would have heeded the call by now. I can't imagine what delays her. She has plenty of crystals. The last I knew, she kept a pouch of them strung around her neck."

"Is it possible that she has found the lost crystal?" Indigo asked.

"Sadly, no," Aubergine shook her head. "She has gathered many fine crystals, but I don't believe she has that one."

"What about the answering fire?" Wheat brought up. "Since none of us ever cast the cold-fire crystals skyward, we must assume they are intact. Could we use them in a simmer?"

"Certainly." Aubergine studied the faces around the dye pot. "Who had the tinderbox last?"

Ratta shook her head. "Neither Mamie nor I."

"Don't look at us," Indigo said, indicating herself and Esmeralde. "If we had answering fire, we would have used it. Do you think we like getting pulled around like puppets?"

"The last anyone knew, Sierra had that box." Aubergine glanced toward Skye.

"Sierra is not here," Wheat remarked. "What would you have us do now?"

"Is that why you said my mother might come, but would be too late?" Skye asked Lily.

"Sierra had the answering fire," Lily confirmed. "She had the duty of releasing the crystals skyward at the first sign of Aubergine's summons. Then those here would know that we had seen the fire and would answer its call."

Aubergine rose and reached into the shelves of dyestuffs behind her chair. She pulled down the empty tinderbox that had housed the crystals she had thrown into the sky to create the summons. She held out the silver box toward Skye. "It was a seamless container, the match to this one."

Trader looked at Skye. "That is your box," she whispered. "The one you have hidden in your mother's knits."

"I have it," Skye said eagerly. "It's in a rucksack upstairs in my room. My mother sheltered it in a bundle of crystal-dyed garments she had a friend hide for me when she was arrested at the fairgrounds."

Indigo turned on her. "You had the answering fire this entire time and you didn't let us use it? Do you realize the bother you could have saved us on the road?"

"I didn't even know what it was," Skye answered. "I slept on it once by mistake and the hard edges gave me a crick in the neck."

"Fetch the box," Aubergine said.

Skye hurried toward the dye shed door, which burst open before her so quickly that she ran straight into a young man in a Northland Guard uniform.

From her vantage point at the cauldron Winter Wheat noticed the military intruder first. "Soldiers!" She warned, reaching for her staff.

The cabochons hit and sparked, chittering like squirrels as they illumi-nated the doorway. Wheat deftly dipped the crook of her staff, focus-ing the light from the amber crystals into a blinding beam and aimed at the emblem sewn on the breast of the Guardsman's tunic.

Smokey Jo, fascinated, crowed, "Fall back!"

"Keep out," Ratta raged, whirling to bar the soldier's entrance. "Men are not allowed here."

"What a surprise!" Skye gave the young man a joyful hug, and then turned to the others. "I know he looks like a grown man and a Guards-man, but he's just my brother."

"He's still a boy," Ratta glowered, as Skye tried to pull Warren past her. "He can't come in."

Suddenly the lamp on the stand by the door began to wobble, before spilling a trail of oil across the worn planks. The burning wick ignited the oil, which erupted in a curtain of flame across the doorway.

"What in cracked crystal?" Warren shrank back from the fire.

"The magic of men is not welcome here, now or ever!" Ratta snarled.

"Ratta, the boy could not have known," Lily said.

Warren looked from his sister to Lily. "I swear I did not knock it." As he bent to steady the hissing lamp, green flames burst anew from its chimney and singed his fingers.

Warren leapt back, shaking his hands. "Shards!" he swore.

"Leave it be! You've caused enough damage," Ratta shouted, coughing. Scowling at him, she reached for the blazing lamp. Almost immediately the fire subsided. She surveyed the doorframe, which continued to smolder and choke the room with smoke. "Look what he's done!"

Smokey Jo jumped down from her stool. "Stand aside! I can put it out." Armed with a remnant of damp carpet she saved for such occasions, Smokey Jo scurried to the doorway and beat out the remaining flames.

Before she was quite done, they heard more commotion in the hall, the sound like a cornered cat, spitting and fighting. The noise grew louder. A cloaked figure stepped through the hovering smoke, dragging a small form dressed in an oversized army jacket. The scraggly thing shrieked terribly.

"Noooooo," it yowled, struggling like a trapped animal. "No, no, no."

A tall Northland woman yanked the creature unceremoniously into the room. "It was all I could do to coax her back here again," she said to the youth.

"You should have used the rope," he replied, loosening the coil from his climbing belt.

The feisty thing kicked at him. "No!" she spit. "No!"

Shrinking away from the braided hemp, she turned with a baleful stare, noticing the others. The group of witches stood in a semicircle to each side of Aubergine, struck silent by the scene before them.

"Mae?" the old crone said.

From the far side of the bubbling pot, Aubergine's eyes rested on the heavy pouch hanging from a cord around the scrawny neck. "Greetings, Lavender Mae. You are just in time for the simmer." She smiled and held out her arms. "Welcome, Sierra Blue."

Sierra bowed her head. "We apologize to the Twelve for our tardiness." She stroked the top of Mae's head to calm her. "We had an unavoidable delay."

"Mae," the crone agreed, clinging to Sierra with her eyes shut tight.

Sierra shot Aubergine a troubled glance. "I could not answer your call. I no longer carried the fire."

"Mother?" Skye whispered. "I have the box."

"That's your mother?" Trader asked.

"Yes." Skye went to embrace Sierra, but stopped short because the creature by her mother's side looked like she might bite. "I barely recognized you," she confessed.

"Nor I you," Sierra said. "You look like a woman grown. Are you well?"

Skye nodded solemnly. "Garth is in the kitchen. We never found father." She dropped her eyes. "I have your place in the circle now."

"That is as it should be," Sierra said gently.

"How have you fared?" Esmeralde asked, taking in Sierra's lined face, her soiled cloak, and the addled crone clinging to her. "When we learned you went to the fair, we feared the worst."

"As well as could be expected, given the circumstances. I escaped imprisonment in the Burnt Holes only to find my son, deserted from the army and wandering the lower caves of the glacier with Lavender Mae."

Lily shook her head sadly at the wizened witch whose face was buried in the folds of Sierra's traveling cloak. "It's hard to believe she is our Mae."

"It's more difficult to believe that the two of them arrived without being covered with bites and scratches," Indigo said.

"She bit." Warren pulled up his sleeve to reveal a small crescent on his wrist above angry red claw marks. "And scratched. She ran off twice."

"We've had a trying time," Sierra said. "I eluded my captors only because they feared a dervish that flew north past us. They decided to retreat to the safety of the garrison. In the fray, I was able to slip deep into the ice caves." She gave Warren a curious glance. "There I discovered my son, whom I have not seen in months, leading one of our own like a pet on a leash."

"That's no stranger than Wheat's antics." Ratta snorted. "In her room, she harbors a sheep that she mistakes for a lap dog."

Wheat glared at her. "You find that peculiar? Really?" She looked back at Sierra. "When I met Ratta on the road, she was carrying Mamie's body around in a shawl, like a baby."

"Enough," Lily warned.

Not to be outdone, Smokey Jo raised her hand and waved it wildly. "I toyed with Wheat's staff until it turned me into smoke," she blurted. "I stole Teal's jacket unchallenged and that made her mad."

"We all have tales to tell," Aubergine said, with a sharp glance at Ratta. "One of us in particular."

Sierra surveyed the room. "Does anyone know anything about a dervish?"

Wheat raised her staff. "A few days ago, I freed a dervish from a block of ice some Lowlanders hauled out of the glacier."

Sierra smiled. "You will be glad to know that he made it back safely."

"Excuse me, but should I still get the box of answering fire?" Skye asked in a timid voice.

"There is no need now," Aubergine said. "I trust Mae has more powerful crystals." Her eyes rested on the outlandish witch. "Can you behave as one of the Twelve? You are still one of us, after all."

The crone raised her head to peek at Aubergine. "Mae," she agreed in a small voice.

"Then come." Aubergine clapped her hands. "Come to the circle."

Mae picked her way meekly toward the empty space to Skye's right. Sierra hesitated. Only two vacancies remained; the one to between Skye and Trader that had been Tasman's and the other, between Ratta and Indigo, which was Mamie's. Ratta shifted from foot to foot, defending her territory like a protective dog.

Aubergine stood before the steaming cauldron. Her mantle fluttered around her shoulders as she raised her hands high. "I name Sierra Blue Keeper of the Tales, and bequeath to her all the duties that position entails," she announced.

As Sierra tried to pass, Ratta barred her way. "That legacy was Mamie's to bestow." She shot Sierra a hateful glare. "As her ward, I stand to inherit."

"Keep your place," Aubergine warned.

"I speak the tongue of the ancients," Ratta argued. "I'm the only one who has that skill." She turned to Lily. "I cared for Mamie twenty-five years. Her heritage is mine by rights."

"You are here in your own stead, remember?" Lily shook her head in regret. "Bar Sierra's path and you will share the fate of Tracery Teal."

"Step aside," Aubergine commanded.

Ratta reluctantly made way. Sierra brushed past to stand between Ratta and Indigo Rose.

"The tale will be told, then?" Sierra asked lightly.

"It will be told," Ratta fumed. "But you will not like the yarn, nor the destiny it holds for you."

Aubergine gave Ratta a stern look. "If you have ever hoped that Mamie Verde would pass from this world peacefully, you will recite the yarn exactly as she uttered it."

"Why must I, when I have funeral raiment for her?" Ratta pulled out the shimmering Land-of-Dreams scarf that she had taken from Esmeralde's cottage. "This should be enough to guide Mamie safely to the land of dreams."

"Where did you get that?" Esmeralde narrowed her eyes.

"A scarf has little power to aid one of the Twelve, in this world or the next." Aubergine told Ratta coldly.

"I challenge you!" Esmeralde pointed at Ratta, but spoke to Aubergine. "The scarf is not hers. I dyed that alpaca in a color I call Winterberry, because as all know berries do not grow or ripen in the season of snow. I knit the star design myself to sell to a certain someone who was to meet me at the Middlemarch fair. The funeral scarf is mine."

"If what she says is so, give it back," Aubergine ruled. "Time grows short. Tell us the tale."

"As you wish." Ratta handed the scarf to Indigo, who passed it to Esmeralde. "But first the boy must leave."

"I'm fed up with banishment," Warren said. "I see the fossicker known as Traitor. What makes him special enough to be here?"

"I recognize you too, sledder," Trader jeered. "I beat you handily at dice in Winter Watch not long ago. My specialty lies in the fact that I am a maiden and you are a boy, easy to fool."

"It is so," Lily confirmed to Warren. "We do not condone the magic of men here."

"What magic?" Warren asked. "Does it have anything to do with this hat?" He pulled the Snowflake watch cap from his head. "Mae let me wear it. It's not mine."

"Keep the hat." Aubergine shot a questioning glance to Sierra, who shook her head slightly. "Join your brother in the kitchen," she said to Warren. "The maid can fix you a plate. Then send her in to stoke the fire."

As soon as Warren left through the still-smoking doorframe, Aubergine addressed the others in earnest. "Tonight we have serious work to conduct in our simmer. The fate of the world hangs on what happens here among us. The vision we seek starts at the secret entrance to the glacier. Northlanders call it the Blind Side, because each morning the sun striking the ice is fierce to the eye. To discover this passage unnoticed, we must conjure from our dye pot a colorway in the likeness of multicolored flames licking frozen outcrops."

"Fire," Smokey Jo breathed, "with ice." She relished the words. "We shall call the new colorway Fire and Ice."

"Mae, select for us a series of crystals." Aubergine beckoned Mae to the table beneath the shelves that had housed the dyestuffs. The crone pulled a handful of crystals from her pouch and set them on the shelf. As she did so, she seemed almost sane. Next Aubergine turned to the shepherdess. "Winter Wheat, where is the fiber?"

"Ready." Wheat withdrew a snowy fleece from a burlap sack. She laid it on the table. "It is freshly scoured, long-stapled Suri alpaca," she said, pleased with her find. "It should suit nicely."

"We will dye it and then spin it into fine yarn for a shawl," Aubergine decided. She turned to Smokey Jo. "The shawl, as well as its color, can be called Fire and Ice."

Sierra looked at the fleece approvingly. "I shall spin and ply this fiber into lace weight yarn myself," she said.

"No," Aubergine said gently. "Only Skye can treadle fiber from our simmers now. You shall touch neither spindle nor wheel, for now you will tell the story of each yarn, as Mamie Verde did."

Sierra lowered her eyes. "As you wish."

Mae rummaged in her pouch again and produced an amber crystal, which she placed next to the raw ruby and topaz stones already on the dye table. Humming to herself, she reordered the gems several times before she reached to the shelf behind Aubergine's chair for the mortar and pestle.

"Let's begin." Aubergine lifted a heavy hourglass from the dye shelf and set it on the table. The bottom of the clear glass container was filled with fine shards of broken crystal that had not been disturbed in years. "Esmeralde, bring the mordant," she said briskly. "Indigo, the assistant."

Esmeralde stepped forward to fill a gallon pail with clear vinegar, which she poured into the cauldron. A cloud of steam rose. Indigo sifted a measure of sea salt into a silver scoop and sent it cascading into the pot in an arc of white granules. Together, the two witches took the long-handled wooden paddle and began to stir the liquor slowly. The pungent smells of weak acid and salt water permeated the air.

Aubergine beckoned to Ratta and Lily. "Bring what remains of Mamie to the simmer," she commanded. Silently, Lily went to the back of the room, where the old woman's body lay in the shadows. Ratta followed slowly, unshed tears welling in her eyes. Together they lifted the still form and brought it to the circle just as Mae came forth with the ground crystals, arranged in salt dishes. "Mae?" she asked, recognizing the old woman's likeness. She gazed up at Aubergine. "Mamie?"

"Yes," Aubergine said. "Do you remember what to do?"

Mae nodded solemnly. She sifted first golden grains of topaz, and then burnished bits of ruby, and finally dark amber ground fine as silt, into the iron kettle. Esmeralde and Indigo stirred the bath unceasingly, trading the paddle between them, until the crystals dissolved. Multi-colored ribbons swirled through the current they created, before each in turn disappeared into the vortex.

Smokey dragged her stool closer the pot and climbed back up so she could peer into the steaming mixture. The shaded water pooled and repooled in a medley of colors as it simmered, seeking fiber. "The pot is ready," she announced.

"Wheat, it's your turn," Aubergine said.

Winter Wheat lifted the mass of curly alpaca from the table brought it toward the dye pot where it glistened in the candlelight.

As Wheat lightly held the shining Suri over the steaming cauldron, Aubergine began the incantation. "Tonight we circle the great pot, seeking to wield the power of the ancient stones, much as the First Folk did, as we have practiced countless times before. Over a shared vision we shall meld crystal to fiber. From this we will spin a magical yarn that will someday become the fabric of our story.

"Just as the natural world draws upon elements of earth, water, wind, and fire to flourish, so do we channel the lore and legend gleaned from this circle. Above all, know this: Fire and ice can be used to destroy the lands, but never to rule them. If the Middlelands freeze, or if the Lowlands burn to fuel the Northland wars, we shall all die.

"What happens next is up to the Twelve," she concluded. Scanning the small gathering, she tried not to dwell on the gaping hole between Skye and Trader. Only eleven witches, she thought, only eleven stones.

The pot began to boil.

"Wait!" Smokey shouted. "We are not enough!"

But Wheat had already released the fleece into the simmer. "Fire and Ice," she whispered.

"Fire and Ice," Aubergine declared.

With a flick of the paddle, Esmeralde coaxed the mass of fiber into the swirling liquor. She handed the heavy oar to Indigo, who stirred the whirlpool of color until the fiber spun deep into the dye bath. When she pulled the wooden stick from the pot, nothing clung to its dripping edge.

The bubbling liquid sent up surges of steam, redolent of ground stone, vinegar, and wet wool, as Indigo stowed the paddle and she and Esmeralde resumed their places in the circle.

As the vapor above the vessel began to collect into an opaque cloud, Aubergine continued. "Now it is time to let Mamie pass from this world, if she will." She turned to Trader, who was watching the ceremony in awe. "Little Teal, upend the hourglass," she instructed, beckoning the girl to the table. "You will mark time."

Trader regarded the mound of crumbled crystal in the bottom of the hourglass and her eyes flew to Aubergine in alarm. "I don't know how to tell time," she protested. "I never learned."

"Gifts are not taught," Aubergine said brusquely. "They come from within. Approach." Trader moved forward, slowly. "Young Teal, you are called to count down time, as Tracery Teal did before you. Turn over the glass. When the last grain of crystal falls through the funnel, time will stand still. Mere shadows of Mamie Verde will remain, and you alone shall witness what comes to pass." Aubergine looked to Ratta. "Free her."

With Lily's help, Ratta lifted the sparkling shroud tenderly from Mamie's stiffened form. As the fabric fell to the floor, the glittery pinpricks of light began to burn out, and Ratta understood that from this moment on the wrap would be just a shawl, no longer infused with magic to stall passage between life and death.

As the last light winked out, Aubergine directed, "Lay her body across the bed of clouds."

As Lily and Ratta lifted the frail form over the roiling steam, Aubergine gestured to Trader. "Mark time now," she said, hoping the billowing vapor would hold.

Trader reversed the hourglass, surprised to find it was heavy, and carefully set it back on the table. Tiny fragments of amethyst began to sift through the narrow neck, slowly at first. Now and again the jagged shards caught on each other, threatening to clog the funnel, but somehow they kept slipping through.

Standing tall, Aubergine raised her arms. "Let Mamie go," she said at last. "Let her go."

Tears streaked Ratta's face. Lily gently pulled her own fingers away from Mamie's feet and stepped back. Seeing that the body remained aloft, Ratta let go of Mamie's head and wiped her eyes. The old woman's frame drifted lightly above the pot, pillowed by the steam.

"Tell the tale for all that is true and good," Aubergine told Ratta.

Ratta's eyes flitted to the witches waiting in the circle. "Nothing's coming back to me."

"Start somewhere," Lily said softly. "Anywhere."

"I was a girl when Mamie told me the lost yarn," Ratta said, sounding desperate.

Aubergine clapped her hands. "Everyone, help her remember."

"This legend, does it have a name?" Wheat prompted.

"Guardian of the Crystal Caves." Ratta replied.

"Ask her the question," Lily urged Ratta. "You promised me."

Taking a deep breath, Ratta looked directly at Sierra. "Do you know such a story?"

Sierra shook her head slowly. "Not at all," she said raising her eyes to the group. "It must be the one."

"Mamie had already begun to leave this world when she revealed the lost tale to Ratta," Aubergine observed. "Only the fact that we did not yet have it, tethered her here."

"Her demise was slow." Ratta felt the familiar prick behind her eyes, feeble at first. She gazed sharply toward the body cushioned on the cloud, but the vapor obscured the form that rested there. "I should have let her go years ago."

"Her failing health was impossible to diagnose," Esmeralde added. "Nothing in my Possibles Bag helped."

"We all tried to ease those days," Lily said quietly. "When she ceased to walk with her cane, I cleaned out that old study to bring her bed downstairs."

"I took her favorite rocker to the workshop and made it into a rolling chair to wheel her from table to bed, yarn shop to dye shed." Ratta closed her eyes as a faltering hand fluttered like a butterfly through her mind. "It's coming now," she breathed. "Keep on."

Sierra took up the thread. "Mamie began to sleep more, converse less," she recalled. "When she stopped talking altogether, none of us were surprised—it seemed the natural order of things."

Esmeralde shrugged. "I never knew there was another tale."

"Oddly enough, although she no longer uttered sounds, I still heard her words in my head." Ratta's voice grew stronger with the memory. "I named her silent language Mind Speak, unaware that the Guardians had called it so since time began."

She scanned the group. "Do you remember how you taunted me? Calling me a kitchen wench, and laughing when I answered my lady's inaudible questions aloud. You, Winter Wheat, went so far as to burn holes in my clothing with your bejeweled beetle staff. One day I finally realized that I was the only one who could hear Mamie's words. I stopped voicing my replies. I understood that we could converse in silence, and you would not know. None of you would."

Wheat and Indigo began to speak at once, in what might have become an argument if Aubergine had not held up her hand to stop them. "Let Ratta continue," she said.

"No one realized that Mamie spoke to me. I didn't realize at first that she used the ancient way of the Guardians because she was destined to become one someday," Ratta said. "Later, this was a connection I became aware of, but still do not understand. All these years I have kept her shrouded in a magical cocoon to keep her from death. All I really did was suspend her between this world and the one in which she belongs."

Ratta raised red-rimmed eyes. "I acted selfishly. Although it was time for Mamie to claim her legacy as the next caretaker of the ancients, I was unable to bear the thought of being alone. Her time here was done twenty years ago. The Guardians revealed the tales of old to her, and she fulfilled her pledge to pass them on to us. Who is her successor? You think you know, Aubergine, but I fear you do not. You named Sierra Blue, but I am doubtful, because that tale is yet to be told. Mamie is fated to dwell in the Crystal Caves with the Watchers, safeguarding First Folk secrets, until her stewardship is complete. Only then shall we see who succeeds her—or not."

Aubergine looked around the hushed circle. "Ratta speaks the truth. Our future is far from certain. I have summoned you all here to free Mamie. Once she assumes the Guardianship, she may be able to lead us to the ancient crystals. Then perhaps we will possess renewed power to fend off the Lowlanders and the Northlanders.

"We must act swiftly, for the Lowlanders have broken into the Crystal Caves from the Blind Side. Before long they will plunder the ancient tombs. Secrets of old could easily fall into the possession of the Dark Queen, who might then find a way to use them against us. The present Guardian's watch was up twenty years ago. Who knows if he still safeguards the First Folk remains? Who knows how much longer he has been able to wait?"

Esmeralde looked at Aubergine in disbelief. "Men guard the ancient graves?"

"One did," Aubergine affirmed.

"But no more?" Indigo asked.

"Mamie should have been able to release him twenty years ago, as she promised."

"He was just a man," Ratta tossed back.

"He was my husband." Aubergine's voice vibrated with anger. "Tell the tale."

"I do not claim to understand the Lost Tale, because I discovered it deep inside Mamie's failing memory," Ratta said. "Over the years, she unraveled the lost yarn in fits and starts, while the rest of you stood by, unaware, murmuring your regular incantations. For me, time stood still, and images started coming to me like a waking dream. Nothing I saw made sense, but I was so delighted to have Mamie back again that I didn't care. I didn't realize then that she would never show me the tale again, so I failed to ask questions." She searched the others' faces. "I was young, and thought I had all the time in the world. So much of what Mamie offered seemed like addled mutterings, that I didn't pay enough attention, much heed. I should have told you the story at once, even though I couldn't make sense of it. I knew it had to be important, and I knew that Mamie spoke nothing but the truth."

Trader tapped gently on the table, as a signal that the sands of time were half gone. From her perch on the stool, Smokey peered into the pot. Locks of dyed Suri alpaca fleece had begun to float to the surface of the dye bath. The tendrils reminded Smokey of mountain maples touched by first frost, their leaves streaked fuchsia and gold, scarlet and rust. As the fiber took up the colors, the liquid surrounding the fiber had begun to lose its brilliance and its scent was becoming less heady.

Smokey hopped off her stool and took a birch log from the nearly empty wood box, to toss into the flames under the pot. "We need more sticks for the fire." She bustled to the doorway and looked down the hall. "Where is that girl?"

"Continue," Aubergine prompted Ratta.

"We all know the tale of the Ancients' Folly from Sierra Blue," Ratta said. "In that yarn, the First Folk tried to bend nature to their will and succeeded only in destroying their suns before perishing in a world covered by ice. This is all any of us knew, and we assumed it was Mamie's last legend. Now you will hear the companion tale, that of the Guardian of the Crystal Caves."

Smokey burst back into the room carrying a few sticks of kindling, followed by the kitchen maid, who hauled an entire armload of firewood. Smokey thrust her bits into the blaze under the cauldron while the girl dropped her logs into the wood box. The pot boiled more vigorously, sending up fresh clouds of steam that further blurred the edges of Mamie's body. Smokey resumed her place in the circle. With a fearful look at the vapor swirling above the cauldron, the girl backed away, but only until she disappeared into the shadows at the edge of the room.

Aubergine adjusted her shawl and reached her hands toward the pot. Across from her, Ratta closed her eyes to focus her sight inward. Between them, the air trembled with energy, like lightning generates before a storm fully breaks.

"Show us," Aubergine said.

"We are but eleven," Smokey warned.

"Hush," Aubergine said sharply.

Over the cauldron, the air crackled. When Ratta spoke, the voice that came from her mouth sounded as if it came from some place far away, perhaps even dead. "After their suns turned black and fell from the sky, the first few folk that froze to death were placed in tombs by those who survived," she said, as the smoke cleared to reveal the vision that she had begun to see in her mind's eye.

Skye gasped, while Trader smiled broadly, as they realized they were able to pick out images in the swirling vapor. There was a collective intake of breath. The group watched as sulfurous chunks of great burnt rocks, once suns, smashed to the ground. Still smoking, the boulders scattered across a broad valley edged by snaking rivers.

"It's working!" Smokey cried. She gazed at the empty space beside Skye. "We must be Twelve. Could Teal have joined us?" She asked Aubergine, peering up at the ceiling in search of green haze. "Or did Mamie herself, perhaps?"

Troubled, Aubergine shook her head. "I don't know. Watch and see."

Ratta rambled on as if reciting by rote. The witches paid rapt attention as the story unfolded. "The ancients honored their ruling-class dead by building crypts, embellished with carvings of their suns and of the rivers that crossed at each end of their valley. With these folk they buried pets and riches, clothing and small statues, all signifying their wealth and social standing. These items were intended to accompany the dead into an afterworld they had hoped existed. None of these families wished for less importance in the land of dreams than the station they had possessed in their dying world."

Ratta revealed a scene in which tombs dotted a low bluff overlooking a barren landscape. Piles of uncut stone heaped nearby suggested that more crypts had been planned, but never finished.

"The First Folk were proud and clever," Ratta recalled in her vacant voice. "The death of their suns was neither the beginning nor the end of the damage they wreaked. They used the powerful crystals mined from the riverbanks to defy natural law in other ways.

"A group called the Rainmakers learned to manipulate the change of seasons. By releasing cold-fire crystals into the air, they forced summer to lengthen and rain to fall only on command. Several of the Rainmakers' wives went on a rampage to exterminate bothersome insects, ignoring the plant life that depended upon such flying pests to carry their seed, as well as the birds that starved without such bugs to use for food.

"Another band of First Folk so altered the natural chain of life and death, growth and regrowth, that the seasons ceased to follow each other in order. Fish and fowl became barren, and grains and grasses dwindled to extinction. Instead, there was an endless supply of things the First Folk favored: fragrant blooms, heady wines, and blazing days of sun and sand along the Tigris and Eye. Fertile gardens fell fallow, unable to produce the hardiest grain or root vegetable."

Captivated by the scenes in the haze over the dye pot, Skye saw families reclining on woven mats spread along a glittering beach, beneath sunflowers whose heads were so large they provided shade. Beyond, untended fields held stunted crops.

"Finally the suns, overworked by the constant demands of the First Folk, died. And the world quietly froze." Ratta's vision showed them the river valley growing ever colder. The flowers had shriveled and turned brown, and the beaches were bare and windswept. The twined rivers iced over and snow began to fall.

"Additional First Folk perished from frost and famine. Few remained to bury them. Bodies lay frozen where they had fallen, for the last wolves and carrion birds to ravage. The Guardians of nature observed all this. Although they had pledged never to interfere with those under their watch, they decided to scour the lands clean once more. So began their process of encasing every last sign of the ancients' folly in a mausoleum of ice, which today we call the Northland Glacier."

Within the swirl of smoke, a huge mass of ice formed over the frozen valley. It began to slowly grind south, growing in size as it scraped up every vestige of civilization in its path.

"So began the Age of Ice," Ratta recited. "When young, the glacier was small. As it grew, looming ever larger on the landscape, wind began to sculpt its peaks, and to carve icy spires known as the Out Crops of the Northlands. The glacier itself molded the gentler foothills to the south, where later the freshets of the Crystal Lakes would pool."

Wheat found that she could distinguish familiar features of the glacier that she saw on her return from the Western Highlands each spring. Although there were no Burnt Holes yet, Sierra recognized the eastern bluff of ice that came to house them.

"What the Guardians forgot was that nature always seeks to renew itself," Ratta continued. "Ever so slowly, the world warmed. Eons passed before the season we call spring returned. By then, the Guardians had completely forgotten about our land. When its rebirth came to their attention, they looked upon it favorably. They blessed us with a new sun—but just one, and they kept it far enough from our reach that half of each day remained dark and cold. They hoped that if we had no perpetual sun, as the First Folk did, we might be thankful for time well spent in the light of day."

As she spoke, a new day dawned over the great pot, bathing those within the circle of Twelve in its rosy halo. From the back of the room, the maid crept closer, drawn to the vision like a moth to flame.

"As the temperature rose, more of the world awoke," Ratta went on. "Delicate grasses pushed through the snow, and ice melted into streams that became rivers. The lands became greener again, and the Guardians peopled it once more, taking care to spread us further, from the Lowlands to the Northlands, from the Western Highlands to the Far East and beyond.

"All was true and good until Nature began to unbalance for a second time. Drought and famine in the Lowlands forced a quarrel with the North, and we in the Middlelands became caught in between. Were the Guardians testing us and tiring of us? Or had they merely forgotten us and moved on?"

Ratta opened her faraway eyes to scan the circle. "Baited, one of us aligned herself with the South. With the support of the Lowlands, she seeks to rediscover the power of the First Folk, and to tilt nature to her will as they did. That is another tale, a future yarn that perhaps none of us will live to tell."

As the others began to protest, Aubergine raised her hand to silence them. "Let Ratta finish. She has not yet completed what Mamie Verde wants us to know."

Ratta waited for quiet before speaking again. "As the world thawed and the people began to wander, the Guardians grew concerned. They watched from afar as trade routes sprang up along the rivers, and bridges were built across them to neighboring villages. Knowing what had transpired before, the Guardians feared to expose these new folk to the ancients' folly, or let them stumble across powerful crystals unaware. They decided that one of them would have to keep the remains of the First Folk hidden for all time."

While the witches watched, rivers flowed south from the melt-off. Beyond the glacier's shadow, new grass sprang up in the foothills and fish jumped in the colorful pools that formed the Crystal Lakes.

"This special Guardian was appointed to protect the ancients and their lore, frozen deep within the glacier, among a chain of caverns called the Crystal Caves. According to legend, these vast chasms and passageways formed naturally as the world awoke. Glaciers have life cycles of their own, melting and moving during the warm season and refreezing when it turns cold. Each spring thaw, melt-off from the Northland Glacier carved new caves and tunnels, riddling its under-belly with passageways. Minerals tinged some of the ice caves green and others blue. Underground rivers rushed through fissures to forge tunnels, while air pockets widened into caves.

"Each spring thaw, fragments from the First Folk civilization melted free to tumble through the freshets flowing south, and bits of cracked crystal began to appear in the rivers and lakes. We call these shards. Even now, fossickers occasionally find bits of limestone emblazoned with sun rays or twined rivers."

Within the steam over the dye pot, ice sculptures of fantastical size and shape formed in an immense cavern, its ceiling studded with dripping stalactites. Beyond, ice melted from ancient First-Folk holdings, exposing brick and crypt, cudgel and crystal.

"To keep signs of the ancients safe from discovery, the Guardians salted the passageway to the Crystal Caves with false entrances and blind tunnels," Ratta said. "The Guardians cursed the Caves with the voices of the frozen dead and appointed familiars as Watchers. If disturbed, the ceaseless sound of First-Folk murmurings would drive mad any living being who dared to enter the passage leading to the cave after cave of rubble and relics that held the crystals."

Ratta lifted her chin toward Lavender Mae, huddled in her army jacket. "If you disbelieve me, look no further than our Mae. It is not the smoke of glacier weed or the years spent as a river rat searching for the lost crystal that has addled her brain. Ancient voices echo inside her head. None but a Guardian can cure her."

"Finally the Guardians sealed the Crystal Caves. Their cautionary tales are designed to keep those of us born in more temperate times from being tempted to repeat First-Folk Folly. With each generation, the old stories are told by one who is destined to become caretaker of the First Folk. Each Keeper of the Tales dwells among us for a time to tell the yarns, as Mamie Verde did around this very pot. When the final tale has been uttered, the Keeper of the Tales must name a successor and then assume the Guardianship. While the next Keeper of the Tales spins the yarns of the First Folk anew, the caretaker dwells and keeps watch in an antechamber outside the Crystal Caves."

Trader tapped the table again, more loudly, as the last amethyst shard sifted through the neck of the hourglass. She looked to Aubergine. "The glass is empty. What should I do now?"

Aubergine did not answer, for like the others, she stood frozen. Just to make certain, Trader reached for the old woman's arm. It was cold as stone. Panic-stricken, Trader realized that Aubergine's prediction had come true. Time was standing still. She looked around the circle. All of the witches had turned into statues. Then she noticed something even more shocking. While the witches in the circle had been entranced by Ratta's vision, the kitchen maid had crept close enough to join them. As frozen as the rest, the girl crouched in the vacancy half-hidden between herself and Skye.

Trader searched the shed wildly, uncertain of what to do. She wondered if time had stopped for everyone, or just in this room. And why she herself did not seem to be affected. Holding her breath, she listened intently, relieved to hear the sound of a wagon picking up trash in the back alley.

Trader turned to the cloud of fog encasing Mamie to see if it held clues, but the steam had dissipated and the old woman's remains seemed to have gone up in smoke as well. Or had they? Trader looked closely. She discerned the faint outline of a body drifting over the great pot. It hovered, as if waiting. Taking a wild guess, Trader hefted the hourglass and inverted it again, gasping at what she saw.

"Hold it up," Aubergine said, as if nothing out of the ordinary had happened. "Hold the glass for all to see."

Trader held the heavy timepiece with both hands. Wisps of fog lifted from the dye pot and seeped inside the glass, obscuring the purple shards with smoke. As that enclosed fog cleared, the witches watched a vision in the timekeeper itself, as crystals trickled down through the waist of the glass below the image of a young woman entering the Crystal Caves. Her body had a radiant glow that lit the dark halls of ice.

"Who is that?" Smokey whispered.

"Mamie Verde," Aubergine said. "She is passing through to the Crystal Caves to assume her role."

"That can't be Mamie," Ratta said in disbelief. "She is younger than I."

"And will be forevermore," Aubergine affirmed, with a raise of her eyebrows.

As the witches peered intently into the hourglass, the young Mamie came to a small antechamber, dark and dank with disuse. To one side, a tunnel stretched away into the ice, unguarded.

"Mae," Lavender Mae shouted out in warning, as she recognized the caves. "Mamie!"

"That must be the Guardian's dwelling," Lily surmised. "But where is the Guardian?"

"No longer there, it seems." Aubergine said, shaking her head sorrowfully.

"Perhaps Mamie waited too long," Winter Wheat said.

"Perhaps Ratta did," Indigo added.

"The cycle of the Guardians may be as broken as our circle of Twelve," Sierra said, "because Mamie did not leave us to assume her watch over the First Folk in time."

"She may surprise us yet." Ratta smiled, observing the lithe young woman in the hourglass as she searched the anteroom. Finding nothing, Mamie disappeared into the tunnel and the glass dimmed.

"It looks like we are in the dark again," Esmeralde muttered in disappointment.

Indigo narrowed her eyes at Ratta. "That's no surprise."

"Enough," Lily said. "Before any of you faults another who stands around this pot, know this: We few are charged with our world as it is, and we few will determine whether it survives."

"Listen and learn," Aubergine admonished with a stern look. "There is no need to blame the war between North and South. It does not help to bicker with each other. Do not confuse our gifts with the might of men, who vie with each other to rule. For, as we all know, they cannot."

Mae's gaze was fixated on the hourglass. In the dark, she glimpsed one spark after another. Soon the entire bowl erupted in pinpricks of light. "Maaaaeee," she groaned. "Maaaee."

"What is it?" Esmeralde asked, glancing toward her. "Is she sick?"

"Mae recognizes the sparkle of the crystals," Sierra answered. "This is one tale I do know. Magic crystals from ancient caves wink even in the black of night, each orb infused with its own light. The pink quartz beacons that we use to show our way through dark paths at night come from such caverns, as do the cabochons tied to Wheat's crook. Mae knows. She has been through the caves herself, many times."

Lily tore her gaze from the fireworks inside the hourglass to look at Aubergine. "Judging by the starburst, my guess is that the Guardians have welcomed Mamie into the Crystal Caves. She has begun her watch at last."

Aubergine nodded with satisfaction. "It is just as I had hoped."

"When must I relieve her?" Sierra asked.

"When the last tale is told," Aubergine said. "With Mamie's help we may yet be able to wield the crystals, even from afar. By the time you assume your watch, if fortune goes our way, our powers will be rekindled and we may rule once more. That is what the Northlanders fear most; otherwise they would not have outlawed the use of magic and hunted us down as witches."

"We shall wield the crystals?" Sierra gave Aubergine a look of concern. "No yarns predict that—not even the Lost Tale. Legend suggests that it is our purpose to keep the crystals out of the hands of those who would use them to wreak havoc on the world."

"It depends upon how you read the stories," Aubergine countered. "Isn't that so, Lily?"

Lilac Lily nodded. "The art of using crystals to bend natural law may have been buried with the First Folk, but it is not lost. We have employed such stones for similar intentions in small ways."

"If we use the crystals to rule all, we are no better than the First Folk," Sierra disagreed. "We are as ill-purposed as the Dark Queen."

"We already use the crystals. Think on it," Lily said. "Here in this shed, as we circle this cauldron, the shards we use to dye yarn are fragments of the rock of the ancients. Aubergine found such stones in the Crystal Lakes when she was young. Over time and quite by accident, she learned to harness some of their magical properties."

"That was different," Sierra protested. "It was innocent. When I discovered crystal rock flour in the Lavender Rill flowing by my farm, I dissolved it and used it to dye whimsical cloaks and caps. No one was more surprised than I to find that my garments allowed their wearers to remain serene or to pass unseen, and offered some of them the power of persuasion."

"Innocent or not, you used crystal power to bend others to your will," Lily pointed out. "It is the same."

"All of us wield magic crystals, some more than others," Aubergine pointed out. "Esmeralde gleans cracked crystals from fossick boys who scavenge the flooded freshets each spring. Finely silted stone laces her tinctures, allowing her to strengthen her remedies and better practice her lore. No wonder that her medicines heal like no others. Indigo Rose's greenhouse grows exotic plants far from home. She chops the odd rock and uses it to fertilize fantastical seedlings, which later grow into fruit out of season, much as the First Folk did."

"The ancients ruined their world," Winter Wheat objected.

"We may yet do the same," Aubergine shot back. "With or without the crystals."

"Wheat, you burn holes with your clacking amber beetles, which also light up when they sense danger," Lily pointed out. "Crystals placed on my bed stand at night enhance my ability to ken what you all think. Smokey Jo can start a fire from nothing and sometimes disappears into wisps of smoke. Ratta cannot only hear but recite Mind Speak, which is none other than the language of the Guardians themselves. Poor Mae is far gone, for the voices of the ancients murmur in her mind, but she would find us the missing crystal if she could. Her goal is to make Aubergine's amethyst necklace whole again, so that we may rekindle our lost power."

Suddenly the raven-haired kitchen girl stepped from hiding and fully occupied the remaining place in the circle between Skye and the spot where Trader had stood. In the hourglass, the young woman who was Mamie turned and stared. In return, the serving girl laughed loudly, a sound out of keeping with her submissive appearance. Mamie's shape began to blur. The hourglass went dark. After waiting a few seconds, Trader set it slowly down on the table.

"Mamie disappeared," Trader raised her eyes toward the stranger who stood before her. "Why would she do that?"

"Only with twelve in the circle can the simmer succeed," the maid said. She eyed Trader intently. "But more than one of us is not who she seems."

"No!" Aubergine's eyes raged violet. In one swift move, she jerked Trader away from rejoining the circle. The frightened girl stumbled to her side, knocking the dye table. The hourglass upended once more. It tumbled to the floor and the purple shards scattered. Glaring at the infiltrator, Aubergine shielded Trader with a protective arm.

"What in cracked crystal…?" Wheat began. The words died in her throat. As the witches watched, the kitchen maid shifted shape before their eyes, maturing from a servant girl into a regal woman. She grew taller and more imposing. Her gaze turned from reserved hazel to cold green, while her hair darkened to the intensity of coal.

Smokey Jo plucked at Aubergine's sleeve. "Who is she?"

"You," Ratta uttered, staring at the dark-haired woman in disbelief. In her features Ratta recognized the probing eyes of the man at the stagecoach inn, who had flipped a piece of Lowland gold to a wandering bard for tales of the Twelve.

The stranger's mouth widened into a cruel smile. It was then that Esmeralde saw something familiar, too. Wasn't this woman's profile stamped on the magic coin she'd found at the Banebridge Trading Post?

"Who?" Smokey pestered again.

Sierra looked at Aubergine in disbelief. "Hiding in plain sight," was all she said.

Without answer, Aubergine crossed possessive arms around Trader's shoulders. The unknown woman offered them a defiant stare saying, "Mamie may be safe within the Crystal Caves at last, but the path you seek is more impossible than you can imagine."

The Fire-and-Ice Shawl

A SHAWL PATTERN

This experienced-skill-level shawl has wonderfully intricate stitchwork throughout, and is designed to keep you sane in a world of discordant voices. It measures 75" wide by 41" deep.

The pattern will be available between books for a special Knit Along where you can add your own magical touch to the mix and knit up this gorgeous shawl for yourself or as a very special gift for someone you want to protect.

Sign up for the Potluck Yarn newsletter so you don't miss our announcement for the Knit Along!

ABOUT THE AUTHOR

Cheryl Potter is a fiber artist and author, but is best known as the founder of Cherry Tree Hill Yarn. She has a BA from Middlebury College and an MFA from the University of Arizona. *The Broken Circle* is her seventh book and first novel.

ABOUT THE TYPEFACE

An Old-Style serif typeface, Janson was cut by Hungarian Miklós Kis in the late 1600s. The version used in this book was produced by Hermann Zapf in the 1950s, based on Kis' original matrices. Janson's strong stroke contrast, sharpness, and legibility are just three reasons why this Humanist typeface is popular in book text.